FIRE

Also by C. C. Humphreys

The French Executioner
Blood Ties
Vlad: The Last Confession
Absolute Honour
The Hunt of the Unicorn
Jack Absolute: A Novel
A Place Called Armageddon
The Blooding of Jack Absolute
Shakespeare's Rebel
Plague

As Chris Humphreys

The Fetch
Vendetta
Possession

FIRE

C. C. HUMPHREYS

CENTURY

1 3 5 7 9 10 8 6 4 2

Century
20 Vauxhall Bridge Road
London SW1V 2SA

Century is part of the Penguin Random House group
of companies whose addresses can be found at
global.penguinrandomhouse.com.

Penguin
Random House
UK

First published in Great Britain by Century in 2016

www.randomhouse.co.uk

A CIP catalogue record for this book is available from the British Library.

ISBN 9781780891453 (Trade paperback)
ISBN 9781448164226 (eBook)

Typeset by Palimpsest Book Production Ltd, Falkirk, Stirlingshire

Printed and bound in Great Britain by Clays Ltd, St Ives plc

Penguin Random House is committed to a sustainable future for
our business, our readers and our planet. This book is made from
Forest Stewardship Council® certified paper.

MIX
Paper from
responsible sources
FSC® C018179
www.fsc.org

To Simon Trewin

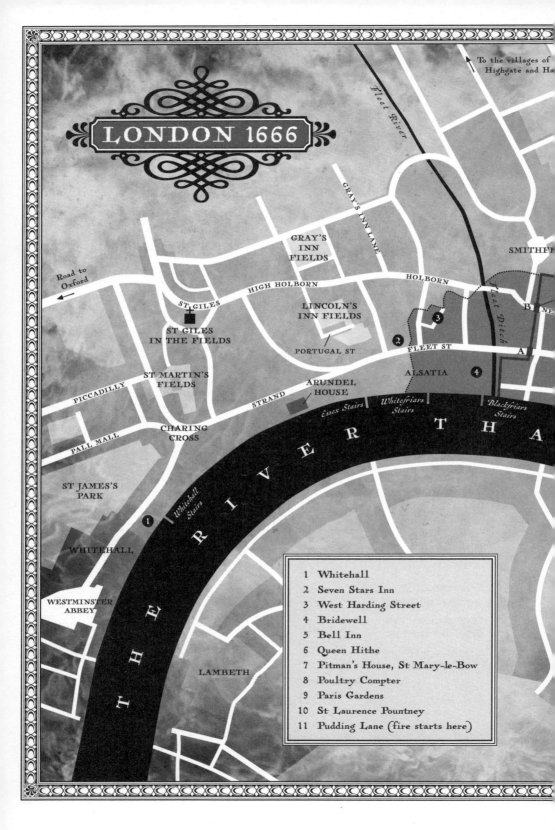

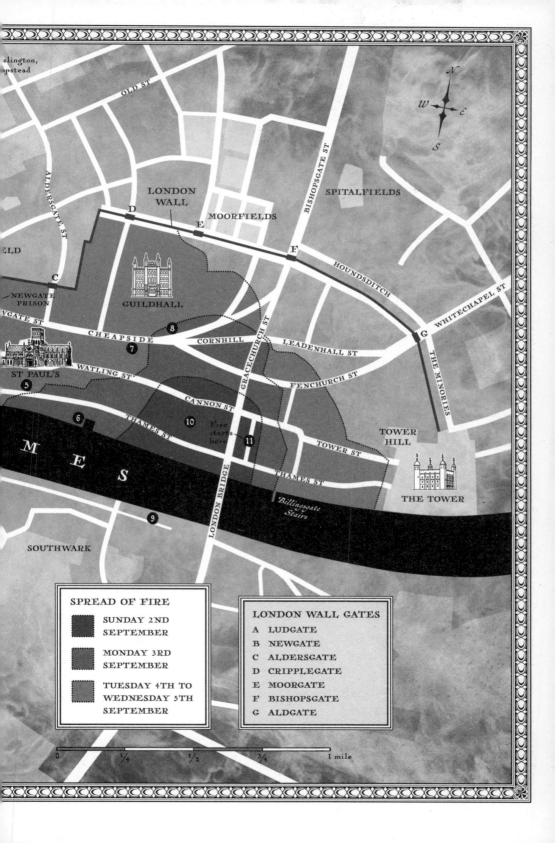

SPREAD OF FIRE

SUNDAY 2ND
SEPTEMBER

MONDAY 3RD
SEPTEMBER

TUESDAY 4TH TO
WEDNESDAY 5TH
SEPTEMBER

LONDON WALL GATES

A LUDGATE
B NEWGATE
C ALDERSGATE
D CRIPPLEGATE
E MOORGATE
F BISHOPSGATE
G ALDGATE

0   ¼   ½   ¾   1 mile

Dramatis Personae

THE THIEF-TAKERS AND FAMILY
Captain William Coke
Dickon
Pitman
Bettina Pitman
Josiah Pitman
Grace, Faith, Benjamin and Eleazar Pitman
Allsop
Friar
Deakins

THE COURT
King Charles II
James, Duke of York
Sir Joseph Williamson, spymaster

THEATRE FOLK
Sarah Chalker
Thomas Betterton
Mary Betterton
Aitcheson, theatre attendant
Hutchins, theatre attendant

THE FIFTH MONARCHISTS
Captain Blood
Thomas Blood, his son
Simeon Critchollow, puppeteer
Daniel
Samuel Tremlett, master builder
Isaiah Hebden

Colonel Rathbone
Colonel Danvers
Chambers
More
Hopkinson

AT sea

Rear-Admiral Sir George Ayscue
Lieutenant Hardiman
Boatswain
Admiral Robert Holmes
Wilbert Bohun
Squires, gun captain

THe POULTRY COMPTer

Jenny Johnson
Mary Johnson
Jenkins
Baronet de Lacey
Eye-Patch and Son
Wallace, master turnkey
Joan
Midwife

THe FIre

Salmon, constable
Thomas Farriner, baker
Sir Thomas Bludworth, Lord Mayor of London
Citizens of the City
Samuel Pepys, diarist
James Morrow, headborough
Tom Walker

OTHERS

Woodstrode, barrister
Thom Peterson, landlord
'Jeremiah' Peckworth
Aaron Bastable
Mad Moll
French wine merchant
Young Samuel Tremlett
Isaac ben Judah
Rebekah bat Judah

1665. The Great Plague ravages London. One
hundred thousand die, horribly.
1666. The plague passes. Citizens resume their lives.

Six years after his restoration to his executed father's throne,
following twelve years of Puritan glumness, King Charles is
called 'the Merry Monarch' with reason. He carouses, he plays
pell-mell, he attends the theatre, he beds his many mistresses. For
him, and the very few very rich, 1666 promises to be another year
of pleasure.

For most Londoners, though, the year will offer no more than
another battle to survive. And for a radical few, it means something
else entirely. For 666 is the number of the Beast – when Satan, as
foretold in the Books of Revelation and Daniel, will return to
battle the armies of Christ at a place called Armageddon; when
Jesus will triumph, raising up the Elect – the chosen, living and
dead – to dwell forever in the New Jerusalem. However these
'Saints' do not simply sit and pray. By their deeds will they end
the Fourth Monarchy of Man, and hasten the Fifth Monarchy of
Christ.

September. The year of the Beast is three-quarters done and
the Devil has not had his due. It has not rained in five months.
Warehouses are stuffed with combustibles: coal, hemp, tobacco,

brandy, parchment, silks, gunpowder. Each wooden house lights a fire daily, while bathhouses, bakeries and breweries stoke furnaces for their labours.

London is a tinderbox: politically, sexually, religiously – literally. And it is about to burn.

AND WHOSOEVER WAS NOT FOUND WRITTEN IN THE
BOOK OF LIFE WAS CAST INTO THE LAKE OF FIRE.
The Revelation of St John the Divine 20:15

PROLOGUE

Fire. Vulnerable as any newborn. Like a child, you give it life, pray that it will thrive and repay your care. Yet how will it survive its first moments in a harsh world?

Take the lit taper from a neighbour. Softly now, softly – even in the few steps to your room, it has so many ways to die. Despite your cupped hand, draughts beset it. It flickers, shreds, re-forms in waves, bends to you as if craving protection, shrinks. You think you've lost it, you stop – and it revives, rising straight again, a final boldness. Now you must be quick.

Over the threshold, across to the stub of candle on the mantel, lower flame to wick. So – it catches! Dropping the taper's end onto a pewter plate, you cross and close the door. The swirl of your motion blows a tiny ember to the floor. You do not note its fall. How can it matter anyway when it is all but dead?

The flame lives now in the candle. You could snuff it in a cone of metal, extinguish it with a snap of fingers, destroy it with a breath. Instead, you pause to admire the yellow spear with cobalt at its heart, the burning eye of the wick. It streams high in three slender fingers and you give thanks to God for life renewed, for warmth, for heat. Now you will be fed as you have fed.

You transfer fire to the grate. Kindling catches and flames move upon the small logs you offer it. You bend to add breath. The chimney draw is not enough, so you cover the hearth with a blanket, seal it from the room. Silence – then a whoosh. Through threadbare wool, you see fiery arms reach high. Folding the blanket fast, you smother any new life within it.

Larger logs now – and your tender babe becomes a brawling youth. As it grows, so does its appetite. Soon it is all the fire you need. You swing a pot over the flames and cook your supper.

Heat makes you drowsy. But you know that unattended fires can be dangerous. You add one last, larger piece of wood to see you into the night, put a metal guard before the hearth and sink into your chair.

You doze before the dwindling light. And though some worry tugs at the edge of your mind, you lose it in sleep.

That ember. That tiny ember from the taper. That orphan. Most orphans in this city perish and this one would have too – if it had not fallen first onto a fragment of leaf, shifted onto an edge of rug, finally settled onto a dropped wool stocking. There a little draught reaches it, gently, and the ember glows and grows ever slowly into the night. Until it is hungrier.

Then it moves more quickly. Consuming all that is beside it, it begins on everything beyond. It reaches out to its cousin fire almost faded on the grate. Revives it, becomes one with it. Smoke fills the room. You, the parent before the hearth, are dead before you are consumed.

The window's lead is melting, its glass is bowing out. Within the plaster walls, horsehairs crisp in filaments of fire. Soon there is nothing left of the room – wood, wool, flesh, all gone. So now, like any living thing, flame has a choice: feed or die.

Across the threshold, a city sleeps.

Part One

I WILL RENDER VENGEANCE TO MINE ENEMIES, AND
WILL REWARD THEM THAT HATE ME.

Deuteronomy 32:41

1

TO KILL A KING

Of all the drunk men in the Seven Stars that noontime, he was undoubtedly the drunkest.

The tavern was one of several close to the law courts but was favoured above others for the quality of its sweet sack, its beef and kidney pudding, and for the several snugs where lawyers could meet their clients or each other in relative privacy. Matters could be discussed with discretion, bribes subtly transferred from cloak to cloak.

The drunkard disturbed their equilibrium. It was not that the legal profession in London was any less inebriated than any other. Indeed, few of them would dream of venturing into the courtroom entirely sober; given that the judge, the juries, most plaintiffs and all defendants were unlikely to be, what would be the purpose? Despite that, most in the tavern comported themselves with decorum, keeping their voices low, their movements minimal.

Unlike the tall man whose long black hair – filigreed with silver and uninhibited by judicial wig or even ribbon – flew around him as he danced to music only he could hear. The man had tried to engage another in his dance, pulling him close, whirling him around again and again before being shoved aside with an oath. Rebuffed, he began to punctuate his jig with short snatches of song, and clapped a-rhythmically along to his stamping.

It was the jarring quality of this last that finally provoked a corpulent barrister named Woodstrode, three bumpers of sack the worse for the morning and so finding it hard to grasp the exact amount he was being offered to lose his case that day, to bellow, 'Christ's mercy, Peterson. Throw the bedlamite out!'

Thom Peterson, landlord of the Stars, had been contemplating doing so since the man began his jigging. But the only part of him that was large was his belly; he'd strained his back shifting barrels earlier in the day and he'd dispatched his tapster, Smythe, who enjoyed hurting drunks, to fetch more offal from the Fetter Lane shambles. Still, with the tavern now suddenly quieter and his regular clients regarding him, he knew he must do something.

Stepping from behind the trestle, he warily approached the man who, on the lawyer's cry, had ceased singing and taken a few unsteady steps back to the crook stool he'd risen from to dance. He swayed above it now and, just as the landlord reached him, flopped onto it.

'Now, listen to me, you –' Peterson began.

'Grash,' the man slurred.

'What's that, fellow?'

Another unintelligible word came, whispered this time while the drunkard also reached up, took the landlord's hand, tugged him down until their heads near touched. Peterson, bending to listen and consider how, with his back, he could lift the larger man from his seat and run him out the door, then realised that there was not just flesh between them – there was metal as well. The man was turning his hand slightly, not letting it go, just enough to reveal that the metal was silver, and had His Majesty's head upon it.

'Leave me be,' the man whispered, releasing the coin over, retaining the hand, 'and I vow I'll be good.'

Between the half-crown in his palm and the pain in his back, Peterson came to an immediate decision. 'See that you are, ye dog,' he declared into the silence that lingered, looking around to add loudly, 'He sued his wife for criminal conversation – and he lost! I've told the poor cuckold he can rest here if he makes not one peep more.'

A few laughs came, along with expressions of wonder – it was rare for a husband to sue a wife for adultery in an adulterous world, rarer still for her to win. Wondering which lucky lawyer it was who had thus triumphed, Woodstrode and the rest turned back to their hushed negotiations. The hum returned to the tavern, the landlord to his trestle, the drunkard to himself. Indeed, the cuckold was now completely, contemptuously, ignored.

Which is just as I want it, thought Captain Coke, as he peered through the falling veil of his hair at the man who'd been his brief and unwilling partner in the dance. Use all your senses, his tutor in crime had told him. The man we seek will be unusual. He will stand out, e'en as he seeks to blend in. Something will distinguish him, give him away. Above all, he'd said, use this. And he'd tapped his nose.

He'd not meant it literally, of course. 'Sniffing out villainy' was a phrase as old as villains and those who hunted them. And yet?

Coke inhaled. The air was fragrant with so many things. Smoke overlaid it all – from the hearth, where sweet applewood burned to stave off the chill of this raw April day; from the clay pipes at which every second man puffed. You could tell the quality of the clientele by the quality of what they smoked. In an alehouse in Wapping, the seaman's rough shag would make all eyes run. However the tobacco in the Seven Stars was finest blended Turkish leaf, purchased on the Haymarket or from Louis on Fleet Street – gentle on nostril, throat and chest.

Deeper, thought Coke, taking another breath which brought . . . the pungency of kidney from one of the establishment's famed puddings, an example of which lay open and ravaged on the table to his side, wafting its flavourings over: nutmeg, cinnamon and black pepper. It brought perfume too, for near all men wore it, in different notes. Within his, bought at considerable expense from Maurice of the Strand Arcade, sandalwood predominated – a good, masculine smell, he'd always felt. Other perfumes nearby were not so nice. He smelled rosewater; then bergamot, lavender and lily.

He looked across the tavern again. The man he'd danced with smelled of none of these. Or rather, anything he wore was overlaid with something far stronger.

The scent of terror.

The man was now looking towards him. Muttering, Coke lowered his head into his hands, looked to the floor – and smiled. Though it was half hidden in floor reeds, had been trampled in muck and had a boot heel's mark obscuring some of the words, the rest of the paper was clear – and told that at two that same afternoon at the Duke's Playhouse, not three hundred paces from where he now sat, Thomas Betterton, 'the prince of players', would give his Hamlet, the prince of Denmark, for the very first time.

And though there was no other name upon the bill, Coke saw one there anyway. For Sarah Chalker, who he hoped one day soon would be Sarah Coke, would be giving her Gertrude.

Smile changed to frown. He wasn't well read in Shakespeare. But he knew that Gertrude was a widow. And 'the Widow Chalker' was what Sarah was called by many. Her husband had been slain, brutally slain, but eight months before. She'd told him that she was reluctant to marry again so soon before she had fully mourned. But Coke feared otherwise: that even though he knew she loved him, he also believed that the child that she carried, that they had created, made her wary of a life with him. He did not blame her – for what prospect was he? How could he provide for her and the babe? What was he, after all? A disinherited knight. A man forced to give up the one trade he had any skill in and exchange it for another which was . . . what? Sitting in a tavern, sniffing men? Seeking . . .

'Do not turn about.' The voice came low from behind him. 'Or at least if you do, do so slowly and in your current – and masterly, may I say – personation.'

Coke continued slouching forward for a further half minute. Then, yawning widely, he turned about, laid his head upon the forearms on the table and closed his eyes. He'd seen all he needed.

Pitman was a big man, taller by half a head than himself, and half as broad again. Yet while Coke had jigged, the man had contrived to cross a crowded tavern and insert his large self into the corner of the settle unobserved. This quiet way of being there and yet not seeming to be was just one of several skills that Pitman had been trying to teach his new partner, which the thief-taker alluded to now.

'I see you took my advice about hiding in plain sight,' he said. He tamped then lit his pipe from the table's candle, exhaling a plume of smoke – shag, Coke thought, coughing, the man had low tastes in some things – to add to the fug. 'Well done, William.'

Coke sighed. The lessons were good, and well received. Yet sometimes they were delivered in the tone of a schoolmaster speaking to a particularly dense child. 'Nay, sir,' he replied without raising his head, 'that's a catch I learned all by myself – perhaps on the score of robberies I undertook *in plain sight* while you and all the other thief-takers chased my shadow.'

The big man chuckled, scratching under his luxuriant beard. 'Ah, Captain Cock. Would you rather be holding up coaches still than about such subterfuge?'

'I would rather be about what we agreed.' He sniffed. 'Using our respective skills to hunt and snare my former fellow road knights. Splitting their bounties between us.' He coughed again at Pitman's execrable tobacco. 'This is not the king's highway, sir. We will find no highwayman here.'

Pitman stopped smiling. 'No. But we may find someone else. And there's money in him, have no fear.' The thief-taker leaned forward to rest his elbows on the table, hands and pipe bowl sheltering his mouth. 'Have you found him out?'

'I believe so.'

'Is he the short young fellow in the brown doublet sitting directly behind you across the tavern?'

Coke opened one eye. 'How do you know already what I have only just discovered?'

'He is one of the few here not in company. His clothes, though plain, are better cut than most. His wig is certainly more expensive. And he has just pulled out his timepiece for the third time in as many minutes. He is waiting for someone.' The pot boy placed a tankard on the table and moved away. Pitman took a large swig. 'And I was told the rendezvous would be in the Seven Stars.'

'By whom? For Chrissakes, Pitman, who is this bloody fellow? Why are we concerned with him?'

The questions came fast, borne on irritation. Pitman shoved the pint pot across. 'Drink, Captain, while the fellow scans behind him now and pays us no nevermind.'

'But —'

'Season your impatience with ale and I will answer you — as far as I am able.' As Coke obeyed and drank, he continued, 'I'll tell you this, though — find him out and we will be wealthier for it at twenty guineas a man. Nay, I do not know who he is, Captain, if that is what you would ask. Neither does our employer —'

'Employer! We work for no man —'

Pitman raised a hand, interrupting the interruption. 'Alas, Captain, but in this case we do. He is —' Pitman took a deep breath. It was the information he knew he'd have to share with his friend. It would not please. Marry, it did not please him. Nonetheless. 'Sir Joseph Williamson. He is the Under-Secretary for —'

The expected reaction came. 'I know who he is, sir,' hissed Coke. 'For any fancy title he possesses, he is still England's spymaster. What have we to do with such a man?' His eyes widened. 'Pitman, you do not say —'

'I do.' Pitman took a big swallow before he continued. 'We are summoned to the service of the state. Again.'

'Shit.' Coke reached over and took Pitman's ale from his hand, near draining it, before setting it down. 'And what service are we doing it in this tavern, pray?'

'According to the whisper Sir Joseph heard, we are here to thwart a conspiracy that will begin here.'

'Its aim?'

'To assassinate the king.'

Strangely, Coke felt his anger leave. Perhaps it was the ale. 'Oh. Merely that?' Coke laid his head back onto his forearms. 'You make me tired, Pitman. We are not spies, nor government agents, nor guards of the king's person. Why would Sir Joseph seek our aid?'

It was another thing that Pitman truly did not wish to discuss. Yet he must. 'Because he believes the conspiracy is hatched by our old enemies, the Fifth Monarchists. That the man over there still checking his watch, and this other he awaits, are both members of that infernal crew.'

The captain reached up to pinch between his eyes. And so it circles back, he thought. The fanatics who made Sarah Chalker a widow, who near killed us all, now seek to kill the king – again. 'Other? What other?'

'It was the one additional whisper that Sir Joseph's agents had caught. The arrival in London of a most dangerous man. So dangerous he does not have a name. Merely a nickname.'

'Which is?'

'Homo Sanguineus.'

Coke frowned. 'I ever regret that the late deplored wars forced me to exchange further classical education for bullets and blades. But does that not mean "man of blood"?'

'It does.'

'I see. So what now, Pitman? What would our master have us do? Play the role of damned spy? Observe, report? Arrest? I am not a constable, sir. Unlike you.'

'I fear, as does Sir Joseph, that the affair might be more pressing than that. Do you know what today is?'

'The sixth of April.'

'And what does that signify?'

'Just tell me, man, before I lose the will to live.'

'Very well.' Pitman glanced across the room, to the man now scratching hard under his expensive wig. 'In '61, Major General Harrison was executed. You may have heard of him.'

'He was a regicide, was he not? Signed the death warrant of our late king, Charles I?'

'He did. And suffered the fate of a traitor for it. He was hung, drawn and quartered. Yet 'tis said that, despite the horrors visited upon his old body, the general never stopped singing hymns. Right up to the moment when they were extracting his guts with hot tongs . . .'

Coke raised a hand. 'I beg your favour – you can spare me the details.'

Pitman smiled. 'I always forget what a weak stomach you have, Captain. Odd for a military man. Well,' he continued, 'that was five years ago to this very day.'

Coke lifted his head. 'You do not mean –'

'I do.' Pitman nodded. 'Sir Joseph believes they will attempt their revenge on the anniversary of Harrison's . . . martyrdom, as they would have it.'

Coke frowned. 'Easily countered. His Majesty may spend the day cavorting with one of his many mistresses in his

11

apartments at Whitehall with a troop of cavalry to guard each door.'

'He may, but he will not. For he has an appointment.'

'Where?'

Instead of answering, Pitman bent and plucked something from the floor, and laid it on the table before Coke. It was the playbill he had but lately been perusing. Announcing a performance to be given of the *Tragedy of Hamlet* – in less than one hour's time. 'Betterton is His Majesty's favourite player. He never misses his first assay of a role,' Pitman added.

Coke barely heard him. He rose.

'Calmly, man. Where do you go?' Pitman said.

'To the playhouse. Sarah's there. And if these fanatics are there as well –'

He half turned – and Pitman reached and seized his arm. 'They are not, man. They are here. And our best chance to intercept them is –'

He was interrupted, not by Coke's argument but by the main doors beside them banging open, and by the shout given by the man in a long, black cloak who entered. 'The judges are returning!' he yelled. 'The courts are in session. All persons with business before their Worships to come forthwith.'

Where there had been quiet, now there was noise, as lawyers, plaintiffs, defendants, all rose, drained tankards and loudly made their last points. Where there had been space, it was now filled as men flooded the area before the Seven Stars' trestle. Coke and Pitman turned, seeking through the sudden mob. But as the smoke cleared through doors flung wide onto the street, and as the lawyers streamed out, they saw that the man they'd been watching so assiduously had gone.

'The back door, swiftly!'

There were still enough customers to hinder them and despite his size it took near half a minute for Pitman to push through, Coke in his wake. The back door gave onto a dank alley. But its only occupants were five men adding to its reek by pissing against its walls. The man they sought was not one of them.

'The playhouse!'

Coke set off at a good pace, Pitman level with him. 'Tell me,' he said, as they dodged between the yellow puddles, 'how did you single out this fellow amongst all the others? Did you take my advice?'

'In a way. I used this.' He tapped his nose.

'Ah good! Your sixth sense.'

'No. I used *this*.' He tapped again. 'The man reeked.'

'Not uncommon in London. Marry, my Bettina says that if I do not take my fortnightly bath –'

'You mistake me. This was a particular kind of smell. Such a one as I have scented only one place before. You will have smelled it too.'

'Where?'

'On a battlefield. In the late king's wars, you may have fought for Parliament and I for the King, but I wager our comrades smelled exactly the same going into a fight for the first time. I know I did. It is the scent of terror,' he nodded, 'and this man reeks of it.'

They rounded the corner and were gone.

Had Pitman not been so distracted he would have noticed something in the alley – for he was famed for his seeing of even the smallest detail. And this was not even that small, truly. A man near as large as the thief-taker, leaning against the wall, unbuttoned. A man engaged in the act of pissing yet voiding nothing. A man who tucked himself away now, buttoned his breeches and followed, at a steadier pace, those three who hurried to the theatre. The ones he'd spotted immediately in the tavern as they looked elsewhere — for he had a good eye for an enemy, born of the experience of having had so many.

He need not hurry, knowing he had ten minutes before the new rendezvous he'd arranged in a swift whisper with the man who — he had to agree with the government toady — smelled none so well. Though he wished the time were shorter so that he could relieve himself of the large metal ball that pressed against his spine.

Shifting it a little, the man known as Homo Sanguineus walked slowly towards a royal death.

2

PLAYHOUSE GHOSTS

'Do you see nothing there?' he screamed, arm flung out, eyes wide in terror.

Sarah knew what to say. Knew that she was meant to deny the ghost – and she could not. Because there was one there – the ghost of a man who was not dead. The ghost of William Coke.

Thomas Betterton, his arm still thrust before him to ward off the spirit, looked down at her upon the bed. His eyes narrowed.

Speak, she thought, and still couldn't. Not when it wasn't Bill Tarbuck the actor gazing at her from the far side of the stage but the man she loved. The man whose child she carried, who had left their bed not three hours before. His eyes, that had always held pain deep within them, were clear of it now. He even had a slight smile upon his lips. In another moment perhaps his laugh would come – so rare, and doubly prized for its rarity. But what made the apparition even stranger was that he was not dressed as he had been when he left her that morning. Then he had been attired in his customary black – while his spirit was bare-footed, wore a patched grey shirt, knee-length breeches, every item as soaked and dripping as his hair.

'Mrs Chalker!'

She couldn't look away. Not yet. Not when the spirit was turning and she saw . . . that the right side of his face was freshly scarred.

'Ah!' She could not help her cry.

'No!' Betterton slammed his hand onto the bedpost. 'You are not meant to see him. Only I am! You know this!'

Sarah forced her gaze up. From the grey, calm eyes of the man she loved to the black and angry ones above her.

'Are you pausing for effect, madam?' Betterton continued. 'I forbid it. I have told you – this exchange must build swiftly to the point of the ghost's exit,' he hissed. ''Tis why we are rehearsing this bit – yet again! – with the doors of the playhouse to be opened in a moment to admit the audience. To admit the king, damn me.' All restraint went. 'For the love of God, ye dumb whore, just say your fucking line!'

It was as if he'd slapped her and, by the way he waved his hands, he looked as if he ached to do so in more than foul words. It made her take a breath – another, yet deeper. The first restored her to the place and time she was. The second mastered her anger: there was no good to be gained from fighting with the leader of the company, however insulting. Not with his new production of *Hamlet* about to open in half an hour.

Her third breath, the deepest yet, allowed her to look across to where Coke's ghost had stood – and see no ghost there – or at least only the actor playing Old Hamlet. 'I am sorry, Thomas,' she said. ''Twas your performance, seeing your father's spirit. I swore I saw him too.' It was not the most heartfelt of her deliveries so she hurried on. 'I apologise.' She looked across at Tarbuck. 'And to you, Bill. May I try again?'

With a grunt, Betterton resumed his position and flung his arm out. He said his line, she replied promptly, and carried on thus to the end of the scene. The feeling did not matter, this last rehearsal was about precision not passion. The audience, it was hoped, would stimulate them to that. It was understood in the theatre that all final run-throughs must be poor to make the first performance great.

The scene ended. It was the last one they would rehearse. 'To your preparations, all. Admit the audience!' Betterton bellowed and as other actors hurried away, he took Sarah's arm, ungently. 'And you, ma'am, get some food into you. Every moment I think you are going to faint upon the stage.' He looked pointedly at her belly. 'Your baby still irks you?'

It was said with no concern for her, only himself. He had been persuaded that Sarah's illness was a passing thing and that she could undertake roles still. She had to maintain him in that belief. She did not know what she would do for money if she could not act, with the babe's birth still five months away and Coke in his new and uncertain trade. 'Nay, 'tis fine, Mr Betterton,' she said, patting her stomach and smiling. 'Indeed, I am quite recovered. You are kind to ask.'

It was the best performance she'd given that day. Betterton walked away, muttering. And as soon as he did, Sarah moved to the opposite side, to the bucket she'd discreetly placed there, parting her long auburn hair just in time to void a thin stream. She crouched, awaiting more, remembering. Why had her William's shade visited her like that? He was not dead. She would have known it instantly if he were, Coke's presence being as strong as that of their child within her. She may not have had all her mother's gifts as a cunning woman, a communicator with the departed, but she could still tell a ghost apart from . . . a premonition? What had he been trying to tell her, this future William? He was clad as if for the sea. Must he go abroad? Must they?

Shivering, she bent again to heave nothing into the bucket.

She felt a hand, gentle upon her back. 'Sarah?' came a voice as soft as the touch.

'It's all right.' She raised herself, managed a little smile. 'I'm well.'

Dickon's eyes wandered as they ever would, as did his other hand through his hedge of wheaten hair. William had rescued the orphan from his doorway three winters since and had restored him to health, though his full wits would probably be ever beyond him. 'You are s-sick, Sarah,' he said.

'I am.' She put her hand over her belly. ''Tis the baby.'

'The cap'n's baby.' He smiled, then frowned suddenly. 'The cap'n –'

Chill, brought by the memory of a premonition, displaced the heat on her brow. 'Any news?'

'Nay, n-none.'

The boy would get upset too long apart from his 'cap'n' – especially if he suspected his guardian was in any peril. 'All is fine, I am sure,' she said quickly. 'They are celebrating success in some tavern, sure.'

It worked. 'In some tavern, sure,' Dickon repeated, then frowned again. 'The b-baby? Why does it make you sick?'

'I do not know. It was not so last year . . .' She cut herself off. She did not want to think of that lost child, nor of the man who had fathered the babe, the man whose name she still carried – her late husband, John Chalker. There were enough ghosts about the stage of the Duke's Playhouse already, especially as she had last seen him, a torn and bloody carcass.

She closed her eyes, rose from her crouch, mastered her stomach – for from a few feet away came excited voices, the first of the audience jostling for places on the front benches in the pit.

Dickon straightened too. 'C-candles,' he said. She had got him the work behind the scenes at the playhouse and he took his job – mainly the trimming and setting of the candles in the chandeliers that would light the scenes – most seriously.

He moved away but she paused to listen beyond the shouts and arguments in the pit. Words came clear, from a multitude of voices.

'Your Majesty!'

'Your Royal Highness!'

'Huzzah! Huzzah!'

There could be no doubt. King Charles, together with his brother James, Duke of York, had arrived at the theatre's doors. He's early, she thought, gathering her dress to squeeze between the painted wings depicting Elsinore's battlements and bedchambers. She had work to do – to eat if she could; and to paint herself so that she looked as if she could be Hamlet's mother, though Betterton and her were of an age, both twenty-eight. Still, she knew she looked how she felt: ill and old. Very little ceruse would be needed for which she was grateful – the scent of the white lead paint always made her giddy. And she knew that seeing Coke's spirit had left her quite pale enough.

'Your Majesty!'

'Your Royal Highness!'

'Huzzah! Huzzah!'

The man of blood watched them, a little sheltered from the downpour beneath the branches of a sycamore, his cloak tight about him and his uncocked hat pulled low. He did not join in the cheers that greeted King Charles and his brother as they stepped from the coach. He observed – Charles's finery, a scarlet coat whose colour was near suffused in all the gold trim and creamy lace; the king's four guards, men as large as he with the same gimlet stares; the mistress Charles handed down, who shrieked at the rain, its effect on her elaborately set coiffure, tendrilled and tonged for hours, and ran under the theatre's portico. Laughing, Charles acknowledged the acclaim again with a smile and a wave. Then he and his brother strode down the avenue his guards had created through the mob which folded after them like the Red Sea closing after Moses and Aaron.

He turned away to lean against the trunk and listen to the drops patter onto his hat brim, thinking of the last time he'd seen the king. Five years before, in 1661, when he'd been one of a party of Irish Protestant landholders who'd come to petition the newly restored monarch to not return to the Papists the land that had been stripped from them and given to God's own people – themselves. To no avail. Too many Catholics got their land back. Too many of the righteous lost theirs. And his own hatred was kindled for the betrayer, this Stuart king, this Charles whose mother was a Papist, who was said to be a secret one himself, intent on restoring more than himself upon the throne; restoring alongside himself the Antichrist himself, the Devil in Rome, to rule over them all.

He raised a hand. He was surprised to see it shaking. He was surprised to feel tears in his eyes. Seeing the king had done that to him. He breathed deeply, then prayed. "'And God shall wipe away all tears from their eyes; and there shall be no more death, neither sorrow, nor crying, neither shall there be any more pain.'"

He watched his hand steady, his tears dry up. Well, he thought, rubbing his eyes, there will be more death before the glory, if God has chosen this day, and me as his instrument. Me – and this man whose footsteps I hear now.

He softly spoke a name. 'Jeremiah?'

"'Tis I.'

'Prove it.'

The voice that came was high-pitched and tremulous. "'Thou . . . thou art," ah! I am sorry, I –' He broke off, cleared his throat and tried again. "'Thou art my battle axe and weapons of war: for with thee I will . . . *will* I break in pieces the nations. And with thee will I destroy kingdoms.'"

It was close enough. This fellow, nicknamed for the prophet who wrote those words, was an apprentice in the cause. His nervousness was understandable. As long as it did not prevent him doing the Lord's work. 'And here is *your* weapon of war,' the man replied, reaching inside his doublet to the object that had caused such chafing to his back. He grasped the metal sphere, withdrew it, held it still under his cloak. 'Make ready. We do not want any part of this to be exposed to rain, even for a moment.'

'I see. I –' 'Jeremiah' swallowed. 'It will not go off?'

The man grunted. It was extraordinary to him, he who had spent his life at war, that any man could be so ignorant. 'Nay, sure. For that you must introduce it to flame. Swiftly now. We must not linger here.'

21

The transfer was quickly made, though Jeremiah's hands shook as he took the ball. 'And how must I –?'

'Put it away, fool!' The man took another deep breath to quell his irritation, reminding himself that this youth had been chosen by Brother S partly because of his inexperience, the fact that he was not known to any – along with a type of fanaticism that only came from the very newest of converts. Besides, it was all in God's hands – not his, not this Jeremiah's. Though the young man would hurl the grenado, it was God who would decide if the time was right by guiding his aim. God, with a little help from his Saints. 'You remember what is planned?'

'I . . . do?' It came out more like a question and he chewed at already ragged lips. 'I am to wait until the first scene is playing –'

'Do not tell me,' the man interrupted, 'for I do not need to know. My task is done and all is now in God's hands. Trust in him, brother. Praise him!' He turned to go.

Jeremiah grabbed him. 'Tell me, please!' Tears spilled out of his eyes. 'I will do this. The Lord will guide me, I know. But in my desire to serve Him, I seem to have forgotten some . . . some details.' He reached up, wiping his eyes. 'When I light the . . . the fuse, is it? . . . how long must I wait before I throw the grenado? I was told that too soon and it would go out, too late and . . .' He broke off, gave a strange, choked laugh. 'I have forgotten the count.'

The man stared at the youth. When Brother S, his sole contact among the Fifth Monarchists in London, had asked for help with this plan, he'd thought it a weak one. He thought so even more now. How many more times would the great cause be betrayed by poor planning and cowards? Still, in the end, did it require him to believe it would work? No. It only behooved him to believe that God would decide if it did. His only task? To do his utmost to help Providence fulfil itself.

He smiled. It was not a natural set for his long, lean, much-scarred face and the youth blinked up at him. 'Brother,' he said, letting his rough voice go soft, 'it is very simple. When you are ready you put the fuse,' he reached under the other's cloak and tapped it, 'into the candle's flame, see? I am an expert, and fashioned the paper myself, with just enough gunpowder in it so sparks will come. At the first flash you count – one chicken, two chicken.' He said them slowly, steadily. 'Then you simply reach over and lay it into the king's box. As soon as you have done so, you turn, and run from yours. The grenado will explode on six and with God's favour you will be clear of its blast by then. If not,' the smile came again, wolfish, 'you will the next instant be at His right hand in heaven.' He reached over, gripping the other's forearm. 'Pray with me. Our father, who art in heaven . . .'

Jeremiah joined in the only prayer God's saints would countenance. He saw that it steadied the youth, and in his eyes he remembered when he'd first truly heard the Word. As if Jesus himself had come and whispered it into his ear. He would have done then what this 'Jeremiah' was about to do now. Yeah, he thought, with a song of praise on my lips, I would have done it.

The prayer finished, the Amens spoken, he continued, 'I will tell you what I will do. I cannot come inside. There are those who might know me. But I will wait for you here, beneath this tree. Come to me straight when you have fulfilled your vow and I will spirit you to safety. And if you do not come . . .' – he clasped the other's hand – 'why then, I will go and join with all your other

23

brothers in praising your name. And see you again at the resurrection which cometh soon. Amen!'

'Amen!' The youth stepped away. His eyes were clearer now. His hand did not shake as much. 'Bless you, brother. Praise God!'

With that, he turned about, crossed the roadway and pushed his way into the theatre. The man of blood watched him, his strange smile still upon his lips – which vanished when he saw the two men he'd last seen in the alley behind the tavern come from opposite directions and meet before the playhouse. A boy emerged from it to join them there. He capered about, full of jerks and shakes like one palsied. After a moment he dragged the cavalier, the one who'd feigned drunkenness in the Seven Stars, into the playhouse, leaving the huge man to turn and stare.

3

A DEATH AT THE PLAYHOUSE

Pitman looked about him, studying faces, not seeking the man from the Seven Stars but wondering if he could spot his accomplice. He was sure some detail would give him away, some tic, some cast of face or demeanour. But no one stood out among the theatre-goers – men and women, most of them of the well-dressed, middling classes, with the odd nobleman and his lady or mistress distinguished by their even finer apparel and the falsely careless way they wore it, as if they did not court the crowd's admiring gaze. A few, a very few, wore the less fancy attire of trade. Yet all of these, men in the main, had the same expressions of excitement that the buzz of the playhouse gave to all classes – one they'd been deprived of while the plague had raged and all places of entertainment had been shut. Any one of them could be 'acting' of course. Yet Pitman, his own sixth sense highly developed, did not believe that any threat stood near him now.

He glanced across the cobbles to the edge of the park that was Lincoln's Inn Fields. Vendors stood there, men and women, their cries cutting through the chatter of the crowd. 'Seville oranges! Juicy and sweet!' 'Nuts! Nuts! Nuts!' 'Milk from the teat!' Beyond these, others sheltered 'neath the sycamores and cedars, getting what little protection from the still-steady rain that a tree in April could offer. He saw couples entwined, some 'business' being conducted under cloaks; men, single and in pairs, simply regarding the world. One figure especially drew him – a large man whose face was completely hidden between cloak edge and hat brim. There was a quality to his watchfulness. One he recognised in himself.

Pitman took a step.

The bugle blast made him jump, coming so near his ear as it did. The bugler, a young and fresh-faced lad, grinned at the flinching he'd caused, then shouted, his accent of the local streets, 'Ten minutes! Lords, ladies, gentlemen, to your places. Whores? Finish 'em off, will ya? The play's the thing!'

Another blast and the boy slipped back inside, others now jostling to follow. The clothes parade was done, though more posing would take place inside. The main business of the day was about to commence.

Pitman looked back across the street. The watchful figure had gone. He shrugged and, using his bulk, forced a swift entrance into the playhouse.

'Cap'n's here!' Dickon cried, pulling Coke in by his arm.

She cried out, as she had before when she'd seen his shade upon the stage. In a moment, she was up and in his arms.

'Ha!' said Coke, startled by the force of her assault but happy in it and to hold her as her hands moved up and down his arms. 'Madam, are you verifying that I still have all my limbs?'

Sarah pulled back to stare up at him, searching his face. 'You are well. You are here.'

He frowned at the statements, yet smiled at the same time. 'As you see – and feel, chuck. Why would I not be?'

'You left so early. And about some danger.'

'Not truly –'

She stamped. 'Nay, do not try to deny it, sir. I am not a child. I am not!'

Her concern had turned to sudden anger. She was prone to such instant switches, especially recently, her moods changeable. Now he was torn – he wanted to warn her of what might happen today in the theatre. He'd even thought to beg Betterton to at least delay the play a little while he and Pitman searched. One swift glance at the player told him, though – a man does not play Hamlet every day. And not before his king. The king who stood beside him now, his brother with him, all laughing at something the player was saying.

Coke turned to Dickon. 'Do you not have work to be about, ye rogue?'

'Aye, aye, Cap'n.' He laughed, saluted and scampered away.

He turned back to Sarah. Her eyes searched his. He had little more facility with lies than he did with compliments. But he must try – and he was better, anyway, with action. 'Nothing so dangerous, sweet. We track a villain whose taking may fill our purses. And we think he may even be here in the playhouse.' So far, so good. 'And now I must join Pitman in the pit to continue the hunt. I just came to wish you good luck for the performance.'

Her face softened. 'You do not wish an actress luck before the play. It is bad luck to do so. You wish me an injury.'

'Ah.' His ignorance had won him a smile. He furrowed his brow. 'I am sorry. I do not think I could ever wish you any harm.'

'Then go, you goose.' She slapped his arm, then took it more gently, adding softly. 'But with care.'

That look in her eye was back. He did not understand it. Then again, in this field, he truly understood so little. So he just bowed and said, 'Always. And good –'

'Go,' she said, slapping him again.

He went.

Sarah watched him all the way to the door, through it, staring at the space for a long moment after he left. Then, sighing, she turned back to her mirror. He is safe, she mouthed to her image in the glass. All is well.

'Pray, Mr Peckworth. Allow me.' The attendant reached past the young man who was trying with just one hand to draw the curtains that backed the box. 'There's a trick to it – la!' He pulled the heavy cloth aside. 'Please, enter.'

He did – still holding one arm in the manner of a wounded bird, Aitcheson observed. Blinking like one too, in the sudden bright light of a thousand candles from the auditorium, and in the waft of warmed air bringing a thousand smells. He swayed, and Aitcheson reached out to grip him. 'Steady, there. Are you well, sir?'

'Thank you. A small fever is all. Quite well.'

Aitcheson dropped his hand quickly, wiping it surreptitiously on his breeches. Though the plague that had killed so many the previous year was said to have entirely passed – which was why the theatre had been allowed to open again only this week – there were rumours that people still died of it in the poorer parts of the city; that not every house had the red cross painted out. He forced another smile. 'And will your eminent brother, Sir Walter, be joining you shortly?'

'Yes. No. I . . . I d-don't know,' the young man stammered. 'Perhaps.'

'I doubt that Sir Walter, for all his care for the city, would miss Master Betterton playing Hamlet, eh?'

'Hamlet? Oh, is that what's on?'

Aitcheson took a small step away. They were too close anyway, for the other still stood nearer to the corridor than the box's front. He might not be plagued but he was certainly mad. Not know what was playing? Or perhaps he was drunk? And speaking of – 'What refreshment would you care for, Master Peckworth? I have some fine canary –'

'No, no wine. Maybe later, ah? But you could bring me a . . . a –'

Nuts, oranges, a whore, thought the attendant. But the reply surprised.

'A lantern.'

'A lantern?' The youth, his eminent brother notwithstanding, was starting to annoy him. 'You will see the stage well enough, sir.'

'Ah, but I . . . I wish to read. And my eyes?' He waved his one free hand before them. 'Not so good, do ye see?'

'I will attend to it forthwith, sir.'

'Oh, and take this to see that I am not disturbed.'

Aitcheson put out his hand – and the man put a gold guinea into it. It was new minted, shiny, King Charles's profile handsome upon it – which reminded him. 'And sir, you do know that His Majesty will be in attendance this day? And that the royal box is next to you here, closest to the stage?'

'I do know.' For some reason Peckworth giggled. 'I am counting on it.'

Definitely mad, Aitcheson thought, as he stepped into the corridor. There was a small window right opposite the box for the rich to gaze upon those still arriving. He looked out at the crowd still pushing in. A full house, he thought to himself with satisfaction. Lots of money to be made today.

He descended to the small room where the attendants kept their properties. His colleague Hutchins was there, pouring canary into flasks. 'Got another bedlamite in the box next to the royal one,' Aitcheson said, his accent relaxing into his native London 'Indeed, it could be an outer cell of the asylum.'

'Same box that, whatsisname, that Lord Garnthorpe had last year? The one what tried to kill the Duke of York?'

'It is.' Aitcheson found a lantern, lighting the candle within it with another. 'And compared to him, this one's a mere gibberer.'

'Anything?'

Pitman stood in the stairwell of the pit, unmoving as a rock in an ocean of people. They bounced on him, off him, squeezed around him, cursed him. He ignored all, continuing his scan of the house. 'Nothing,' he replied to Coke who'd shoved through to him. 'I have not seen our man. But not all have arrived yet. Not even the king.'

'He's behind the stage, talking with Betterton.'

Pitman pointed. 'They've moved the royal box. 'Twas on t'other side last year.'

'You're right. And they've taken the pause of the plague to gild it up. 'Tis twice as plush now.'

'They court royal favour. It draws the fashionable crowd. See how the other boxes are crowded with the nobility.' He swept his gaze in a circle about. 'Except for the box next to it. It's yet unoccupied.'

'Not for long, I'm certain. Sarah told me that every seat for this was taken up weeks ago.' He glanced around. 'There is a buzz, is there not?'

'Aye.' Pitman's gaze went around the auditorium once more, then settled on his friend. 'Earlier, Captain, at the tavern? When you were close enough to the man we've lost to smell him, did you happen to feel if he had any weapons concealed?'

'Marry, I gave him some gropes I'd have hesitated to visit on a mistress. I would swear he had none. Mayhap a dagger in his boot cuff which I did not see. But Charles's guards would never let a knifeman near him, for sure.'

'Nay, they would not. Yet a weapon of some kind could have been prior concealed about this place, awaiting him.'

'Something I do not understand.' Coke pulled the larger man to the side of the stair, easing through another flood of play-goers. 'This place. The fellow could not have chosen a more public setting for his attempt on the king's life. How could he hope to get away with it?'

'Killing a man in public is difficult – but not impossible, as many examples have shown us. And if by getting away you mean the assassin surviving the attempt, I do not think that concerns him.' He ceased his surveying, turning to look at Coke. 'Remember, his entire life is dedicated to God, to do with what He will. His death entirely in His hands also. He may wish to live and continuing worshipping, but if he dies as a martyr then –' He shrugged.

'He will speed to God's right side and dwell forever in Paradise. For he will have hastened the return of the king, Jesus, to rule us all.' He looked about him at the bustling, smiling play-goers. 'And he will not care how many sinners are sacrificed in that cause.'

'Another man driven mad by faith. I am ever thankful that I have none.' Coke shivered. 'We saw many such fanatics in the wars, did we not? Mainly on your side, I have to say. How did you avoid it, Pitman? You were fanatical in your time too, were you not? Even one of these same damned Fifth Monarchists for a while?'

'I was. But I decided that Christ, in his wisdom, will choose the time of his return entirely without my intervention. So I will worship him – but I will save my love for my family. Ah,' Pitman pointed with his chin, 'he comes.'

In the royal box, previously empty, a soldier in the scarlet coat of the King's Life Guards now stood. For a long moment he surveyed the scene below. Then he turned to the back of the box and nodded. At the same moment, three musicians walked out upon the stage and began to play a royal air.

The next moment Charles was there, standing at the very front of the box. Those who had sat in the auditorium, in the boxes, now rose and joined those still standing. Huzzahs came, shouts of 'God save Your Majesty!' and 'Health to Your Majesty.' The Duke of York joined Charles and the acclaim slackened a little – His Grace's dull brown clothes made him a pigeon to his brother's peacock, and he was an avowed Catholic to boot. A lady joined them, masked, and the house erupted in twittered speculation as to which royal mistress was present. All three waved, looked about them, bestowing nods on a favoured few. Then, suddenly, all sat. The musicians changed their tune as they marched off, moving from celebration to a softer, sadder air. An actor, carrying a spear, walked to the centre of the stage, to applause. But he did not, to Coke's relief, start making an over-solicitous speech of welcome as was customary. As the music ended with a flourish, there was a last rush of play-goers past them, forcing themselves onto the pit's benches, to cries of outrage and much jostling. The actor waited, allowing all to settle. Then he bowed briefly to the royal box, turned to the right and hissed, 'Who's there?'

'Do we sit, Pitman?'

'Let's keep afoot and light upon 'em, too. Something's amiss, I can sense it.' He looked up, to the box next to the king's. 'And why is that the only damned seat not taken in the house?'

Coke peered. 'Nay, but it is. There's someone there, sitting a little back in the gloom. Can't quite see him –' He leaned closer. 'Ha! Did you observe our man smoke a pipe in the tavern?'

'He was one of very few who did not.'

'And I smelled no smoke upon his clothes.' He started, clutching the other's arm. 'So answer me this: why did he just ungate a lantern?'

Pitman did not reply. He just set out at a run for the front of the playhouse.

Upon the stage, and to many gasps, a ghost appeared.

'I'll make a ghost of him – of all the Stuarts. Ha ha! And the Whore of Babylon beside.'

Simon Peckworth giggled as he fumbled open the gate of the lantern. But he did not grab the candle straightway. His hand was shaking so much he feared he would snuff it out. Flame was so fragile – this one anyway. But this little spark would soon conjure a greater one that would send Charles to the flames of Hell.

'The Lord is my shepherd,' he breathed, 'I shall not want.'

The psalm soothed, as it always did. He'd been frightened when the king's guard had thrust into the box, demanding to know who he was. The attendant had saved him, vouching for him as Sir Walter Peckworth's brother. Sir Walter was one of the king's staunchest supporters in Parliament. The guard had withdrawn and never noticed what the cushion concealed.

He reached for the grenado now. It was lighter than he remembered, but solid. Better to put it to the flame than the flame to it.

As he reached to the lantern, words came as if from far away.

'But soft, behold, lo, where it comes again!
I'll cross it though it blast me.'

He smiled. The words were appropriate for what he was about. But he had even better ones by heart. 'Yea though I walk through the valley of the shadow of death, I will fear no evil: For thou art with me, thy rod and thy staff they comfort me.'

He felt comforted. He stopped shaking and pushed the fuse into the flame.

A guard was at the top of the stairs. 'Stop!' he shouted, reaching for his sword, as Pitman and Coke charged up.

They could not. 'The king!' Pitman cried and hurled himself at the man, pushing his sword back into its sheath, grappling him.

But the guard was of a size with the thief-taker and had his duty. Both men went down.

Coke vaulted them and ran on down the corridor. As he neared its end, another guard emerged from the royal box, sword drawn. 'Hold there!' he cried, levelling. But Coke did not halt, nor explain. Slapping aside the rapier's blade, he threw back the curtains of the last but one box and stepped inside.

A man stood there. He stank. He had fire in his eyes, fire in his hand and it was that fire that Coke looked at, for it spluttered. 'One chicken,' the man said, and giggled. 'Two chicken.'

He was just beginning to turn away when Coke reached and wrapped his hand around the flame. It burned him but he did not let go, not until he'd jerked the steel ball clear of the other's grip. Then he dropped it.

The man punched him, but on the top of the head, enough to make him stagger. Coke bent, hands raised against further blows – and saw that the fuse to what he knew now to be a grenado was not entirely out, a red glow near its base. He shot his hand down, snatched the weapon up and, just as the guard disentangled himself from the curtains and thrust in, stepped under the guard's raised sword arm and hurled the ball at the window opposite.

Glass shattered. The grenado dropped just below the sill – and exploded.

The window frame and a huge chunk of the lath and plaster wall burst in, knocking both Coke and the guard to the floor, covering them with choking dust and horsehair. The explosion had near-deafened him and the shouts that were now coming from box and auditorium seemed very far away; he could barely see, through the white clouds, shapes moving. He glimpsed what he thought was Pitman, still locked on the floor in the guard's embrace. He looked the other way – to the king emerging from his box, mouthing words.

It appeared that the only sense that was fully functioning was in his nose. He felt, rather than saw, a shape pass above him. But he certainly smelled him, as Simon Peckworth leapt over him, over Pitman, and ran down the stairs.

The explosion was loud. Too loud, he thought. If it had happened within the building, the noise of the grenado would have come to him muffled, a dull crump, and screams hard upon it. This had been a sharp crack following the smash of breaking glass.

Had he lost his nerve? It was likely. The man had reeked of fear. Though it was odd that he would have gone as far as the lighting of the fuse which, surely, was the most terrifying thing? To have changed his mind at the last moment? To decide that even though it was this spawn of the Antichrist that he was to kill, he had not the nerve to be a killer? Many had not. He had not, once.

Now I will know, he thought. The doors are opening, the sinners are flooding out of their place of sin; there is lamentation. But it is made of fright, not horror. No one has died this day. Not yet.

Among the very first to appear was Jeremiah. The man of blood shifted slightly and prepared to meet him.

The youth staggered across, collapsed onto him. He was weeping, snot running from his nose, snail trails glistening on the white powder of plaster that covered him head to toe. 'Help me!' he cried. 'They will come. We must flee.'

The man prevented him easily with one hand. 'You failed.'

'I was thwarted!' Peckworth wailed. 'Those men. The ones in the tavern. They —' He used the other's arms to drag himself upright, until their faces nearly touched. 'Help me!' he beseeched.

'I will.'

There wasn't a question. Once more, Jesus had been failed by a man who had not the will to succeed, to do what must be done. A man who, even if he managed to get away now, would be taken soon. It was clear in his voice, his eyes — his stench. Broken easily, he would betray them all.

It was harder than it appeared, to kill a man with a knife. At least he had found it so, once. The weapon was important, a thin, well-tempered steel blade the best — a stiletto, where the edges were naught, the point everything. It was this he drove up, once he'd discovered with a fingertip the right spot between the ribs. Then it was easy. He burst the heart, red surged from the mouth and drowned the 'why' the young man would have spoken.

'Peace be with you,' the man of blood murmured, holding the other until the fire in his eyes went out. As he lowered the martyr to the ground, as he sheathed his knife, he felt that peace descend on him.

'Next time, Lord,' he said as he walked away from the screams and the shouting, 'next time.'

4

THE TRACT OF TEARS

Pitman had always believed that ghosts were nothing but Catholic superstition; that none would rise from their graves to walk again until the last trump sounded and Christ returned to judge both the quick and the dead.

Well, bugger I, he thought, I've turned Papist. For there are ghosts before me now.

He watched them from where he lay in the playhouse corridor, each figure shimmering white and moving as slowly as if underwater, their every sound half-drowned, barely piercing the sharp whine that had taken near all his hearing. Yet this was not unfamiliar, this scene, this sound, and he suddenly recalled the cannon that had exploded next to him on the ramparts at Brentford. It had made ghosts of all its crew and nearly him as well though he didn't see them.

And the king hadn't been there. This king, indeed, would have been a child then and so unable to stride down the corridor, bend and shake him, mouthing words that slowly, slowly began to penetrate the whine.

'Pitman? Pitman? Are you hurt? Pitman?'

He swung onto his knees, bent his head, and thought he was going to puke. But the king's hand was now upon his back, and the king's voice was becoming clearer. 'Rest easy, man.'

Instead of vomit he managed spit. His mouth was filled with plaster and he voided it onto the floor. 'Your pardon, Majesty,' he managed to croak.

'Take your time.' Charles turned. 'You there! Bring wine.'

Pitman rolled and placed his back against the wall. One of the king's guards approached flask in hand and he gulped the canary gratefully, swilling his mouth clean. His senses were clearing, he could smell the wine now, and the king's cologne, even through the sulphurous reek that dominated the air; he could hear other voices down the corridor and even a greater murmur from beyond it, from the auditorium. With returning senses came memory. 'Captain Coke?' he gasped and tried to rise.

'I am here.'

His partner knelt beside the king, who said, 'Do you have him, sir? I should show myself or the crowd may panic.'

'I have him.' Coke smiled. 'And we have Your Majesty's canary, so we will be fine.'

'Keep it,' said Charles, rising. 'Recover – and remain, if you please. There are matters here I do not understand, such as your presence – again – when me and mine are under threat. I would discuss it.'

With that he was gone, into the enfolding arms of his guards, several engaged in brushing the plaster from their scarlet coats. He swept into his box, and they heard the upsurge of voices that greeted his reappearance and then his reassuring tone. 'Calm, ladies, gentlemen, I pray you, calm. I am quite well.'

Someone pulled the thick box curtains closed, and Charles's voice came to Pitman muffled through them. It let him concentrate on the man before him. 'You do not look like a ghost, Captain,' he croaked, coughed and drank.

'Ghost?' He looked down. 'Oh, the powder. Nay, once I'd flung the bomb through the window, I retired swiftly into the shelter of the box.'

He reached down and began to dust Pitman's shoulder, but the larger man took and held his hand. 'And the bomber?'

'Fled. Out the front.'

'It was our pigeon from the tavern?'

'It was, aye. But I have his face fixed. We'll find the rogue again.'

'Indeed. I would ask him some questions.' Pitman drank, shaking his head hard. 'Captain, my hearing is still a little affected. But is that . . . screaming I hear?'

Coke stood, stepped towards the large hole that the grenado had torn in the wall. ''Tis. A woman's and in front of the theatre. She . . . she's screaming blue murder and –' he turned, 'and real murder too. Someone's dead out there.'

'Help me up.'

Pitman thrust out a hand and Coke pulled him to his feet. 'Are you sure you are able?' he asked.

'My body feels like a thousand horses have trampled upon't. But I'll manage, on your arm. If there's murder outside the theatre, it must be connected with the attempted murder within it. Let us see it before some fool interferes with all the evidence.'

They were halfway down the stairs, moving slowly, when the voice halted them. 'Is all this mayhem to do with the pair of you?'

They looked down. Sarah was at the bottom of the stairs. But she was up them in a moment and her arms around each of them. 'What happened? What was the explosion? Are you hurt?'

The story, what they knew, was swiftly told as they descended and then stood before the theatre and the mob that milled there. Relief shaded quickly into anger. 'And you, sir,' she said, striking Coke on the arm. 'You try to fob me off with reassurances that your work is none so dangerous?'

'Most is not, Sarah. Besides, we need –' He broke off.

'The money. I know.' She touched her belly. 'But our child would rather have a father than a full purse.'

He laid his hand on hers. 'He shall have both, love.'

'Oh? You are certain that I carry your son? Marry, sir, it is far –'

'Peace, both!' Pitman interrupted. 'Delighted as I am to witness that you love each other enough to bicker so, we have work here to do.'

He said this as he began to move through the mob across the cobbled lane that separated playhouse and park. But the mob was thickest before one tree – the tree, he now remembered, behind which he'd seen that cloaked and muffled figure before the play. 'Make way, there,' he called and, when the backs did not shift, added on a bass bellow, 'Headborough of the parish! Make way!'

Most parted then, enough to reveal the body on the ground – and a man crouched over it, who looked up now. 'Not this parish, Mr Pitman. I'm headborough around here.'

He looked down at the man he'd known a little when they were both constables in adjoining parishes in the city. The fellow who'd been plump then was huge now, though his formerly ramshackle beard had lately been trimmed to a regal moustache. 'Congratulations on your promotion, Mr Deakins. Oh, and it's Pitman, as you'll remember no doubt. Plain Pitman, without the "Mr".'

'Ah, yes. "Plain Pitman" indeed.' He extended a hand which Pitman shook. 'How's the watch in St Leonard's?' He looked at the other's clothes. 'Or have you given up crime for plastering?'

'Nay, still in the field. But at St Mary-le-Bow now.'

Deakins whistled. 'Now there's an elevation, sure. Richest parish in the city? Headborough?' The other nodded. 'How d'you swing that?'

'I did the state some service. My reputation –' He shrugged.

'Oh yes. I heard something 'bout that. Saved . . .' – he looked around at the jostling, whispering crowd – 'someone's life, eh?' He sucked air between his lips. 'Well, you always had an eye.' He jerked his head. 'Care to cast it over this here?'

Pitman nodded, and the two men knelt. 'Stabbed,' Deakins said. 'Right in the heart. Killed him straight. A lucky jab for both, for sure.'

Pitman stared at the man he'd last seen alive in the Seven Stars tavern. Death had smoothed his features, stilled his wild eyes – though it had done nothing to lessen the stench Coke had talked of. Rather the opposite. 'May I?' He gestured at the blood-soaked clothes.

'What you will.'

He felt the wetness. Yet warm, not surprising since he'd fled less than ten minutes before. There was a lot of it too, and its source was confirmed as he pulled open the slick buttons of the doublet and reached inside the lawn shirt. Deakins was right, the heart had been directly punctured. But he was also wrong. The wound was neat, minuscule. No luck was involved here. Not for the victim — nor for his killer.

'Rest in peace,' he murmured, reaching up to close the youth's eyes. Yet as he did he glanced down, and noticed it: the corner of paper sticking out of a pocket in the doublet he'd folded aside; he'd nearly missed it because it had soaked up the blood and so was blended into the cloth. He did not reach for it, though, not yet. Some things needed to be kept to oneself. Instead he turned. 'Have you constables to take him to the mortuary?'

'Aye,' Deakins replied, rose and called out, 'Egbert! Fleetwood! Here!'

As soon as the man turned, Pitman reached both hands to the corpse — one to prise open the pocket, one to withdraw the paper. A little split off but he got the bulk out and swiftly tucked it away inside his coat.

The watchmen arrived. Sharp orders overcame their reluctance and the wet body was soon slung between them, the crowd parting to let them through. 'Anything to identify him, Pitman?' Deakins asked.

'Nothing.'

'Ach, we'll find that soon enough. He's well dressed, so someone will be missing him. Probably a jealous lover, eh? He must have been pretty enough once to woo the ladies — or the boys,' he added with a wink. 'Yes, I'll be studying the mourners careful. Good fortune, man.'

He left, following his constables, the small crowd moving away to reveal Coke, Sarah and others. Standing with them were two men: one, tall and hefty with the same hard look as one of the king's guards, who was looking around as one of the guards would do, searching for threats; the other Pitman had met for the first time only the day before. He was, Pitman supposed, their current employer. Under-Secretary for State, he was also the nation's spymaster. 'Sir Joseph,' he said, coming to them. 'I did not know you liked the theatre.'

'I loathe it.' Williamson was long and skinny, bent forward like a heron poised above a fall of water, though not a crested one, his hair long since having retreated over the high, bald dome of his head. He was a Cumbrian by birth, his native vowels further clipped now by his impatience. 'I would much rather be at my desk and about my business. But something told me I should attend this day. And was I not right?' He pointed with his chin to the body being carried away. 'What news?'

'Have you met Captain Coke and Mrs —'

'What news, sirrah?'

Pitman had never been a servant and disliked being treated as one. It confirmed what he'd half decided anyway: to withhold whatever his pocket now held. It might be nothing; that he would decide once he'd seen it. Besides, possession of information only he had meant power now — and perhaps coin later. 'Only this, sir. The would-be assassin is dead. Killed within minutes of his attempt by . . .' he hesitated, '. . . by someone who knew what he was about.'

Williamson's eyes narrowed. 'By someone, er,' he glanced at the others then back to Pitman, '*sanguine?*'

Pitman shrugged. 'Perhaps.'

'Hmm.' He stared for a moment longer. 'We will discuss this

further. Tomorrow. Nine o'clock. My office. Whitehall. Bring all your thoughts there. Oh yes. Then there's this.'

He nodded to the guard who reached beneath his cloak, undid a pouch from his belt, then held it out to Pitman. 'The sum agreed,' his employer said, and when Pitman took it, he turned again, taking a step, his guard a shadow on his shoulder. 'You may go.'

Pitman's voice halted him. 'Thank you, sir. But the king ordered us to remain and speak with him.'

The minister stopped and turned. 'The king has changed his mind. He is ever . . . changeable. And he would see the end of this play.'

It was Coke who spoke, in surprise. 'After this?'

'Especially after this. He would not have any say he is afraid. Indeed, he delights in bravado. It can make his safety a little, ah, difficult to manage.' He sniffed. 'However, I am sure the players will struggle to match his sangfroid.' Finally, his gaze alighted on Sarah. 'Means "cool blood", girl. Think you can muster some for His Majesty?'

He spoke as if to a child. Sarah let her accent slip back to the streets she was born in. 'Oh, I think I might manage it, cock. So 'ow about you pop in after and warm us back up again?'

She was rewarded with the faintest rose on the pallid cheeks. 'Interesting,' the spymaster said, before walking away.

He'd merged into the crowd at the playhouse doors before Coke and Pitman broke into laughter. 'I suspect there's few who can make that man blush, Mrs Chalker,' Pitman commented.

'Ah, he's just a man in the end. Easy to judge, like all of you.' She looked to the theatre. 'Here we go.'

The bugler had stepped out again. His blast was less assured now, his voice wobbly. 'The p-play. Back to the play. It rec— recommen— starts again.' The bugler slipped back inside.

'I will see you later. Here, or at our lodgings?' Sarah said to Coke.

'Nay, here,' he replied. 'Indeed, I'll come in and watch. If the king has sangfroid then, damn me, so have I. Pitman? Pitman?'

'Hmm.' The thief-taker's gaze that had been up to the sky returned to them. 'Er, no. I have matters to attend to. I must go home and see my Bettina. She will have an unguent for my side which still aches from the blast. Maybe she can candle my ears, for they still ring. I will see you both later.'

They went, and Pitman turned his gaze heavenwards again, closing his face to the rain. Sangfroid, he thought – cold blood. He had no doubt that the murder had happened coldly. Blood, still warm from the side of the dead man, soaked into the mud before him.

He stepped under the scant shelter of the same tree and carefully pulled the damp paper from his cloak's pocket. Unfolding it tore it slightly more, as he was surprised to find that he could not control a palsy in his hand. Yet he was still able to recognise what it was: a prophecy tract that some millenarian had printed up on cheap paper and sold for tuppence. Here, one 'Hebediah Baker' had set down his visions. Reading was not one of Pitman's strengths and he pieced it together slowly, his finger tracing the words, his lips moving.

'A fire, a consuming fire, shall be kindled in the bowels of the earth which will scorch with burning heat all hypocrites, unstable double-minded workers of iniquity. Yea, a great effusion of blood, fire and smoke shall increase up in the dark habitations of cruelty, howling and great wailing shall be on every hand in all her streets.'

'Blood. Fire. Smoke,' he mumbled.

He had seen such tracts as this before. They told of the destruction to be visited upon that modern Babylon, that seventeenth-century Sodom and Gomorrah, that London. Yet this one, stained red by a man who, howsoever deluded, considered himself a martyr, disturbed him as no other had. He raised his eyes to the sky and closed them to the chill rain. And felt it — another crease in the paper. He looked down.

Someone had written in ink a date at the foot of the paper. September the third 666. Not 1666. Just those three numbers that everyone knew — numbers and a date he now watched run from the page in blue and red, and made no effort to stop their blurring.

5

PROPHECIES

Two days later

From its strings held high, the marionette twirled slowly. With its huge hook of a nose, vast eyes that were nearly all whites, horse-hair eyebrows like a tavern door's boot-brush, a red slash of a wildly grinning mouth, it was a spinning grotesque. Yet when it settled, it was beside a face that many would find just as disturbing.

The man knew it. 'Are we not a match, Punchinello and I?' Simeon Critchollow asked, laughing, his voice a deep roll. 'Mind, I never was handsome. When I began in the theatre, all I played were servants and roughs, not once a noble lord.' He reached up, ran a finger across the bright scar that bisected his twisted nose. 'So, in some ways, that cavalier at Naseby did me favour. I would have starved as an actor. Yet now I am a leading player. Or rather, my friend and I are.'

The puppet's face swung again. For a moment the two grotesques were in profile. When it swung back, it spoke, its voice a screech. 'Eh, eh eh? 'andsome boy? Take me. Take me!'

Daniel carefully placed one hand atop the puppeteer's where it held the wooden struts, reaching the other to the huge wooden arse under the wool pantaloons. 'Ooh! 'elp me, master,' the puppet yelped, jerking forward. ''andsome boy's feelin' us up!'

When Daniel blushed, Simeon laughed. The younger man took the puppet and carried it across to the boxes, laid it gently down in its cradle, pulled the blanket across, tucking it around. Finally, with a certain relief, he covered the wickedly grinning face. He took the wooden lids, slid them into their grooves on each box. Punchinello now slept in his coffin, alongside his wife, the judge, the hangman, the brat, in theirs.

'We did well.' Simeon yawned and shook the purse.

Daniel hesitated. He did not often question the man who'd raised him from degradation, who'd led him from darkness into light. But the puppet-master seemed relaxed tonight. 'Why did you choose to play in this tavern, master, now the theatres are open again? Would you not have taken more money at the Moorfields playhouse?'

Simeon took a swig of ale. 'Undoubtedly. But here better suited my plans. No musicians to hire, save you on your flute. No ticket men, ale men, fruit sellers. Besides, the innkeeper here is a brother Saint. He could use the trade and we – we needed a meeting place.' He looked around the large upstairs room. Chairs were scattered about and the floor was awash with the audience's leavings – peanut husks, orange peel, chicken bones, bungs from bottles. He frowned. 'Tidy, boy.'

Daniel fetched a broom and began to sweep, pushing the detritus into great piles, moving chairs to the side, save for the six that would be required for the Council of the Great Ones, while his master sat, sipping, watching him, reviving.

He truly is a handsome lad now, Simeon thought. Such contrast to the thin, scabbed and desperate wretch who'd begged a coin from him last year, while the plague raged. Simeon had given him more than silver. He'd given him hope and a cause – the greatest, the only one: the return of King Jesus. A second coming to be hastened tonight in the resolutions of his Fifth Monarchist brethren.

The room was near swept clean when Simeon heard boots upon the stair. He frowned. A bell in the nearby church had only just struck eight, and there was yet an hour until the meeting. 'Daniel,' he called, 'come stand beside me.' As the footfalls neared, he reached into his bag, pulled out and cocked a pistol, keeping it below the table.

However, it was neither a pack of constables, nor an eager member of the Six who came through the door, but a man he'd been thinking much on lately – one that disturbed and excited him in equal measure. Uncocking, then putting his pistol back into his bag, he rose. 'Welcome, Mr Morton and, er, you have brought your friend, Master Hunt. I am pleased to see you both well.'

The men stopped on the threshold and the elder spoke. 'Since there are none but friends here, you may call us by our God-given names, Critchollow.'

'Very well then. Blood – *Pater et fili. Capitanus et –*'

'And you can stop the Papist talk,' replied Captain Blood, striding up to the table. 'Plain English is the Lord's true tongue.'

Simeon gave a faint sigh. He was as rigorous in God's work as any man alive. But a touch of lightness in discourse surely offended no one? Yet the big Irishman and his hulking son, who

50

was perhaps fifteen, had no lightness about them at all. 'Fetch the Bloods that jug of beer, Daniel,' he said, 'and the bread and cheese too.'

Daniel brought both over and the two sat, quaffed and ate as if they hadn't for some days. Maybe they hadn't. Simeon had no idea where Blood stayed in London, or even if he did. He came, he went. He knew only this: where the man had been two days ago. And he needed to know more about that. 'Take the young gentleman downstairs, Daniel,' he said. 'The captain and I have matters to discuss.'

The younger Blood looked at his father, who nodded. Cramming another hunk of cheese between two thick slices of bread and grabbing his pint pot, he went out of the door. Daniel followed, closing it quietly behind them.

Simeon watched the man eat for a few seconds more before he spoke. 'Well?'

It was obvious what was being asked. 'He failed,' Blood replied through a full mouth.

'Since the tyrant was observed playing at pell-mell only this afternoon I surmised that much. How did he fail?'

'How?' The Irishman's green eyes swivelled onto Simeon's. 'Want of will.'

Simeon frowned. 'That puzzles me. For I recall him being most willing – fervent, indeed. His eyes shone with his desire and with the holy spirit. He would have given everything, including his life – which he did.'

Blood drank, then set down his tankard. 'It is one thing to be willing in the chapel, in fellowship, your ears ringing with God's praises. You will find it is quite another thing out there,' he jabbed a thumb over his shoulder, 'to discover the will to kill a man.'

'Oh, trust me, brother. I have killed my share,' Simeon replied softly, then touched a finger to his scar. 'And I did not get this in a chapel.'

The two men stared at each other for a moment – until Blood spoke. 'Well, some men can and some can't. He was one of the latter.'

'Yet he died in the act?'

'Did he?' Blood took up his tankard, sat back. 'Blown up, was he? I tried to explain the timing of the thing –'

'Not blown up. Stabbed.'

Blood paused for a moment, then shrugged. 'I suppose it's why the king employs his guards. To stab assassins.'

And Simeon thought, Oh, I see you, sir. In a lifetime spent in lies he knew how to read them. So he knew who had killed Brother Peckworth. He knew why – the man before him would leave no trail to follow. He also knew that, in God's great plan, it mattered not a jot.

Reaching for the jug, Blood poured himself more ale. 'There's something you need to know. Jeremiah was followed. Someone had wind of the thing.'

Simeon frowned. Peckworth had been chosen for this task because he was a 'white lamb' – new to the cause, unremarked by the state, untainted. And only a tiny few knew of this venture – the Council of the Six, due to meet there that night. If one of them was a traitor . . . 'How do you know this?'

Blood snorted. 'Marry, brother, I haven't survived this long at this game without having my senses about me. I spotted your fellow straightway. 'slid, he gave himself away with his fidgeting. So I bided a while – and soon enough saw the two who watched him.'

'King's agents?'

'Perhaps. Though unlike any I'd seen before.'

'How so?'

Blood leaned back, staring at the ceiling. 'One was big, in every way. Bald as a billiard ball but with a huge beard that came to here,' he put fingers to the chest, 'while the other . . .'

'. . . had long greying hair and a moustache.'

The words were spoken so softly, so coldly, that Blood looked down sharply. 'You know them?'

'Oh, I know them.' Simeon looked above the other's head. But he did not see a tavern's wall. He saw a dead man. He had a broken wrist, a knife wound in the side and chest blown open with shot. This had killed him. But then his corpse had been subjected to the further horrors visited upon all traitors. Like the deceased regicides who had signed the first Charles's death warrant – dug from their graves on the second Charles's restoration six years before, beheaded, quartered, their several parts distributed through the land as warning – so had his comrade's body been treated. He had gone to watch this second martyrdom. Borne witness. Testified. Six months ago, almost to this day.

'Critchollow?'

Simeon's eyes focused again. The man of blood was staring at him. 'These men,' he said softly, 'are named Pitman and Coke. The one is a thief-taker, the other a reformed highwayman. And together with Coke's whore, one Sarah Chalker, they managed to snap one of God's brightest blades, even in the moment before His triumph –'

He broke off, words and memories choking him. 'His name?' Blood asked.

'You may read it in the book of martyrs,' Simeon replied. 'Garnthorpe.'

'The man who nearly killed the Duke of York last year?'

'The same.'

Blood whistled. 'Would he were alive today to aid us in this great work.'

'Amen. But he is not. While these foes, these sinners, these servants of the Antichrist,' Simeon took a deep breath, 'they appear again to thwart us. To thwart God's plan.' He shook his head hard, reached for the jug, topping up both tankards, and raised his. 'Will you toast our dead brothers for their sacrifice?'

'No.' Blood did not raise his mug. 'I will not toast stupidity.'

Simeon glared. 'Killing the king is stupidity?'

'Failing to kill him is.' Blood slammed his mug down. 'Listen well, man. I was willing to aid you, given my newness to the town, and my knowledge of matters explosive. But I always thought it a poor shot. Christ's mercy,' he cried out, 'sure and have I not had enough of this in my native land? Where every other madman thinks that all success demands is courage and God's name on his lips? Answer me this – why should the Almighty help those who have not proved themselves deserving of His help?'

'He –'

But Blood was not seeking a reply. Tapping the side of his head, he continued, 'The Almighty gave us dominion over the earth when he gave us reason. Yet we squander that gift again and again,' he slapped the table, 'on petty actions. 'sooth, I'm done with such toys. I will never again risk my life, nor my son's, in any foolish endeavour. From now on, what I want is a plan. Cunningly reasoned, skilfully executed, and above all this.' He leaned forward, his eyes boring into Simeon's. 'To only venture at a time that God has already marked out for success. Then will we be proved worthy of God's blessing. Then will the Saints inherit the earth.'

Simeon was used to testifying. He did it himself. But the man was right – too often, it was dreamers who did it, who knew not how to do more than recount their dreams. Yet here was a man who did do more. Had done more – in Ireland in recent years. In London two days ago. A man willing not just to talk but to act. 'Amen, brother,' he said. 'I am one with you for that. Reasoned plans require time spent upon 'em.'

'They do.'

'You speak of a time foretold. Has God not set down certain times in his books of prophecy?'

'He has. You know he has. This year –'

'Is 1666. Praise him!'

'Praise him indeed.' Both men nodded, caught up in it now.

'And 666 is the number of the Beast.'

'Aye, the fourth beast. The fourth kingdom upon the earth. The one spoken of in Daniel, in Revelation – destroyed this year. This one! Destroyed by the Fifth Monarchists. By the Saints.' The puppeteer's voice soared. 'When King Jesus returns to lead us – in the flesh!'

'"And I saw heaven opened,"' cried Blood, '"and behold a white horse. And he that sat upon him was called Faithful and True, and in righteousness he doth judge and make war."'

'Amen,' Simeon said. 'He will come. Yet you were right before. We have to earn our place in Christ's army by our deeds. By our reason. And we must seek to find in our prophet's words, just when the hour is to come.'

'Have you calculated it, as many have tried to do?'

'I rely on wiser heads for that. But this I know: there is one date that appears again and again in prophecy. Mother Shipton set it down. The astrologer Lilly, whom all revere. The Saints' own seer, Anna Trapnel. All have marked this day.'

'Name it.'

'September the third.'

Blood thumped the table. 'By heaven's blessing, I knew you'd say that! For I'll tell you something else of it.' He leaned in. ''Twas on September the third that Oliver Cromwell died.' He raised a hand as if to halt a protest. 'I know. Many believe that Cromwell did not go far enough to usher in a truly godly republic. But, by heaven he guided us to holy victories over the old tyrant Charles Stuart. Yeah, and guided him to the block.'

'He did. And do you know what else our Lord Protector did on the day we speak of?' Simeon smiled. 'He defeated the Scots at Dunbar in that mighty fight. And then he also defeated the tyrant who rules us now, the second Charles, at Worcester in '51. Both upon that same special day. And I was with him at both.' His voice dropped to a whisper. 'Never was a day marked out in a year so oft foretold.' He sat straight. 'Never has God set it out for us more clearly, to use both our reason and our faith – to kill a second king. To bring about Armageddon,' he held out his hand, 'on the third day of September, in this the year of the Beast.'

Blood held his gaze for a further, long moment. 'September the third,' he said at last, taking Simeon's hand, shaking it and rising straightway. 'Five months gives us time to plan the thing well, as God would have us do. Gives me time to go to Holland to organise the weapons we will need, as I planned before I was . . . distracted by your scheme. Since the Dutch, a godly people, fight the English upon the sea, they would be delighted to see their brothers in Christ bring disaster to their enemies.'

Simeon rose too. 'Will you not stay a time? We would benefit from your advice.'

Blood eyed him. 'There's danger wherever I stay. How long?'

'A week, maybe two. To allow me to prepare some real plans for your perusal. Unless you care to wait tonight? The Council –'

'The Council may be compromised and you must look to that. Someone betrayed Jeremiah, remember. Besides, I do not wish to be caught up in debate. Come up with actions and I will play my role in them. Two weeks?' Blood tipped his head to the side. 'Hang a blanket from this window on the morning of the meeting. Send your boy to meet mine at Eleanor's Cross on the Strand at four that afternoon to let me know the where and when.' He nodded. 'Until then, God's blessings upon you.'

'And you, brother.'

Blood crossed to the door, then halted there and turned back. 'One last thing. Those men who thwarted us this time, who thwarted you before. You should not let them interfere a third time in our work. The solution is simple – find men who know how to use a knife and kill them, that's my advice. Kill them soon.'

He left. Simeon stood a while, staring at the door. Men who know how to use a knife, he thought. Like you.

A vision came to him then – of Peckworth, his eyes shining

with the light of Christ's word received, and of his comrade, Brother Garnthorpe, his body torn apart. Both their deaths caused by two men, Pitman and Coke, and one woman, Sarah Chalker. A knife for each of them? It was possible – though given how much these enemies had survived, he knew it would not be as simple as Blood thought. Also he had few Saints to spare, men he would need on the great day to come. Besides – and this he felt clearly, sharply, suddenly – a knife in some alley was just too paltry a revenge for his dismembered dead comrades.

He found he was standing at the little stage again, with no clear memory of crossing to it. Before him were the boxes, like miniature coffins. His puppets were within them and he ran his fingers along each of them.

On a sudden urge, he slid down the lid of one, then pulled down the soft covering to reveal the twisted features of Punchinello. Gently, he lifted the puppet from his bed, unravelled the strings, dangled him from the wooden strut until his feet touched the floor, turning him from side to side and making his gnarled hands rise and fall in greeting. How the room had throbbed with laughter not one hour before! How skilled he was, the master puppeteer!

When the thought came, it brought a smile as twisted by his scars as the puppet's was by paint.

Why shouldn't God's vengeance be spectacular?

Part Two

><-><-O-<>-><-<

AND IN THOSE DAYS SHALL MEN SEEK DEATH, AND
SHALL NOT FIND IT; AND SHALL DESIRE TO DIE,
AND DEATH SHALL FLEE FROM THEM.
The Revelation of St John the Divine 9:6

6

SIREN CALLS

'And what is that?' Coke asked. 'The small square that abuts the main bedchamber?'

The builder peered. 'That, sir, is a second privy office. You do not wish to be feeling your way downstairs in the middle of the night, nor be groping for pots – neither you, nor especially Mrs Coke.'

Coke grunted. Sarah did not hold that title yet. His hope was that today's enterprise might convince her to assume it. Still, he hesitated. It was a great deal of money, this business of buying a house.

'These lines?' he said, jabbing down.

'Water pipes.' It was the second man who replied. He had not been there with the master mason the first time Coke had visited the site. His assistant no doubt, a strange-looking fellow with a nose that had once been badly broken by a blade, probably in the late king's wars. Coke had the odd sensation that they had met before, but he put that down to his nerves. They had probably fought against each other. The fellow had the crop-haired look and sober demeanour of an old Parliament man.

He continued, his voice a smooth roll. 'Master Tremlett has contracted with the New River Company to supply each of his houses on West Harding Street with water. Think, sir! Fresh water flowing into your home all the way from the pristine meadows of Hertfordshire via the reservoir in Islington. No more going to the parish pump for water that may well have come straight from the murky Thames.'

Running water, thought Coke. It would be pleasant. Sarah would find it pleasant, surely?

He nodded, looking also at the area map beside the house plans. Really, he was asking questions merely to delay a decision now. Everything had been explained twice. The location was excellent. Not far to the north, there were bowling lawns and some pasture still; to the west, a short walk away, the more urban pleasures of Covent Garden and indeed, Lincoln's Inn. Would Sarah wish to return to the playhouse after she was delivered? She'd joked that actresses were known to drop a child at eleven of the morning and be on the boards playing Juliet by one. He hoped that she would not desire it. His own mother had never worked, being the lady of the manor, but that was not it. Sarah's 'manor' was the streets of St Giles, the toughest in the city.

He knew he could not make her into something she was not. But the theatre, where all women were treated like the whores several of them had once been? Was she so enamoured of the life that she would insist on going back to it? It had been a step up from the slums, sure. Marrying the son of a knight, albeit one who had lost both title and lands in the wars, would be another. And owning a new house, perhaps, the last?

But who would own it? 'Sir, a question. Can a second also sign here, and be a part owner?'

'What second?'

'My . . . a woman.'

Tremlett pursed his lips. 'A woman? It would be highly unusual. And if you are referring to your wife, well,' he smiled, 'it is simpler, more expedient, to specify her as your heir in your will, sir.'

My will, thought Coke. The next paper I must draw up. 'You will take a deposit now, you say?'

'Indeed.' The florid-faced mason beamed as he unbent from the charts. 'A quarter on signing, a half when the hearth joist is laid, last quarter upon completion.'

He decided. 'Well,' Coke straightened too, 'I have the first with me.'

His share of the reward for the thwarting of the assassination was in the purse he now placed upon the house plans. Tremlett tipped the contents out, spreading them to be sorted. These were mainly the new coinage, milled-edged, with Charles's profile handsomely embossed – though, given the continual shortage of coins, there were the usual foreign ones, too: Spanish ducats, French crowns, Dutch florins. Still, a swift tally left both men satisfied.

'And now, Captain,' said the broken-nosed man, after the other had swept the coins into a box, 'your signature?'

'Captain?' Coke halted his reach for the pen. 'Who told you I was called so?'

There was no hesitation in the man's reply. 'I am sure you did, sir. Maybe to my master here, at your previous meeting.' He smiled, crookedly. 'Or perhaps it's just your military bearing.'

He held out the pen again and Coke took it. He was trying

to stop people calling him Captain, without much success, even with Sarah, or his ward, Dickon. The wars were long over, and he was no longer even a highwayman, where every 'knight of the road' assumed what had – for him at least – been a genuine rank. 'Plain Mr Coke will do,' he muttered and, dipping the pen in the inkwell, leaned down. This is it then, he thought, the full nib hovering over the line. The last contract I signed was the one that joined me to the regiment. And look where that led!

Then a vision came – of Sarah, smiling. He took a deep breath and signed, both the mason's copy and another that he would take.

The second man scattered some sand to blot the ink. All three smiled. 'Bravo, sir,' said the mason, reaching out a hand to shake. 'You will not regret this for a moment.'

I already do, Coke thought, his head curiously light. Though when he reached, it was only to pick up and roll his copy, not to snatch both and destroy them. Tucking it into his cloak, he bowed his head. 'Gentlemen,' he said, and left.

Only when the footfalls on the stair had entirely faded did the man with the sabre scar breathe out a satisfied, 'Excellent.'

The mason exhaled too, though his face was a frown. 'Are you sure, Brother S? It seems . . .'

'What?'

'Elaborate.' He grunted. 'Are there not simpler ways of being avenged?'

'A blade in an alley, perhaps, Brother Tremlett?'

'That's one.'

Simeon Critchollow shrugged. 'Where is it written that vengeance be simple? When God's light shines on a world of such glorious complexity and richness, why should revenge be taken only in the dark?' He smiled. 'When you told me that this Coke had come to you, I thought it a coincidence. Until I remembered: there is no coincidence in God's great plan.'

'Praise Him indeed. But how will this proceed?'

'Slowly.' Simeon licked dry lips. 'If I were still a gambling man, as in my days of sin and ignorance I was, I would wager I know whither the captain is now bound. He goes to see a Jew. And he will find us waiting.' He reached for his hat and stick beside the paper. 'Ha! I've just noticed something. Talking of God's providence. How have I not noted this before?' He laid the tip of his stick on the charts. 'Do you have Latin?'

'Enough for my trade. Customers like it on the plans.'

'Look at this wonder.' Simeon tapped the chart's masthead. 'If you were to lay out every Roman numeral, what is their total?'

'Let me see.' The mason's brow furrowed. 'M is a thousand. Add five hundred for D. C is a hundred. L is, ah —'

'Fifty. X is ten, V, five. One is one.'

'So?'

Simeon beamed. 'Add them together.'

'One thousand, six hundred and . . . Oh!' Tremlett's eyes widened. 'Their total is sixteen hundred and sixty-six.' He raised his hands, palms up. 'Praise God!'

'Praise him indeed,' Simeon nodded, 'for this, another example of His providence! God's plan is so far-reaching that two thousand years ago he made the pagan Romans adopt numbers that would add up to this year. The one foretold. The year the Fifth Monarchy arises.' He went to the door and turned, his eyes ablaze. 'Oh yes, brother. With yet another example of the Lord's infinite precision revealed, I believe we can allow vengeance to be . . . a little elaborate, don't you?'

The flute was beautifully played, its notes piercing even the din of Little Eastcheap at full trade. The player, Coke saw, was a handsome lad of about twenty or so, with some admiring servant girls gathered giggling before him, and coins in his cap that both music and looks had earned. Coke added another before he strode the few steps further on and entered the premises of Isaac ben Judah, goldsmith.

But his friend was not behind the counter. Another of the tribe was there who related the disturbing news: Isaac was ill and in his bed, three doors down the street.

There Coke hastened, the sound of the flute following him.

'Mr ben Judah.' Coke threw his cloak and hat upon a chair, leant his stick, then knelt by the bed, taking the hand of the man upon it. 'You are not well.'

'I am not, Captain.' The voice was weak, his long grey hair lank, his face pallid. He began to cough, a dry scratchy sound. From the corner of the room came a young woman Coke had not noticed. She carried a mug, bent to lift Isaac up and held the vessel to his cracked lips. When the cough was stilled, and Isaac lay back down, the girl began to adjust the blankets.

'You have not met my daughter,' Isaac said. 'Rebekah, this is Captain William Coke. A special friend.'

'Honoured.' Coke rose and bowed. He guessed the girl to be about fifteen, though she could have been older. Tall for her age, she had midnight-black hair within a headdress, thick dark eyebrows, a straight nose and firm mouth. There was no make-up on her face at all and her paleness, especially against the hair, was severe.

She regarded him with as bold an appraisal as he gave her. 'Sir,' she said, her voice low, executing a short curtsey before turning back. 'Father, since you have a friend here, perhaps now would be a good time to run my errands. To fetch you medicine and the house some food.' She turned back to Coke. 'Are you able to attend him while I do so, sir?'

He nodded. Even if he was keen to get back to Sarah, there was something about this girl that could not be denied.

'Out and straight back,' her father called as she wrapped a shawl around herself and crossed to the door. 'No footling.'

She smiled. 'I am not sure, Father, I know what that is. So how shall I avoid it?'

With that, she was gone, and Isaac, who'd raised himself upon an elbow, sank back. For a moment both men listened to her footfalls on the stairs and, beyond them, the flute's rising notes.

'Your daughter is most lovely,' Coke murmured, drawing up a small stool and sitting.

'She is. She is!' Isaac sighed. 'The very picture of Leah, her mother. Indeed, since my wife's death, I think my daughter is becoming more like her every day. In looks at least.' He coughed again but waved Coke down when he rose to fetch the mug. 'I fear her character is not as calm as her mother's, though. She is . . . wilful. Too tempted by what is out there. I do not like to let her go onto the streets alone. But with my sister in York, and me here —'

'And why are you here, my friend? You were not sick when we spoke last week.'

'I was, though I was at pains to disguise it.' A slight smile appeared. 'We were doing business after all, and no man wants to seem weak when conducting that.'

'Did you think I would exploit you?'

'Nay, Captain. You are one of the very few Gentiles I know would not. Habits of a lifetime, eh?' He shrugged, winced. 'But this sickness can no longer be concealed. Especially since I may die of it. Or of its cure anyway.'

'Do not say so.' Coke reached to take the man's hand again. He did not have many beyond acquaintances in London and though he did not know the Jew well, they had always been plain in their dealings and their mutual regard. He liked the man. 'And tell me how I may help?'

Isaac glanced to the sword at Coke's side. 'How delicate are you with your blade, Captain? Could you cut me open and extract the root of my malady?'

Coke whitened. 'If I could, you would not want me to. For a man who was so often at war, I have a devilishly weak stomach for some of its consequences.' He nodded downwards. 'So it is the stone?'

'Aye. My old problem.' Isaac winced again, as a spasm shook him. 'Each time before, I have, with some difficulty, managed to piss it out. Not this one. My physician tells me he must cut to cure.'

Coke took a deep breath. 'Many undergo that operation and live. Is your surgeon good?'

'He is, and of my tribe. But as you know, howsoever good, many, indeed perhaps most, patients do not survive this.' Isaac shrugged. 'As ever, I am in God's hands. So, Captain, shall we leave me there and turn to you?' He nodded to the table in the corner. 'I was not so ill that I could not deal with your affairs.'

Coke rose, went to the table. A purse was there, the contents of which he knew he need not count. He tucked it into his cloak. Their contract also lay there. Second in a day, he thought, though now he picked up the pen with no hesitation.

'You should read it again, sir,' Ben Judah called. 'I have had to alter it slightly due to my illness. I have specified to whom your debt must be paid, should I, ah, be unable to collect.'

Coke looked at the second page, where a name had been written in. Rebekah bat Judah. The correction was initialled and he added his 'WC'. Did the same on the second copy, then signed both. 'There, sir,' he said, putting up the pen. 'I am in your debt.'

'You are. Do you know when you will be requiring the last payment?'

'The builder said on completion. He seems to have many labourers so it may be within the fortnight. Of course, I may have earned the money ere then but if not –'

'If not, you will find the sum here. Though it may coincide with my operation. I will leave word if . . . well, if.'

Coke looked across. The man did look ill. 'I meant what I said before . . . Isaac.' He used the man's given name deliberately for the first time. 'How may I be of help?'

'If the need arises, you could – you could look to my daughter.' He came up on one elbow again, though it pained him. 'Most of our family is in York. In Rotterdam. She may need some temporary protection until they can be summoned should anything . . .' He trailed off.

Coke came over, knelt and took the man's hand again. 'And she shall have mine, Isaac. You may trust me on that.'

'Very good, Captain – William. Then I shall.'

The two friends sat silent for a while, listening to the high, beautiful notes sounding nearby.

The youth did not need to cease his tune to smile. But he did to speak.

'Hello again,' he said, lowering his flute.

'Keep playing,' replied Rebekah bat Judah.

He did, just as beautifully. Several people paused to listen, to tap a foot. Some dropped a coin into the cap on the cobbles before moving on. Rebekah did not move, or sway, just stood regarding him, her dark eyes wide.

The tune ended on a single high note, wonderfully sustained, clinging in the air a long moment after he lowered the flute. A passer-by threw in a last groat. The player knelt, running his fingers over the coins, then looked up at her, his blue eyes dancing under his shank of golden hair. 'A goodly haul,' he said. 'May I spend a portion on you, Rebekah? Buy you a drink?'

Her face stayed grave. 'You know that is not possible. I do not go anywhere, with anyone. Especially –' She gestured at him. 'I do not even know your name, though you stole mine.'

'Stole? Nay,' he laughed, 'I took it in exchange for my heart!'

'Tut!' she scoffed, though she was pleased. 'Your name, sir?'

He rose, his face serious now. Pouring the coins into a pocket of his coat, he clutched the hat before him. 'Daniel,' he said, and gave a formal bow.

'Daniel?' she echoed. ''Tis a name . . . a name of my people.'

'I know. My parents honoured them. As do I. I wish –' he hesitated, 'I wish I could be one of them – of you. Especially now.'

'Why now?'

The smile returned, the face lit. 'Because then maybe you'd let me buy you that drink.'

'Tut,' she said again. 'Are girls of your people allowed to do such things with a stranger?'

'No. Though I would not truly know. I have had little to do with girls. I haven't wanted to until –' He broke off, his shy smile returning. 'I have brought you something. A token.'

'What?'

He looked around. People were staring at this young couple, both handsome, so different. The Gentile and the Jew. The light and the dark. 'I think some of your tribe are disapproving that we talk so long. Come.'

He stepped away. She did not move. 'Where?'

'Just a few paces.' He pointed to an alley's narrow entrance. 'There.' When she still did not move, he smiled. 'Come. Do not fear. We will stay near the entrance, in the light.'

'Tut,' she said, for the third time, though there was little disapproval in it now.

He led her two paces into the alley, halted, delved into his coat and pulled out an object.

'A banana?' she exclaimed, then laughed. 'It is not even heart-shaped, sir!'

'Have you tried one? The queen eats little else, they say, since they came to the realm but recently.'

'I have not.' She reached, drawing her hand back. 'We are not allowed to eat many things.'

'But this is a fruit, not – not a pig! Here,' he broke the skin, peeling it in four sections, broke off a nub and offered it to her. When she shook her head, he ate it himself. 'Hmm! Delicious. Are you sure?'

He tore off a much smaller piece, held it out. She shook her head again, so he ate her piece, folded up the rest of the banana in its skin and put it away.

'Well, sir,' she said, taking a step, 'if that is all –'

'Nay. That was just . . . lunch.' He reached again into his coat. 'This is dessert.' He held out a paper-wrapped package. After a moment she took it and held it.

'Open it,' he said.

She unwrapped it and gave a little cry – of delight. In her hand, was a tortoiseshell object the size of her palm. Delicate teeth curved down; while above, on the main body, a pattern of flowers, iris and bluebell, had been inlaid in some shining shell.

'It is to hold the hair in place. The seller named it a barrette and told me that this,' Daniel ran his finger across the blue-green shimmer, 'is "abalone", a sea creature from across the globe, from the land of Mexico.' He took her hand, tilting the shell to the light. 'Can you see those southern seas, its blues and greens, in its sheen?'

'Oh, I can. I can.' She tilted it herself, delighting in it, then stopped as she became aware of his touch. Withdrawing her hand, she continued, 'I may get a chance to see them by candle-light and in their proper place when my father has gone to sleep. I – I thank you. But I should –' She took a step back. His cry halted her.

'By candlelight? Hidden in a room for only yourself to see? Nay, I beg you. Let me see it.'

'Now? It is not possible. I must keep my head covered.' She touched her shrouding headdress. 'I cannot —'

'One glimpse?' His blue eyes beseeched. 'A small enough return for my heart, surely?'

She went to say 'tut' but could not. Instead, and after a long moment, she looked around, then passed him the barrette and reached up to her scarf. When she had taken it off, she hesitated again. But his eyes were wide as he stared up, and she reached again, releasing the tight ball of hair allowing the thick coils to burst upon her shoulders like waves on a midnight shore. She shook the tresses, smoothed them down and looked up. Wordless, he handed her back the barrette.

She placed it in her hair, taming one small part of the wild. She swept it around, turning for him to see, one eye upon him. 'Well, sir?' she said. 'Well — Daniel?'

He did not reply — only raised his hand. When his fingers were a palm's breadth away, she moved her head back slightly. 'You should not do that,' she whispered.

'Then tell me to stop.'

Their gazes held. She did not speak again. He moved the little distance and ran his fingertips beneath the barrette and up into her hair. She closed her eyes to his touch.

7

SUBTERFUGES

The Merry Monarch was anything but. 'No, Sir Joseph.' The king slapped the table. 'I tell you, no. I cannot make myself plainer. I will not cower. I never have and I never will. By God, 'tis not the Stuart way.'

'I only suggest it for a time, Majesty.' The Under-Secretary of State took off his spectacles to pinch the deep red grooves at the bridge of his nose. 'Just until these flames,' he gestured to the papers spread on the table before him, 'are snuffed out.'

'Flames? These are sparks alone, man, nothing more. If I was to take to my bed each time some bedlamite threatened me in misspelled prose or execrable verse, marry, I'd never leave its confines.' He sniffed. 'Now while that might please my Lady Castlemaine or my sweet Winifred, it would not me, especially when my inaction would be construed as cowardice.' Charles turned, fixing the thief-taker with his unnerving stare, the one eye bright, the other dulled with a cast. 'Do you not agree with me, Mr Pitman?'

It did not seem the right time to remind His Majesty that he went by 'Pitman' alone, he thought. Nor was it in his own interests to agree with the king and contradict the minister – who, he reminded himself again, was his current paymaster. Neutrality seemed appropriate. 'I believe Sir Joseph refers not to the broadsides but to other information he has there.'

'Oh yes, the letters from his informers – paid rogues who puff up their roguery to be better rewarded.' Charles dug in his pocket and pulled out an ornate ivory box. 'How much silver would they receive if they sent word: "No threats. All is peaceful in the realm." Hmm? Snuff,' he added, flicking open the box lid, offering it first to Sir Joseph, who declined, then to Pitman, who accepted. Monarch and subject snorted in each nostril, then sneezed simultaneously into mouchoirs. Pitman was surprised to note that his was far cleaner than His Majesty's. But that's my Bettina for you, he thought.

'It is true, sir,' Sir Joseph continued when the echoes had faded, 'that some agents might exaggerate. But rarely all, and at the same time.' He riffled some of the papers before him. 'These speak to a pattern of violence building. This is a special time, after all. This year –'

'Yes, Williamson. Yes. I know. But I do not suppose either Pitman – ha, yes, sir, you see I remembered! – either my good Pitman here nor I need a sermon on 666 and the year of the Beast.' Charles mimed a yawn. 'Really, they have been spouting similar nonsense for years, with every comet foretelling the doom of kings, and Christ's return in the flesh. And here I am . . . and Christ is not.' He cleared his throat. 'I mean no sacrilege in that remark. Only that I am certain in my belief that, with God's good grace, I will see my saviour in heaven after my death and not here before it.'

'It is the possibility of your death that concerns us, Majesty. If you would but –'

'Truly!' exclaimed Charles. 'I do not understand why these fanatics mean me such harm. All know how I wanted toleration for every man's belief on my restoration. It was not my fault that forces, especially in parliament, overruled me.' He reached to scratch under his luxuriant, curled wig. 'I will try again, when the time is right for it. I believe every man and woman should be allowed to peaceably – peaceably, mark you! – worship God in his own way. Why, my brother is a Catholic, as is our mother, and I would have him and her as free as any.'

The royal family's Catholicism, as well as the suspicion that Charles himself harboured desires that way, was a reason so many feared and hated him. Pitman wondered how the minister would handle the subject, now it had been raised.

By ignoring it. 'Sire,' Sir Joseph's voice was quiet, but firm. 'These people do not want universal tolerance. They hate it as much as they hate restriction – nay, they hate it more. They do not care for freedom of worship. They want only one way of worship – theirs. They are fundamental in their beliefs and they will kill any who oppose them, especially –'

'*Try* to kill. They have failed utterly, and will fail again. Men like you and our Pitman here have seen to that, and will each time.' Charles stood, so both the others did too. 'No, sir. I will not be hidden away in a box. Marry, I'd die of boredom and do their job for 'em.' He pulled out a pocket watch. 'I am late for . . . something. I will leave you to discuss how best to counter these threats.'

Both men bowed. 'Majesty.'

Charles walked to the door and opened it. In the corridor, two of his guards immediately stood to attention. He paused, his hand on the door edge, and looked back. 'Let me leave you with a story, gentlemen. 'Tis of my father.' He swallowed. 'The morning of his execution was bitter cold. So he asked his groom to lay out two thick wool shirts. He was not afraid, knowing as he did that heaven awaited him above. But he did not wish those who watched to mistake any shivering for fear.' He nodded. 'That's how we do it in our family. So I will not cower.' He smiled. 'But I may, upon occasion, wear an extra shirt.'

He was gone, leaving the door ajar. Sir Joseph crossed to it, held it a moment, then closed it softly. Without turning, he spoke. 'You see with what I must contend.'

Even with the king no longer in the room, Pitman still did not see why he must take sides. He was not there to ingratiate himself. He was there, in the end, for gold. 'How may I be of service, Sir Joseph?'

The Cumbrian turned and peered over his spectacles, looking even more like a heron about to stoop for a fish. 'I wish you to help protect His Majesty, Mr Pitman.'

'Just Pitman, begging your favour. And both my partner Captain Coke and I have been offered such positions before. They are not –'

He paused. He was about to say 'lucrative enough' and go on to explain that with his family of five and one more on the way, with Coke becoming a father and buying a house, that they had to return to their primary business of taking highwaymen . . . when, fortunately, he was forestalled.

'I do not mean as guards for his person. He has many as capable as you for that pass. No, I want you to exert your special skills — to sniff out these rogues and apprehend them far from His Majesty.' Sir Joseph came back to his desk, sat behind it, ordered the jumble of pamphlets and papers before him and drew one out. 'I have word of a gathering. It is of the group known as the Council of the Six, also sometimes called the Council of the Great Ones.' He snorted. 'How they puff themselves up, these builders and brewers and tanners. Have you heard of them?'

'Yes. They are the leaders of the Fifth Monarchists.'

'Five of them are. One of them is my agent. A somewhat reluctant one and so not always reliable but –' He pulled out another paper. 'This meeting will take place in three days' time somewhere in the city. I do not know where yet and may not discover it as my informant writes but sporadically. So I am hoping you would exert your special skills, sniff out the place — and arrest them all.'

Were you indeed, thought Pitman, but said, 'The report you have of this clandestine meeting. Does it not give a more accurate account as to numbers?'

Sir Joseph shifted a few papers on his desk, jabbing his finger at one. 'The Council, so there's six. There will no doubt be a few other conspirators. So six — five, if you take away my man — and a few.' He peered over his spectacles again. 'Shall we say ten?' he added, taking out and glancing at his pocket watch.

We can say hens make holy water, thought Pitman, but it wouldn't make it true. Instead, he replied, 'I'll only have my six constables from the parish –'

'And the troop of His Majesty's Life Guards which I will assign.'

'That, sir, is a problem. You know that the City aldermen are

78

prickly about soldiers within the walls, ever since the late king's wars. And twenty cavalrymen would be hard to conceal. They may frighten off the very pigeons we seek to trap.'

The Under-Secretary put away his watch and took off his glasses. 'Then what is it you suggest?'

'Leave off the soldiers. Let me recruit discreetly among local parishes. I warrant I can raise a force that will suffice.'

'In three days?'

'Aye, the shorter amount of time the better. For you, sir, are not the only one with informants. But they'll want paying.' He nodded. 'As will I.'

'I wondered when money might arise.' Sir Joseph sat back. 'How much?'

It didn't take excessive haggling. Figures were written down, scratched out, revised. In the end, Pitman got rather more than he'd first hoped for. There would be thirty guineas apiece for him and the captain and ten for each of the men he'd hire – if all the pigeons were caught.

The deal was concluded with a nod. Pitman didn't think to offer his hand – the Under-Secretary did not look like someone who spat and shook. Dismissed, the thief-taker tucked the paper into his doublet, rose – then paused. For he'd remembered something else. Someone else.

'Sir Joseph?'

'Hmm?'

'In our discussion with His Majesty of the events at the theatre, you did not mention the man you believed behind them.'

The Under-Secretary looked up. Lamplight reflected in his lenses. 'I did not. I do not believe the king should be burdened with everything.' He sniffed. 'Besides, word has it that "Homo Sanguineus" is gone. Indeed, many say he was never here at all.'

'I have a feeling that he was.'

'A feeling?'

'Call it a sixth sense.'

'Really, sir! We deal in facts in this room.'

Pitman continued, unruffled. 'And if he still is? If indeed he attends this meeting of the Six —?'

He left the sentence unfinished. It was the way to draw certain men out, he'd always found. And it drew Sir Joseph, who squinted up at him. 'If he does, and you take him, you would find me most generous, Mr, er . . . no, just Pitman, isn't it?'

'It is indeed, sir,' Pitman smiled and took out the paper again. 'And I wonder if you'd just add to the bottom there *how* generous?'

'Where are you taking me?' Sarah said, stopping to lean against a door post. 'Really, William, I do not need this exercise.'

Coke looked back. He wished she felt better. He wished the rain had not begun so suddenly and continued so hard. He wished he'd conceived a different plan than the one he was executing now. But he hadn't, and time was now against them. Though he'd vowed to give up all gambling, and had succeeded in forsaking cocks and dice, he was still throwing for the hazard here, the stake higher than it had ever been.

He moved back to her, unclasped his cloak at the neck, reaching half of it around and over her. 'There's something I must show you, love. Come, it is but a little further.'

He knew that after a performance, if she was not rehearsing

for the next day, all she wanted was to go back to their lodgings in Sheere Lane and sleep. His urgency moved her, though. She sighed, but set off.

Coke glanced back. Trailing them by twenty yards, as wet as a dog on a chase, was Dickon. Yet no weather concerned the boy as long as he was near his captain. Especially now, as he had shared what he planned to do with the lad, who loved Sarah near as much as he. Dickon stuck both thumbs up and grinned. Even in the rain, something sparkled on one digit's end.

They turned, stepping out of the slight shelter of Cursitor's Alley, and onto the more open Fetter Lane. The rain grew heavier, thudding into his cloak in damp explosions. He felt her pace falter again. 'Close, love,' he whispered. 'Very close.'

They turned into West Harding Street. There, to the distance of some hundred yards, the old houses had been cleared away on both sides and new ones begun. Scaffolding was everywhere, several derricks swung around. Coke led the way to the tallest structure – a brick chimney, smoke curling up from it, black against the grey sky.

They halted beside it, and before a site that looked as if it had been recently forsaken. Trowels and hammers lay about, alongside a mound of mortar with a shovel shoved in it. Bricks rose to the height of a tall man, a first level attained. To the side, Coke saw a great beam of oak resting on trestles: the house's hearth joist, ready to be raised.

Here was the moment he'd anticipated. Dreaded.

'What are we looking at, William?' Sarah had leaned away from him when they halted. Her eyes were not filled with tiredness now but alertness. Her voice was stage sharp.

He assumed that she would probably have already guessed. But he said it as a surprise anyway. 'Our house.'

Her gasp was gratifying. 'What? How?'

While she had rehearsed her plays in their two rooms, he had practised a speech. But he was not trained as she was, and all he wanted to say came out now a-jumble. 'The joist is there, about to be raised. The second payment is due. The house may be finished in a month. There's a privy office upstairs. We can move in shortly thereafter. Not into the privy. We –' He swallowed. Damn me, he thought, give me a pistol at a roadside and a lord to rob any day. Then he remembered – there was a movement he'd practised to precede the next words.

He dropped suddenly, to kneel in the mud at her feet. 'Will you marry me?' he said.

They weren't a shock, his words. The house was – and the sudden surge of delight it brought was immediately washed away by fear. Who was she, Sarah Chalker, born in the lowest parish in London, St Giles in the Fields, a tenement urchin who'd struggled from the filth to stride the playhouse stage, to own a house? A new one too, brick-built, with – with a privy upstairs, is that what he'd said?

She began to laugh, raising a hand to stifle it. His face! Looking up at her, a hank of his thick, black-silver hair plastered to his forehead, raindrops running through his moustache. The appeal in those grey eyes, the ones whose deep pain she'd noted from their very first meeting, the ones she had not allowed herself to love until later because she'd been married then, though her husband was killed, cruelly killed, shortly thereafter. And even though she knew she loved Captain Coke, loved him in a way she had not loved John Chalker, she had not thought to marry again. The life within her had not changed her in that opinion. It was neither the playhouse nor the St Giles way.

And yet? Here he was, the best man she'd ever known, kneeling before her because that's what he'd seen her stage lovers do. More, doing it before the house he'd bought to shelter her, shelter the life inside her that they had made. What could she say, as she had so often said upon the stage, but – 'Yes.'

'Huzzah!' he cried, but then did not move when she expected him to stand and sweep her into a kiss. Another movement made her start – and remember that he had planned all this, and was not done with his scheme yet. For Dickon was suddenly there, wide-set eyes afire, mouth spread in a grin. He held a thumb up as if to cheer them, and she saw something glittering upon it. Coke reached for it now and, lifting her left hand, placed the ring upon her third finger.

'Dickon is our ring-bearer now. As he will be on Sunday.'

'Sund—' she began, incredulous, but then he was indeed up, catching her in his arms, stopping her words with a kiss. Beside them, Dickon cried joyfully and began to caper about. Within it all, she was aware of many things: the rain, ceasing as suddenly as it had come; the sun coming out, dazzling them, like a shift of mirrors behind the wings of the theatre. It made her laugh again, joyously, within his kiss, so she broke away and laughed too.

There were so many surprises to discuss, she began with the most recent. 'But how can we be married this Sunday? The banns must need be read the two Sundays preceding.'

'They have been.' Coke's expression changed, a young boy

caught out in some mischief. 'I knew your reluctance, ma'am. I thought to circumvent it with haste. Not to give you a chance to change your mind.' He looked sheepish. 'Was I wrong?'

'You were certainly assured, sirrah!' she said, with a touch of asperity. 'A woman likes to make certain preparations for such an event and you have given me little time.'

'I believe Mrs Pitman has taken care of many things you may require,' he mumbled.

'Oh, so all the world knows of your plans aside from me?'

'Not all. Dickon, the Pitmans –'

'Truly?' Something about the day came to her. 'Wait! This Sunday? Are you not about an enterprise with Pitman on Saturday?'

'I am.'

It was not the sun vanishing again into a cloud, withdrawing its heat, that made her shiver. It was the ghost of a memory – and the memory of a ghost. She no longer saw him there as he was, cloaked and booted, but as he had been upon the stage two weeks previously – barefoot and in rags.

As she swayed, he reached for her, and she gripped his arm hard. 'Postpone it, sir. It . . . it seems an ill venture to me.'

He frowned. 'How so? You know nothing of it.'

'It is . . . just a feeling. I –'

'I cannot. I am pledged.'

'Withdraw. Please, sir!' She dug her fingers in. 'I fear you may make me a widow ere you make me a wife.'

His eyes narrowed and he reached his free hand up to run thumb and finger either side of his moustache. After a moment, he shook his head. 'Madam, much as I respect your . . . feelings, I cannot. Pitman and I . . . this is what we do, after all. And both of us need the rewards it will bring. For with his Bettina pregnant too, as you know, he will soon have five mouths to feed. While I –' He looked first down at her, then about. 'I am committed here, to provide shelter to our joy.'

'But –'

'Nay, Sarah,' he said sharply. 'I cannot be argued out of it.'

For a moment she saw a hardness come into his eyes. This was a man, she knew, who had not only fought throughout the late king's wars and endured long years of hard exile after them, he had also earned his living as a highwayman. And though what she mainly saw in their daily contact was her gentle William, she knew he was something else as well – and that this look could not be gainsaid. So she took a breath. 'Very well, sir. If you promise me –'

'Sure, it's none so dangerous. Some rogues is all. Pitman always says that, in the event, they come as quiet as lambs.' He smiled, the hardness displaced again. 'With our customary good fortune, their fleeces will provide the other payments on this house.'

She could not smile. Was there a softer way she could yet win this argument? But she was forestalled in trying by another voice.

'Mr Coke! Come to chivvy us for our slow progress?'

Sarah turned to see a heavy-set man in a much-stained apron.

Coke stepped away from her and spoke. 'Ah, sir! Not at all, I think what you have achieved so far is remarkable. May I present, ah –'

'Mrs Coke, certain.' The man swept off his cap and bowed. 'Samuel Tremlett.'

'Not certain. Though now I suppose I have little choice.' Sarah smiled at the man's querying frown and nodded in greeting.

'May I show you, ma'am, sir, what we have achieved so far? It is quite different from seeing it on paper, I assure you.' He squinted up into a sunbeam. Behind him, steam rose from wet piles of brick and mud. 'The Lord smiles on us now, sure, and we can be speedy again. I warrant we'll raise the joist on Saturday.'

'And may I bring you the payment on Monday, sir? I am some-what –' Coke glanced at Sarah, 'engaged this weekend.'

'Monday will be fine, sir. Please!' He led them through the open doorway. For the next quarter hour, as they moved from one marked-off or half-finished room to the next and Tremlett described the modernity that would soon stand where they did, Sarah leaned on Coke. His solidity gradually dispersed the shade of him she'd recalled. Finally, and for the first time in an age, standing in a house she would soon live in, give birth in, she felt entirely well. More than that, she thought, for the first time since John Chalker was buried, I feel entirely content.

8

THE RAID

'Brother Isaiah, will you lead us in the prayer?'

'Right gladly, Brother Simeon.' The hefty tanner stood and raised his hands, palms up. 'Our Father –'

All rose and Simeon walked from his place at the table's head to stand behind his comrade. He rested a hand on the man's shoulder and thought about how long he'd known Isaiah Hebden. He recalled how they'd waited patiently in the ranks of Christ's army as the king's cannoneers and musketeers slaughtered their fellows. How they'd charged and slaughtered in their turn. How they'd knelt and prayed and wept among their dead. How, on the battlefield at the very moment of victory they'd received the true word that the Fifth Monarchy was nigh. And how, in all the years of oppression since they'd striven side by side in the Council of the Six to hasten the day of reckoning, that day had been brought ever closer by their good works, by all that had been discussed and decided tonight. Sad then, thought Simeon, after all that, and when we are at its gates, that only one of us will enter the New Jerusalem.

With that thought, and in the moment between the ending of

the prayer and the first Amen, he slipped the garrotte over his friend's neck.

He knew what he was about; he had done this before. He knew that the man would always reach for the cord that he had no chance of undoing instead of using his last of breath to fight. And though Isaiah was a large man, Simeon had strength that came from God, not his trade. So he turned, bent down and heaved the tanner onto his back, as if he were a sack of coal, or a pig's carcass in a slaughterhouse; facing away, dragging the rope down, taking small steps to steady himself as his brother jerked and bucked and strove to break free, kicking the table and sending the tankards crashing to the floor – though the smell of spilled beer was swiftly overlain by something foul. Through it all, through the frantic tugs that diminished gradually to shudders and then to nothing at all, Simeon held tight. He tried to pray for the sinner as he died. Yet he found it difficult. For the thought kept intruding: that Isaiah Hebden was another of his puppets, dangling on a string, playing before a crowd.

He turned to that crowd now, as he loosed the cord and stepped away, letting the body slip to the ground. 'Amen,' he said, finishing the prayer, though none of the surviving Six joined in – the two colonels, Rathbone and Danvers, Chambers the lawyer's clerk, More the chandler. Their faces were all aghast. He looked at the other men there last. The youth's big face was stretched by an excited grin. His father's face betrayed nothing, neither joy nor horror. Only, after a moment, as their eyes locked, did Captain Blood give a small nod.

Silence had held sway until then. Now the room exploded with oaths and questions. Simeon, used to commanding from a pulpit or in a playhouse, ended them with a loud command. 'Quiet!' As the hubbub lowered, he continued, 'Brother Hebden was a traitor. He was observed in conference with agents of that demi-imp Sir Joseph Williamson only yesterday by our new comrade. Then I found hidden papers, silver. Not quite thirty pieces. Not much less.' He gestured to the Irishman. 'Captain Blood offered to deal with the man himself, somewhere dark. I told him that the Council of the Six would deal with their own Iscariot, and in the light.' He gestured to the corpse, curled over and reeking on the floor. 'Witness how we have.'

Horror had held them all immobile. Now they all moved at once. 'Betrayed?' Colonel Rathbone yelped, and reached for his cloak across a chair back. 'We must flee.'

'Aye,' cried Danvers, seizing his cloak too.

'The back stairs,' cried Chambers, taking a step.

'No cause.' Simeon's voice was softer, but it halted them and he continued, 'As you know I changed our meeting place to the Bell Inn only this morning – and I made sure that Brother Isaiah never left me, though he desired it, at any moment.' He gave a short laugh. 'He must have thought it odd, that I pissed every time he did.'

'But what are we going to do . . . do with the body? It's too far to the river and –' the lawyer's clerk, who had never served in the army, was looking down, his jaw loose.

'That's another reason I chose the Bell. The landlord is a sympathiser. And he keeps pigs.'

It took the clerk a moment to understand. When he did, he staggered to a corner and vomited.

Somewhere close, a church bell began to toll the hour. Simeon looked again at Blood. The man had told him that he and his son would ride for Harwich and take a ship for Holland straight after the meeting's business was concluded. 'God's speed on the road, Captain,' Simeon said. 'I look forward to our reunion. In September.'

Both men knew what was meant. 'In September,' Blood echoed. He had put a monocle into his left eye to study some papers. He had left it in to witness a death. Now he tucked the glass into a doublet pocket. But then, as he reached for his cloak, he paused. There were footsteps coming fast up the stairs, though the landlord had been up not ten minutes before to replenish their jugs.

'Who's there?' Simeon called.

When the bells of St Matthew's began their slow toll to ten, Pitman checked that his pistols slid easily from their holsters, spat on the cobbles and stepped out of the shadows.

As he crossed, he looked up. Captain Coke flashed a thumb before disappearing into the gloom. Pitman hoped that the position he'd assigned to his friend would not be tested; that the conspirators would take the backstairs that led to the small yard where most of his men waited in ambush. The window that gave onto Coke's roof was small, not an obvious exit if they panicked. With fortune, the captain would not even need to draw his rapier – and the bridegroom's skin would stay intact for his wedding on the morrow.

Surprise and speed were required – and numbers. At least he had the latter – ten hard men, constables and former soldiers too, all from Parliament's army in the late deplored wars. Ten roundheads then – and one cavalier, he thought, licking dry lips as he entered the tavern's side stairs.

Like the highwayman who jerks open the carriage door, going in the front was always going to be the most dangerous act. But Pitman was the leader, and he had the armour, such as it was. Bettina had had one of her 'turns' and insisted he wear his old breast-and-back plates. He hadn't the heart to tell her that these rarely stopped a bullet at close range. He also had the blunderbuss which he pulled off his back now. 'Follow me,' he said to the two waiting men, Allsop and Friar. He took the stairs two at a time, but they were still half a dozen steps away when the door above was flung open and a large man stepped out. He had a pistol.

'Drop it!' bellowed Pitman, but the man did not. Instead, he pointed and pulled. There was the spark, the flash and the report loud in the narrow, wood-lined stairwell. Pitman ducked but Allsop did not, crying out and reeling back. Amidst the gun smoke, Pitman saw the figure slip inside again and heard the man's cry, 'The watch!' With the landing clear above, Pitman pulled his trigger. He had loaded it with scrap, for the sound and the fury. He wanted them alive. Justice required it. His purse did too. Sir Joseph paid more for men he could question.

The hot metal tore great chunks from the wainscot at the stair head. Laying down the blunderbuss and coughing in the smoke, Pitman drew one pistol and charged up the remaining stairs. He knelt and shoved his face around the door jamb. As he had hoped, the back door was open, and men were already crowding it, trying to flee. One turned and raised his arm. Pitman threw himself back as another shot came and wood exploded in splinters above him.

Friar knelt beside him. 'Allsop?' queried Pitman.

'Shoulder,' replied Friar. 'Think the bullet passed through.' He gestured with his head. 'Do they take the lure?'

'I think so, aye,' Pitman cocked his head. 'As long as our friends below bide —'

Dick Cleethorpe, who'd stood next to him in the push of pike on battlefields across England and never flinched, was in charge below. They were well sheltered down there, behind the beer barrels. Now he heard his comrade's cry, 'Surrender! You are surrounded!'

More shots spoke to this, more replied, and the room that had gone quiet filled with noise again. He risked a look, saw three men rush back into the room. One had a blunderbuss much like his own and discharged it at them now; the door slammed back, coming off its hinges to fall onto the constables crouched there. The sound of smashing came, glass first then wood. Pitman uncocked his pistol, holstered it and grabbed one end of the door. 'Take it up,' he cried, and Friar did. Holding it before them like a shield, the two men moved into the room.

Shot slammed into the door. Pitman heard a shout of 'With me!' Risking a peek, he glimpsed a smaller man slipping through the window. The other two were big, one a youth, one older. This was the man who'd shot at him. He had little doubt now as to who he was.

'Halt!' he cried, throwing off the door, drawing and uncocking a pistol. The father snarled, turned back and raised a gun even as the son disappeared. Then suddenly the room was filled with men again, as four conspirators burst back in, blocking Pitman's sight of the window. He swung his muzzle, as did Friar beside him, and all the men's hands went high, one of them crying out, 'Don't shoot!'

Pitman did not – but Captain Blood did. Aiming at the thief-taker, he hit one of the men there, his body hurled forward onto Pitman. At the same time, the rest of the constables ran in from below.

By the time Pitman had disentangled himself from the body and the crowd, Blood had disappeared through the window.

Captain, he thought to cry, but didn't. He hoped Coke would have the sense of any bridegroom and lay low on the eve of his wedding. At least until Pitman could push through this crowd and aid him.

When one man came through the smashed window, Coke drew his cudgel. When the second did, he exchanged it for a pistol. When a third joined them, he added his sword. 'Hold there!' he cried, stepping forward so the weapons in his hands would be clear even in the murky light. And they did, for a moment, all three staring at him. 'Drop the gun,' he yelled.

With a snarl, one man part-obeyed – he flung his weapon hard towards Coke. Coke used his own pistol to bat it aside but pulled the trigger in error. The gun fired, the bullet flew above the three men who, held now only by bared steel, all drew blades of their own – two rapiers and a short-bladed cutlass between them.

Coke heard Pitman shouting in the room behind the men. 'Clear away!' The thief-taker would be there promptly, he was sure. So he need only delay these gentlemen for a short time. Yet if he hoped to do it with conversation he was immediately disappointed when the first man, has face hidden by a scarf, slashed the cutlass across his chest and the youth charged at him.

Coke stepped fast back, avoiding the swung steel, then brought his sword hard across to guide the rapier past his side, the body following and aided in its acceleration by the foot the captain stuck out. The youth yelped and crashed onto the slick roof tiles. But the last, biggest man now lunged hard for Coke's chest and he was only just able to get his own sword back to parry the thrust, taking it over his shoulder. This brought the man close enough for Coke to see, even in the poor light, the fury in the green eyes. Fury, but little fear.

The gaze held but a moment before Coke shoved the steel hard away, dropped his wrist, and tried to pop the pommel of his sword between those furious eyes. But the man had seen it, raised his other hand and caught the pommel – though the force of the blow banged his knuckles into his face. His fingers fastened, he tried to wrench the sword from the captain's hand, but Coke jerked it hard back, using the movement to retire two steps, just in time to duck the cutlass the scarfed man swung at him a second time. However, Coke's retreat had taken him close to the sprawled youth who reached and grabbed his legs. Swaying, Coke swung his sword in a great circle to fend off the other attackers while he fought for balance – a fight he lost, tumbling down even as the elder man lunged again, the fall saving him.

Coke freed a leg, kicked the son hard in his chest, rolling to the side to dodge, yet again, the scarfed man's cutlass. As it smashed onto the tiles beside him, he swept his rapier across, forcing both the standing men back, kicking his legs hard, heels scrabbling on the roof, propelling him away from the men who looked as if they were going to come again . . . and then didn't.

'Hold there!' yelled Pitman, his great boots reducing the window frame to further splinters. He pushed one leg and half his big body through, his pistol leading. With one glance at him and another to the rising captain, the three conspirators ran as one for the roof edge and hurled themselves over it.

Pitman was beside him in a moment. 'Are you hurt?'

'Only my pride.'

Pitman offered an arm and hauled Coke up. 'An unusual guard, Captain, sitting on your arse,' he said. 'Learn it in France?'

'Are we after them?'

'We are – for that's two-thirds of our bounty escaping.'

'Fast then – I've house payments to make.'

The two men leapt the small parapet between roofs just as their quarry's coat-tails disappeared over the next one. Coke and Pitman followed fast, dropping to the cobbles. The pace of hunter and prey was evenly matched as they splashed through the garbage-choked kennels of the ill-lit alleys, weaving westwards.

Pitman began to labour. ''Tis my armour,' he gasped at Coke's querying glance. 'Not meant for running.'

'Can you slip it off?'

'Too troublesome,' Pitman grunted. 'Come! Last gasp or lose 'em.' And with that, the bigger man sped up.

They drew close enough to hear the heaving breaths of the men ahead. This alley was narrowing, darkening, the jutties over-head nearly joined into a single roof. But then, around another bend, the way ahead lightened, for the alley's end gave onto an open space, and a vast structure ahead.

'The cathedral!' wheezed Coke. 'Do they seek sanctuary?'

'They'll find none,' came the grunted reply. Taking the lead, for two men could not clear the entrance together, Pitman burst out into St Paul's churchyard, the captain a pace behind him.

There was enough of a moon to turn the biggest building in the city into a hulk of shadows and gloom. Scaffolding was everywhere, propping up walls that had long leaned precipitously outwards, allowing for sailcloth and wood tiles to block vast sections of the holed and sagging roof. While two of the pursued ran straight for the wooden struts at the church's eastern end, the third turned right, speeding up, heading north to Blow Bladder Street and the cramped alleys beyond.

'Yours,' said Pitman, nodding after the man.

'And leave you two? Nay!'

They'd paused. The men ahead had started to mount the scaffolding. 'I'll have 'em,' said Pitman, patting his chest. 'I've two primed pistols here, and I am certain they have discharged both theirs. Drag your man back here, if you can.'

In matters of pursuit, the highwayman had decided to defer to the thief-taker. With a nod, he obeyed.

Pitman reached the base of the eastern wall in a dozen strides, just as the men above him slipped through a gap of crumbled masonry. He grunted. A climb in armour did not appeal. He looked through the wooden poles, noted a small door like a sally port in the bastion of a castle. He slipped into the scaffolding, reached for the door's handle. It gave way easily to his twist and opened silently outwards. He stepped inside.

He stood just inside the doorway, allowing his eyes to become accustomed to the gloom. There was some light within the great hall; lanterns burned at a few points, a little moonlight came through such of the stained-glass windows that had not been shrouded in sailcloth for their protection. He did not know the cathedral well – he was a man of the dissident meeting house not the great churches of state. But he had been there during Cromwell's Commonwealth, when soldiers more radical than he had desecrated a building they saw as verging on popery. They'd stabled horses in the chapels and played ninepins in the nave.

From what he could see – and the view of most of the church was obscured by the great screen that separated this space behind the altar and the choir beyond – St Paul's was not in a much better state under the king than it had been in Cromwell's day. Wooden poles rose above him, with platforms at various levels, propping up walls that bowed out. The altar step was there, but the altar was not – as any services held within were now confined, he knew, to the chapel below, at the level of the crypt, St Faith's, a parish church within a cathedral.

He waited, mastering his breath. And then he heard a whisper, a young man's voice, and his older companion cutting him short with a harsh, 'Shtt!' The scaffolding creaked above him. The men were descending. But unless they knew of the sally port, there was only one way for them to leave the church and that was at its western end, through its main doors.

Passing through the rood screen, into the choir, Pitman found a place for ambush: the tomb of some ancient prelate, his form atop it, stone hands clasped over his belly in piety. He slipped into its shadows, stumbling a little at the rear of the sarcophagus where his feet encountered some pieces of masonry fallen from it. Then he heard again the creak of wood, and boots dropping onto flag-stones. He drew both his pistols and several deep breaths.

The men came into the choir. They hesitated for a moment at

the gap in the rood screen, then strode swiftly forward. A few moments would bring them level with the tomb. Regretting the necessity of the sound, Pitman full cocked both his guns.

A voice came hard upon the sound. 'What make you here? Murder, what ho!'

Pitman swivelled around fast – to find a man, with the collar of a priest, rising from one of the choir stalls close by, where darkness had concealed him. 'Quiet, sir –' Pitman began.

There was a rush of footsteps. 'Hold!' Pitman cried, swinging back his guns.

Too late. They were close and had drawn their weapons. Pitman raised one pistol. But the youth knocked it aside, and the elder lunged.

The blade's thrust came low. The breastplate deflected the point from his guts – but guided it into Pitman's thigh.

He cried out, stumbled backwards, stepping onto the piles of broken stones. Wobbled upon them, trying to twist around and keep his pistols levelled at his enemies; he fell. There was a crack, bringing searing pain to his already wounded, twisted leg. Yet Pitman managed to raise one pistol and fire, aiming he knew not where.

He hit neither man – but the explosion echoed hugely in the vaulted chamber. Shouts came, and the man who'd startled him stepped up. As Pitman raised the second pistol, the priest grabbed his arm. 'This is the house of God! Thieves! Murderers! Ho!' he roared. From further down the nave came more shouts, along with the sound of running feet. Pitman jerked his pistol free. 'Stop,' he cried, trying to struggle up, causing agony by his movement. But if his quarry heard they did not heed him, sprinting towards the approaching torches, crying out to make way.

Pitman fell back heavily, laid the pistols down beside him and reached to his leg. His fingers came away sticky. 'Help me,' he whispered, holding the blood up to the priest who bent over him now, before the darkness came.

Coke walked back into the cathedral yard, shaking his head. He had lost his man in the twisting alleys. To some tavern perhaps, or the sanctuary of one of his fellow Saints. He could only hope that Pitman had done better, and that their purses would yet be filled.

He came in through the west doors, pausing to lean against them and take still more deep breaths. It's a younger man's game, he thought. Ten years ago I'd have caught the rogue.

There was only gloom around the entrance; but further down the great nave, near its eastern end, he saw a circle of lights. A murmuring came to him and he smiled. No doubt Pitman was there, standing over the shackled villains, holding forth on how God's providence had manifested in his life again, delivering the realm's enemies into his hands. He likes an audience, Coke thought, speeding up. Don't want to miss the sermon.

A crowd was gathered, but not around Pitman – at least that was Coke's first thought – his friend would tower over everyone there. But then, as he pushed through, he saw the thief-taker – propped up against a choir stall, his face in the lamplight chalky white.

Coke was at his side in a moment. 'What is it, man? You are hurt?'

'I am.' Pitman groaned.

Coke looked down. His friend had a grey rag shoved against his thigh. Even in the dim lamplight, the deeper stains were obvious. 'Bullet or blade?' he asked.

'Blade.'

'May I see?'

A faint smile came to Pitman's lips. 'I do not think your battle-field skills will serve me here, Captain. And do you not faint at the sight of blood?'

'It's more guts I have a problem with. You are not —'

'Bowel pierced? Nay. But there's a lot of blood and I do not dare remove the bandage for fear of issuing more.' A spasm of pain came and he gripped Coke's arm. 'Get me home, for mercy's sake. Get me to Bettina.'

Three hundred paces away, three men sat in the ruins of a different church.

'This was once the liberty of St Martin's Le Grand,' said Simeon Critchollow, patting a tumbled, ivy-covered stone. 'If we'd fled here in the reign of Good Queen Bess, we might have cried sanctuary within its bounds and defied our enemies.'

'I doubt that would have stopped the thief-taker,' muttered Captain Blood.

'But a blade did, Father,' said his son. 'You stabbed that bastard good.'

'Good enough to kill him, think you?' asked Simeon.

'Mayhap.'

'If it is so, you have done our cause great service. This Pitman has been a mighty enemy of the Saints before this night and would be again.'

'And who was the other? The one we fought on the roof and who pursued you?'

'His name is Captain Coke. He was a knight of the road. Now he catches them. And he fornicates with –' He paused, licking his lips. This was not the time to discuss again how these three had thwarted the Lord's great work before. '– a veritable whore of Babylon. An actress, Sarah Chalker.'

'Chalker. Coke. Pitman. All bear the mark of the Beast, that's for sure.' Blood tapped his hat. 'And they are also marked in the book of my head. I will punish them if I can.'

'Oh, do not fear for that.' Simeon put out a hand and the younger Blood pulled him up. 'I have a plan afoot will bring these enemies low. Even as soon as tomorrow.'

'Assassination?' asked the younger Blood.

Before his father could reply, Simeon did. 'Nay, not killing,' he said, 'not yet.' Then he smiled. 'Something far better than that.'

9

A WEDDING

There was a ghost in the church.

Sarah did not turn to seek it out. Felt it only, a presence behind her. It could be . . . anyone. Her mother, who'd had the second sight far stronger than she did, always said that marriages and funerals brought the spirits out – and not just the unquiet dead. Conjured from the graves beyond the church's doors or from the richer tombs within, some worthy burgher whose charity had so benefited the parish would return to gaze with satisfaction upon his works. Or his relic would sit again in her reserved pew to lady it over all others.

This feeling was not like that. She feared that she had brought this spirit with her. It nearly made her look, the thought of him – John Chalker. But the image that came was not as she'd last seen him – in a coffin, a barely recognisable mass of wounds and blood – but as she'd seen him when he'd been the man standing before her at the altar rail. He'd played so many ghosts in performances they'd done together, why would he not show up to be in this one?

Sarah closed her eyes, and swayed. Immediately she felt the

captain's hand upon her arm, steadying her, as he'd had to do all morning. She'd woken feeling nauseous again, the first time in a fortnight. She'd eaten nothing that she had not voided straight-way. She looked up at William now, took more steadiness from his eyes, his grey eyes that oft held a remembered sadness, yet now were filled only with love. A love returned, so different from the one she'd had for John, whom she'd known from childhood, a brother from the foul streets of St Giles. They'd risen above them together, all the way to the playhouse, and married on a whim.

William's look, his arm, centred her. Face forward, she commanded herself. Listen to the words.

'I require and charge you both,' continued the priest, 'that as ye will answer at the dreadful day of judgment when the secrets of all hearts shall be disclosed, that if either of you know any impediment, why ye may not be lawfully joined together in matri-mony, ye do now confess it.'

Was a ghost an impediment? Should she declare him? Oh God, let me not laugh! The line between her laughter and her tears was as thin as a St Giles leper these days.

The priest spoke on. It was time for questions, for commitments, for words that she could speak, in reply to William's, delivered so fervently, when he took her as his wife.

'I will,' he declared.

'I will,' she replied.

Their love had banished all shades. She was ready now, feeling stronger by the moment.

Until the priest asked the next question, 'Who giveth this Woman to be married to this Man?' and she remembered that it was not only the dead that walked. Sometimes the living did too, away from their bodies.

It was meant to be Pitman who gave her away. But he was home and delirious with a fever from an infected wound and a badly broken leg. He could not come – and she did not want to see him there. For her mother had told her that the imminently dead would come to say goodbye to those they loved.

It was a relief then that it was Thomas Betterton who stepped up now – though his face showed that he knew, by the lateness of his casting, that he was undoubtedly an understudy. '*I* do,' he said, taking his place at Sarah's right. He put his hand under Sarah's other elbow, and made a small gesture of moving her towards the priest.

It was the time for lines again and her captain spoke boldly. 'I, William Coke, take thee, Sarah Chalker, to my wedded wife, to have and to hold from this day forward, for better for worse, for richer for poorer, in sickness and in health, to love and to cherish, till death us do part, according to God's holy ordinance; and thereto I plight thee my troth.'

Sarah took his hand, said her not entirely similar words. Then the priest called for the ring.

It was brought on a yell. There was no question as to how alive the ring-bearer was. All attempts to smooth down Dickon's hair had failed and thick clumps of it stood up on his head like wheat sheaves in a field. They had purchased him new shirt, doublet, breeches and stockings. All had been in alignment when they'd entered St Clement's; all were now askew. Meanwhile the nuts that he consumed in quantities that would have fed herds were evident in the bits of shell on his lips. 'Here it is, C-cap'n,' he cried, brandishing the gold band aloft. 'As shiny as that one we took off the Marchioness of Guildford –'

'Thanks, boy,' interrupted Coke loudly, taking the ring, as sniggers came from the pews. He placed it on Sarah's finger, repeated the words. 'With this ring I thee wed, with my body I thee worship, and with all my worldly goods I thee endow: In the name of the Father, and of the Son, and of the Holy . . . *Ghost.*'

She could not help it. The word took her away from all the other words. She said her lines, though it was mainly the vicar now, intoning prayers, citing scripture, urging her to obedience, to the reverence of the man who gripped her again as she swayed.

She was certain who was behind her now. But she waited until the last pronouncements were made, until the chapel erupted in cheers, before she turned to confront him. She understood. She was to see him for this last time. And bid him farewell forever.

And yet it was not her murdered husband. Not the dead who walked there but the living. Dressed as he'd been when she'd seen him upon the stage three weeks before.

It was the man she'd just married. William Coke, who stood in finery beside her, shaking hands – who also stood in rags, dripping water, staring at her. He nodded once before turning and walking through the shut door.

Her eyes rolled. Darkness came.

'I shall summon a chair.'

'Nay.' She gripped his arm as he tried to rise from the bench outside the church. 'I am quite recovered. It was only my . . . you know what it was.' She smiled. 'Truly, I am well. And it is but a short walk to Covent Garden.'

'Are you certain? Then we will take it slowly.' He stood, bending down for her. 'Come . . . wife.'

They rose and she clutched him. Yet they'd gone but a half dozen paces when they were halted by a chair-man. Coke waved him away but the man did not move from the path. ''Tis not a fare I seek, sir,' he said. 'My fare would speak with you.'

Coke bent to look – and the sight drew a cry from him. 'Isaac? You came.'

Isaac ben Judah leant forward, though even the small move-ment caused a spasm of pain to possess his face. 'Alas, I am not here for your nuptials, Captain Coke. Would that I were.' He leaned back, a small cry escaping as he did. 'I have come to beg your help.'

Coke straightened. 'Dickon,' he called. The boy was beside him immediately. 'Take Sarah's arm,' he said. 'Help her to the inn. I will follow fast.'

'Follow? Nay, we'll wait.'

'Sarah, you need to sit, to eat.' He reached up to touch her cheek. 'I will talk with my friend here briefly and catch up with you before you even get to the Hare and Hound.'

'What does this man want? Really, sir, this is not convenient.'

'That I am to discover,' he said gently, lifting her hand and placing it on Dickon's arm. 'Go. I will be but moments.'

Reluctantly, Sarah allowed Dickon to lead her away and Coke swung himself onto the bench opposite Isaac. It was one of the smaller chairs, and the tall captain was wedged into a corner, his knees shoved high near his chest. 'You should not have come forth, my friend,' he said. 'I would have come to you.'

'I had to,' the Jew wheezed. 'I could not be certain that any messenger would move you from your wedding day. Besides, I could not write down my sorrow for others to see. I had to come.'

'Tell me your sorrow then,' replied Coke, 'and how I may allay it. Is it to do with your daughter?'

'It is. It is!' A tear stole from the older man's eye. 'Oh, William, I have been so sick and unable to keep my usual attention on her. And with my sister dead, and my family scattered –' He winced again, balling a fist into his stomach. 'She has strayed, sir. Strayed from me and, I fear, our faith. There is a man –'

'Not one of your tribe?'

'No. I know little of him. She mentioned someone who was kind to her, who made her laugh. And then she started wearing a –' He gestured to his head. 'I do not know what they are called. In her hair, hidden under her scarf, but I saw it and asked her. She said it was gift from a friend. I was angry, and my fear made me more so. I shouted that she was to take no gifts from anyone I did not know. She was dutiful for a few days, if sullen. And then,' he reached out to grip Coke's arm, 'she was gone. A day, a night. I tried to rise but it hurt so. I sent out friends to seek her. They had no success.' He reached into his coat pocket. 'This morning, there was a knock. No one was there. But this was.'

He pulled out a piece of grubby paper, handing it to Coke, who took it and spread it out. There was printing on one side, handwriting on the back.

Your daughter is saf. She is comin to no God. If ye wish to see her, come today, at the hour of three, to the Black

Cat Tavrn, Maiden Lane, hard by St Lennard's, Eastcheap.
Come yourself, or send someone with twenty gold
guineas. One man alone or you shall never see her more.

Coke looked up. 'Three o'clock? But that is less than two hours
away.'

'Aye, Captain. Do you know the tavern?'

'I can find it. But is it not close to your lodgings?' Isaac nodded
and Coke studied the paper again. 'They ask that you send
someone?'

'Rebekah must have told them I cannot walk.'

Coke looked down again, frowned. 'What is this about coming
to "no" God?'

'I think they mean "know".' Isaac swallowed. 'Turn the paper
over.'

Coke did and drew in a harsh breath. The words at the top
were in large font and in Hebrew of which he had no knowledge.
But he knew these anyway, as many did.

'Mene, Mene Tekel, Upharsin,' he read aloud.

'It is from our Book of Daniel,' Isaac said. 'The invisible angel's
finger writing on plaster at Belshazzar's feast. "God hath numbered
thy kingdom and finished it."'

Coke glanced at the rest of the words. He did not need to read
them; he had seen many of their like before – in tracts and
pamphlets proclaiming the approaching apocalypse, the death of
King Charles, the return of King Jesus. He paused only at the
numbers at the bottom of the paper. 'Do you know what these
are?'

'They are also from Daniel – verses.' Isaac cleared his throat, spoke softly. '"The Saints of the most high shall take the kingdom forever, even for ever and ever."'

Coke went cold. 'The Saints?'

'It is why I brought this to you. None of my tribe would be, er, capable. For you know them, do you not?'

Know them, he thought. Aye, as well as one can know men who have tried so hard to kill me. Not only last year, with the monster that was Lord Garnthorpe. Just the previous night, with the Bloods and a scarfed man, stabbing at him on a rooftop.

He didn't say any of that, only, 'Aye. And the one thing you can be certain of, at least, is that they revere your people. I doubt they will have harmed your daughter.'

'There are many ways to harm an innocent girl of our faith,' the Jew replied softly. 'And they are asking money to have her returned, so –' He broke off. 'Will you go and get her for me? It is much to ask on this of all your days, I know, but,' he sighed, 'I do not know anyone else who has had dealings with . . . such dangerous men.'

He had met Isaac the goldsmith to their mutual profit in his days as a knight of the road. But he had liked the Jew from the off and had grown to like him more since he'd left that profession. There was also the small matter of the money Isaac was lending him for the house-building. Still, he would not undertake such a thing on his wedding day for money. Friendship, however?

'Of course, I will aid you.'

The relief on the man's face was clear and immediate, then clouded with a frown. 'Your bride?'

'I will explain. She will understand.' He held up the paper. 'May I keep this?'

'Of course. You will need this also.' Isaac reached into the deep pockets within his cloak and pulled out a bag that clinked. 'There's thirty guineas there. The extra for you, if you –'

Coke shook his head. 'I will take it in case there's any more bargaining to be done. But I will return you the remaining coins when I bring you back your daughter.' He held up his hand to forestall protest. 'It is agreed, sir.'

Isaac sat back into the chair seat, a brief smile displacing the pain on his face. Coke unwound from the cramped space. When he was standing outside again, he leaned down and said, 'I will bring her to you in a few hours, my friend.' He straightened up, tapped the roof. 'Take this gentleman home.'

Coke watched the chair-men bobbing their way through the other chairs, coaches and pedestrians until they disappeared from sight around the corner of the church. Still, he did not move. It was not how he wanted this day to proceed. He wished to celebrate with his bride, to bring her later to their lodgings. To lie beside her all night, making love – or not, as her condition allowed, he was content either way. Well, perhaps he could yet do that last part. A bit of business in the city, swiftly concluded, and then he would return.

He drew his sword an inch, felt it slide easily in its sheath. He did not reach for the dagger in his boot, though he felt it there. With fortune all would go well and he would have no need of a weapon. However, this he knew: with the Saints involved it was best to be most cautious.

He strode fast towards Covent Garden and caught up with the wedding party on Southampton Street. As the others waited, he took Sarah aside.

'You are going *now*?'

'I cannot delay. I am obliged to Isaac and –'

'Obliged?' She was aware of the shrillness in her voice. Nearby, Mary Betterton looked at her. Sarah continued, in a lower key. 'And your obligation to me? To this day? What is so important that you can neglect that?' She saw the hesitation, the same look on his face as when he was off to catch thieves with Pitman and wished to spare her the fear of it. 'Nay, sir, you will tell me. Else how will I explain to our guests the bridegroom's sudden absence?'

More actors were looking now, so he took her further aside. 'You need say little more than I go to aid a desperate friend. With fortune I will be back even before the feast's end.'

'But there is danger in this aid, is there not?'

'Not so much –'

'Come, sir, I will not be treated like a child. Where do you go and upon what cause?'

'I do not treat you like a child, Sarah. I try to spare you –' Her hiss made him stop, take a breath. 'I go to aid my friend. His daughter is missing but he knows where she is and I will go to fetch her back. That is all.'

'Is she pretty?'

'What?'

'I cannot believe you would be so gallant on your wedding day for a homely girl.'

The words were out. She would have them back – and yet not so. They'd just got married. How dare he be the courteous knight for someone else?

'She's, er, fifteen. I –' He flushed. 'Lady, what are you saying?'

Behind them, one of the actors had pulled out a fiddle and struck up a reel. Dickon was there in a moment, capering to cheers. They both looked, and when she'd turned back she saw that his eyes had hooded over, in the way they did whenever she tried to probe something painful from his past. She had not seen that look, that absence, for a while.

He spoke first. 'You are being absurd.'

'Am I?'

'This is something I must do. So I will go, and I will return, either to the inn or to our lodgings.' He bobbed his head. 'Keep Dickon with you.'

He walked away. She took a step after him. But her legs wobbled and she had to lean against a wall. She took a deep breath, and another, until her head cleared a little. Why was she behaving like this? Why? She knew who he was. 'Captain?' she called him by his rank, the only name she'd used for the longest time while she was trying not to fall in love with him. But her voice was faint. He rounded the corner and was gone. Gone like . . .

It was then she remembered what her anger and confusion had masked. William Coke, in rags, pallid as any ghost, slipping away from her. She felt a sudden clutch inside. Not the pain of her pregnancy — worse.

'Sa-sarah?'

She turned. Dickon was there, concern on his face. She smiled for him, hard though it was. 'All's well. The captain will be back soon.'

'The cap'n?' Maybe he saw the ghost behind her smile. He took a step.

There was nothing she could do now. She did not know where

he'd gone or exactly what he was about. She could only bide, hope – and keep Dickon safe. 'Nay, boy,' she said, taking his arm, pulling him towards the fiddler. 'You owe me the first dance.'

10

A RECKONING

He held the last note of the song, plangent, sorrowful, beautifully sustained. He let it slowly fade, as if disappearing into the air above her head.

'Again,' Rebekah said, raising her hand above her as if reaching up to trap the fleeting strain. 'Play it again.'

Daniel lowered the flute. 'Nay, lass. That was the last time – for now. Till after we are done. But then,' he smiled, 'then there will be more songs. Of praise. Of love.'

'And will there be more of other things?' She stretched a hand to him, running her fingers down his naked shoulder, the blanket that had covered her own nakedness falling away. She didn't prevent it falling, enjoying the way his eyes widened at what was revealed. 'Come,' she said, pinching his flesh now between thumb and forefinger. 'There is time enough, surely, for that?'

He laid the flute down, turned to her. But just as he did, the bell struck twice in the tower of St Leonard's. So he took her hand from him, kissed it and set it down. 'You are a wanton,' he said, as he rose from the bed.

'If I am, 'twas you made me so.' She came up onto her knees.

'A week ago and I was ignorant of everything. You taught me all.' Her lower lip thrust out. 'Teach me more now.'

But he was pulling on his breeches. 'It is time for God's lessons now, child,' he said. 'God's judgments.' He thought of Simeon. 'You know what you are to do?'

She flinched at the change in his tone, covering herself with the rough wool blanket. 'You have told me, aye. I still do not understand –'

'You do not need to understand,' he replied, his voice still firm. 'Which of us truly understands God's ways? We only need to have faith.'

'I – I have,' she said, lowering her eyes, shivering. 'You have brought me to that, too. It is just that this captain was always my father's friend –'

'And our Lord's most accursed enemy.' He pulled on his lawn shirt, tucked it in, then bent to her, putting his hand under her chin, raising her face up. 'Do not question what greater wisdoms than ours have ordained. He has been judged. He will be punished, and the way of it will be both a sign of God's favour and a warning to other sinners.'

'I know. I believe. Yet –'

Daniel lifted his hand from her face and slapped her, hard enough to sting. 'No more questions,' he said, his voice harsh now. 'You have your task. Do it.'

Tears ran down her nose now. But as he stepped away, she grabbed his hand. 'I will! You know I will.'

He pushed his hand into her tumble of thick hair and she bent her face against his palm. 'I do know,' he said, his voice soft again. 'Both love and faith convince me.'

She kissed his hand then, and he leaned down, pulling her lips to his. After a moment he stood straight. 'Be ready,' he said, and left the room.

Daniel shut the door, propped himself against it and closed his eyes. He regretted much: the sin of fornication, if not its pleasure; the sin of the hurt he'd done her. But his master, who had brought him to faith, had assured him that these deeds were nothing in the infinity of God's plan. That when the last trumpet sounded – so soon! – and Christ came to judge them all, his service would be weighed against his sin. And the laying low of so great an enemy would tip the scales heavily in his favour.

He reached into his pocket, feeling the apothecary's vial there. One more task, he thought, starting down the stairs, and it is done.

The Black Cat Tavern was at the end of an alley that ran alongside St Leonard's church, into Pudding Lane.

Most taverns stank of sour beer. Coke assumed the Vintners must own this one, for the scents of Rhenish wine assailed his nostrils from the moment he pushed through the door. It made him thirsty, even as it filled him with regret – he should have been toasting his bride in the stuff right now.

He scanned the crowd. He did not know who he was to meet. He could only presume that they would know him.

Someone did. A young man had risen in a corner settle and was signalling. Coke did not go over straightway. These were the Saints he was dealing with, after all. But everyone around the youth appeared to be boisterously engaged in their own company. Keeping his hand on the pommel of his sword, he crossed the rush-strewn floor.

'Sit, sir. Take some wine.'

The young man seemed familiar to him but he could not remember where he'd seen him. Still, familiar or not, he was not there to drink with him. 'There is no need for me to sit,' Coke replied curtly. 'Only for you to rise and take me to the maid.'

'Her whereabouts I do not know. Truly, Captain, if I may call you so. My friends told me you were a dangerous man and might try and trick us. You might even, er, attack me.' He gestured again to the stool opposite him. 'So once our business is concluded amicably here, another will lead you to your prize.'

Coke *had* considered violence as an early resort. He had no scruples about dealing harshly with these rogues and kidnappers. But his first duty here was to Isaac, and the safe return of his daughter. So he sat, glancing around as he did, again trying to spot the man's confederates. No one immediately offered themselves.

'Drink, sir, please,' said the youth, waving at the glass before Coke. 'We have a little time. And you are paying for it, after all.'

Coke, who had picked up the glass, now put it down without sipping. 'You say someone will come and lead us to her? So she is not here?'

'No, indeed, sir. Your health.' The youth raised his glass.

Coke leaned across the table. 'Now listen to me, you puppy,' he said, his voice low. 'I do not pledge the health of a villain. What you have done to a sick old man is cruelty itself. So the sooner our business is done and the girl returned to her father, the sooner I can drink with whom I choose.' He pulled out Isaac's purse from which he'd removed the extra ten guineas. 'Count this and be damned.'

He threw the guineas across. The youth paled. 'No villain, I, but only God's true servant.' He opened the purse string, emptied the coins out onto the settle seat beside him, counted, then swept the coins back into the cloth bag. 'All there,' he said.

'Then will you signal the blackguard who accompanies you and let us be about it.'

'We will await him, sir. I can do no more.'

The youth sat back and stared at him sullenly. Coke slapped the table in frustration; then suddenly recalling his thirst, he picked up the glass and threw the contents back. It was Rhenish all right but not as good as he expected in the Vintner's own tavern. There was a slightly bitter tang to it that had him running his tongue over his mouth. The youth had clearly paid for only the cheapest stuff.

He looked behind. The young man's glumness cleared, as he raised his eyes above Coke's head. 'There,' he said.

Coke turned and looked back. A stranger stood in the tavern's doorway, staring at them. He gave a nod, and stepped back into the street.

Coke crossed rapidly to the door. The other fellow was a few paces down the cobbles. The young man came up to the doorway. 'How far?'

'Not far, Captain, not far at all.' The young man's gloom had entirely gone for he grinned now and gestured. 'Mind your step.'

They went down Pudding Lane a little ways, then turned right down an alley that ended on Fish Street. The bridge was at the end of that and they made for it. For a while he thought they might take him across it and into the stews of Southwark, a suitable place for such villainy. Instead they turned north, cut up

Crooked Lane, through St Michael's churchyard and on up to Great Eastcheap. Yet instead of continuing west or north, they cut immediately east again, heading back in the direction they'd just come.

'What is this?' demanded Coke, halting. 'You are leading me on a dance.'

'Not at all, sir, not at all,' replied the young man. 'Perhaps you don't know this part of the city. So many alleys, they are often dead ends.' He stepped closer, peering into Coke's face. 'Are you alright, sir? You seem hot.'

'I am fine,' answered Coke, reaching up to his forehead to find it slick. But it was a warm night, and his cloak his fancier, lined one. He'd intended it for a wedding not a chase. 'Proceed, damn ye,' he growled.

'Right you are, Captain. This way.'

They turned south towards the river then, but just when he thought the water would appear to his sight, they cut north again. It was true, he did not know this part of town very well. He was damnably lost and he wished he could take off his cloak. 'Heh,' he said – tried to say. His tongue felt thick in his mouth. He spat onto the cobbles, looking up to the men who had stopped before him. They shifted to his sight, then doubled. 'Heh,' he said more clearly, drawing himself up. 'I remember you now. You make music outside the goldsmith's. You play the –'

He couldn't remember what instrument the young man played. It went from his mind, along with his knees from under him as he sank onto the street. He did not halt there, but continued a slow fall until his face was pressed into the cobbles. Figures moved about him then, several more than two now, he thought. His hand closed over his sword's pommel but he had not the strength to draw it. Someone else did.

He was lifted and sagged between two men. He heard the young man's voice again, but it sounded far away.

'Hurry.'

A flute. That's what the youth had played outside Isaac's house. He remembered it on waking because he heard one in the dream that roused him – a pleasant one, as pleasant as the reality he woke to. He must have fulfilled his mission for the Jew for he had returned to his own bed. A body lay next to him, as naked as he was. A woman's, by the scent, the soft skin.

'Sarah,' he breathed, though he wasn't sure the word came out, as his tongue seemed as thick as before. And there was something wrong with his eyes, a stickiness to them. He tried to reach a hand up to wipe them, but someone was holding it.

'I'll fetch them,' he heard a familiar voice say. The sound of boots on a wooden floor came, then faded down some stairs.

'Hurry, he stirs,' said Sarah.

Not Sarah. It was wrong: the voice, the scent, the skin – he freed his fingers, lifted his hand and dropped it higher up. Onto a breast.

Her scream was loud. Not Sarah's. It made him jump, launching him into wakefulness. He forced his eyelids open, even as he threw himself backwards, toppling over the edge of the bed. He landed on his back and lay there like a crab unable to do more than wriggle his limbs, unable to focus on more than the person above him on the bed. It took him a long moment to recognise her, even though she was the one he'd sought. For he'd never seen Rebekah bat Judah without her head covered, her hair hidden. And he had never seen her naked.

'Help!' she screamed, pulling a blanket over herself. 'Help me!'

Coke lurched onto his knees, though when he did it was like someone had driven a spike through his forehead. He reached out to her. 'Maid! Shh! I am here to –'

Her heels dug into the bed, kicking her back to the headboard. 'No,' she screamed once, and again when he somehow got onto his feet, though swaying as if at sea. She thrust out her hand before her eyes and turned her face away, crying.

He looked down. He was as naked as she. How was this possible? How?

He looked around. His clothes lay a-tangle on the floor as if hastily ripped off and cast aside. He bent to the breeches, tried to pull the stockings from them and place his foot. The movement made him nauseous and he paused to still his heaving stomach. 'Maid.' He tried again. 'Rebekah. I am come to aid you . . .'

'Help!' she screamed once more, and he realised it was not his aid she sought. Her face was now turned to the door, and the sound of running men came from the stairs.

Again Coke tried to get his foot into his breeches; again he failed. He had no time for a third attempt because three large men rushed into the room.

'I am –' Coke began but got no further. The first man had placed a hand against his chest and pushed him hard. His legs were shaky enough and could not hold him. He crashed back onto a small table there. It collapsed under him and he fell to the floor.

'Stay there, ye bastard. I am a constable of this parish and I order you to do so,' his assailant shouted, hefting a large cudgel before turning to another man who'd gone to the weeping girl on the bed. 'Is it her?'

'Dunno,' the man replied, bending till his head was level with hers. 'Is it you, sweetheart? Are you the Jew's missing daughter?'

She lowered her hand from her face. 'I am!' she cried. 'I am Rebekah bat Judah.' She raised a hand, pointing at Coke. 'And this man . . . this man!' She sobbed and buried her face again.

The first constable turned to the third man there. ''E's three doors along. Fetch 'im! And you,' he whipped back to Coke who'd been trying to rise, 'just give me a reason to beat ya. Though I don't need much – rapist!'

'No!' Despite the raised cudgel, Coke rose to his knees. 'I am her father's friend –'

'Some friend,' the man spat. 'Now you just bide.'

He had no choice. The second man had come closer, also with a club, and looked as keen to strike as the first. Moving slowly so as not to provoke them, he managed to disentangle his stockings from his breeches. The men glared but did not forbid it and he began to slide them on. 'That's right,' said the second constable. 'Put it away, ye swine. Now you've 'ad your fun.'

Everything was wrong. But Isaac would speak for him. Isaac would come and tell them.

Except the next footsteps up the stairs were not Isaac's. Another Jew entered the room. He was a little younger than the goldsmith, though his hair was as grey under his skullcap.

'Uncle!' cried Rebekah, rising up off the bed, then realising her nakedness and falling back to cover herself up.

'Child!' the man strode across. 'What has happened here?'

122

'He —' She pointed her finger at Coke, then screamed the next words. 'He kidnapped me. He . . . ravished me.'

She dissolved again into sobs. Her uncle lent to her, taking the blanket up, covering her. Then, bending, he lifted her off the bed. She drove her head into his chest. 'I will take her to her father — though I fear this news will hasten his death, sick as he is.' He looked for the first time at Coke. 'Constables, I beseech you, do your duty.'

'We shall.'

'This is wrong.' Coke stood up now, despite the clubs raised menacingly again. 'I came to help her. Her father sent me. She's lying. I did not touch her.'

'You did not touch whom?'

The voice came soft from the doorway. But an actress did not need to speak loudly for her voice to carry.

'Sarah!'

Like any piece of theatre — a puppet show or anything put on at the playhouse — it is always a matter of timing, he thought. Every performer got it wrong sometimes. But when God orchestrated the piece . . .

In the shadows of the doorway opposite, Simeon heard Coke's impassioned cry of his bride's name. Getting her there had been difficult, a message sent from 'a concerned party', arriving only an hour previously at the wedding feast, when the drug looked like it was wearing off. He'd been worried that Sarah Chalker — Sarah Coke — would not make it in time. It wasn't vital — but it would be an extra delight.

The Lord hastened her. That and the wild-eyed boy she leaned upon guiding her there. 'Just in time,' he whispered. A thought he never shared with his ever-sombre, most literal brothers was that God was a puppet-master just like him. Why, did he not set fire to a bush, trap a ram in a thicket, part the flood? So why wouldn't the Almighty relish a moment as perfect as this?

He wished he could have witnessed the newlyweds' reunion. But Coke knew him now, from the building site, and he did not wish to confuse the constables. Still, he thought, I never see the faces of my puppets below me on the stage; yet I can hear the effect they have. Like the woman's sobbing.

You'll cry more tears, Mrs Coke, ere God and I are done.

11

THE PRESS

'No, you don't!'

As two of the constables began to drag his cap'n from the room, he ran at them. One raised an arm to fend him off, but he dodged it easily, then grabbed the man's hand and wrenched it back against its inclination as his cap'n had showed him when they wrestled for sport. The man didn't think it sport and gave a great cry as he fell back.

Maybe I twists it too hard, Dickon thought. But no one 'rests my captain.

The second man swung a fist at him but he was old and fat and slow and Dickon ducked and put his own fist in the man's ribs, just a jab, sharp though, and the man wheezed and let go of his prisoner, which was the point.

'Run, Cap'n,' Dickon shouted, but his guardian just sagged and almost fell. Something was wrong with him and when Dickon reached to hold him up, the third constable who'd gone to the door crossed back and fetched him a great buffet across his head, knocking him onto the jumbled bed, making his ear ring. Still, he'd have been up in a moment, bells or not, to fight 'em, if'n the cap'n hadn't cried, 'No, Dickon! Sarah!' and pointed, and he'd turned back and seen Sarah sagging almost like the cap'n, like they were both drunk, which he'd never seen, though he'd seen plenty of others so, including those who'd left him in the doorway two years before all cold for the cap'n to find.

He could only choose one, for now. And Coke had always taught him to look to ladies first. Being 'gallant' is what he called it. So Dickon was gallant and went to catch Sarah just before she fell and had to hold her up and get her to the bed, even though his head still rung, even though the three officers were running his cap'n out the door now, though the one was not helping much but holding his hurt hand.

Sarah sagged onto the bed. He helped her as best he could. 'Look up!' he called, alarmed at the fluttering of her eyes.

These steadied for a moment at his voice, and she stared up at him. 'William?' she whispered.

He had been gallant. Now he had to go. He ran for the stairs.

She tried to rise. She wanted to follow, but her legs would not answer her will.

I am not a woman who faints, she thought, grinding her teeth, taking a deep breath and placing her hands beneath her. I am not.

She pushed. For a moment she hovered at the balance, neither up nor down. Then with an effort she stood. She was up, but she could not move, not yet. It took more breaths, more steeling, and when she walked it was more a lurch and she had to catch herself at the door. The stairs required still more time, more effort. It took too long for her to reach the street. Coke, the constables, Dickon, the Jew and the girl – all were gone. A man was staring at her from the doorway opposite. 'Did you see? A man? A prisoner? Which way?'

Her words came out jerky, on heaved breaths. But the man only shrugged before walking away, a smile on his broken face.

She did not know where to go. She did not have the strength to go if she did. She would need to rest and then set out. Sinking down onto the doorstep, she tried to steady her breathing, though that was so hard with her jerking thoughts.

What had just happened? Her husband of only a few hours, her lover. The man who had given her the child that so weakened her legs now. With another? His friend's young daughter? And she had screamed of ravishment. Sarah had heard her as she'd slowly climbed the stairs to a room that stank of fornication. With William and the girl half dressed within it.

None of it was possible. And yet?

Someone thought him guilty, else why were constables there? No. She would not, could not believe. Not until she looked him in the eyes. If she knew little enough about this man she'd married, at least she would know if he lied to her.

Determination steadied her. There was only one place a rapist would be taken in the city. Rising, she took the first shaky steps towards Newgate prison.

There was no purpose in attacking again. Dickon wasn't afeard; but even if he managed to free the cap'n from the constables, twist the other two's wrists as well, it didn't look like his guardian could run away fast enough, to escape the halloo that would follow. He was still sagging in the men's grip. Maybe they'd hit him before he'd been able to catch up. He'd pay 'em if they had.

At least they'd allowed him to put his clothes on. It was sad to see them, his wedding garb, new doublet and lawn shirt all askew, his fine brown breeches stained with something, his rich cloak showing the street filth it must have fallen into. At one point his silk scarf fell, unnoticed by any of the men. Dickon just beat an urchin to it and tucked it away into his own bright new breeches.

He followed, taking care that he was not seen. Along Watling Street, a roadway so old and narrow the houses' eaves appeared woven together and no daylight fell onto the dank cobbles, the party met another group of men coming the opposite way – eight men with cudgels who had others in their midst. Prisoners, Dickon thought, though these men were also dressed in Sunday finery as if they'd come straight from church.

Dickon slipped into a doorway to watch. All this ballyhoo, he might have a chance to cut his cap'n free of the mob. Truth to tell, Coke looked as if he was recovering, just a little. As the two groups met and overlapped, he stood a little straighter. And when Dickon gave a whistle, the same alert that they would use when they were about their work on the king's highway, he saw Coke turn his head.

Through the fog that still shrouded his mind, something pierced – a whistle he knew, alerting him to danger on the road. But of all the robberies he and Dickon had undertaken, he did not think they'd encountered any danger as great as this. For if he'd thought that being dragged to Newgate prison for a crime he knew he had not committed, while still trying to shake the last effects of the damnable drug they'd slipped into his wine, would be the ultimate horror, he was now learning that he was wrong.

For the leader of the group they'd merged with was passing the constable a flagon of rum to sip, while making a proposition. 'Rape? What punishment is he going to get for that?' The man had skin that looked like it had come from a tannery, dark-hued by all weathers. Such teeth as he had flashed bright against it when he smiled. 'Was she a looker at least?'

'A peach,' replied one of the parish constables. 'Jew's daughter, dark as sin.'

The other man laughed. 'A Jewish peach? Now there's a fruit I wouldn't mind *pluck*ing.' More men laughed too and his deep voice rose above it. 'But there's yet another reason to listen to my offer,' he continued, waving the flagon back as the constable tried to return it. 'We all know the Jews are still barely protected at law. This 'ere ravisher? A gentleman. They'll probably congratulate him on his fortune, pat his back, send him home.' He shook his head. 'Don't seem right. So should we not show that all peoples get justice here in our realm? Sometimes we citizens have to see right done, right? Like we did for the good old cause.'

There were grunts of assent at this, as the rum flagon went around again, for they were all Parliament's men in the late wars. When it reached the leader of the constables once more, he swigged and said, 'What is it you propose?'

The dark-faced man put his shoulders back. 'See here. I am recruiting for His Majesty's Navy. These men –' he gestured at the four dressed as they would be for church, but who were shackled at wrist and whose faces bore the signs of both tears and ill usage, 'are eager volunteers to fight against the Hogen Mogens, those dastardly Dutch what threaten our liberties. Yeah, even the liberties of the Jews in our midst.' He sucked his lips between his ramshackle teeth. 'Now I've a bet on with another petty officer that in one night of pressing I could bring back more than he to St Katharine's Dock. I know for a fact he only brung back four. So I am still one short.' He grinned. 'So how's about you sell me you'rn, give the Jew justice, and the Hogens one more reason to fear.'

One of his subordinates pointed at Coke. 'Bit old, ain't 'e?'

'Wonder if the Jewess thought so?' The petty officer bent and shoved a coiled whip under the captain's chin, forcing his head up. 'Nah. In his prime, I'd say.'

Coke had been slowly gathering himself. Whatever the drug had been that they'd given him a few hours before – five, he realised as a church bell tolled eight nearby now – still had a grip on him. He knew he could not fight even one of these men. He could not run. But at last his tongue was free again for him to talk. 'Friends,' he said, straightening, 'I am a victim of a foul plot. I am not –'

He got no further before hoots drowned him out. 'Oh, I am sure that Delilah plotted your fall,' the petty officer said, then looked around. 'Yes, "Delilah". I am a Bible-read man. And I also remember this.' He cleared his throat, spat on the cobbles, stood straight. '"Vengeance is mine, saith the Lord." Well, I am his weapon. His will be done,' he bent his face closer. Coke smelled rum, tobacco, foul teeth, 'and you are coming with us.' He looked at the constable. 'Subject to suitable recompense, of course.'

Coke thought of his father, dead these several decades. The last of a long speech of advice the old man had given him when he set out for war was this: 'Be wary of drinking with strangers – and always keep a dagger in your boot.'

If I failed to heed you in the first, Father, he thought, I did not in the second. He bent, gripped and as he pulled the dagger clear gave the same whistle Dickon had given him: Be ready. Then he straightened and placed the blade against the nearest constable's throat. 'You will all –'

It was as far as he got. The swarthy man hit him across the face with his whip, the coiled and tarred cords as solid as any wood. White exploded in Coke's eyes and he fell sideways, dropping the dagger, plunging back into the darkness he'd only just risen from. Words faded to mumbles above him. He was lifted and shackles were placed on his wrists. Then he was shoved into a stumbling walk. He was aware that they were moving back the way they had come. Aware of the river drawing nearer. Aware of a bird's whistle nearby that a bird did not make.

When he was thrown into a wherry, his face landed in a pool of stagnant water. He turned his head and gasped a breath; struggled to open his eyes, managed it only for a brief moment. But long enough to see a face he knew, wild-eyed beneath a thatch of corn-coloured hair. A cheer came, as someone slipped onto the bench above him and laid a hand upon his shoulder.

''S'aright, Cap'n,' Dickon whispered, as the boat moved out onto the choppy waters of the Thames, 'I'm 'ere.'

Part Three

﹥─◆◎─◆─﹤

AND THE SECOND ANGEL POURED OUT HIS
VIAL UPON THE SEA; AND IT BECAME AS THE BLOOD
OF A DEAD MAN: AND EVERY LIVING
SOUL DIED IN THE SEA.
The Revelation of St John the Divine 16:3

11

DEBTS

Three weeks later

They came for her at dawn. She was already awake. The life inside her had made sure of that, shifting around, pressing her belly out with what she thought could be an elbow or a heel. She was always grateful for the touch. He – she sensed it was a 'he' – had gone quiet for a couple of days and she had scarcely slept at all, sure that she had lost him, as she had lost the other. Then the pushing out, the shifting, came again. A sunbeam in her darkness.

Her babe woke her; her thoughts kept her so. What am I to do? she wondered. What in Christ's holy name am I to do?

Thomas Betterton had made it clear two nights before. If he occasionally admired her talent, he never really liked her, she knew. Only a few days after the murder of her husband John Chalker the previous year, he had renewed his attentions. Seeking to console, he'd said, pressing her into corners. You needs must forget, he'd said, bending to kiss her. A sharp knee to his heated groin had put him off – and then it was back to resenting her, the laughs or tears she could conjure from an audience. Davenant, the manager of the company, had always sheltered her for her talents. But he was abroad, leaving Thomas in charge.

'It is with deepest regret,' he'd said, the glitter in his eyes showing the opposite, 'but you know your condition is affecting your playing. Affecting your looks too.' He'd smirked. 'We cannot pay you to play maids and fishwives, Mrs Chalker – ah, apologies, Mrs Coke.' There was relish in the way he said that too, naming her missing husband. 'Return when you have spawned. No guarantees, but there may be opportunities – maids and fishwives.'

Did the men now hammering on her front door know that she was without employment, she wondered as she raised herself off the bed, pausing to sit on its edge to let the dizziness, and the nausea it brought, settle. Probably. Betterton had no doubt told them – with the deepest regret, of course. And now her income had been taken away, the last barrier she'd had between herself and her debt was gone too. With employment she'd been able to offer gradual repayment. Without it . . .

She heard the landlady descending the stairs, then heard her loudly command the men to cease their kicking. Her own door was bolted, but only to give a little more time if she'd happened to find the balm of sleep. Awake, she only had to dress to be as ready as she would ever be.

She rose, removed her night shift, put on a freshly laundered one and a clean smock over that. She doubted there would be much opportunity to keep her clothes clean where she was bound. She could at least begin well.

Bolts were drawn below. The volume of argument rose. She moved across to the large bag she had kept packed these several days, folded her still warm night clothes, cramming them atop the other items she would take, most of which she hoped to sell. She heard the clink of glass, two bottles of 'Mrs Pitman's Famous Elixir' rubbing together.

'Ask three shillings for one, and drink the other yesself. You'll need to keep up your strength,' Bettina had said when she'd called round the day before. She'd cried as she said it, trying to keep her tears hidden by bustling about and adding items she thought might help. She'd even tried to slip in a gold crown, but Sarah had refused it. The Pitmans, the breadwinner still laid up in bed, fevered and with his leg in splints, needed all their little money for themselves, what with four hungry children and Bettina also expecting. 'Praise God that the parish is letting us stay in the house while Pitman recovers. They may yet change their minds and then,' she'd wiped her eyes, 'well, then we may be joining you. The whole bloody lot of us!'

They were coming up the stairs now. Sarah reached and wrapped her shawl around herself though she did not need its warmth. London was as hot as she could ever remember it in May, with no rain for a month, and none on the horizon. But weather changed and she did not know what the rooms would be like. Nor how many seasons she must go through in them.

She ran her hand over the rich, patterned material. Yak's wool, whatever a yak was. An early present from the captain, purchased from the Jewish merchants he'd befriended, who'd brought it from afar along their trade routes to the east. He'd got a bargain, he said, laughing away the expense, its price discounted for certain kindnesses of his.

What other kindnesses had he given and received of Jews? She shivered, but not from cold. From the memory of two days before, when she'd gone to Isaac the goldsmith to beg him to wait for the money Coke had borrowed from them, a debt too great for her to repay now, when other debts pressed. But the man she'd seen had had no kindness in his eyes. He was Isaac's cousin, he'd told her, deputed to take care of his relative's affairs while God decided if the goldsmith would live or die following his operation. The prospects were not good, though; an inflammation had set in and fever followed, as oft occurred after cutting for the stone. In which case, the man had said, it is the daughter's affairs I must attend to. And the mention of Rebekah had made Sarah look away, though not before she'd seen the cold fury in the man's eyes.

She shivered again. She did not know what to believe. She'd married a man she thought she loved. No – did love, she was sure. But she also recognised that she barely knew him. There was so much of his history that he had never revealed in confidences that she had seen only in fleeting shadows within his eyes. He'd suffered in the wars, she knew. He had seen friends die. And he had killed. He had lost everything – home, every member of his family. A woman he'd loved, whose name he never spoke awake but cried out sometimes in his sleep – Evangeline. He never talked about her – or about any of it, though some nights she held him when he cried in his dreams. What must a man like that have seen? What could a man like that do, when the darkness came?

The men were at the door of her room now. There was muttering beyond it, and then loud knocking. She had a moment left in the place they had shared together. And this she knew: only if she could look him in his grey eyes and ask him, would she discover the truth of that room, that girl. But she could not. For where was he now, her captain, her husband, her stranger? Where was William Coke?

There was no one to tell her for Dickon had not returned either, another ache in her heart. She had found the strength, gone to Newgate prison to enquire – only to discover that he had never reached it. It took three more days to track down the constables who'd arrested him and learn the truth, though the man could not meet her eyes when he'd told her.

'The press took him. Maybe he'll atone for his sins by serving his country against the Dutch.'

Maybe, she thought, as the hammering increased. Or maybe he'll die. And I will never get to ask him.

It suddenly became the worst thought of all. Worse even than what awaited her beyond the door. Sarah crossed to it now, shooting the bolts and stepping back.

The door swung in. Three men were there, different from those who had dogged her at the theatre. The one at the front with one hand still raised to knock held a rolled paper in the other. 'Mrs Sarah Coke?' he asked, though it was clear he knew.

The title still sounded strange to her. But she could not deny it, nor him. 'Yes.'

'Wife and sole heir of William Coke, Esquire, of this parish?' 'Yes.'

The man unfolded the paper. 'I have a warrant here for your arrest for failure to pay your family obligations of forty guineas, entered into with one,' he squinted down at the paper, 'Samuel Tremlett, master mason, for the construction of a house on West Harding Street. Also, the sum of forty guineas to one Isaac ben

Judah, goldsmith.' He looked up. 'Do you have the money to pay this debt now?'

'No.'

'Then you are obliged to accompany me to debtors' prison, there to remain until you are able to discharge your obligations.' He rolled up the paper again. 'Come.'

Sarah picked up her valise. 'Are you taking me to the Fleet prison?'

'No. The debtee is resident in the City of London and you will bide near him.' He gestured to his two men to step aside and allow Sarah out. 'So you will be lodged at the Poultry Compter.'

She'd heard of it. The name still struck her as absurd even though she knew it was just the name of the street the debtors' prison was on. Though jokes and puns were her strength as an actress, she now found that she could not come up with a single one. Could only pick up her bag, walk out of the room, not look back.

He knew it was wrong. He was weak still, but his senses had returned. Bettina, who had nursed him so carefully with her herbs and potions, did not want to believe it. ''Tis your fever fancy, Pitman. And look at you, you've lost so many pounds from a fortnight's lack of food, *all* your bones feel funny. Especially that one.' She'd pointed to his leg. 'Now you just drink some of this while it's hot.'

He had; but he knew even his wife's mutton soup would not cure what ailed him. It was her fear of what he'd recognised that blinded her to it. For the consequences were dire. If he could not be up and about his parish duties soon, not to mention his other activities as a taker of thieves, they would not be able to pay for this house, the ingredients for her elixirs, the food for their table. She needed him whole and mended – which he would never be with a broken leg that had been wrongly set.

He had seen too often, in the late king's wars, the consequences of that. Comrades hastily splinted in retreat, the breaks neglected later. Limping forever after, discharged back to lives they could no longer take full part in. He needed to be able to run, to chase down villains; to stand tall and impose himself on rogues who would face him down. He could do neither leaning on a crutch.

He pulled himself onto his elbows and listened to Bettina below, bustling about, tidying their brood. It was the Sabbath, so she was bound for the meeting house and then to the Strangers' Market, where those who worshipped a different God were happy to sell on the Lord's day. There she would spend some of their diminishing stock of coin wisely: to buy meat just on the turn, vegetables only a little bruised. 'Off out, my love?' he called down the stairs.

'Off out, Pitman. All of us. Do you want anything?'

'Leave me Josiah. I have an errand for him to run.'

'But the Sabbath?'

'I know. But this is urgent parish business and cannot wait.'

'Very well.'

The girls were gathered – Grace and Faith carrying the infant Benjamin. All came to kiss their father goodbye, to have him admire their Sunday best, the ribbons in their hair. The front door cut off their pretty chirping and in a few moments, his son was there. 'What errand, Father?' he asked. Pitman could see Josiah was not unhappy about missing chapel.

He studied his son. The boy was twelve now, and tall with it. There was a stillness to him, quite unlike either parent. A haunted look, not uncommon in London that year. Pitman knew the boy had seen too much, things he wished he had not. A slaughtered body on a road in Finchley. Too many other bodies on the plague-ridden streets, including a sister and baby brother carried away on a death cart. Josiah had had the plague himself, but lived. It would scar anyone, and he spent much of his days just staring out of the window. An occupation had to be found for him, an apprenticeship. It was time he began to make his way in the world. But that was not why Pitman needed him now.

'Do you recall the stables where we hire horses some time?'

'Cripplegate Without?'

'Aye. There's a smithy beside it. The smith's name is Aaron Bastable. Tell him that Pitman needs to see him urgent, and bring him straight back.'

'Aye, Father.' Josiah turned to leave, then turned back again. 'But 'tis the Sabbath. Will he not be in church or chapel?'

'He will not. He may be in the tavern next door, the Woodcock.' He raised a hand, forestalling his son's protest. 'I know, taverns should be closed this day. Some are not, for those who do need a drink on the Lord's day.'

His son gave one of his rare smiles. 'And how would you know that, Da?'

'Never you mind. Tell him to come quick.'

'And if he won't?'

'He will.'

Josiah nodded and left. Pitman lay back down, staring at the ceiling. He hoped Bastable was still there. It had been a year since last he'd seen him and the plague had taken so many. If he was, he would come. For friendship, sealed in those years after the war when they'd all – he, Aaron and Bettina – been part of the mad crew, the Ranters, praising God in the open field, with drink, with dance, with . . . love – but for comradeship too. He'd saved the man's life on the ramparts at Turnham Green – twice, and on the same day.

'I will ever be in your debt, Pitman. You have but to call,' he'd said.

Now the debt would be repaid. For Aaron Bastable, blacksmith, was the best breaker and resetter of bones he'd ever known.

He dozed, his dreams a haze of tobacco smoke, fiddle music and naked flesh under a full moon. Stairs creaking woke him. Voices on the landing.

'Goliath laid low, eh? I told you no good would come of forsaking sin for righteousness.'

The man grinning in the doorway didn't look much different than when Pitman had last seen him. Still the insolence in the close-set eyes, one straight on, one askance, as if always both questioning and mocking the world. Both under a thatched roof of thick black hair, eaves silvered, above a face that was all folds and creases, every one lined in the residue of smoke that was the smith's trade.

Peering in at his elbow, eyes bright, was Josiah. 'Off to chapel, boy,' Pitman said, raising himself up.

'But, Father, I'd rather stay and hear you tell your old war tales. Master Bastable told me a few coming over and –'

'Did he, by God? Then you already know more than you need. Off with you now.'

'Father.'

Reluctantly, Josiah turned about. The front door closed. 'Have no fear,' Aaron said as he came into the room, 'I told him naught of consequence. Didn't even mention that time when you and I was so drunk we dressed up as Catholic priests and went and took confession up at his Lordship's manor house.' His offset eyes filled with light. 'By God, those Papists had stored up some sins, hadn't they? We had to set unusual penances, did we not? For the maids anyhow.' His voice went high. ' "Oh no, Father Evelyn, I shouldn't touch that. But I will, if you'll only forgive me. Ooh, Father Evelyn!" ' He tipped back his head and guffawed. 'By God, you had four and I had five before his Lordship cottoned on. I think it was her Ladyship's cry of "Father Evelyn, what's that under your cassock?" that tipped him off.' He feigned a limp around the room, rubbing his backside. 'We was lucky his blunderbuss was only loaded for starlings, I tell ye. Though Bettina was picking shot from our arses for weeks.'

Pitman laughed with his friend. His memory of the night, indeed of most of the three years he'd spent as a Ranter, was hazy, lost in smoke and debauchery. 'I've a feeling you are overestimating our conquests – and our capacity, man. And only you took the shot, if you recall. You were never the fastest over a wall. You'd proved that at Turnham Green ramparts.'

Aaron pulled a stool to the bedside and sat, running his hand through his thick hair. Coke dust rose and fell in sunbeams from the window. 'You're right there, Evelyn, and I still thank –'

'Sht!' The thief-taker's hand shot up. 'You know I never use my given name. Few remember it now. It's Pitman to you, Pitman to all.'

Mischief returned to the eyes. 'But it's so pretty a name. Why, any maid would be glad to own . . . erk!'

Pitman had extended his raised hand, grabbed Aaron's throat and squeezed. His friend slipped free, fell back, choking and laughing. 'Very well, very well, Corporal Pitman. Tell me what means this summons.' He glanced down the bed to the bandaged leg, an eyebrow raised.

It was all swiftly explained, as much as Aaron needed to know. He knew Pitman's other trade, indeed was one of those the thief-taker would recruit from time to time when he needed men. He'd been away at the recent raid, else he'd have been on it. 'Tut, these Saints, eh?' Aaron shook his head. 'Fucking madmen. I mean, I think doom is coming, right? Just don't reckon Jesus is on his way back to rule us.'

'Well, they do. And they are a danger. And I need to be strong enough to face them.' He gestured down. 'Take a look at my leg.'

Aaron rose and undid the bandages. When the flesh was exposed, he winced. The skin was still a brownish yellow, with purple lines running like rivers on a map down to the knee. 'Bullet or blade?'

'Blade.' As Aaron bent to sniff and wince again, Pitman continued, 'It went bad. I had a fever, just come out of it two days since. Bettina attended me.'

'With her own potions? She did not let a quack near you?'

'She'd bite his bill if one tried. But I think in tending the flesh she missed something else. I'll show you. Help me sit.' With his arm around his friend's neck, and despite the pain, he managed to swing onto his rump. The leg was stretched out before him. 'D'ye see?'

Aaron did not need to bend again – the angle of upper leg to knee was obvious. 'Certainly broken,' he said. 'Lie back and let's see how bad.'

Pitman chewed his lip to still his own cries as the smith probed, turned the leg, lifted it. Finally, when his brow was wet with sweat, Aaron laid the leg back down, sat on the bed's edge. 'The good news is that it's none so bad – a clean fracture, it feels. But it's already started to knit together and it's knitting wrong. That's why you're angled and it'll never have the strength to bear you true. Also, you get up onto it too soon and it could break again – worse, maybe even pierce your skin – and then,' he shrugged, 'not even Bettina's potions would save ye.'

''Tis what I thought.' Pitman nodded. 'Can you reset it?'

'I can. I will –' he raised a hand, 'but not now.'

'But I need to be about quick. This will take some healing.'

'It will. But trust me, we have one shot at getting this right and I will not rush it. It's still inflamed at the break, which I do not like. That needs must settle, and I'll show Bettina ways of aiding that.' As Pitman came up on his elbows to protest, Aaron put a hand on his shoulder and pushed him gently back down. 'No, man. You will bide. A week I say, at the least. Then I will return, with a leather strap for your mouth, a sleeping draught for your mind and a couple of stout fellows to hold you down as a caution.' He rubbed at his jaw. 'I'll never get those teeth back you knocked out at Newbury when I put your shoulder back that one time.' He winced. 'Nay, I vow I'll fix ye,' he continued, a smile returning, 'or your name's not Evelyn.'

12

SEA FIGHT

3rd June 1666

'Fire!'

As the gun captain shouted and plunged the slow match into the top hole, William Coke stepped to the side, turned away and, taking a deep breath, shoved his fingers into his ears.

The culverin roared, lurching back on its carriage, the breeching ropes straining to their limits. Smoke poured from the muzzle, obscuring everything, but Coke did not need to see, so often had he done this now. As other cannons followed, firing the length of the gun deck, he grabbed the pole, stepped up to the cannon's mouth, shoved the stick and its wet cloth all the way in and swabbed it up and down. After the ceaseless broadsides of the last two hours, there was so much powder scattered over the deck that one spark could be a disaster.

'Load again!' yelled the gun captain, removing the wedge at the cannon's rear so that the barrel angled up. As Coke stepped away, the second captain came forward with the cloth cartridge bag. Laying the pole down, Coke bent and lifted the eighteen-pound smooth iron ball with a grunt. Another man, Forbes, should have been doing that; but Dutch shot had carried away both his legs, together with the head of the man beside him, and the fingers of a third, one ball halving their crew from six to three. Each of them now did all the tasks. Death had promoted him from second sponger and second loader to the first rank of both.

As he waited for the second captain to shove the cloth bag of gunpowder down the muzzle, Coke glanced out of the gun port and through the gunsmoke shredded by the wind of their passage. The aft of the enemy ship was just passing, perhaps seventy yards away; close enough so that he could read, amidst all the gilt of the decoration, the Dutch lettering. Apparently the Hogens he'd been trying to kill came from their main province of Amsterdam. He'd spent some years in that city, when in exile during Cromwell's protectorate. Now he wondered if he'd just helped murder someone with whom he'd once drunk jenever.

'Bill, you dozy cunt!' The second captain slapped his shoulder. 'Load the bastard.'

'Aye, aye.'

'Belay that!' It was Squires, the gun captain, who'd counter-manded. He'd been leaning into the splintered gap that the enemy's ball had opened in the ship's side, peering out. Now he straightened up, which, at maybe five foot, he was just able to do; while Coke, closer to six, held the back of his head to the ceiling, forever hunched. 'It's the last of 'em, for now. No doubt the admiral will turn us round to 'ave another go at the herring fuckers. But we've some time afore that happens. Let's get the gun cleaned and squared away.'

Another go? How many more can we have? Coke thought –

but did not say. He'd learned in his four weeks aboard that a landsman voicing any opinion at sea received mockery, extra tasks, even punishments. He'd seen what happened to others swept up in the press like himself who questioned or whined. So he'd curbed his temper, shed only hidden tears, and did what was asked of him. As now.

The officer in charge of their gun deck bellowed out what Squires had already guessed. 'Clear away. Make safe!' the lieutenant called. Coke fetched the cartridge out of the gun with a hook, then plied a broom until all the powder scattered near him could be scooped up and stowed. Other men appeared from above, and the bodies they'd been unable to shift during combat were carried away – many in multiple pieces. Coke looked in the opposite direction. He knew he mustn't glimpse any of the guts that were being dumped in buckets. He would probably spew. He usually did.

'Cap'n?'

The word accompanied a tug on his arm. He turned – and there was Dickon. Only exhaustion had prevented Coke from fearing for the lad during the previous two hours of fight. Now he had to resist the urge to sweep his ward into his arms. Instead, he whispered back, 'It's Pa, or Da. Remember that. No rank here.'

'Pa-pa,' the boy stuttered, then offered up a water flask. Coke took it and drank deep. Four weeks at sea and the water was on the turn, but it tasted like nectar right then. He looked at Dickon as he drank. It had seemed like some small way of protecting the lad, if Coke claimed paternity. His size and quietness made men wary of him. But truly, Dickon needed little protecting. Indeed, all had taken to him, treating him almost like a luck charm, many tousling his thick corn-stalk hair as he passed by. For the boy was always grinning, laughing, capering. Nothing daunted him – not even his first two days of battle, it appeared.

'Are you well, son?' Coke asked, seeking in the wide face for any hurt or terror.

'Aye, aye, Cap . . . Pa! Ca-pa! Capa!' Dickon laughed. 'Whoa! The bangs, the whizz, the fire!'

A voice intruded. 'When you're done, all topside. There's grub and beer.'

The lieutenant's call started a rush. Men swiftly finished the last of their tasks and soon Coke, bent over, was following Dickon to the stair, up and through the next gun deck and out onto the main deck of His Majesty's Ship *Prince George*. He took deep breaths of the salty air, paradise after the hot and smoky hell below. He took more when he glanced over the rail and noted that the enemy fleet, who had passed the English line, was tacking about. He was bound for hell again, and soon.

There was little more than hardtack biscuit to eat, with the beer as sour as the water, but he wolfed both down as Dickon prattled. He'd spent the entire fight aloft on the foremast. If the Dutch had decided to disable the *Prince George*, it was up there they'd have concentrated their fire. But as they passed, they'd gone broadside to broadside with the English and Dickon, when he was not trim-ming the rigging, repairing ropes and swinging around the sails, had had a true bird's-eye view.

'There was some Ho-ho-hogens we hardly hit at all, Capa,' he grinned again at the new title he'd made, 'and others we fair bl-blasted. Mind, they blasted us too.' A brief darkness clouded his eyes. 'I feared for ye, Cap, ah, Pap!' The eyes brightened. 'But you are whole. Whole and not h-holed!'

He laughed and Coke could not hold back his own smile. The boy he'd found frozen in his doorway two winters before had been barely able to speak. Now he could talk, even read. And make jokes. 'Not quite,' he said, touching his own cheek. It may have been lost to the black powder that had near transformed him into a blackamoor, but he had a splinter the size of a finger there, delivered by that same Dutch shot that had carried off his comrades. Considering what it had done to them, he was thinking of leaving it in as a charm.

'Belay that!' yelled Dickon suddenly, squirming wildly. And a moment later a face popped out of the boy's collar, all wide eyes and chattering teeth. 'Now, now, Tromp,' Dickon said, and reached up to bring the little spider monkey from his cave. The animal swung out but wrapped arms and legs around the boy's neck. Four equally wide eyes now stared up at Coke but he knew better than to reach a teasing finger. The monkey had already bitten him twice; indeed, it would bite anyone except his new master, his old one having died of a fever as the voyage commenced. Dickon, though, had discovered a common passion – which he produced now.

'Nuts!' he said happily, holding out a handful of peanuts. Tromp – named for the Hogen admiral they fought – grabbed one and shelled it rapidly between little teeth, pausing only to hiss at Coke when he took one too.

'How the devil do you get these, Dickon?' Coke asked, crunching.

'Friends, friends,' came the reply. The boy nodded past his captain's shoulder. 'Are our other friends leaving the p-party, think you?'

Coke turned. Were the Dutch manoeuvring to leave or return? Had they won? He truly did not give a fig for England's cause. He didn't know what it was and he had been kidnapped to fight for it. But he would have liked respite from both the work and the danger. Especially from the empty feeling in the stomach that was always there as he helped hurl death at the Dutch, as he awaited a death hurled back. Two days they'd been fighting, with endless shifting to get the wind in their sails. 'Shifting' was not the term, he knew; but he'd resisted learning any more of the language of the navy than he needed to operate the gun he'd been assigned to, as he was considered far too old and rigid to work aloft. But at least he knew that the wind behind them was called the weather gauge. Sudden attacks happened when they had it, terrible defence when the enemy did. But surely, whoever had it, no battle at sea lasted longer than two days? Yet even if it was over, what would happen then?

A similar, yet different flutter came to his stomach. There was a perverse part of him, he knew, that enjoyed combat for this one reason: during it, he could think of nothing else. It had been the only time in the four weeks since his pressing that he'd thought of anything other than home.

But he did now. While Dickon and the monkey ate nuts and chattered, the boy telling more of what he'd seen aloft that Tromp had missed being tucked inside his shirt, Coke could only look to the sea and watch the rolling ships' masts transform into London church spires. One he especially noted – the narrow tiered column that rose from St Clement Danes upon the Strand. The last church he'd been inside. The one where he'd married Sarah Chalker. He closed his eyes – and saw her, facing him at the altar rail. He tried to hold onto that vision, to see only her, her and a moment, that one when he had realised, when he'd known that he was truly, completely happy for the first time since he had departed for the late king's wars.

He could not hold it long. Other visions came to crowd it out. Many were jumbled together, and as blurry as when he'd been cozened and betrayed. The taint of the sleeping draught not quite disguised by sack; the touch of Rebekah's naked skin on an attic bed; her cry of rape as the men burst into the room; and the worst, by far the worst: Sarah's cry when she saw him there, on their wedding night, naked with another. The way he couldn't speak, deny, unable to raise his thickened tongue from the base of his mouth. The blow from the presser's coiled whip had sent him back into a darkness that lasted for so long and only ended when sea water was dumped on him and he'd awoken aboard the *Prince George*.

He lifted his shut eyes to the north, trying to reach beyond sight. Where are you now, Sarah? In the theatre? Still working even though you are so ill? I'd hoped to let you leave there, if you chose, to rest and deliver your baby – our baby – safely. In the house I'd bought you – the house that must have been sold again, since I failed to make the last payments. Are you still in Sheere Lane then, acting by day, resting at night? Or has Pitman, recovered by now, taken you in because Bettina insisted? Because he insisted too? I pray so, though I have rarely been a praying man. Above all, I pray that I survive this battle and the next and them all and can somehow get back to you *whole*. To explain the foul conspiracy that took me. To ask forgiveness for my foolish-ness. Simply, in the end, to love you.

The tug on his arm had become too insistent to ignore.

'Cap'n,' said Dickon, in a low voice. 'Something's happening.'

Coke opened his eyes, and even though they were a landsman's he could see that things had changed. The Dutch ships that had broken through the English line were re-forming to port and they would have the weather gauge, the wind bearing them down to the attack. But he saw on the starboard side that there were other Dutch ships there, a smaller group. And that same wind could blow the English upon them like a vengeful storm.

It was this that the man who'd climbed from the quarter to the poop deck now turned to address. 'Hearken, my steady lads,' bellowed Sir George Ayscue, Rear-Admiral of the Fleet, in a voice well used to reaching over wind and water, 'you've given the Hogen Mogens hellfire, and they've run off – for now. But a Dutchman's memory is as short as his cock,' laughter came at this, which Ayscue topped, 'and no doubt Admiral de Ruyter over there,' he gestured to port, to the ships that had broken through, 'will be upon us soon. But why should we wait when there,' his hand waved to starboard, 'lies Admiral Tromp a-wallowing, with only twelve ships at his command. If we get among 'em, the Hogens will find it hard to fire without hitting their brothers. If we get among 'em, me boys,' his eyes gleamed, 'there's prizes to be had.'

A cheer came at this. Coke shifted on his bare feet. Even his poor share of the takings of an admiral's flagship would give him a bag of guineas – money for bribery, perhaps, to fund his escape?

Ayscue continued. 'Now, you know you can leave the way of it up to me. And the first thing I want to do is preserve your lives to partake of the bounty.' Another cheer. 'So my gallant Lieutenant

Hardiman here,' he turned and clapped the shoulder of a tall young man beside him, 'is going to take yon sloop *Antelope*,' he waved to a vessel paralleling their course to port, 'into the heart of 'em. Break 'em up and make them easy takings. For the *Antelope* is the finest of His Majesty's purpose-built –' he paused a moment, 'fireships!'

If men had been prepared to punch the air and cheer the admiral's soaring voice, they dropped their hands now. A fireship, Coke thought, glancing to the vessel. Even he could see now what he had missed when glancing at it before – the wide doors aft; the longboat chained and trailing at them. He'd heard the talk below decks, the way of it. A skeleton crew would sail the swift vessel, packed with combustibles, at the enemy. At the last possible moment they would climb into the longboat, light the fuse and cast off. Though it was a tactic that had had some success – for living in a floating tinder box, there was nothing a sailor feared more than fire – it was the opinion on the gun deck that the skeleton crew would be true skeletons ere long.

Hence the sudden drop of enthusiasm, the looks anywhere but at the poop deck – and at the admiral who knew what they thought was coming, and spoke it anyway. 'Yes, hearties, I know what you think: he's about to call for volunteers. Even if,' he leaned onto the rail, his eyes hawk-bright, 'even if I only have to command men aboard. But we all know it takes nerve to hold a fireship steady, to withstand the shot of the enemy, to repel any attempt at boarding. Such nerve is not possessed by reluctant men. So let me offer this.' He raised both hands in the air. 'We do not need, and cannot spare, many sailors. But the *Antelope* lost its gun crew to a stray Hogen ball. So we need five men who can handle a cannon and who can fight – five landsmen then. And I can promise them –' he paused, 'a double share of any prizes the *Prince George* takes. And, of course, a king's and a nation's eternal gratitude.'

There had been a shifting, as the admiral spoke, with the sailors stepping away from the landsmen. Coke found himself among those who, like himself, did not have the wind- and rain-beaten faces acquired by years before the mast. Some, indeed, who still wore vestiges of the clothes they'd been pressed in, many like him on a Sunday, with their best doublet now a tattered thing, their finest lawn shirts darkened with tar and gunsmoke, their breeches in shreds. They looked around, looked down or to sea, anywhere but up at the admiral; as if not seeing him, he would not see them.

Only Coke looked up. For a vision had come to him – of Sarah's hand in his as he pushed the ring onto her finger. He cleared his throat, so he could speak loudly. 'If it's landsmen you desire, Admiral,' he said, 'why not offer them something they truly want? Not coin, which, odds are, they will not survive the fight to spend. Promise them their free passage home, as soon as the task is done.'

He was surprised they'd let him say as much as he had – a rating daring to talk to a lord. A bellow came from the flag captain of the vessel who stepped up beside Ayscue now. 'Who dares,' he roared, 'to address your admiral thus? Seize that man. Tie him to the grate. I'll have him flogged!'

The other landsmen had scattered, leaving him isolated, save for Dickon at his side. Even Tromp the monkey, sensing the mood, had vanished inside the boy's shirt. Two able seamen strode forward, grabbing one of Coke's arms apiece. But they got no further than that before the first, loudest voice intervened. 'Belay that. Or at least before he's punished, let the rogue speak. Who are you, ye insolent dog?'

In his gambling days, recently put aside for love, Coke would risk his all on a roll, would never back down. And he would throw the hazard now or he would lose everything. So, setting aside the stoop he'd acquired by being so long below decks and despite the restraining arms, he straightened. Setting aside also the rougher voice of the Somerset countryside where he'd been born, he spoke once more as a gentleman. 'My name, Admiral, is William Coke, formerly a captain in the late Sir Bevil Grenville's Regiment of Foote. This is my son, Dickon. And with all respect, sir, I wager I have fought as many battles as you for my king, if not at sea. I will fight this one more, if you will meet my terms.'

The flag captain on the poop looked about to shout again. But Ayscue's raised hand halted him. 'And you were pressed, er, Captain?'

'I was. On my wedding day. And as victim of a dire plot. Circumstances require my immediate return to London.'

Coke glanced to the side. Squires, his gun captain, was staring at him open-mouthed. He looked up again; even at the distance between them, Coke could see the sparkle in the admiral's eyes. 'Do they indeed? Yet do you not think that every landsman here has an equally tragic tale?'

Coke shrugged. What could he add?

After a moment, Ayscue shook his head. 'Well, sir, you intrigue me, I must say.' He glanced to the water, as Coke did too. Tromp's twelve ships were appreciably nearer. 'Can you handle a cannon?' the admiral continued.

Coke looked again at Squires. The gun captain started, then

stepped forward, knuckling his forehead. 'Beg pardon for speaking, Your Worship,' he said. 'But he's been on my crew throughout the fight and he's steady.'

'And I'm even better with musket, pistol and sword if you'll give me 'em,' Coke said. 'Come, Admiral,' he added. 'You have two of your volunteers, for my son comes with me and he's as steady as I. 'Tis in the blood. And we'll both give up our double share of the prize to buy rum for the company,' a cheer came at this, 'if you vouchsafe to send us home once the Hogens are aflame and we safely returned.'

Coke could sense it – for he had seen it on battlefields and in sieges many times before: the mood of the crew, dampened when they thought they might be ordered on this mission, aflame again. He suspected the admiral was experienced enough to sense it too.

He was. 'You know, Captain Coke, I've always liked a bold dog. So I will make the bargain with you, and promise you a speedy return home with your success.' He gazed out again over the whole company. 'Are there three more stout hearts who will take the same deal?'

Coke looked. The dozen landsmen who'd retreated when he spoke out were still near. He could see conflict on their faces – some stared at their feet, their fear ruling them out. Others looked to the heavens, lips moving. Finally, one man, short and older than the others, stepped forward. 'I'm your man, sir. I've two wives with three bairns apiece, all on short rations now. I would get back to 'em.'

Laughter and another cheer came. Two others came forth, then a rush of more. They were taken forward, examined, and three selected. 'Aboard then!' cried Ayscue. 'For the wind is in our sails and we'll be upon the Dutch shortly.' He looked down. 'And, sir, when you return, I'd be delighted to give you a sherry in my quarters and hear your story.'

Coke, with one leg over the rail, paused. 'And I delighted to drink the one and tell the other, Admiral.'

'Very well. God's blessings upon you,' Ayscue called before turning away.

It was only when they were in the longboat, and its rowers pulling strongly through the chop for the fireship, that Coke breathed deep and shook his head. He had rolled and hit the hazard, for sure. But he was also fully aware that Ayscue, in all likelihood, would never have to share that sherry.

13

THE FIRESHIP

'It's the timing of the thing, d'ye see?' said Lieutenant Hardiman, leaning on Coke to peer along the brass barrel and over the beak-head. 'If the Hogens see us too soon, they'll recognise us as a fireship – else why would a two-masted sloop be charging full tilt at 'em? – and they'll rake us so bad they might disable us before we can reach 'em. Or shift out the way and then broadside us as we pass.' He grinned. 'Neither good. But if the admiral shelters us close, as he strives to do –'

He left the sentence unfinished and simply pointed. Raising his head from the gun – he had been trying to remember all that Squires had done in terms of siting the gun, though truly it had been precious little – Coke looked afore. The *Antelope* was tight in the lee of the *Prince George*, scarce fifty yards behind it. The great warship, with a following wind bellying its sails, was surging forward. There were moments when a larger wave in the roistering sea dipped the bigger vessel, raising the *Antelope*, and allowing Coke to see clear to the Dutch fleet. They were still bunched up and struggling to come about, to turn broadside on to their hurtling enemy. Though he found distances hard to gauge at sea, he reckoned they were less than a half-mile away.

Hardiman stood straight. "Tis nearly the moment to let us loose. And we need to slow a little, else we'll be shoving our bowsprit up the admiral's arse.' He slapped Coke's back and stepped away. 'And then we must double our speed to close with the enemy. D'ye like Shakespeare at all?' On Coke's grunt – he didn't – the officer continued, 'We're greyhounds in the slips, what?' He leaned back down for a moment. 'Remember, do not fire until you are on the up of the wave. Aim high, but not too high. With fortune our chain-shot will shred the Hogens' rigging and sail and even snap the main mast. Disable that and it'll slow 'em till we crash into 'em.' He grinned. ''Tis the theory, anyhow. Good luck.'

He walked off the forecastle, bawling at his men to handle the sheets. Men, and one boy – for Dickon was aloft, laughing no doubt, his monkey on his back. Coke saw the immediate effect of the commands, the *Prince George* gaining again, but not too much; the Dutch beyond, appreciably nearer. It could only be a matter of minutes.

It was even less. In one minute, with the enemy perhaps a quarter-mile off, the great ship began its swing to port, the strong wind in its massive sails and four hands on the tiller turning it as easily as Coke could have guided his horse. That same wind carried Hardiman's shouts to him, full sail deployed as the *Antelope* countered, bearing sharply to starboard. The lieutenant had talked of timing and he'd been right – the sloop plunged so close to the flagship's stern Coke felt he could almost have reached over and peeled some gilt paint from its panels. Then, with full sail up, the fireship was driving straight at a Dutch ship, the largest one. He could clearly see the three gun decks, and what had to be close to forty muzzles, like hungry iron mouths now swinging towards the *Antelope* as the English sloop surged on. No shots came immediately, but there was no comfort in that. The Hogens could just be waiting for them to get too close to miss.

Coke knew, from lurid tales told in hammocks around him at night, that though the target of a ship coming straight at you was narrow, if you did hit it, the ball could carry the length of the vessel, smashing gun carriages, splitting beams and shattering wood into a thousand splinters that became missiles in their own right. He reached up and touched his cheek where the splinter he'd received still lay. He'd been lucky. He'd seen men ripped apart by them.

'Please God, keep me lucky still,' he murmured, and smiled just a little. He rarely uttered a prayer, except in battle. During those, like most men, he was a fervent believer.

Three hundred yards now. He grabbed the spike, shoved it hard down into the touch-hole, puncturing the cloth cartridge bag within. Withdrawing the metal, he scattered some powder from a cup into the touch-hole, then reached back to the glowing slow-match hanging on a hook, keeping his arm wide. Just as he did, a huge roar came and he looked up to see a giant cloud of white smoke burst from the ship ahead.

'Fall down!' Hardiman cried, but his yell blended with the balls' whoosh towards him . . . past him, whirling blurs that came and went, barely giving him time even to duck. But not a single shot entered the *Antelope*'s prow; no splinters shredded him. Coke looked again and the Dutchman was still dead ahead, the smoke rising from its sides, its gunners no doubt frantically loading again.

It was close to time. He now uttered a different type of prayer, the kind he would breathe over dice in a gaming club. 'To fortune – and my sweet Sarah,' he murmured. Truly he had no desire to kill any man, and he had no personal quarrel with the Dutch. But he had undertaken to do this, as a means not an end, and do it he would. So now he raised the slow-match above the touch-hole. The *Antelope* was bucking up and down like the creature for which it was named. When it reached the bottom of one large wave, just as the next wave took it, Coke shoved the slow-match into the powder. On the gun deck of the *Prince George*, he'd seen the burn happen instantly, heard it fizz and go out, counted three seconds when nothing happened and then the blast arrived. Here, sparks came on the instant of his touch and were followed, perhaps one heartbeat later, by the explosion.

He could not see, and did not stay to check for success. He was already running, coughing out the smoke, making speed aft. The skeleton crew was already in the longboat, held to the *Antelope*'s stern by a chain. They would wait for him – but they wouldn't wait for long.

'By Christ, man, that was good shooting,' cried Hardiman from the rail.

Pausing to cough and breathe, Coke chanced a look back. The smoke had largely cleared from the Dutch broadside, and he could see immediately what he'd done. Spars, rigging and canvas dangled from the shattered main mast.

'Lively now,' the lieutenant said, ducking at the crack of muskets being discharged, taking Coke's arm to push him firmly towards the net that hung down to the longboat below. Dickon was at the prow of the longboat, the monkey on his shoulder, arm stretched out to his aid. Throwing himself swiftly over the rail, Coke swung down and the boy held him steady.

'Make ready to cast off,' called Hardiman, swinging a leg over the rail. There he paused, a sudden query on his face. 'By –' he managed before blood burst like a fountain from his mouth and he pitched over the side, to plunge into the sea scarce a yard from the longboat, vanishing immediately under the waves.

As Coke bent to seek him he heard the cry of the boatswain, hand on the tiller, 'Rats!' and he turned back in time to see a huge black shape running down the chain towards him. There were others behind and for a moment he was too stunned to do anything but gape. Another seaman beside him was quicker, reaching past him with his oar, swiping them off one by one as if in some strange fairground game. They kept coming; the man kept hitting them, while Tromp the monkey chittered furiously at them, scrambling around and around Dickon's head.

'Sir! Sir!'

The cry came again from the boatswain; Coke, realising he was being addressed, looked back. The man was passing something to the rower before him, who passed it on in his turn. 'Hardiman was going to light the fuse, sir. Now you must.'

Another slow-torch was slapped into his hand. He grabbed it too swiftly, yelped as he was singed. 'How?' he called back.

'There's a hatch between the gun ports. You can see the cloth fuse dangling out.'

Using one hand to steady himself on the boat's prow, Coke leaned forward. A piece of grey cloth hung from a square opening, damp when he touched it, reeking of oil. As the man beside him kept swiping the rats, as the monkey yelled loudly, and as the sound of another Dutch broadside came – this one striking home, he could feel the ship shudder even through the chain – Coke thrust the glowing rope's end into the cloth. There was a fizz, then a flame, which climbed rapidly into the hatch.

'Cast away,' shouted the boatswain and the man who'd been fighting the rats, whose numbers had not ceased, now dropped his oar back into the boat, and reached to unhook the chain's end.

With a loud shriek, the monkey broke from his master's clutch. He leapt onto the chain and onto the first rat upon it, biting down, then ran past him, leaping over others to vault onto the ship.

'No!' Dickon yelled and then hurled himself at the net. In a moment he was up and over the railing.

'Dickon!' cried Coke, rising and swaying as the waves struck the longboat.

'Cast off!' yelled the boatswain. 'You'll have to leave 'im, cap'n. She's a powder keg now.'

The crewman at the front threw off the chain. For a moment, Coke hesitated – but only a moment. Someone had called him Cap'n – and only one person called him that.

He hurled himself across the already widening gap, just grabbed the net, though his feet plunged into the water. He started to climb, ignoring the shouts to return. When he reached the rail, he glanced back. The boat was already fifty yards away, the men's calls lost to wind and wave.

'Dickon!' he shouted. The smoke was roiling up thick through the deck. He'd paid no mind to what had been prepared to turn the *Antelope* into a burning spear. Whatever it was burned fast. He could feel the heat on his bare feet.

Smoke engulfed him. He could not cry out again, just stagger forward, coughing, seeking Dickon in the dense clouds. Then he heard a faint noise above him, glimpsed the soles of two feet on the rigging of the main mast. They were only an arm's reach above his head and, with a leap, Coke grabbed one.

Dickon fell onto Coke, sending both of them crashing to the hot deck. There was a gap of air there, perhaps a foot high. Through their wracking coughs they managed to take a little of it in.

'Come,' Coke croaked, seizing the boy's hand and starting for the stern of the ship. He had no plan, save to go where last he'd seen other Englishmen. His one hope was that perhaps they'd stood off and waited. Yet even as he crawled, palms and knees scorched by the heated wood, he knew this was a faint hope indeed.

They'd got halfway to the stern when the collision came. It was preceded by faint cries, like those of sirens luring sailors onto the rocks, penetrating what had become a roar of fire. Both he and Dickon were knocked onto their sides and rolled down to smash into the rails, which fractured but did not give. Coke looked up through the smoke, some of it dispersing enough for him to see a looming immensity above. Then all was swept away by the decking, which had been bending up as if pushed from below by some living creature, suddenly exploding, with flames shooting up, reaching high enough to seize the sails and tarred ropes which, crisping on the instant, fell upon them like flaming whips.

Fire – above, below, all around. Fire enfolding them. Clothes catching, hair dissolving, skin blistering. Coke took a breath that was near all smoke. In his fading sight, the flames assumed the shape of a beast, rising high, stooping for him with red and yellow claws. For him – and for the body next to him. For Dickon.

It was his last moment, and all that remained of a final breath. He'd curled his feet up, folded in on himself as if that would give him some protection. Now he kicked out, striking the rail hard which shattered under force and flame. Seizing Dickon's collar, he rolled them both off the ship.

The water was freezing, glorious – until he realised he could breathe it no more than he could smoke. Yet it didn't seem to matter. He'd used his last breath well. And as he sank, Captain Coke could only hope that Dickon, who he'd pulled from a pile of snow on a London doorstep, whose shape he saw rising above him, would live to eat more nuts.

14

THE COMPTER

'Captain,' she said, and reached for his hand.

'William,' he reminded, giving it.

Of course. She had called him by his old rank when first they knew each other. It had been a way of keeping him at a distance. But there was no need for that now. Now that they were married.

'Here,' she said and placed his hand on her belly.

His grey eyes went wide. His rare smile came. 'The baby,' he said. 'It lives.'

'*He* lives,' she assured him.

Eyes narrowed. Delight fled them. 'Do anything,' he said, 'to survive.'

'Never doubt it.' She squeezed his hand hard. 'And you do the same. Come back to us.'

He faded then, the grip of his hand, the look in his eyes. He was gone, but as Sarah woke she knew three things.

That William Coke still lived.

That she would obey him, as she had vowed at their wedding.

That today was the day she turned whore.

It was the first of August, the date she'd marked weeks ago, thinking it so far off, believing that something must happen before it arrived, praying that it would. But no saviour had come. *He* had not come, except in dreams. He was so welcome there; for she knew when she saw him, knew beyond any doubt, that he was innocent of the foul accusations made against him. It had been the one light in the darkness of her prison, that certainty. That, and the babe even now kicking within his own cell of flesh.

Though dawn's light now poured through the high, barred window, it was still quiet on the women's side of the Poultry Compter, a rare thing. Early enough so that no babe cried, no child moaned his hunger, no inmate silenced them with a hiss or a blow. Beyond the bars, she could hear the first signs of a city stirring, the first citizens going about their business. Iron-rimmed wheels ground over the cobbles of the alley beside the prison as deliverymen went about their work. This one was carrying bread, fresh from the baker's three doors down. The savour flooded her mouth with saliva. She swallowed it back; but the sharp hunger it provoked only made her more certain. This day I will have fresh bread. This day I will survive.

Her bed companion giggled. Sarah raised herself onto an elbow and peered over the bare shoulder next to her. Jenny Johnson still slept, caught in some happy dream. Pulled tight to her, her three-year-old daughter Mary stirred but did not open her eyes.

The bed was narrow. Sarah's arm had been pressed to the top of Jenny's back, skin to skin above their shifts. It came away with a wet sucking. August followed on from July in heat. No breeze relieved them from the high, narrow window. No rain for three months.

She inhaled again. But the cart had moved off and only the ward's and her own rankness filled her nostrils now. She would have to wash. If she was going to do this, she was going to do it well. Years as an actress had taught her: gentlemen pay more for a better performance. Though many of her colleagues in the playhouse had happily straddled the border between player and prostitute, she never had. But she had observed who earned better and how. Who fucked the dukes rather than the draymen. Over on the men's side, the Knight's as it was called, there were several gentlemen. There was even a baronet. All debtors too, but still able to afford the extra shillings for a room, for better food. If either was lying around she would take it, silver or bread or both. Thievery and whoredom went hand in glove.

Another shifting came, this time within her. She laid a hand on her belly, felt the welcome kick, kick, kick. 'You are why I do this,' she crooned softly. 'You and William Coke.'

''Allo, luv,' Jenny said, smiling up at Sarah. 'Been awake long?'

'A while. Thinking.'

'Dangerous.'

'Maybe.' Sarah took a deep breath. 'Today's the day.'

'Yes? Well, 'bout time.' Jenny slid up the bed now, to rest her back against the stone wall, Mary rising with her. She was fastened as ever to Jenny's breast, even though there was no milk. 'I've told ya. There's nothin' to it.'

'Nothing?'

'Well –' Jenny shrugged. 'Not much. They're all so drunk over there it's over in moments and you walk away with a shilling. Or more.' She smiled again. 'And look what sometimes 'appens. You get a lovely little thing like my Mary 'ere. Who would wish that away?'

She bent down to kiss the top of her daughter's head, hair as red as the mother's. Sarah shook her head. 'That's not my plan.'

'Nah, you'll have to clear your oven before you stick in another load of buns.' Jenny cackled loud. Immediately a voice came from a nearby bed. 'Will you two poxed whores cease your blabbing? Some of us are trying to sleep.'

'Pot calling the kettle black, Jane Warren!' Jenny retorted. She lowered her voice, not much. 'Sixpence she charges. Lowers the price for all of us, the cheap trull. Lucky everyone knows she's got the Covent Garden gout, so not even the turnkeys'll touch 'er.'

'Oi!' Jane screamed, and that woke the whole cell. There was an immediate Babel of competing voices – yelling mothers, crying children, single women complaining.

'Come on,' said Jenny, popping Mary off her breast and pulling up her shift. 'Let's see if we can get to the pump before the rush. I stinks even to meself.'

Their door had been unlocked at first light. It gave directly onto the yard, as did the others on either side. Some of these were already open, some women and children about, some ahead at the pump. Sarah looked to the main gate which opened onto the narrow lane that led down to Poultry and the city beyond, watching the first few debtors slip out, some to work, some to beg, some to whore. Every man and woman was allowed to leave to earn money by whatever means to repay their debt – though few earned more than the wherewithal to survive. The 'garnish', as it was called, charged by the gaolers – for a roof and a bunk, by the bailiffs for clothes and sundries, by the attorney-at-law who would offer hope of freedom with legal quibbles that went nowhere – sucked away everything.

'We're on,' Jenny said, jolting Sarah from her stare. Jenny stepped up and pumped the water. It took a while, for the pressure was low for the lack of rain. She filled and tipped a bucket over herself, a second over Sarah and then, to her squeals, a third over Mary. 'I've this,' she said, producing a nub of soap which she began to wash her daughter and herself before passing the little that remained across. Sarah scrubbed all over under her shift until the block dissolved. As she passed across her distended belly she felt a hardness pressing out. Elbow or heel she wondered, rubbing at it. One pail between them sluiced them down.

There was a rectangle of sunlight at the western end of the yard. They went and sat in it, enjoying the warmth on their cooled skin, knowing they would be sweating again all too soon. 'You sure about this?' asked Jenny, pulling Mary tight to her.

Sarah sighed. 'Were you sure the first time?'

'What, back in the reign of Good Queen Bess?' She laughed. 'First time? Well, my ma was in the trade so –' She squinted. 'Nah, didn't like it. I remember that. But you get used to what you must, eh? And that was "first time" first time. Won't be yours,' she gestured down, 'unless that's the result of you coupling with the 'oly spirit.' She cackled again, crossing herself at the same time. Jenny was a Catholic and on her knees each night before she climbed into their cot.

'Nay, indeed.' A brief vision of William came, as he'd been in the dream. Survive, he'd said. Survive, she would.

Jenny reached out and touched her arm. More gently now she said, 'I was born to it, but you was not. Is there no other way? Your cousins in St Giles?'

'They spared me all they could, which was not much, for they are near as hungry in those tenements as we are here.'

'Try the playhouse one more time.'

Sarah shook her head. They would not let her act any more. Indeed, Betterton disliked her so, for always refusing his advances, that he would not even let her sew the dresses. Others had helped, sparing what they could from the little an actor earned. But, like the pump soon would in the Compter's yard, that course had run dry.

'No one else?'

There'd been one other source that had sustained her until now. Bettina Pitman had been a weekly visitor, always bringing something – from her table, or her stove, for she was a marvellous creator of cordials and elixirs. But at the last visit a week before, she'd wept at the little she could offer. 'Since the pestilence departed, few buy my plague water,' she'd said. 'And Pitman's pittance of a constable's salary is putting little food on our platters.' She'd dabbed her eyes, tried a smile. 'But his leg's set, and he's up on two feet again, though moving slowly, the great cabbage. Perhaps he'll be agile enough to take us a thief ere long and all our problems will be solved.'

Sarah looked back at Jenny. 'I can rely on no one else.'

Her friend took her hand. 'You can rely on me, love. I'll see you through it.' Without letting go, she rose. 'Come, let's beautify.'

They borrowed a brush, pulled it through each other's hair, shaking off lice at every pass. Sarah's had lost all the blonde dye

173

she'd used as an actress; it was auburn again now, though she knew well enough that silver wound through it too. They mixed charcoal from the long-dead fires with spit, making a paste that would substitute for kohl and highlighted their eyes and eyebrows. They even giggled as they did each other's, though Sarah fell silent when she remembered that these preparations were not leading to the stage. She stayed silent as she pulled on first her other, better shift, then her second dress, the one she had worn only when calling on friends to beg for money. She'd had to let it out, of course, and had done that enough so that her pregnancy was not immediately obvious. There was no mirror to look at herself in, for which she was grateful. She felt like a foaling mare.

Jenny seemed more pleased with herself, in her Sunday best. She twirled and said, 'Shall we go pay a call?'

'At this hour?' Sarah raised a hand to the sound of the bell in St Olave Old Jewry only just then sounding nine.

'The best time to catch them. The sots will have drunk the night through and those who are still awake will be lusty – lusty and largely incapable.' Jenny giggled. 'Doesn't matter, s'long as they pay us ahead.' She moved to the door. 'We'll go see the baronet. He's got a lovely room.'

They crossed the narrow yard to the Knight's side. On the ground level, either side of an archway, one on each side, were cramped cells just like the women's; from which, if possible, an even greater stench emerged. Men crowded the windows, leaning there with mouths wide to catch some fresher air. One called out, 'Avast! A fine pair of frigates hoving to!' and a few others then thrust their faces to the bars, whistling and blowing kisses. Just inside the main doorway, a gaoler had a key in the lock, about to turn it. Sarah knew that the men were only locked in to prevent them wandering at night, causing a disturbance in the streets and getting up to various villainies. By day, like the women, they could leave in search of the means to pay back their debts. Like the women, they all returned at night. For if they absconded, and were likely caught again, they would be Newgate-bound, that prison an even lower level of hell.

'Now there's a pair of fishmonger's daughters if ever I saw 'em,' said the gaoler, straightening up. 'Who're you off to jilt?'

'We're jilting no one but playing upon the square. The baronet sent for us.'

'Did he? Wonder how he managed that since he was snoring not five minutes past. I look after his door so —' He scratched at his unshaven chin. 'Wha's in it for me to let you up?'

Jenny glided close to him, grabbing him through his breeches. 'Somethin' on account, Mr Jenkins?' she purred.

'Leave that,' he growled, slapping her hand away. 'I'm a God-fearing and a married man.' He shoved her back. 'But I'll take me cut.'

Jenny sucked at her teeth. 'I've already got a mackerel,' she said. 'Bully Davis, in charge at the 'ospital. Shall I tell 'im you was trying to squeeze us?'

The man whitened. 'On your way,' he muttered, and turned back to the men's door.

Jenny led the way up the stair. 'Mackerel?' asked Sarah, as they rounded the corner.

'Pander,' Jenny replied. 'I ain't got one in 'ere, but Bully Davis is mad so 'e believes 'e is mine if I give 'im the odd free fondle.

Kill a man if I asked.' She paused before a door. 'So 'ere we are. You sure you're ready for this?'

'Yes. Why?'

'Because you've got a face like a smacked arse. Can you fake it?'

Sarah smiled. 'My dear countess, it's what I've been doing all my life,' she said.

'Good girl. Tits up. Tally ho.'

She pushed the door. The first thing Sarah thought was, lovely room? With mould blooming on bare plaster between strips of torn wallpaper; the floorboards that were splintered and cracked; the single, sagging bed; and the same overflowing slop bucket that reeked in the corner of the women's ward. But then she remembered: one man has all this space to himself. He had a table, two chairs. There was a moth-chewed rug on the floor, but a rug nonetheless. Above all there was the open window. Higher up, a breeze reached through it, slightly tempering the heat of the morning.

There were three men in the room. One upon the bed with his forearm across his eyes; two at the table, face down. There were bottles upon that, dice – and some silver coins. Sarah indicated them with her chin. Jenny mouthed a 'no' and crossed to the bed. 'Sir Knight,' she said softly, running her hand down his chest. 'Coo-ee there, Dickie bird.'

She rested her hand on the man's crotch. He jerked awake. 'What?' he screeched. 'Egad, what means this, ha? Who the devil –'

Jenny had leaned out of range of the flailing. Now she caught the knight's hand. ''Tis I, Dickie. Your sweet Jenny.' She kissed his finger, lingeringly. 'You sent for me.'

'Did I?' He swung his feet onto the floor, sat up, clutching his head with a yelp of pain. Sarah could see that he was a man of middling years, his face florid with drink, his nose a small purple cauliflower. Hair ringed his bald head like a grey coronet.

''Ere, sweetheart,' Jenny said, rising and fetching a mug from the table, ''ere's fur of the same wolf what bit ya.'

As the baronet gulped greedily, Sarah looked at the two men at the table, both of whom had sat up. The younger one was already appraising her from under a thatch of black hair. The elder had an eye-patch, in which the missing eye was marked out in tiny glittering gems. Sarah had a vague recall, of someone William had talked of, a dice sharper whom he disliked. Then she shook herself. Do not think of Captain Coke, she thought. Do not.

'Are these the buttocks we were promised, Father?' said the youth.

'I do not know, my boy,' Eye-Patch replied. 'Are they, de Lacey?'

The baronet squinted. 'Don't know that one. Who's she, Jenny?'

'A friend. You said you'd like somethin' new.'

'Something new, indeed.' A gleam had displaced the torpor in his eyes. He stood, wobbled, then steadied. Took a step forward.

'Oh, but Dickie!' Jenny cried. 'Aren't you going to offer the ladies a drink? A bite? You are always so gentlemanly.'

'Gentlemanly,' drawled the younger man, rising, 'to a pair of painted punks? There's only one part of this gentleman they'll get.'

'No!' the baronet roared. 'You do not live here, sir, and I do. We'll have our fun, never you fear. But we'll do it in proper style.'

He bowed. 'Ladies, help yourself to whatever's here, while I relieve my beastly bladder.'

He staggered to the corner, turned his back and fiddled with his breeches. After a while a trickle came, the sound enough to provoke the others. They lined up behind the knight, turning their back on the two women.

Sarah looked at the table. The remains of several partridges were upon it, not completely picked clean. She tore into them, glancing about, and saw, upon the sill, a basket of fruit. Still chewing, she moved over and recognised greengages. Throwing the partridge bones through the open window, she lifted one and bit into it. It was young, a little sour. She didn't think she'd tasted anything so delicious in her life. The only fruit they got inside the Compter was the kind that pigs rejected outside it.

She ate three standing there, pausing only to throw a greengage to Jenny who caught it in one hand, while she swigged from a bottle in the other.

'And now, my dear.'

His voice made her turn back. The baronet crossed to her. 'My, but you're a plump one, girl,' he said, running his hand over her breasts. He mistook her pained groan. 'Like that, d'ya? Hmm!' He squeezed harder and then his hand journeyed down. 'See if you like . . . Egad!' He jumped back as if he'd placed his hand on a hot hob. 'By Christ! By Jesus! You are with child.'

Sarah remembered what Jenny had said. What she had decided herself. She was there to – act. Which she could do. 'Never mind that, sir,' she said, letting her voice go deep as she stepped forward, reaching towards him. 'There's plenty of things –'

'No! God, no!' He stepped away. 'Can't stand the stench of a

woman with a babe in the breech. Reminds me of her Ladyship.'
He shuddered and turned. 'Jenny, do ye seek to gull us here?'

'Nay, indeed, sir –'

'It does not matter to me.' Eye-Patch's voice was as smooth
as the baronet's had been agitated. 'I doubt it will to my son.' He
smiled. 'Do you take your old moll, de Lacey. Let us handle the
brood mare.'

Jenny turned to the men. 'Do you suggest one after the other
or both at once? That'll cost ya more –'

'Quiet, whore,' Eye-Patch snapped. Then his voice returned
to silk. 'She will be well rewarded, I assure you. For I stint nothing
in my boy's education. Why, has he not just come down from
Oxford?' He reached into his doublet, pulling out a leather purse
and placing it on the window sill. 'What's within will also pay for
whatever de Lacey wishes.' He chuckled. 'Even deeper in my debt,
old friend, what?' He turned to his son. 'And I think, both at once,
don't you?'

'Really, Father?' The youth laughed. 'You are better than any
tutor at Oxford.'

Sarah swallowed. She wanted to run – from the coolness in the
single eye of the older man and the heat in the eyes of the younger.
But the purse? There might be a month of food within it. For her,
yes. But more importantly for her baby.

Act, she told herself again and put a smile on her face. 'Whatever
you desire, gentlemen.'

Eye-Patch picked up the wooden platters on the table and tipped
the scraps out of the window. 'What I desire is that you remove
that hideous dress and lay yourself on the table.'

With a last nod at her, Jenny led de Lacey to the bed. With

some difficulty, Sarah pulled her gown over her head. Then, clad only in her shift, she hoisted herself onto the table. Survive, she heard her William say.

'Knees up,' Eye-Patch said, reaching for the buttons of his breeches.

As the bell sounded the quarter in the tower of St Olave's, Pitman limped into the yard of the Poultry Compter. He leaned there on his great staff and looked about.

There but for the grace of God go I, he thought, eyeing the wretches around him. He wondered if the proverb was biblical, and decided not. It was true nonetheless. How far had he and his been from such degradation? Not very far, was the answer. But that was all changed now.

He did not find whom he sought. But there was a turnkey on the Knight's side whom he'd dealt with before approaching the gateway now. 'Jenkins,' he said.

The man jumped. 'Jesu mercy, but you frightened me, Mr Pitman. Why are you lurking there?'

'That's Pitman to you. Pitman to all, king or commoner. And I lurk, as you put it, because I need to see a debtor.'

'What's his name?'

'Hers. Sarah . . . Coke.'

'Sarah – ?' The man rubbed his chin. 'Old? White hair? Missing an ear?'

'Nay. Young enough. The actress.'

'Oh, the whore.'

Pitman stepped closer to grab him by the collar. 'They are not always the same, Jenkins. And you would be advised to speak most carefully of a friend –'

'No, no, no! I assure you.' The man wriggled, unable to break the grip. 'The actress. She is ab-ab-about the other business now.'

Pitman frowned, loosening his hold slightly. 'What mean you?'

'Up-up there!' He pointed to the men's side. 'She and the other moll, Jenny Johnson, they went up to visit the baronet not five minutes since.'

'Which window? Which?' Pitman shook the man hard.

'Th-there!' the man whimpered. 'Above the centre stair.'

Pitman released him and moved faster than he had until now, feeling the strain in his newly knitted bone, pivoting off his great stick to relieve it. As he came under the window, something struck his shoulder and stuck there. Looking down, he saw that it was the gnawed leg of some bird and a fruit stone. He flicked them off and charged in.

The stair was harder, though he managed it, and in just moments he stood between three doors. Then, from behind one of them, he heard a laugh. There was something nasty in it, so he pivoted on his staff and used his good leg to kick in the door.

For a moment there was no movement in the room but the door flying in to crash against the wall — no sound but its smash. The five people just stared at him, united in shock. There was a flame-haired woman kneeling at a bed, a man seated before her. The woman was not Sarah. Another woman was lying on her side on a small table at either end of which stood a man — one older with an eye-patch, the other younger. Both had their fingers on the buttons of their breeches, and one apiece undone.

It took Pitman a longer moment to recognise Sarah, for he had not seen her in a while, laid up as he'd been; and Bettina had not told him of her changes. But he doubted that even his wife would

181

have recognised her instantly, what with her eyes so painted, her hair falling so about her.

She gave a cry, rolled off the table and stepped into a corner, her back to the room. The older man cried too, differently. 'Who the devil? Dog, how dare you? Burst in upon gentlemen, will ye?'

The younger man, closer to Pitman and nearer his size, did not yell. He growled, a beast interrupted; he stooped, slipped a hand into his boot cuff and pulled out a knife.

A blade always focused Pitman's attention – especially thrust at him. Placing both hands on his stick, he slammed it sideways into the man's wrist then smacked the top of the stout ash pole between the younger man's eyes.

He screeched, dropped the knife and fell to the floor. His father shouted, 'Do you know who it is you cross here, wretch? By God, I'll have you flogged –'

Pitman brought the stick over in a great arc and slammed it on the table. 'You are the ones who will be flogged,' he roared. 'For I am constable of this parish and I have caught you in the act of fornication!'

It wasn't his parish, and the rules against fornication were rarely enforced when the king was the acknowledged master fornicator of the realm. But Pitman's size, his fury and the loud moaning of the younger man, together with the blood oozing between his clutched hands, cowed Eye-Patch's fury. White of face, he went and helped his son rise, and then, pausing only to snatch up his purse, he hurried him from the room.

'Wha-what do you mean by this, sir?' The man on the bed's anger was countered by his quavering voice. 'These were my friends.'

'Are you their mack? Their pander? Will you join them in the stocks?' Pitman found that his fury had no bottom. Not while he could see Sarah turned away still in the corner, her shoulders shaking. He took several deep breaths and steadied himself. When he was sure his voice was calm, he took a step towards her and said, 'Mrs Chalker?' She didn't move. 'Will you come with me?'

She turned suddenly. Snatching up her fallen dress, she passed him without looking up and exited the room.

He followed her down the stairs and outside. 'Mrs Coke,' he called, cursing himself for always forgetting her change of names. Still she did not turn back, did not stop until she'd reached the corner of the small yard from whence there was nowhere else to go. There she froze, lifted the dress she carried and thrust her face into it.

He reached out, but stopped his hand its own breadth from her back. 'Mrs Chalk— Coke . . . Sarah. I —'

He paused, uncertain what to say.

Her voice came low. 'So, Pitman, you arrived in the nick. Like something in a play. You have preserved my honour.' She gave a humourless laugh. 'And you may have doomed me – us.' She broke off, pushing her face back into the dress.

'It was the first time you —'

He stopped. He so wished Bettina had been there. In situations like these, words were not his strength.

It took a moment for her to speak again. 'The first time, aye. But it will not be the last.'

He looked up, searching for the right words. He saw faces there in the cloudless blue sky, as he sometimes did. 'Necessity is a hard master, Sarah. It forces us to do things we know to be sins against

God. Against man. In the late wars it forced me to kill. To steal. To –'

He paused, and she spoke. 'How do you live with that?'

He sighed. 'I had to make my peace with what was necessary.'

She turned to him a little. 'And did you succeed? Do you forget?'

He looked down, away from the faces of dead men in the heavens. 'Not always. Nor do I want to, entirely. For then, what will goad me to make myself better? I try to forgive my enemies.'

'Forgive?' She half-turned to him then. 'Can you forgive me for what you saw up there?'

'Did Jesus not say: "Judge not, and ye shall not be judged; condemn not, and ye shall not be condemned; forgive, and you shall be forgiven."' He nodded. 'And remember I arrived, as you say, in the nick. You committed no sin.'

She turned fully to him now. 'This day. But I would have. I will. You have but delayed me. Cost me, sir! For necessity drives me still. *This* drives me.' She laid her hand on her belly. 'I would do anything so that my child survives. All that you did in war, and more besides.'

He could not help his smile. It was partly for the return of the old Sarah he knew, not the one turned away, ashamed. The one facing him, determined and fierce; the one who, a year before, had loaded a gun with double ball and blown her husband's murderer to hell. But his smile was also for what he could tell her now. 'I cannot speak to all the future. We are each of us in God's care. But for now I can remove "necessity" at least.' He glanced at people coming close to listen. 'Is there anywhere in this palace where we can converse in private? I have food here, which I fear these loiterers would snatch at,' he tapped the satchel at his side, 'and news also. I would give you both alone.'

Her eyes brightened. 'News of William Coke?'

'Concerning him, aye.'

She pointed behind her. 'There's a storeroom here. They call it "the hole". If it is not occupied by a debtor under torment for some crime, the turnkeys will use it for,' she flushed, 'various things. But it is locked.'

Pitman turned, saw it and called out, 'Jenkins?'

The gaoler approached, taking care to keep beyond Pitman's long reach. 'You found your, er, friend, then?'

'I did. And I would like a private word with her.' He pointed at the lock. 'You have this key?'

The meaning of the man's smirk was obvious. 'Oh, I have.' He took out a bunch, selected one and inserted it. He pushed the door, beckoned to them to enter, then closed it behind them.

The room was dim, its only light filtering in from a small window high up. A sunbeam came through it, amply lighting piles of boxes, clothes spilling out of them, bottles in others, firewood in stacks and falling directly onto other things.

'You know what they are,' she said, following his gaze.

'I've seen 'em before,' he replied, going to them, lifting the thumbscrews, the head vice, irons for ankles and neck, putting them out of sight behind the boxes.

'You can hear the cries some nights. A debtor who's offended a gaoler, or is hiding money.'

'This is a terrible place indeed.' Pitman reached into his satchel and withdrew things to place on the cleared box-top: a loaf of manchet, a block of ewe's cheese, some nuts and oranges.

Sarah began to eat. 'And we must find ways of easing your time in it.'

'But not getting me out?' she said, through her crammed mouth.

'Alas, the bounty that pays for this food does not run to forty guineas apiece for the builder and the Jew. But I had luck, and took a twenty-guinea thief on my first day afoot. With husbandry, Bettina reckons we can feed you at least, and perhaps get you better quarters for a rest.' He produced a small purse. 'This may pay for a room for a week or two and I will endeavour to get more now I am about.'

'A room, even for a few days, would be luxury. But I will share it with Jenny and her daughter. She has saved me in here.' She hesitated, then reached for an orange and began to peel it. 'You said you had news of my husband?'

'Not news exactly. But I have unravelled part of the mystery around his disappearance.' He cleared his throat. 'Captain Coke is innocent.'

She paused in her eating and looked at him. 'I know.'

'You do? How –'

'Because I have seen him.' She tapped her head. 'In here. In my dreams. I doubted for a while because I felt I did not know him well enough. But I do.'

'It is good you have faith, Sarah. Because –'

'Tell me.'

'He is the victim of a plot. The same terrible plot that sees you in this place.'

'Go on.'

'You remember the girl he was, uh, caught with?'

'It is unlikely I will ever forget her.'

'Yes. Ahem. I believe I am a good judge of character, and this never did fit with Coke. Something always stank about it. But the girl vanished, as completely as the captain did. Her father was cut for the stone and was so ill for a time he looked like he would die. I could not question him.'

Sarah finished the orange, reached for a second, then drew her hand back. 'This must all be saved for little Mary,' she murmured, then looked up. 'Isaac lives?'

'On the mend, I hear. And only yesterday his daughter returned in secret to see him.'

'In secret?'

'Aye. I do not think she intended to stay long, and she had relatives with her. I believe they plan to take her out of the country. But I'd set Josiah to watch and he brought me the word –' He broke off. 'To make swift report, I went and examined her. The relatives, her father, were reluctant to let me. But I can be,' a little smile came, 'forceful, or so my dearest chuck tells me.' A frown returned. 'The story is unpleasant, and reveals a damned conspiracy. Against the captain. Against you. And against the Jew too. It would have taken me in too, no doubt, if the conspirators had not thought me already dealt with by Captain Blood's sword.'

'Conspirators?'

'Our old foes – the Fifth Monarchy men.' Over her gasp, he continued, 'This Blood is one and I have discovered that Tremlett, who you owe the debt to, is another. He denies any plot and I cannot touch him – yet. This flute-playing youth is also one of the damned crew, by the texts the girl said he quoted. He vanished, of course, to her great distress. She is young, and was much in love, I fear. I cannot find the seducer, but I will. But behind them all, there's someone else, some . . . damned puppeteer who jerks all the strings. He is the orchestrator of this vengeance. I haven't been able to pin him yet, but by God I will. I promise you that.'

'And I promise you – these so-called Saints are not the only ones who know about vengeance. As they have already discovered.' She reached for the satchel and started putting items back into it. 'May I keep this?'

'Indeed. There's a fresh bottle of Bettina's elixir in there too, for your strength – and for the babe's.'

She paused as she handled the bag of hazelnuts. 'Dickon. No word of him either?'

'Nay. Though I think we can guess that wherever the captain is, there he'll be too. He's a spaniel, truly. I never saw anyone so loyal.'

'Except perhaps yourself?' Sarah finished stuffing the bag. 'But where might they be now? I know he was pressed.'

Pitman exhaled loud. 'A big battle was fought against the Dutch over four days in June. It was claimed as a great victory, though time proved that as false as dicers' oaths. Many men were taken prisoner –'

'Many killed?'

'Aye. But I do not believe it of the captain. That man has survived worse, in war and in peace. Why, did he and I not rise from the plague pits of Moorfields, like lazars from the dead?'

'I agree.' She shook her head. 'Alas, I inherited a poor fraction of the gifts my mother had as a seer. I cannot call a number on a dice table nor the winner in a cockfight. But I've always known when someone is dead. My William is not.'

'So he's either still at sea with the fleet, or in some Hogen prison on land.' He grinned. 'Trust me. He will return, Mrs Chalker.'

'I do trust you, Pitman. Ever,' she said, wiping her eyes and shouldering the satchel. 'And that's Coke to you – to all. Mrs Coke. I will be a wife again before I am a widow.' She smiled. 'For if you recall, the captain owes me a wedding night.'

15

BLOOD

Terschelling, Holland, 9th August

Keep your head down. He will not know me. He saw me but for a few moments, in the dark and over blades. Like the smiting angel he rants about, he will pass me by. But pray God, let it be soon. I am not sure how much more apocalypse I can take.

Through his hands, resting on the pew before him and raised like many of the prisoners around him in an attitude of prayer, Coke risked a look. The man who had been haranguing them for half an hour from the pulpit of the small Dutch church showed no signs of flagging. The only hope that he might make an end of it soon was how the verses were coming more regularly, each delivered with ever-increasing fervour. Coke had suffered enough sermons in his life to recognise their shape — and to identify, too, a skilled preacher from a poor one. Captain Blood was one of the best.

'"These have the power to shut heaven,"' the Irishman cried, '"that it rain not in the days of their prophecy; and have the power over waters to turn them to blood, and to smite the earth with all plagues, as often as they will."'

Most of the English prisoners of war were sailors: practical men, who also were keeping their heads down. But there was a sizeable group of landsmen, pressed like Coke, their lives shattered by fate. These men, in the front two pews, had a different take on the words. These men yearned for certainties.

'It has not rained in London these four months,' cried one.

'They say so many died in the four-day battle that the sea turned red,' added another.

'And all know how many were lost in the great plague last year,' cried a third. 'My father, my —'

'Aye, brothers!' Blood leaned over the pulpit now towards those who were swaying. 'We know the inevitable. What we must know now is our part in it. For the Lord wants servants who will labour for him, even to their utmost, yeah, even to the end of days. To hasten *His* kingdom with righteous acts. This is what we must plan for now, against the day foretold, that is nigh upon us.' He looked at them all, each in turn. 'What are we to do?'

'Fight?'

'Aye, brother. Fight!' Blood slapped the pulpit before him to halt the muttering that followed. 'And that is why I have come to you. To offer you the chance to join the warriors of Christ in the waging of this holy war.' His eyes gleamed. 'There's eighteen thousand veterans from the late civil wars already formed into regiments, many under their former commanders from the good old cause. Ready to come, with the Dutch ready to transport 'em.' He raised both hands. '"For thou art my battle axe and weapons of war; and with thee will I break in pieces the nations."' He pointed at one man. 'Will you be my battle axe?' At another. 'Will you join me and break in pieces Satan's nation? Will you battle and conquer the Beast and prepare the way for King Jesus?'

'Aye! Amen! King Jesus!' The men in the front pews rose as one. 'Praise him! Hallelujah! Hallelujah!'

Blood now looked from those who praised to those who did not. Coke lowered his head again. It is done, he thought. Now, for mercy's sake, let Christ's recruiting officer move on to the next prison camp and leave me be.

'Come, comrades!' Blood's voice rose again. 'Our Dutch brethren in Jesus have laid out a feast for those who will join in this crusade. Come and partake.'

Two soldiers now opened the chapel's doors. Coke and the rest waited as the men from the front poured out. All had seen the tables covered with food – hams, sausages, fruits – rewards for the recruited. There was even beer, sore temptation for the sailors who had spent a dry time in Terschelling among the ever sober Dutch. But though Coke was as thirsty as any man there, he would bide – first here in the church as everyone else left, then in the barn that served as barracks. Later, he would go and work again in Gerrit van der Woude's fields to earn the simpler fare that kept him and Dickon alive. He liked the old man and had got to know him better as the only prisoner of war who spoke some Dutch, learnt when he was in exile in Holland during the Protectorate. Perhaps Gerrit would share some jenever with him later if Greta was not about. It would be better than the sour Dutch beer.

Noises faded. He thought he was alone and was about to rise – until he heard the voice.

'Not joining us, brother? Are you not a disciple of Christ?'

The Irish voice was gentle now it was not ranting. Coke was tempted to keep his head down and mumble, but that might seem suspicious. Besides, how could the man recognise him? He was much changed from their few exchanges on the tavern's roof – one side of his face still livid from his burns, hair and eyebrows scorched away on one side, growing back in stubble. Nonetheless he let his native Somersetshire accent thicken. 'No. For I'm Jewish, zee,' he replied, looking boldly into Captain Blood's eyes. The Irishman stared a moment longer, laughed and left.

In the doorway, he passed someone else coming in. 'Cap'n!' Dickon cried, running up to him. 'I b-brought your ointment.'

Dickon was the only one to be excused the meeting, for he could never sit still and his cries of ecstasy were not ones that any preacher would have appreciated. Now he sat down on the pew beside his guardian and handed over the familiar jar.

It was filled with pig grease, its rank smell alleviated a little by the flowers that Greta van der Woude crushed into it. It was part of his fortune, he felt, a sign that gave him hope. For when the Dutch had pulled him and Dickon from the sea and taken them aboard their ship, their surgeons had, of course, treated their own sailors for their burns first, and in approved style – pouring scalding oil over the wounds to puncture the blisters. Many men had died screaming on the spot, several others a short time after. He'd been transferred to smaller craft and then, after three days, to Terschelling before the physicians could attend him. So it had been left to Greta to treat him with the foul ointment. He had stunk since then. But he had healed too.

As he smeared it on, Dickon jumped up and ran to the chapel's door. The sounds of celebration came through it. 'Beer, Cap'n?' he called. 'Shall I fetch ya some?'

'Nay, lad. It comes at too high a price.'

'Does it?'

That voice was back. Coke turned.

Blood was in the doorway. He was holding Dickon by the shoulders, the boy squirming under the grip. Behind the Irishman was a tall young man, perhaps fifteen years of age. Behind him were the two soldiers. 'Part of my trade requires a prodigious memory, for I write little down,' Blood said. 'Codes. Holy texts. I remember them all. Faces.' He smiled. 'Yours confused me for it is altered since we exchanged blows. But your boy here, who I saw just the once in your company before the theatre,' he moved his hands up to Dickon's neck, 'now he hasn't changed a bit.' Then, without turning, he barked, 'Seize him!'

The soldiers came fast. Coke wondered if he should fight, realised he could not – not with Blood's hands clamped now around his ward's throat. He was grabbed, his arms pinioned behind him, and marched to the doors. 'There now,' said Blood, easing his grip on the wriggling boy.

It was a mistake. Loosed, Dickon swung his knee up and hard into the Irishman's groin. Blood yelped, released him, and Dickon was gone, sprinting across the chapel's yard, through the gate, into the town.

The young man started after him. 'Shall I chase him, Father?' he cried.

Blood was bent over, his eyes pained. He shook his head. 'Let him go,' he gasped, then slowly straightened up. 'We have who we want.' Then he drew back his fist and round-housed Coke. It was a good punch from a big man and the captain dissolved swiftly into the darkness.

Water woke him from a dream of fire.

'Wake up!' someone bellowed, and Coke blinked away the liquid, opening his eyes. They were still filmy from the blow and the light was poor in the hut, a single gated lantern on a hook above him. Focusing, the two shapes before him resolved into the Bloods — father and son.

'By, and it was a good hit, Pa,' declared the younger, bending close to study Coke's jaw. 'Did you break it, d'you think?'

The elder bent too. ''Tis a fine thing, sure, the judging of that. I'm hoping not, for I'm keen to hear clearly what yer man here has to say, the many things he has to say. Relieve our concerns, Captain Coke. Can ye talk?'

There was no point in denying it. It would not long delay what these men had in mind. Probing with his tongue showed that a tooth was loose and that his jaw had swollen mightily; but it was not broken. Indeed, the greater pain for now was at his wrists which someone had tied so tightly behind him that he could not feel his fingers.

He rocked forward and the chair creaked. 'I can,' he replied.

'Splendid. Then we can begin.' Blood pulled up a chair to face him, while his son still stood by. 'I am sure you know how this goes, Captain. We will ask you questions. Depending on your answers, we will cause you pain or not. Do you understand?'

Coke squinted at him. He didn't know what he had to tell. But since it was fairly certain that he would be killed at the end of his telling, he knew he must drag out this session until something else came up – though what, he had little idea. Perhaps his gentle host Gerrit would object. This was Holland, after all, not Ireland. 'I do,' he said.

'There. No pain for that reply. Simple, is it not?' Blood smiled. 'How long have you worked for Sir Joseph Williamson?'

'But I do not work for him. I –'

The nod was imperceptible. But the boy reacted as if he'd been waiting for it all this time and hit Coke hard with an open-handed slap right on his swelling jaw. It may not have been broken but the bruise was tender and white agony overwhelmed him. He also felt something give. The chair rocked with the force, and returned. Bending over, he spat the tooth at Blood's feet.

The Irishman peered at the floor. 'It's either my old eyes, or the room's dim. Ah!' He bent, picked up the tooth and stared at it. 'I sympathise, man. I've lost too many of these to blows and battles. Gets harder to chew meat each day, don't it? Nevertheless,' he put the tooth on his thumb and flicked it into Coke's cheek, 'unless you want to eat naught but soup for the rest of your life, you'd best be answering truthfully now.'

Coke took a deep breath. 'I do not work for him,' he saw the boy's arm raise, 'except upon occasions.'

The hand stayed high. 'Like when you heard rumour of an attempt upon the king's life?'

'Then we are summoned.'

Another nod, and the hand lowered. 'We? That's you and this thief-taker, this Pitman, hmm?' On Coke's nod he continued, 'In London, a fellow Saint told me much of you two. You thwarted a holy plot last year, didn't you? Killed one of our brothers? You two and this whore you both straddle?'

'She's no whore, you Irish pig —'

The slap came fast and harder; this time the chair crashed to the ground and he struck his head. 'Dear, dear,' said Blood as he stepped to help his son right the chair and the prisoner. 'Did I not tell you that insults would be punished the same as lies?' Coke was flung back onto the righted chair and Blood bent closer. 'No, I can't see his eyes, which I need to. Else how can I tell his lies from his truths? Light another candle, Tom, will ye?'

His son reached up to the lantern and unhooked it from above the chair. When the warm metal passed close to Coke's face, he couldn't help but flinch. Blood's eyes narrowed. 'Those are some nasty burns you have there. I was burned once myself, at a siege. The skin remains sensitive for a time, does it not?'

Coke ran his tongue around his bloodied gums. 'Is that a question you would like answered?' he said.

'Oh no, sir,' Blood replied, 'that one I can answer for myself.' He reached back, grasped the candle in its pewter holder that his son had lit, then frowned. 'What's that?' he said.

Perhaps it was the ringing in his ears that prevented it the first time. But Coke heard in a moment what the other two already had.

'Thunder?' said the younger.

'No,' said Blood, standing straight. 'Cannon.' He waved with the candle at the door. 'There's our ship and many others in the Vlie channel. Go and see if for some reason they have chosen to practise their gunnery at night.' The boy nodded, unbolted the door and stepped out. Blood turned back, bringing the flame near again. 'Now, where were we?'

Through the open door, the noise of cannon fire came, more

of it and louder. There were shouts now too, and the sound of running feet. 'Father!' The younger Blood ran back in. ''Tis the English. They're raiding the fleet.'

'What? Probably just one of their damned frigates.' Blood hesitated, then put down the candlestick and unhooked the lantern. 'No, I'd better see. Come.' He looked back. 'Pleasure delayed only, Captain Coke.'

They went out, slamming the door. He heard a key turn, and the growing noises of attack beyond. Then something nearer. A scratching. 'Cap'n,' came the familiar voice.

'Dickon!' He twisted around to the sound. At the window, high up and barred, fingers waved. 'Dickon! Try the door, did they leave the key in it?'

A moment and then his ward was at the front. 'N-no. Shall I smash it in?'

In the flickering light, Coke could see that the room was small with stone walls and a thick oak door. It would take even a strong man time to knock that down. And he suspected he did not have long. 'Are we close to the van der Woudes'?'

'Aye, it's just down –'

'Find the Menheer. Bring him. He may be able to stop this. Fast now.'

'Aye.'

He heard the boy step away. 'Dickon?' he shouted. The footsteps returned. 'Have you your knife?'

'Aye, Cap'n.'

'Drop it through the window.' A moment later the knife clattered down. 'Now go.'

He rose and looked at the knife. He did not see how he could cut himself free with his wrists so bound. As he wondered, he heard the sound outside change. The cannons had ceased, and a different weapon commenced. 'Muskets,' he breathed. These did not come in the ordered volleys he had heard on battlefields across England. There was a crack, a crack-crack, more shots, singly and in pairs. There was only one reason for firing muskets. Men were landing to raid. Other men were resisting them.

He knew suddenly, clearly, what this would mean. Captain Blood could not risk being taken here. He would flee. But he would not leave his enemy behind.

Coke's eyes were drawn to flickering light. Ever since his burning he'd kept away from flame. Now, with no choice, he went to it.

He burnt himself the first time he placed his hands there and knocked the candlestick as he jerked away. But it tottered, righted and, after an agonising moment, the yellow cone again streamed high. Taking more care, he pushed his hands closer, slowly. He cried out as his skin heated; then, turning very slightly, his pain diminished as the flame settled on the rope. It took a while, and his hurt only grew. He stifled it, biting his lip until the blood ran, humming tunes – and finally, only by concentrating entirely on Sarah: remembering every detail of her face, of her body; remembering her belly kick when last he'd placed his hand upon it. Kicked by his son.

The tarry rope was raising lots of smoke before he felt it give. He pushed out against the bonds, grunting with the strain of it. Slowly, slowly, he felt the strands part and dissolve. Breaking his hands free, he tucked both wrists under his arms until the agony abated.

The musketry, which had multiplied along with cries and wailing, was growing louder, getting nearer. In moments he heard English shouts in the distance as well as Dutch, and the running of feet. Then, under those, a more measured tread. 'I tell you no, boy,' said Captain Blood. 'You will fetch our sacks and bring them here. Swiftly now.'

As the key turned in the lock, Coke snatched up Dickon's knife, then slumped back into the chair.

The opened door admitted more shouts, more screams, more explosions. 'I am sorry our acquaintance must be so brief, Captain Coke,' Blood said, entering, then closing the door. 'Sorrier still that I will not hear more of what you would be telling me. Know my enemy is a dictum I have long lived by. And with what we have planned –'

He tipped his head back to the sound of combat. 'But that's your lads coming fast and in force and I must be gone.'

He put down the lamp, extinguished in his journey. Only the candle now lit the room, and just the part around the table – the two men in a small circle of light. Blood reached to his belt, to the pistol there. Even without the gunpowder, Coke would not have staked much on himself in his weakened state, against a man as powerful as Blood. Unless he evened the odds.

Leaning forward, Coke blew out the candle.

There was an oath, a spark, an explosion. Flame shot from the muzzle, the ball preceding it, smashing into the chair – that Coke was no longer in. He moaned loudly anyway, then rolled to place his back against the wall beneath the window. 'Captain?' came Blood's voice. 'Are you hurt?'

Coke inhaled softly. Beyond the room, the noise of combat

continued, drawing nearer. Within it he could only hear the Irishman's harsher breaths – and then the sound, always distinctive, of a sword clearing a sheath. 'Captain,' Blood called again, then said, 'Shite!' as he banged into the table. Two swishes followed, a rapier slashed back and forth through the air.

He kept his breathing steady still as he heard the Irishman shuffle forward.

'Coke,' whispered Blood. 'Let's be reasonable here. You must be wounded. I'll fetch you a physician. You've trumped me, and I respect a bold enemy.' The man shuffled closer. 'What's say we call a truce, eh?'

He was right before him. So Coke lifted the candlestick he'd picked up and threw it into the far corner of the room. With a cry, Blood swung about, slashing before him. And Coke, putting all on the hazard, threw himself up and stabbed right where a man's waist might be.

His blade entered flesh; which part he could not know. It left flesh too, as the man leapt forward with a shriek. Coke did not pursue – a good choice as he felt the wind of a sword cut in the air before his face. He moved swiftly left, found the back wall, slid down it. And listened with satisfaction to the swift breaths of the other man.

'By God, I've not been stabbed in twenty years,' Blood gasped. 'I doubt it's mortal, Captain. But now we both bleed, cannot we say we're even and call that truce?'

'What makes you think I am bleeding?' said Coke, moving again as he spoke.

There was a roar, a rush, as Blood leapt to where he'd last heard sound. He crashed there, his breathing ever more laboured.

By God, I might even have the fellow, thought Coke. He came onto his knees and changed his grip on the knife. Now he could stab down.

Perhaps he would have if the door had not burst open at that moment. If Blood's son had not been standing there, screaming 'The English!', and if Blood, instead of using the little light to hunt down his enemy, used it instead to stagger to the door and through it.

Coke put back his arm to throw, then didn't. Partly because he suddenly thought it better to retain his weapon against his enemy's possible return. Mainly because he saw where the Irishman clutched himself and the sight weakened him for just the moment of decision.

For it appeared that he had stabbed Captain Blood in his arse.

Admiral Robert Holmes was as fierce as his reputation – and as much a man of mode. He stood now in the great cabin of his flagship, the *Tyger*, in his famous gold suit, his hair falling in styled waves to his shoulder, his beard and moustaches waxed and pointed to a fine brush's tip. 'It is an astonishing story,' he boomed, stepping forward to refill their three mugs – for Wilbert Bohun, who'd found Coke and Dickon in the town, stood beside him. 'No wonder that Ayscue made that promise to you. You are a bold dog indeed. And I speak as a wolfhound mesself. Huzzah!'

While Holmes drank deep, Coke sipped his sack. He'd grown unused to liquor in his time with the sober Dutch, and he'd been forced already to pledge the king, damn the Hogens and drink two down. He also wanted to be clear that he had achieved his desire – and that the admiral would be sober enough to remember it. Indeed, he had told little enough, leaving the full conspiracy behind his pressing murky, speaking more of the fireship attack and its consequences.

'Don't blame your son for going after his monkey, though,' Holmes now shouted, as if his audience was the length of a ship away rather than three paces across a cabin. 'Why, I'd venture over scores of burning decks to save my Achilles, would I not, dear heart?' His Irish brogue deepened as he addressed this last to the boy and the baboon, the latter of whom bared his teeth and chittered at him before turning back to the competition Dickon had engineered over a tray of fruit. 'So I am delighted to reaffirm Ayscue's promise to ye. When the chance arises, you will be returned forthwith to your native shore.'

The chance arising was what concerned Coke. 'Do you have a thought when that might be, Admiral? My need is —'

'As soon as possible, I say, and mean it,' Holmes cried, moving to slap a huge hand on Coke's shoulder. 'But you can hardly expect a fellow to dispatch a warship to take you back there on the instant. Pardon I, but there's the little matter of the Hogens to defeat first, eh?' He slapped him again and turned to pick up his hat, gloves and a map case. 'Which matter I must attend to now, with the other admirals aboard the *Charles*. We've stung 'em at Vlie and by burning Brandaris. Kicked 'em in their purses, which they hate.' He beamed. 'I hear they are already calling it "Sir Robert Holmes' Bonfire". But there's no doubt they'll be coming after us.' He strode to the door. 'When I return, you'll join me for supper and more tales, sir. Though,' he looked Coke over, from his bare feet to his torn shirt, 'I shall require you to dress. Dear heart, have you something close to the captain's size?'

'It will be my honour to find him something, sir,' Bohun replied, bowing.

Holmes swept out. The two men drank off the rest of their sack more slowly, then Bohun beckoned. 'Come. We gentleman volunteers have a nook for'ard, and there's a dead man's hammock for ye, if you like. Dead man's clothes too, for he was of your build. But what of your boy?'

Coke looked back. Dickon was engaged in a tug of war with Achilles over a banana. 'Away, lad,' he called.

'Aye, aye, Cap'n.' Surrendering the prize, Dickon skipped from the cabin.

'I warrant that he will spend most of his time aloft, and sleep beneath my hammock when he needs to,' Coke continued, following.

When they reached the deck, he and Bohun leaned on the rail, watching Holmes' cutter make its way over to Admiral Monck's flagship, the *Royal Charles*. Even with the wind, they could hear the Irishman damning the rowers for their indolence.

'A rare diamond, he,' said Coke.

'Aye, but one who will honour his promise to you when he can. He seems all bluster, but he has a mind like a clock, forever ticking. He'll remember what you told him about this Irish fellow – what, Blood? Perhaps send the news with ye – for cutters go back to England with dispatches, ships of the line need repairs. He'll see you home soon enough. Would I could join you.' He gestured aft. 'Those clothes?'

'Could you give me a moment?'

'Of course. Just ask for Bohun's billet.' He smiled. 'But you'll probably nose it by the rum.'

As the officer headed aft, and Dickon climbed up into the rigging, Coke moved to the other taffrail. Now he was facing away from the lowlands of Holland. Beyond sight, but there was England. 'Home soon, Sarah,' he murmured into the wind. 'Home soon.'

Part Four

A sudden wind, after days of calm, brings so much that is good.

It stirs the sails of merchant ships, makes them pregnant and potent again, powering them across the oceans to the realm's profit. It wakes Admiral Holmes aboard his flagship by the creak of his rigging, has him out of his bunk and shouting, for he knows that if he gets this easterly behind him, he will gain the weather gauge and then may fall like a fury upon the Dutch. It drives a cutter towards the English coast, bearing his intentions to his commander, the Duke of York, and to the king; while in the cutter's hold, a captain and his ward smile at the wind's song, and in spite of a mountainous sea.

In the fields of southern England, other sails that had drooped now fill and spin again. The longest, hottest summer in memory has brought an early harvest and farmers rise early to rush their bounty to the windmills for grinding. After a shortage there will soon be an abundance of flour for the realm's bakers to transform to bread, pasty and pie. Across seven counties, boys rouse themselves, then grin; for this is a wind to fly kites upon, and with their bellies full.

In London, a baker stands on the threshold of his house and his business, his eyes closed, his face turned to the breeze now surging up narrow Pudding Lane. He smiles, tasting the salt in it, thinking of his country's mighty fleet surging across the waters into battle. His interest is not just patriotic – Thomas Farriner bakes the Navy's biscuit. This wind tells him that, even though tomorrow is the Sabbath, yet he must work. Indeed, he must do a double batch of hardtack, for fighting sailors are hungry sailors.

Eager now for his bed, knowing he will be up even earlier than usual, he pulls the door to – nearly to. His beehive oven is cool, only a trace of residue warmth in its brick. He rakes the ashes out into a bucket, yawning as he does; tips them onto the bake-house hearth, and sets a grille before its faint glow. He returns and fills the oven with faggots against the morning's labour and looks about one last time. All is safe. Now the glass rattles in his windows, draughts coming through it. Reminding himself yet again to renew their leading, he picks up his candle and shuffles to the stair.

As he climbs, he is too tired to note that his candle's flame streams away from him, not towards.

He is asleep a minute after he lies down beside his wife. Thus he does not hear the wind's voice still rising; does not hear the front door, that he didn't quite close, blowing open, nor the sound of the very last embers, those he failed to sweep from the oven, reigniting. Fanned into life, they swiftly catch and consume the fuel set out for the morning's baking. Then a gust not only shakes the windows, it lifts a glowing faggot from the oven and drops it onto its fellows in a tub beside. All is gone in moments and flame falls to the floor, seeking other things to feed on.

Thus at two on a Sunday morning, on the second day of September, in the year of our Lord, also the year of the Beast, 1666, London begins to burn.

16

THE GREAT FIRE OF LONDON

2nd September, 4 a.m.

At her third deep sigh, Pitman turned to her. 'Can you not sleep, dearest chuck?'

Bettina sighed again. 'Nay, love, I cannot.' She reached and took his hand, placing it on her vast belly. 'Your son will not allow it.'

It took only a moment for his hand to be almost lifted from her skin. It was a feeling that never failed to thrill him. 'You are sure it will be a boy?'

'This hard a kicker? Aye, I'm certain. Only Josiah beat his poor ma like this. Both our girls were ever gentle.'

He turned on his side. Moonlight through their window lit the fleshy mountain. 'Is there anything I can fetch to ease you?' he asked. 'Some water? Some of your cordial?'

'Nay, it will only make me want to piss like a mare,' she replied, then belched. 'Oh, pardon I.'

Pitman smiled. For all her chapel ways, Bettina was still in some respects the crude-mouthed wanton he'd met in the

Ranters' camp in '47. Indeed, this last fortnight, that same wantonness had returned. If she'd not already been big with child, they'd have made another one for sure. 'Can I rub your back?' he said.

She pushed his hand off her. 'Nay, Pitman, it's too hot for all that nonsense.' She sighed again. 'I tell you what I've been dreaming about, during the odd snatches of sleep I've had. One of Master Farriner's sweet buns, hot from his oven. That, and a pot of tea to dip it in, would do me nicely.'

Pitman laughed. His wife was moderate in all things, and frugal with it, her only extravagance being a new-found passion for tea. It was yet rare and thus expensive, but he could not grudge her it. 'I will fetch you the one, and boil up t'other on my return,' he said, swinging his legs off their bed, sitting up and reaching for his breeches. They both slept naked, especially in this heat, a habit from their Ranter days when they rarely wore clothes be it daytime or nighttime.

'Will he be up, the baker?'

'If not yet, then soon,' he said, pulling his shirt over his head. 'I heard three bells, and he always bakes them buns first.'

'Hurry back,' she said, as he closed the door.

In the other room, he stepped softly past the sleeping forms of his two daughters, Grace and Faith, entwined together on a mattress, little Benjamin between them. Josiah slept in the attic, claiming it was cooler and his sisters too noisy. Pitman suspected it was because the attic window gave onto a window opposite, only a hand's breadth away, and his neighbours there had a daughter, at fifteen just three years older than his boy, and she was wont to leave her curtains undrawn.

Like father like son, he thought, stepping out onto the cobbles of Bow Lane, pulling his door to. The moon was near full and bright, and looked as if it was balancing atop the spire of St Mary-le-Bow right behind his house. He took a deep breath through his nose. There was the faintest tang of a fire. Almost no one was burning them for heat, while the summer continued so hot and so long. Another baker, he thought, setting out. He would pass several far closer than Farriner's. But they had lived near Pudding Lane for a time, and Bettina would know instantly if he brought home a rival's sweet bun. Besides, it was not too long a walk to Farriner's bakehouse. He'd take Bow Lane to Thames Street and walk parallel to the water, and so get the breeze off the river. By the time he got to his destination, his leg, always stiff on waking, would have eased.

He was just crossing Fish Street, pausing to look down it to the bridge, when a swirl within what he now recognised to be a strong easterly wind brought enough smoke to make him cough. Looking ahead and slightly north, he saw, over the warehouses and dwellings on the bridge's approach, a spiralling cloud in the clear sky and, within that, sparks. Coughing again, he increased his pace, using his stick to help propel him along.

The entrance to the road he sought took just fifty of his great strides. Turning the corner, he saw straightway that a building halfway up Pudding Lane was afire.

'Christ preserve us!' he muttered, hastening forward. There was already a crowd upon the street, and he espied a man he knew amongst them, a constable of the parish, one Salmon, who was organising a line of men with buckets. He limped up to him. 'When did this start?'

'Ah, Pitman.' The man wiped a sleeve across his sweaty brow. 'An hour or so since. In the baker's.'

'Farriner's? My wife will be sad to hear it. She most especially wanted one of his sweet buns.'

'Well, perhaps you'd care to reach in and pluck one out?' Salmon gestured to the burning structure opposite. Flames had breached the roof and were spilling out from the burst windows.

'Nay, truly, I am sorry to hear of it. Farriner is a good man. Did he escape?'

'He's there,' replied the constable, pointing to a huddle of people about twenty paces further on. 'He and his family are safe. They crawled out along the eaves, though there's talk of a maid too scared to make the journey. She's within. Or not, now.' He shook his head. 'You'll excuse me? I've a fire to fight. The Lord Mayor's been sent for, so we can hope he'll bring more men. Grab a bucket if you've a mind. Come, lads,' he suddenly shouted, striding off to a bunch of milling men.

Pitman went on, to the next group, arriving in time to hear the baker lamenting. 'I swear 'tis so. I came down at midnight, seeking to light a candle. There was not a flame in the bakehouse to fire it.' He looked up at his blazing home and business and bellowed, ''Twas fired deliberate, I tell ye. Some rival seeks to put me out.'

'Let's have no talk of arson, thank ye,' said another man, coming up. Pitman turned and recognised Thomas Bludworth, the Lord Mayor, who he'd had dealings with in city matters before. It was always best to broach those with him sometime between eleven and one because he was usually drunk by two. He appeared nearly as wide as Pitman was tall, the floridness of his jowly face showing what he'd been up to mere hours before.

He looked less than pleased with what was in front of him. 'This?' he cried, turning to slap hard the shoulder of a man beside him, who cringed and stepped away. 'You wake me for this? Pish, a woman might piss it out.' Salmon came up then, giving the mayor a short bow. 'Have you enough men for this, constable?' Bludworth continued. 'Buckets, syringes and whatcha-ma-call-'em? Have the New River stopcocks been opened for your use?'

'Aye, sir, they have. But we could use —'

'Good, good,' said Bludworth, turning away. 'Then I'm for my bed again. You,' he pointed at the unfortunate he'd slapped before, 'stay here and bring me a full report when it's out. But not before ten, mark ye.' He yawned. 'I think I'll sleep in late on the morrow.'

Salmon went away to organise his men and Pitman was about to join him, when he felt his sleeve tugged. He turned and saw Josiah. 'You're to come straight, Father,' his son said. 'It's begun.'

'All's well?' he said, gripping the boy.

'Aye, but Ma says you're to hurry.'

They set off at a good pace, Pitman making speed despite the odd gait caused by stiff leg and stick. There was an alley three houses up from the blazing bakehouse and they cut left through this, passing a side entrance to the yard of the Star Inn, whose main door was upon Fish Street Hill. Pitman glanced — and saw that the yard was filled with hay, piles of timber to fire the inn's brewery, a wagon loaded with barley. The landlord was there, with some apprentices about him, staring over his back wall at the flames in the sky and the floating, burning debris rising from it. Pitman paused. 'You'll want to shift all that, and have some water ready,' he shouted.

'Go boil your 'ead,' the landlord called back. 'Think I ain't seen one of these before?'

Yet even as he spoke, one of the youths with him yelped and began slapping at his own head. Before he moved away, Pitman saw another pick up a broom and start beating a pile of hay that was against the back wall.

They hurried on, passing the few people who were about and staring up at the over-lit dawn sky, into the alleys of a city still asleep.

The cry greeted him as soon as he pushed open the door. It was one he'd heard many times before. Uttering one himself, he took the stairs in a few short leaps.

'Don't make a fuss, Pitman,' she said. 'This one's making enough for us all.'

Bettina held up the little squalling bundle, then ended his yells by clamping him to one breast. 'A boy, I told you, and so anxious to join us he came in a rush. I barely had time to call the girls up and it was "whoosh, jug, and catch me".'

She laughed, and he did too, kneeling by the bed, one hand for his wife, one for his new child. 'Little Eleazar,' he said, stroking both damp heads, 'welcome to the Pitmans. May God have mercy on you!'

They both laughed then, their children rising to put arms around them and laugh too. Then, while the girls set about tidying and cleaning, Bettina washed the babe in a bucket of warm water Josiah fetched. 'You know, chuck,' she said, scooping the water over Eleazar and rubbing gently, 'my first thought after I knew the babe was hale was of dear Sarah. She was as near her time as I. We oft talked of having our babes side by side, but now with her in that terrible place –' She broke off, sniffed and continued. 'I feel I should go to her, and soon.'

'You will not stir,' he said, raising his hand against her protests. 'Nay, I know you think you're like your old ma in Kent who dropped you in a field, then returned to the hop-picking,' his voice rose over her squawk, 'but I will not risk you on those dirty streets, and in that foul place, where illnesses thrive. I will go see Mrs Chalker . . . Coke! And I will bring her such relief as I am able.'

Bettina sighed, sitting back against the headboard. 'Well, perhaps I do need a little sleep first. But you shall not prevent me bringing her aid on the morrow, Pitman, you shall not. Does Jesus not urge charity for a stranger? How much more so are we urged for such a friend?' She glanced down at the babe, suckling again. 'Mind, I am near as hungry as this mite.' She looked up at him. 'Where's my sweet bun?'

'Burnt.'

Poultry Compter. 9 a.m.

Sarah screamed. Like everything else of the night and the long morning too, it drained her and she flopped back onto the straw. It felt like her guts were ropes being twisted tight between twin devils. Earlier there had been some respite, a few minutes' gap between each bout of torment. The gaps had shrunk in length until it seemed that her insides were being continuously torn apart.

Yet no effort she made could expel what caused the agony. 'I'm worried,' said Jenny, bending to wipe a soaked cloth across Sarah's fevered forehead. 'This isn't right. Your waters haven't come but the cramps are so frequent.' She shook Sarah's shoulder gently. 'Let me fetch her.'

'For fuck's sake, fetch 'er,' yelled someone in the chamber. For the hundredth time, Sarah wished that she'd kept the tiny room the Pitmans' little money had allowed her. But she'd chosen to spend it instead on the one inside her, on more food to sustain him or her, though she hadn't told the Pitmans so.

Other voices came.

'For the love of God, squeeze it out, woman!'

'We can't breathe.'

They'd pressed clothes and blankets into the grille on the door. Even the keyholes had straw stuffed into them. All knew that vapours could hurt a woman giving birth. More of them shouted now, and Jenny turned back into the room and snarled. 'Go into the yard if you want air, you bitches. Leave 'er be.'

'Yard stinks o' smoke, you whore,' said the first woman who'd shouted, coming forward, a sullen child on her hip. 'There's a fire on the river, in case you 'adn't 'eard.'

'Yeah, and you want to let that all in 'ere?' Jenny stood, looming over the other who shrank back. 'Go out, the lot of ya, close the door behind ya – and send in the wise woman.' She said this last as she looked back and down at Sarah.

She'd shunned the midwife so far. As a child Sarah remembered seeing others like her come to their room in St Giles; watched their fumblings, listened to her mother's screams. Not one baby had survived more than a week, since Sarah had been born. But as another surge ripped through her, she moaned and managed a small nod. What choice did she have?

With much muttering, the rest of the women left, dragging

their complaining children. "Ere, take little Mary,' said Jenny, handing her child to one woman who picked the infant up, grudgingly.

Even in the small moments the door was open, Sarah could smell the smoke on the wind. 'Fire?' she croaked, and coughed.

Jenny knelt, helping her raise her head to drink from a flask of water. 'Big one, they say. But she's right, it's down by the river. Never reach us 'ere. Stinks, though, eh?'

The door opened again, admitting more foul air – and an older woman. She had a shawl over her head, wisps of grey hair straying out from under it. Her face was pale, except for two reddened and pockmarked cheeks 'Well, my dears,' she said, smiling, closing the door behind her, 'and about time too.'

She came over to the corner of the room and its bed of heaped-up straw, then, with a little difficulty, knelt. Immediately, the smell of smoke was overwhelmed by the reek of whisky. She smiled, her mouth a wilderness of gum, one tooth on the bottom like a solitary gravestone. 'Let's have a feel then,' she wheezed, as Sarah convulsed again.

Jenny pulled up the shift, and the midwife ran her hands over the distended belly, pressing hard. Then she reached between Sarah's legs. 'Dry as a virgin's slit,' she laughed, then licked her fingers. Sarah winced as first one, then two of them entered her, probing.

'Well,' the woman said, falling back to sit. 'You're this close,' she said, holding up two glistening fingers, 'so you're not that close. How often the pains coming?'

'Near all the time,' Jenny said.

'Truly? Hmm.' She scratched at a mole upon her face. 'It's cos your waters haven't burst. But I can fix that.' She reached within her cloak, fumbled around, finally pulling out a slim, black stick about half a foot long. It had a hook on one end. 'Usually I use this to grab the babe and 'ook 'im out.' She grinned, stabbing the probe down. 'But I can use it to break your bag as well.' Sarah shivered and the woman shrugged. 'If you don't like that, though, I've a coin with sharp edge. It's a milled sixpence from the reign of Good Queen Bess. Her virginity must bless it cos I've delivered ever so many with its aid.'

She laughed again. Sarah was about to protest, but then the woman sat back rather than reaching. 'I'll do either,' she continued, 'after we've discussed payment.'

'You'll get paid,' Jenny said. 'Just do it, will ya?'

'Ahead of time,' the midwife replied. 'Afterwards women tend to forget. If'n they're in a state to remember.' She held out a grimy hand. 'One crown.'

'So much?' Sarah said faintly.

'Course! I've got some drugs for you too, ease the pain. They cost as well.'

'I've only got a half-crown. More later.'

'More now.' When Sarah shook her head, the midwife shrugged and began to rise.

'Wait!' said Jenny. She went to the door, opened it, looked about. 'Jenkins!' she called loudly. 'Come 'ere, love. I want to talk to ya.'

'No, Jenny— '

'Hush now,' said her friend, turning back. 'It's only Jenkins. Be over in a blink.'

The turnkey came over. Jenny closed the door on their hushed conversation and Sarah heard them walking away. The pain doubled again. 'Can you –?'

'Oh, I'll just bide if you don't mind.' The midwife chuckled, then reached again within her shawl, pulling out a flask. 'Drink?' she said. At Sarah's shake of the head, she shrugged and drank deep.

Successive waves of pain took her, seeming to be getting ever closer together, until they merged into one constant agony. Her eyes were closed against it, her hands across her belly and the movement there. 'Come.' She sent down the thought through her fingertips. 'Pity me and come.'

She wasn't sure how long had passed before the door opened again. Not long, perhaps, for the woman still had the flask in her hand.

Jenny entered. 'Told ya,' she said, smoothing down her dress as she crossed to the straw, ''Ere ya go.' She handed her coin to the midwife, reached into Sarah's discarded smock and matched silver to silver. 'Now get on with it.'

'All in good time,' replied the other, secreting the half-crowns within her clothes, then pulling out a little glass bottle. 'Have a swig of this, sweetheart,' she said. 'It'll take all your pains and troubles away.'

As agony surged through her again, Sarah took it, then hesitated. 'What is it?'

'Oh, a very special concoction of my own devising.'

Jenny bent to sniff, wrinkling her nose. 'What's in it?'

'This and that.' She gestured to the flask impatiently. 'Just get it down, will ya?'

Again Sarah raised it to her lips. Again she hesitated. 'What "this"? What "that"?' she said.

'Oh, for Jesu's sake!' The woman raised her eyes to the ceiling. 'It's mainly, you know, the sleeping poppy.'

Sarah frowned, but it was Jenny who spoke. 'Opium? But that'll make her drowsy. She needs to be awake to push. I remember with my Mary —'

'She'll be awake,' interrupted the woman, tetchy now, 'and she'll push. Enough for me to get a grip.' She raised her stick and tapped the little flask. 'Get on, now. There's plenty of others out there who need my services.'

A sudden sharp agony came, greater than any before. Sarah screamed, dropped the flask, to the midwife's loud yelp — but Sarah barely heard her. Through the pain she suddenly remembered another birth she'd attended, one where she'd been the helper — Lucy Absolute's delivery the year before. Lucy had died soon after — not from the childbirth but from the plague that had ravaged the city and killed so many. But what she recalled clearly was her friend, not lying down but squatting with her back against the wall. 'Help me up,' she yelled, and Jenny — big, strong Jenny — reached under her arms, hoisted her and held her against the wall.

'But your waters haven't broken,' the midwife cried. 'Let me —' She reached again with her hooked stick — and Sarah slapped it from her hands. 'Get away,' she shrieked. 'Keep her away from me, Jenny! I swear I'll . . . ahhh!'

Time dissolved, lost to torment. Sometimes she knew she was up and squatting, Jenny supporting her and yelling encouragement. At others she was on her back again, or her side, the pain excruciating and she was screaming to drown out anyone else's counsel. It was half-dream, other women's faces coming, other voices shouting commands, whispering reassurance – her mother's, Lucy's. Then the men came too, where men should never be – Betterton, telling her she was too fat to perform; Pitman, driving off men who would harm her; her husband, her first husband, John Chalker, shaking his full and curly black locks in that way he did, laughing his great, deep laugh; lastly, longer, her captain was there – her William. Telling her to live for him, begging her to await his return, vowing he would be there soon.

A bell shook her, and she opened her eyes. It was the deep toll of nearby St Christopher le Stocks. That deeply religious harlot, Jenny Johnson, had told her all the tales of the nearby churches and the saints they were named for, crossing herself in true papist style as she gave thanks to each one. Christopher was the patron saint of many things, most notably of travellers – and of sailors. Was not her William a sailor now?

The ninth, the final stroke came, and almost upon it came the sailor's child, her child. The head appeared, or so Jenny said, shouting for more. With what she felt would be the last of her strength, she heaved again, felt a terrible burning down there, like the fire that raged on the riverside laid between her legs. Then that passed, and with a last mighty scream the babe passed, and Jenny let her go to catch it. Slipping down the wall, Sarah let more tears fall.

Somehow, through the sobs, she heard the voice. 'Poor thing,' the midwife was saying. 'Poor mite. It happens. But I told ya – if you'd only let me reach in with my little hook –'

Sarah opened her eyes. She'd fallen on her side but she sat up now. Jenny was holding a red and wrinkled thing, slick with blood. It was not human, because it had no face, just skin where the face should be. 'I'm sorry,' Jenny said. She was weeping too, holding the thing – her babe, a boy, she could see that on the instant – up to her.

As the pain in her body receded, her mind came suddenly, completely clear. 'Oh no,' Sarah said, but not in distress as she sat up and peeled the skin from the baby's face.

There was a moment of complete silence within the cell, beyond it, as if all the world went still. And then the baby opened its mouth and yelled; and in that first cry, in that glorious first cry, Sarah heard, unmistakably, that most rare, most wonderful thing – William Coke's laugh. And she knew their child on the instant.

Coldharbour, near London Bridge. 9 a.m.

No toll called the hour from the tower of St Magnus the Martyr. The flames that had run parallel down Pudding Lane and Fish Street Hill had united to ravage the church. Plenty of other bells sounded nearby, though none counted the clock – for their peals were sounded backwards.

The inhabitants of the Coldharbour sanctuary poured towards the docks. From the cramped laneways – Red Cross Alley, Flower de Luce Alley, Ebgate – they came, drawn by the strange peal of those bells, driven by the smoke that was thickening every minute, choking them in their tenements, clutching the few things they were able to save.

A hefty porter came with a harpsichord on his back; a youth with a bookshelf hoisted, stuffed with thick leather volumes. Others brought lesser things, valuable to them – a crate with a single canary; hessian sacks that clanked with plate; an armchair with straw spilling from its split cushions, perched atop a head. Most just carried babes, or small children, or old men and women. Everyone shouted at the boatmen.

'Take me!'

'No, me. I saw him first.'

'Take my daughter!'

'Five shillings.'

'But that's double the fare!'

'I'll give you seven!'

Two more boats swept into the dock, the wherrymen grabbing wood and shouting, 'Eight shillings to Southwark. Eight!'

'Order here, good citizens! Order!'

Members of the watch cried out, trying to control the crowd with staves. They might as well have used them to keep off rain.

'Look at the sinners scramble – as if they could escape judgment.' Simeon Critchollow turned. 'Say it, Daniel. The words I had thee learn.'

The younger man took a deep breath. '"And death and hell were cast into the lake of fire. This is the second death. And whosoever was not found written in the book of life was cast into the lake of fire."'

'The lake of fire.' As he repeated the words, Simeon looked again towards the columns of smoke spiralling up from the city and to the flames, a shimmering line now running from east of the bridge, one hundred yards to the west of it, and as far north.

'But who is in the book of life? What of our brothers, soon to be resurrected?'

They turned to the bridge, the reason they'd come to this viewpoint. Another fire, decades before, had destroyed much of the northern end. There was still a gap and the flames, having nothing to feed on and fought by householders further along the structure, who beat them back with boot, broom and bucket, had been stayed. Southwark, a suburb even more sinful than Coldharbour, had been spared. For now.

Simeon's sight was ever keen and despite the smoke he could still see the gatehouse at the southern end. See the four heads among the many staked upon it. Two were skulls, long since picked clean by crows; the third, hoisted up six months before, had little flesh left about it either. But he, who had been to revere them several times, could tell each from each from their position among the dozens.

'Pray with me, Daniel,' he said, keeping his eyes upon those three. 'Pray for our martyrs impaled there. You know our rallying cry: "King Jesus and the heads upon the bridge." Pray for their remains now. That they are not burned. That their skulls will be fleshed again, their mouths oped to greet their returning souls at the last trumpet, which soundeth soon.' He lifted his hands, palms up to the side, his eyes to the darkening sky. 'Lord, we beseech you to hold close our brothers – Thomas Venner, General Harrison, Colonel Rathbone, sacrificed in your righteous cause,' he intoned.

'Rise again! Amen!'

But it was the fourth skull that mattered to him most. 'And I beseech you to remember most particularly your brightest blade, Lord Garnthorpe. May he rise to wield it again in your cause.'

'Amen.'

'For are their names not written in the book of life? Proven so by this, their sacrifice? All for this time, now. For this day of judgment, come. Amen.'

This last was declaimed loudly, with finality. Daniel echoed it. 'And what do we do now, Brother Simeon?'

The puppeteer smiled. 'Do? We must be about it – fuel, guns, powder. Follow the example of these our martyrs who did not wait but forever strove.'

A surge of people jostled them, pushing and screaming for the few boats. Someone fell in the river to more screams. The watchmen yelled in vain and Simeon looked again at them. 'Witness how all authority yields now to God's. And yet, man will always oppose His will.' He nodded. 'You know who this will draw to the city? One who ever seeks to court the people's love?'

'The king?'

'Aye. Perhaps his brother too. They make such show of care. How could they resist this chance of proving it again?' He dropped his voice to an urgent whisper. 'The Fourth Monarchy staggers to destruction. But it will need a final push. So we will need Captain Blood.'

'Is he returned?'

'You think he would miss this? He knew this date as well as we, remember.' He smiled. 'Do you go and hang a blanket in the Bell Inn's window. He will know by that to come to our meeting house hard by All Hallows the More, where all saints will rally.'

Even in the little time they'd stood on the docks, everything had intensified: the smoke, the heat, the lamentations. Daniel coughed. 'Master,' he said, 'I am confused. Did not the prophecies foretell that September the *third* was the day of judgment? Today is the second.'

Simeon stared at him for a long moment – then burst out laughing. 'You think that the Almighty is bound . . . by a day? That all the prophets – Master Lilly, Anna Trapnel, Mother Shipton – are so scrupulous they could not err by so few hours?' He stepped closer, laughter gone, his eyes dancing with reflected light as he looked up once more. 'This fire is but the forerunner, as the baptiser John was to Christ. This is the first spark, merely. By tomorrow there may be something even greater: the death of kings. So let us be about it.' As he strode away, pushing through the panicked crowd, he yelled, 'Fuel, guns and powder. And Captain Blood.'

St Mary-le-Bow churchyard. Noon.

Clamping his hat to his skull so he did not lose it to the still-raging wind, Pitman surveyed what the church vaults had disgorged. He was not pleased.

This comes of taking the position of headborough without a proper handover, he thought. What annoyed him most was that it was at least partly his own fault. He had been in the post mere weeks when he'd been hurt by that devilish Irishman. And when he'd recovered enough from that, so much other parish business had built up to be dealt with that some things had been neglected. St Mary-le-Bow's arsenal for fire-fighting was one of them.

Such as there was, his men had spread out on the paths of the churchyard. Only two fire poles: one twenty feet, one thirty feet in length, with iron hooks at their ends, and ropes down the side for the pulling down of houses in a fire's path – if the houses had rings in their end beams to hook onto, which was not always the case. There were a mere dozen leathern buckets, and they would not make a very long chain from well to flame. They were better served with axes and ladders, having a dozen of the one, two-threes of the other. But the two brass fire squirts that men would fill with water and shoot over the flames looked as if they had survived from the first James's reign, and had been a habitation for mice ever since. He'd ordered them cleaned out but . . .

He sighed. He'd hoped to take half of his equipment to go and aid in the fight on the river. Now he thought he'd better take only himself and the half dozen constables he'd managed to rouse from slumber or chapel. 'Bring a bucket and an axe apiece, lads,' he commanded, 'and follow me.'

As he grabbed one of each, his hat, unencumbered, flew from his head and out of the churchyard. He did not give chase but went the opposite way. He was aware of the grumbling behind him, but the whistling of the wind drowned the words – though he knew what they'd be saying. That it was some distant parish's problem, at least a quarter of a mile away. That it was only old Coldharbour liberty that burned – so they'd been dragged from church to save the homes of some of the city's greatest sinners. All on their day off too.

He did not feel that way. It is my fellow citizens suffering, howsoever fallen, he thought, as he led his men down Bow Row and onto the Watling Street, my fellow Christians. Charity must be offered, as Jesus taught. He had special reason to give thanks with good works on this, the Lord's day. He had a new son, swaddled up with his mother back at home. Cooing, his mother said, not crying.

It was when he stood at the crossroads with Walbrook and could see along Cannon Street that his smile vanished. The lane was a chaos of carts being pushed by hand and dragged along by horses, with men and women burdened like pack beasts. Smoke was gushing out of the lanes running up from the south, as if each were a chimney funnelling a most ferocious hearth. As he led his men into the mayhem, more and more people kept stumbling from each one, clutching each other and their few meagre possessions. 'You there,' he called to a man newly emerged, who was slapping the back of a woman sitting on the ground, 'where's the fire reached?'

The man coughed, spat and drew breath. 'It's burned through the liberty,' he wheezed. 'Fishmongers' Hall, Dyers' Hall, both gone.' Over the astonished cries of some of the constables, he continued, 'Some men are trying to stop it at Thames Street.' He doubled over, hacking again, then looked up blearily. 'Not many. Most are just running.'

'Why did you not go upon the water, fellow?' asked another constable.

'Take me for a fool? Or a money-bags?' The man emptied his nostrils to the side. 'Bastard boatmen are charging a pound a trip now. But they won't have business for long cos the wharves are all ablaze too.' He helped the woman up from the cobbles and they staggered off.

'Onwards,' said Pitman. If Thames Street is breached, he thought, this is a riverside fire no more.

Through the smoke ahead he saw men a-saddle. Striding closer, weaving between carts and drays, he recognised one of them. He'd seen him earlier that morning. Pitman thought of asking him now if he still believed a woman could piss this fire out. However, the Lord Mayor did not look like a man who would find the question amusing.

'I *have* been pulling down houses, sir. When I can,' Bludworth said, his voice shrill. 'But, God preserve me, people will not obey me, and householders threaten me – with law suits, with violence.' He dabbed the sweat on his brow with a large handkerchief. 'What more would the king have me do?'

He was addressing these words to a man standing by his horse's bridle, a small, neat fellow who looked to be in his early thirties. He had a sharp way to him, as if he noted things others didn't – much as I do, Pitman thought. He certainly was losing his patience. 'He would have you fight the fire, sir,' the man replied, pointedly, 'and he offers you more soldiers to aid in the task.'

'Ah, no! No, Mr Pepys.' Bludworth raised his voice. 'You know that the city is most mindful of its prerogatives. And the King's Guards within the Mile? It speaks to them of tyranny.'

'Tyranny, sir?' Pepys' voice was as sharp but far calmer. 'The only tyrant this day is the fire.'

'Indeed, indeed!' The mayor wiped his face again. 'And I thank the king. But the numbers he has sent so far will suffice. Why, as soon as this deuced wind drops –' He broke off. 'We will have it under control, have no fear, sir. Reassure His Majesty that I will tend to it in person just as soon,' he swayed in his saddle, 'as soon as I have had a little rest.' His voice rose in complaint. 'They woke me at three in the morning, damn it.'

With that, Bludworth flicked his reins and rode off, the other two horsemen following.

'Bloody fool,' said Pepys, not softly.

'He is indeed, sir,' said Pitman.

The fellow turned, without much of a start. 'Ha! I know you. It's, uh, Mr Pitman, is it not? I've seen you in the company of the Duke of York.'

'I've had the honour to do him some service, yes.'

'Some?' The serious face was transformed by a boyish smile. 'Didn't you save his life? From those damned Fifth Monarchists, eh?'

Pitman shrugged. 'Will you be returning to the Palace, sir?'

'I will. The royal brothers asked for immediate report.'

'My suggestion is to bypass Bully Bludworth. More soldiers are essential and bugger the city's prerogatives. And I say that as an old Parliament man myself.'

'I will take the message once I have checked on my home.' Pepys extended his hand. 'They said you were a singular fellow, Mr Pitman. And they were right.'

Pitman engulfed the other's small hand in his huge one. 'That's Pitman to you, sir. Pitman to all, as His Royal Highness will vouch to you.'

'Where do you make for now, uh, Pitman?'

'Thames Street. I have some experience of this kind of fight, sir. If we can tear down many houses afore it, as the mayor should be doing, we may deprive the beast of what it would devour, and curb its appetite. Good luck to you.'

With a shake, he turned and walked down St Laurence Pountney Lane, his constables following. Soon he halted before the church, craning his neck to peer up. In addition to the hill, St Laurence Pountney had one of the tallest steeples in London, and so was visible from all around. Perhaps that was why so many constables had gathered there. He recognised James Morrow, headborough of his old parish of St Leonard's, and was crossing to speak with him when sudden movement drew his eye.

Pigeons were fleeing their roosts on the waterfront. One he noticed was flying most strangely, taking little lurches through the air, flapping hard. Then suddenly it simply ceased flying and plummeted down. If he had not stepped back, it would have crashed onto his head.

Puzzled, he bent down to look — and saw what had killed the bird, beyond the fall. Both its wings and its tail feathers were singed. 'Poor thing,' he muttered, 'did you not think to leave your nest before it burned?'

A cry came. 'The steeple! St Laurence is fired.'

He looked up. One of the tallest towers in London was ablaze. Which was odd, as the fire itself was still three hundred yards away.

He looked again at the pigeon, its feathers still smouldering. Then that same voice who'd screamed out — not 'on fire', Pitman realised now, but 'fired' — shouted again. 'It's the Dutch! The French! They're trying to burn our city down.'

They were wrong. The evidence was at his feet. He tried to bend to pick up the bird but was jostled aside in the rush. When he saw it again, the pigeon had been trampled and men were running in every direction. Several were calling, 'The Dutch! The Dutch are come! To arms! To arms!'

Pitman pushed his way to his old headborough. 'Ah, Pitman,'

the man cried, 'an old soldier like you, unarmed? Go fetch your musket.'

'Mr Morrow, I need no musket to fight a fire.'

'But you do to kill Dutchmen. Or Frenchmen. Or Papists, begod. They say this fire is an unholy alliance of all three. Does this church's firing not prove that there are incendiaries ahead of their forces?'

He looked up, so Pitman did too. The church tower was now strongly ablaze, flames streaming from it and forming a second red-yellow steeple. Both men stepped back hastily, as something liquid fell, splashing onto the ground where they'd been standing. Pitman saw an oily, shiny reflection of fire on the cobbles. Christ preserve us, he thought, the lead's melting.

He took Morrow's arm. 'Hear me. The fire began in a bakery. And it's spreading by flying embers. Or pigeons. I found one burning –'

'Pigeons? The dastards have trained pigeons to burn for them?' Morrow cried.

'You misunderstand –'

But the man would listen no more. 'The devilish Dutch are upon us!' he bellowed. 'They seek revenge for our burning of Brandaris a fortnight past. Back to the parish. Each man to his musket!' He broke Pitman's grip and led his troop away. Indeed, all the constables gathered there were running off, apart from his own, less terrified perhaps of the flames than of their leader's temper.

Householders near the now-fiercely burning church – melting lead must have carried flames down into the body of the building for they were now issuing from the windows – were out upon the street, gazing up in terror. But for every man or woman who seized a bucket and fire-pole, five more ran for their own homes, flung their doors wide, and began to throw valuables out onto the street.

For a moment, as lead continued to drip near him and people ran, shouting all about, Pitman was uncertain where to go. To his own parish where his family was, nursing the newcomer? It was tempting. 'Steady, Pitman,' he said to himself. His home was beyond the reach of any fire – as long as it was stopped. He'd helped fight one in '55 in Threadneedle Street. People had cried then that it could destroy the whole city, but they'd put it out at the cost of thirty houses. Men had rallied then and would be rallying today, and he knew where, for the man who'd stumbled from the lane had told him.

'Follow me, lads,' he said, striding off. 'We'll stop this bastard at Thames Street.'

As they set off, another huge gust of wind rattled the eaves around him, dislodging tiles that smashed onto the cobbles. Even with his great size he felt as if a ghostly hand was in his back, pushing him along. I'd not be on a deck for the Crown Jewels this day, he thought. Alas, poor William. Rather you than me.

Greenwich. 3rd September, 3 a.m.

They left their horses, exhausted from the all-night ride, in the post-house and to the grumbling care of a stable boy roused for the purpose.

'This glow,' said Captain Coke, as the lad took the bridles and prepared to lead the hired nags away, 'we've seen it for the last ten miles. What means it?'

The boy stopped, yawned widely. 'Where've you been?' he paused, looked at the horses. 'Oh, Carabine's mounts. Sittingbourne, eh?' He ran a hand down the chestnut's foamy flank. 'Did you not rest along the way? These uns 'ull not be fit for 'ire for many a day, you drove 'em so 'ard.'

Coke took a breath and kept his temper. He was near as tired as his mount, he'd vouch for that. At his side, Dickon had already lain down upon some alluring hay. And they'd come a lot further than Sittingbourne. They'd only changed horses there. 'The glow, boy. What is it?'

The stable hand yawned again, as he led the horses into a barn. 'It's a fire in London,' he called over his shoulder. 'All the docks are ablaze, or so they say.'

Coke looked down at Dickon in the hay and had to resist the near overpowering urge to join his ward. They'd had maybe two hours' sleep on the entire ride from Dover, though he'd held Dickon in his saddle while the lad dozed. Twice he'd woken with his mount's nose in a hedge, chewing. But he could not stop now. Not when they were so close.

He left his ward lightly snoring and went into the coaching inn. No one was about, but the hearth glow and one lit lantern showed him the main room. He called. When no one answered, he went behind the trestle bar and tapped a jug of ale. There was bread and a chunk of cheese upon a platter and though each looked a little mouse-gnawed, he shoved both into his cloak's pocket. They'd eaten and drunk as little as they'd slept. He thought of leaving coin, but near all of the purse that Admiral Holmes had given him had gone on the post-horses. He might need his last two crowns.

He took his bounty back to the yard, knelt down and roused Dickon, who woke with uncharacteristic complaint. But ale and food soothed him a little and he rose when his captain bade him. 'Let's to the top of the hill, Dickon,' Coke said, 'and see this river fire for ourselves.'

Chewing bread and cheese, they climbed Greenwich Hill. As they neared its summit, Coke became aware of a sound, beyond the whistling easterly that had blown them fast to Dover from the fleet, pushed in their backs during the ride from the port, and now soughed in the branches of the vast oaks they passed beneath. It was like a large body of people were shouting in the distance; or some battle was being fought. Battle indeed, he thought, for within the distant roar he now could hear the occasional punctuation of an explosion.

Yet no battle he had seen – and he'd fought in many – could have overwhelmed his sight as the one that faced them when they crested the hill.

'God preserve us,' he whispered as Dickon cried out and sank upon the turf.

Under a moon near full and as red as blood, London burned, in a great curved bow of flame, its one tip placed near the Tower in the east, t'other – well, he could not tell – half a mile away at least, far past the dark line of the bridge. But the bow's centre was pushed up to – again, he could not be certain; at least as far as Eastcheap. He knew several who lived there – Isaac for one.

Recalling people he knew distracted him from the shock of the spectacle, back to the reason he was there – there, on Greenwich Hill, and not where he needed to be – there, amidst the flames.

He shuddered, then pulled Dickon to his feet. 'Let's see if we can find a kindly boatman to take us upstream,' he said.

However, there was not a boatman to be had, for charity or hire, on Greenwich docks. 'They're all attending the fire,' said a one-armed man they asked. 'Fortunes to be made, 'tis said, for all who dwell near the river are trying to get their goods aboard.' He stretched out his one hand, rubbed finger and thumb together. 'I'd be there mesself if'n the King's army hadn't taken me arm.' He cackled. 'Fortunes!'

'Come, lad,' said Coke, setting out, 'it's Shanks's pony for us.'

From Deptford, which they soon reached, through Bermondsey and all the way to Southwark, the south bank of the Thames had become one sprawl of industry – dockyards, tanneries, distilleries, breweries, glue and paint factories, all jumbled together with the tenements for those who worked in them, and the many alehouses and ordinaries which fed the workers. The road took them parallel to, but a little way from, this crowded riverbank. The closer they got to Southwark, the louder the noise of fire grew – the cracking of timbers, the whoosh of some structure collapsing, with people's cries, like distant birds, caught up in it. The light grew as well, a dawn an hour before it was due. Above the roofs, the vast cloud of smoke was lit by the fires that caused it, reflecting back, making the excited faces they passed as clear as at midday.

When he could see the steeple of St Mary Overies – it glowed, too, in reflected flame as if lit by a theatre's candelabra – Coke turned up the side streets. 'The bridge,' he said to Dickon. 'No coin needed for that.'

But the bridge was closed. Through the grille of the portcullis, which Coke had never seen lowered, a soldier was talking to a small and anxious mob that wanted to get through. 'It rages at t'other end still,' the guard explained. 'If you choose to be burned alive, 'pon your heads be it, I'd let you go. But my captain says no.'

Coke and Dickon moved away from the cajoling crowd. To the west of the bridge, the riverbank was less crowded with buildings – because this was still a liberty, as it had been since Queen Bess's time. The theatres may have moved to the town and indoors, but the bullring, the bear baiting and the cock pits, together with taverns and brothels innumerable, still thrived. Indeed, as Coke led Dickon through the gates of Paris Gardens, it appeared that pleasure was what people still sought here. It was as crowded as a Saturday night: liquor was being sold, chickens roasted, chairs and tables set out, with men and a few women grouped around them. All faced north, gaping at the spectacle.

Coke, most concerned about achieving their passage onwards, kept pushing through the mob. He stopped at the head of the boat stairs, though, Dickon beside him, both men staring in shock.

It was partly the heat. It had been a warm night anyway, the latest in a long line of them. But standing there was like being before an especially well-fed hearth. As the wave of warmth hit him, sweat started running down his head, inside his shirt. He felt also the places where he'd burned aboard the fireship. Greta van der Woude's pig-grease ointment may have healed the worst of it, but areas were yet tender and his cheek, ear and side of his head stung. He took a step back; but he could not mind it for long, so dreadful was the spectacle before him.

The great bow he'd seen from Greenwich was a wall here, stretching either side of him at least half a mile wide. Directly ahead, smoke rose from fires that raged everywhere. He could see by its light that already so much had been burned out, vast buildings that he'd known but perhaps could not name were charred ruins now. Churches were gone, save for a stone tower here and there, all glowing as white as beacons on a dark night.

'Cap'n,' said Dickon, tugging his arm. When Coke managed to look down, his ward pointed. 'Boats.'

'Good lad,' said Coke, approaching the stair again. It was well that one of them remembered their purpose.

There *were* boats. In sooth, he'd never seen so many on what was often the most crowded stretch of the Thames. Large wherries, small skiffs, rowboats of every size and type. All were occupied; indeed, all were crowded, shooting every way over ripples in whose crests the fire danced in reflected yellow. Many had to be refugees from the catastrophe, and boats were continually docking and disgorging passengers clutching a pathetic little – bundles of clothes, some boxes, a painting in a frame, candlesticks. Other boats were landing people who had nothing, save perhaps a tankard or bottle. These passengers did not have the distraught mien of those burned out, but, contrariwise, were talking excitedly about what they had been observing. As if the fire was some exotic wonder like an elephant paraded through the streets.

As enthused a crowd waited to take the place of those who disembarked. Coke, flushing with anger at people who would make a spectacle of others' suffering, pushed hard through the mob, not sparing his elbows nor heeding the complaints. 'Crown for the two of ya,' said the boatman, one foot on the dock, one in his wherry.

It was four times the normal fare, half the paltry amount he had, and Coke felt he would need that. 'I've family over there,' he said. 'I must reach them —'

The boatman cut him off. 'I'm not docking, friend,' he said. 'Maybe later when the prices are even higher. For now —' He looked above Coke and called, "Alf-crown an 'ead. Have your money ready.'

'Please.' Coke stepped a little closer. There was something about the man, a deeper bronze to his face, the cording of his forearms, one of which had a name tattooed in smudged ink. 'For a mate from before the mast?'

It made the man look again at him, appraising him now. His gaze moved over the pair of them. They were dressed once more in the motley they'd got from pursers' slops — worn shirts and breeches, patched short coats, boots that gaped. Coke had decided that the fancy laced and velvet garb the officer had lent him to dine with Holmes was not practical on the trip he intended.

He was pleased about that choice now when he saw the man's eyes light up. 'You served?'

'Even now.' Coke let his native Somerset accent deepen. 'Fresh released from giving the Hogens a thrashing, uz. Trying to get home.' He smiled. 'My wife's expecting me.'

'Yeah, but you're goin' to visit your sweetheart first, right?' The wherryman laughed. 'Go on, then. Keep your coin. Someone did the same for me when I got back from Tangiers.' He glanced back across the water, upstream. 'I'll drop you at Queen Hithe. Not burning for now — but not for long, I'd wager.'

Coke and Dickon got in, settling in the stern. Once the fares had been collected and the goggling passengers seated, the wherry shoved off. The boatman was clearly experienced, threading a nimble route through the throng. Coke did not look at the fire drawing ever closer now. He could hear it. He had also begun to smell it, where the following wind had not really allowed him to before. Mostly he could feel it upon his tender patches of skin.

Close to the dock at Queen Hithe, the boat gave a sudden lurch. 'Way there!' cried the ferryman. 'I'm goin' in the dock.'

'As are we, fellow,' came the shouted reply, 'and a monarch must precede.'

That voice. It startled Coke from the reverie where flame and his own concerns had taken him. He looked up in time to see a barge, with ten oars on each side, drive in front of them. In its prow, standing and peering ahead, hand on brow against the glare and the dawn, was Charles, King of England. Slightly behind him, gazing forward too, was James, Duke of York.

The barge entered the wide indentation that was the dock, the wherry following close to, both reaching the main wharf at near the same time. The royals alighted, and soon after so did Coke and Dickon, about twenty-five paces off. For a few moments, Coke kept his face turned away. He was not sure Charles would recognise it, even though he had asked the captain to join his household six months before. He knew he was altered by war, his hair only just growing back on one side, his moustache and eyebrows not yet at their former, luxuriant length. He was also dressed in sailor's clothes; besides, the king's focus was entirely on the flames that rose north and east less than three hundred yards away, and the men who had obviously gathered to meet him there and receive instructions. Yet to leave Queen Hithe he would have to pass quite close to Charles to exit the gate. And he'd learned in their dealings the year before that His Majesty, for all his reputation as little more than a carousing gallant, missed almost nothing.

He hesitated. He had no idea what was ahead of him this day — what the London he must search through had become. All that information would be given to the king now. It would be useful to be near him when it was. And depending on what he heard, it might also be useful to have some regal assistance.

He decided. 'Your Majesty,' he shouted.

Behind the wooden dock was the market area, a large, now crowded square. His was far from the only voice supplicating. Men were gathered about the king with papers and maps, while several well-dressed noblemen stood in attendance. He pushed determinedly through but, three paces away, one of the five royal guards stepped up to intercept him, large fingers splayed on Coke's chest. 'Sire, 'tis I!' Coke called loudly.

'Eh?' said Charles, looking up from a map, his irritation clear, one eyebrow raised above the eye that had the cast. Then the other eyebrow joined the first in puzzlement. 'Why, I – I know you. You're Coke, William Coke.' The gaze continued down from face to the impoverished clothing. 'Whatever are you dressed as, man? Oh,' the expression changed, 'burnt out, eh?'

'In a way, sire.' Coke paused. He had no desire to explain much of the story. And yet? Some had to be told. 'I have just come from the fleet, sire. Sent by Admiral Holmes.'

'With dispatches for me?' The Duke of York stepped forward. He was head of the Navy, Coke knew.

'Wait, Jamie!' The king raised a hand. ''Od's life, man, but I didn't know you'd enlisted? Last I heard, after you'd turned down my bedchamber post, was that you were going to get married.'

'I did. And was pressed into service the very same day.'

'Out upon you! 'Tis true?' At Coke's nod, Charles whistled. 'You are a remarkable fellow, Captain Coke.'

'When truly, sire, my only desire is to be unremarked,' he replied.

Charles looked to his brother, who was obviously holding back a flood of questions. '*Do* you have news from the fleet?'

'Only that it is scattering before this same wind that acts as such a bellows to this fire,' he replied.

'Aye. There'll be no fighting in this.' Charles nodded at the air, which gusted and swirled about them. 'But we have a battle ahead of us nonetheless. Have you come to enlist for that, Captain?'

'Majesty, I –' he swallowed. 'When I was pressed, my wife – whom you knew as Mrs Chalker – was already large with our child. She may have borne the babe by now and they may be –' he turned and nodded to the flaming city, 'somewhere there. Also she does not know if I am even alive. So let me find her first, see her safe and then of course, I will return to the fight.'

'I understand.' The king sighed. 'I've always regretted the necessity to press men and your example deepens that feeling. These fellows here,' he gestured to several men standing by with papers, 'have the latest reports of the fire's progress. Let them report to me and you may learn a safe route to your beloved.' He beckoned one nearer who held a map. 'Where do you think she might be?'

Coke stepped up. 'Either in her old lodgings of Sheere Lane, near Lincoln's Inn –'

'In which case she is far beyond the wrath of even this inferno.'

'Yet she also talked of laying in with the Pitmans. Mrs Pitman is also most near birthing.'

'Pitman? My loyal follower?' It was the duke who now spoke. 'That fellow, whatcha-me-call-it, uh, Pepys. Navy office. The one who first brought news of this fire to Whitehall. He came again later and told us he'd met Pitman in Cannon Street. That the worthy was going to aid in the pulling down of houses closer to its source and upon, what was it? Yes, Thames Street.'

'According to report, that's long breached,' said Charles, pointing at the map. 'The monster is moving up Gracechurch Street, already creeping, nay, raging northwards, and westwards here to, well —' He broke off and waved at the fiery arch, its edge ever nearer. 'Does that help you, Captain?'

Coke peered. Where the fire had burned was scratched in pencil. He placed a finger at a point as yet unshaded. 'This is where Pitman lives, beneath St Mary-le-Bow. He may be there and so may my wife. Thither I'll go.'

'He has the right idea, your friend,' said the duke. 'Pull down the fuel. Blow up houses. We have begun a little of that but must do much more.' He turned to his brother. 'I am sure Pitman will be about it, Charlie. As must we.'

Charles nodded. 'Away, Captain. We will be setting up fire posts ahead of the flames and in a perimeter around them. My lords here,' he gestured to the noblemen surrounding him, 'will each command at one. Join one of them if you are able. May you have all success and, of course,' his eyes sparkled for a moment, 'my compliments to your lovely wife. Now, sirs —' He turned back to the map.

Coke moved away, leading Dickon to the street gate of the

market. There the fumes were even worse, the wind driving the scent of all it had consumed of the area of the Vintry and below, the twin churches of All Hallows, the Great and the Less. The warehouses there contained much of the city's liquor supply and the sweet stench of burnt brandy, wine and whisky casks stung his eyes. He paused at the gate, coughing. 'Now, Dickon, we need to part –' He took the boy's arm when he began to protest, 'Only till we are sure where Sarah is. Do you go to her rooms on Sheere Lane. If she is there, tell her to remain safe and bring me word. If not, and no one knows of her thereabouts, join me at Pitman's, 'neath St Mary's. Is that clear?'

'Aye, Cap'n. All clear.' Dickon smiled though his eyes looked scared. 'Perhaps S-sarah has some nuts for me.'

'I am sure she does.' Coke squeezed his arm. 'Go swiftly, return faster.'

'I will.' With that, Dickon began his loping run away, west along Thames Street.

Coke soon lost him in the mob. Coughing, he pushed his way through and headed up Little Trinity Lane.

Behind him, a crowd still clamoured around the king as he stabbed at points on the map. But two men did not approach His Majesty, just moved to where they could observe him better from under the market's arched entrance.

One spoke. 'He came, master, as you said he would.'

'Aye, Daniel, he did,' Simeon Critchollow replied. 'Yet it is not I who had the foresight but God who forged the plan.'

The younger man chewed at lips already ragged. 'Do we . . .

is this the moment when –?' He reached a shaking hand to touch the pistols tucked under his cloak.

'Nay, lad, it is not. The king is too well protected here. You know that I would not hesitate to become a martyr. But only if I was guaranteed success. Here, we could easily fail, die in the attempt – and all we'd do is set the tyrant on his guard.' He nodded. 'Do you recall what our Irish friend said when the attack on the king at the theatre was thwarted?'

'Was I there?'

'Ah, no, you were not. He lamented actions taken haphazardly. He wanted a plan. And he said, "We must only venture at a time that God has already marked out for success."' Simeon waved behind him, to the smoke and the fire and the noise. 'That time is now.' He pointed ahead. 'The tyrant will go about into this fire and our moment will come. When it does, he will be like a lamb offering his throat to the sacrifice. But for that we need a single shining blade. Once we had Lord Garnthorpe. Now we have Captain Blood.'

'But where is he? I hung the blanket at the Bell Inn, master. Maybe he will come to the meeting?'

'The meeting house will be ashes by the appointed hour. I have brothers seeking for him. But if they do not find him, well,' he shrugged, 'I have faith he will appear exactly when and where he is needed. Meanwhile, let us about it again. There are small fires to be lit ahead of this great one. There are foreigners to blame and riots to spark.' He grinned. 'Into the city again. Hasten the apocalypse.'

Poultry Compter. 1 p.m.

'You 'ave to let us out,' Jenny Johnson screamed, beating on the door. 'We're choking in 'ere!' Many voices rose, adding their pleas, by those still able to speak. Most, like Sarah, were saving their breath.

There was little enough to sustain them in the cell. The small barred window high up in the outer wall, the foot-square door grille – between them they admitted barely enough air on a hot day, as all the days had been of late. Now, they seemed to let in only smoke – and a nauseating mix of sweet scents. Rumour had reached them that the Royal Exchange, home of the merchant city, where all luxuries were sold in hundreds of shops, was a charred ruin. The spice traders kept much of their stock there, and Sarah's eyes streamed, her nose stung with the roasting of black pepper, nutmeg, cinnamon and other spices she could not identify. But something else had started to perfume the air not half an hour since, thickening the smoke.

'That's Bucklersbury going,' said Jenny, flopping down beside her, coughing. 'The druggists have gone up, and all their potions burned. When will they let us out?'

As if in answer, they heard a shout from beyond the door, over the pleas of the women squeezing arms through the door grille. 'Quiet, ye whoores! We're making arrangements to transport ye, and will have ye oot when we're good and ready.'

With that the Scotsman, Master Turnkey Wallace, crossed the yard and bellowed the same at those beseeching on the men's side.

'They'll sweep us out as ashes!' wailed Jenny. She clutched her weeping daughter to her. 'There's some already gone.'

Sarah looked where her friend pointed. Two of the older debtors, both with jail fever and already struggling each day for breath, had lain down half an hour before and ceased coughing soon after. She looked down again, to the bundle in her arms. Her child – she still had not named him, felt she could not without consulting William – was struggling for breath as any there. He did not want her breast either, the only liquid in the cell for any water was long since drunk. He squirmed and his paleness alarmed her. No, no, she thought, after all this I am not going to lose you.

She handed the child to Jenny, who took him to her chest wordlessly, tucking him next to her Mary. Then Sarah slowly hoisted herself onto her feet and stood swaying, uncertain if she was going to faint, the foul, sweet air making her cough. Her insides felt as if someone had been kicking her repeatedly – which he had done. She looked down at her son in the whore's arms. 'For him,' she said aloud.

'For who, love?' said Jenny, looking up.

'Let Mary take the babe. Come with me.'

'Where to?' Jenny wheezed but obeyed, rising and handing the boy over. Mary took him, drawing him tight to her.

Despite each step of pain, Sarah made it to the door. Jenny followed. The others who'd begged at it had dropped away to cough and weep, so she had the grille to herself. 'Can you get Jenkins over here?' she whispered to Jenny.

'I can try. 'E wouldn't come before.'

'This might persuade him.' Sarah had two things in the pocket of her smock. She pulled one out now.

'You've been keepin' a gold sovereign all this time?' Jenny asked in wonder, reaching towards it.

Sarah lifted the coin away. 'Pitman gave it me. Made me swear I would only use it in direst emergency.'

'What? And your baby's troubled comin' wasn't that?' She snorted. 'I had to suckle Jenkins for the other 'alf-crown.'

Despite it all, Jenny had the faintest smile on her face. Sarah smiled too. 'I tried to stop you. But you were gone about your trade.' The smile went. 'Besides that was birth. This,' she jerked her head into the cell, thickening with smoke, 'this could be death. For us all.'

Jenny nodded. 'What's your plan?'

Sarah told her, in whispers. Then she raised her voice. 'Listen. Listen!' The twenty women in the room looked at her. 'We're going to get this door open. And when it is, they'll try to shove us back in. We have to make it hard for 'em. Scatter into the yard.'

No one questioned. All rose, stood there, grabbing what little they had to take. Sarah nodded at Jenny and the whore put her face into the grille. 'Jenkins!' she called. 'Jenkins, love! Over 'ere.'

They heard his step on the cobbles of the yard. 'I can't let you out, Jen,' he said. 'Orders.'

'Nah! Not that. My friend 'as something for ya.'

Then Jenny crouched, just below the grille. Sarah stepped up, a foot away from it.

'Mrs Coke,' Jenkins said, peering in, an insincere smile on his unshaven, pockmarked face. 'How's the babe? How are you?'

'Choking,' she replied, coughing hard, not needing to fake it much. 'We all need air.'

'I know.' He shrugged in false sympathy. 'Wallace'll order you out soon, never fear. Fire's getting close. We'll need to move you.'

'We need water too. We die as much from thirst. Please,' she coughed again. 'Can you shove a few flagons through here?' She tapped the iron bars, the gaps between them just wide enough to admit flasks.

'I might. Men have been asking too.' He sucked between his few teeth. 'Any garnish in it for me?'

'Yes,' Sarah said, drawing one of the objects from her smock. 'I've been saving this for the right occasion.'

His eyebrows rose. 'Christ's bones! A sovereign? For me?'

'If you'll bring us the water now,' Sarah let the coughs come again, but continued through them, 'and be kind to us when they let us out of here.'

'I'll be most kind, trust me.' He lifted a hand. 'Pass it out, then.'

Sarah bent from the waist, coughing louder. She still held the coin up. 'Take it,' she wheezed, stepping back a little. 'Take it.'

Jenkins reached. He was up to his elbow in, his fingers an inch from the coin when Jenny rose up and grabbed him, using her full weight to pin him. As he yelped, wriggled and could not shift her, Sarah drew the second object from her smock.

It was the midwife's razor. She laid the edge to his skin. 'Cry out,' she said softly, 'and I'll take a finger. If the door's not open straightway, I'll take the whole bloody hand.'

Jenkins jerked, could not shake off the hanging Jenny. 'But I –' he began, and stopped when Sarah ran the razor across his knuckles. He whimpered at the line of blood, and she could see him twist to reach down. They heard the jangle of his bunch of keys, metal thudding into wood as, without looking and whispering pleas and curses, Jenkins tried to find the key and keyhole. At last he got it. The lock turned. The door opened.

Still pinioned, Jenkins was dragged into the cell. Once inside, Jenny threw him down. 'Keep quiet, you piece of turd,' she said, kicking him in the ribs.

Sarah poked her head out of the door and looked to the left. Thirty paces away, the front gate of the Compter gave onto a narrow lane that led down to Poultry. Wallace and two lesser turnkeys were leaning on its bars, staring ahead. Beyond them, flames danced on Bucklersbury. Across the yard, men were staring at her through the bars of their own grille. She put a finger to her lips, then turned back into her cell. 'Quiet now,' she said, 'all out and spread. Jenny, help me with the men's door.'

Jenny took her foot off the whimpering Jenkins and joined her with his keys. The other women came close, stepping on, rather than over, the squirming warder. Mary handed Sarah the babe. She took him, felt his weight now she was standing. She took a breath and looked around. She nodded. 'Let's go,' she said.

They all left silently, spreading out as she had asked them to. She followed Jenny who moved swiftly across to the men's cell door. Jenkins's key bunch was large, and key after key failed. She was not halfway through them, when a roar came from the gate. 'What the –? How the –?' Wallace cried, continuing, 'Ye whoores! Back to your cell.'

Sarah glanced back. Wallace and his two lackeys were trying to push through – but the 'whoores' were not letting him. He looked through the throng, and their eyes locked. 'Oot the way!' he yelled, brandishing his club, striking a woman's arm.

'Hurry!' Sarah said, as the warders cleared their path with blows.

Jenny grunted, key after key failing. There were perhaps two untried, when Wallace reached them. 'Give me those, ye damnable whoore, or I'll —'

It was as much as he said before Jenny left the latest key in the lock, turned and punched him in the face. As he staggered back with a yelp, Sarah reached to the key. Turning it took all her little strength. But it did turn and, a moment later, men were running from their cell, knocking Wallace and his men down, and trampling them before running on to the gates.

'They've forgotten these,' said the last man to leave.

Sarah recognised the voice, then the face when she looked up. 'My, my, Mistress Coke, but aren't you the enterprising one?' As he spoke, de Lacey, the baronet, took the bunch of keys from her and strode off to the main gate.

Someone must have known the right key there, or perhaps were just lucky, for by the time Sarah reached them, leaning upon Jenny — who also carried the baby in one arm and held her daughter in the other — the gates were open and most had already fled. They followed, more slowly, into the narrow lane that led down to Poultry proper. It was thick with choking, cloying smoke. They'd not got halfway down when someone emerged from the clouds and bumped into them.

It was another woman from the cell, Joan. 'King's Head on the corner's ablaze,' she cried. 'Some are running past but it looks like everything beyond burns too.'

There were shops to each side of them, their doors open, the rooms beyond scattered with goods, showing the haste in which the owners had fled. 'There,' said Sarah, pointing into one to their right.

Joan came too and the five of them, babe included, picked their way among the abandoned goods of a grocer's store. Apples and other fruit were scattered about, dried raisins and nuts in bags. They each picked up what they could, storing the food in their smocks. But they could not linger as the store was filling fast with acrid, drug-laced smoke. A door at the back gave onto a rubbish-strewn alley, which gave in its turn onto another. They wound through three more before they staggered out onto a wider thorough-fare. There was less smoke there, and they paused to breathe deeper, jostled by a vast crowd of people trudging north, the numbers making progress slow. All had their arms filled with possessions, or stacked on a variety of vehicles before them.

'Where you goin'?'

The man Jenny stopped was pushing a cart laden with expensive-looking rugs, a small dog balanced atop them. He put it down for a moment and straightened with a groan, a hand to his back. 'The Guildhall,' he replied. 'It's stone, so will not burn. My wares will be safe there.'

He bent, lifted the cart once more and moved off. 'He won't listen,' said a woman following, holding a basket on her head, a large sack in her other hand. 'Only safe place is beyond the walls on Moorfields. Stone will bloody burn but grass won't.'

'My family,' gasped Joan, and ran away west.

Jenny turned to Sarah, who'd leant against a wall. 'What do you reckon?' she said.

Sarah had taken off her shawl and was fashioning it into a sling. She took a deep breath. 'Stone sounds good to me. The Guildhall's close, is it not?'

'Maybe a quarter mile that way?'

'Then let us go.' She reached and took her son, over Jenny's protests. 'Nay, I'll take him,' she said, slipping him into the sling, hoisting him carefully over her back. 'I warrant I'll get us both there if we don't take it too fast.'

'No danger of that,' replied Jenny.

They stepped into the slow-moving tide of people, heading north, their backs to the flames. In his sling, Sarah's nameless son began once more to cry.

Trinity churchyard. 5 p.m.

'Heave! Two three! Ho! Two three! Heave! Two three! Ho! Two three! And . . . *Heave!*'

With his mighty shout on the last word, Pitman and every man on the fire pole's ropes gave one last great pull. ''Ware there!' shouted their watcher and as one the men dropped the pole and ran. It had been solidly built, the merchant's house on the shoulder of Trinity churchyard, but it toppled now as all the others had done, the front wall falling out, the others collapsing in, beams, joists and roof tiles tumbling down, dust rising up. 'Wait!' commanded Pitman, as the youngest and most eager of the St Mary's watch, Tom Walker, took a step back, the word and the hand on his shoulder restraining him. The brick chimney, standing proud of the ruin, looked as if it might stay; some did, he knew. Indeed, across the city they were often all that survived destruction. A great swathe of London was already a wilderness of chimneys and church steeples, like fingers thrust up and appealing to a vengeful God.

He was right to wait. The chimney leaned, swayed and fell. Its crest hit the ground a tall man's length before him, and one brick detached and rolled onto his foot. He kicked it away. 'Another!' he called and the watch of the parish of St Mary-le-Bow moved onto the next house.

He was proud of his constables. The twenty he'd managed to rally had remained with him and they'd worked hard through the afternoon. He knew that many parishes around could not boast such fellows. Too many were looking out for themselves, gathering what little they could carry and fleeing before the ever-encroaching flames. But a short speech had convinced his men. 'We fight it there,' he'd said, in their own churchyard, 'or we fight it here.'

No man wanted to witness the devastation they'd seen in the riverside parishes in their own. They'd come, they'd stayed, they'd fought and now they followed him to the next house. His plan was to pull down all the houses along the east–west line of Trinity Lane. He'd like to have cleared the rubble that remained, for each ruin resembled a well-stacked hearth. But his men could not haul it all away and he had no horses, for these were all hired and in traces, being used to remove the victims' goods. At least, though, he could starve the fire of structures filled with air, for these went up in moments. The roads to the north had more stone houses and would be slower to burn. Any delay could save at least a part of the city. *Until the winds drops*, he thought, looking up. *For I fear that's the only thing that truly will.*

It showed no sign of it. A different world existed thirty feet above the cobbles. More like a sea, with objects caught in eddies and tides – a fire sea, for everything above glowed or burned outright. Papers, wood shingles, cloth bags, all swooped like birds among thousands of smaller sparks, riding the currents until they fell. One cinder landed even now on Pitman's cheek and he slapped at it to put it out. They were all forever slapping – their faces, their hair, their clothes. Each one of them had burns where they'd felt the heat too late; each one had patches of hair singed away.

As they halted before the next house, another three-storey one, large and prosperous, Pitman looked at the men gathered both sides of him. They were all blackened, head to toe, covered in soot, eyes peeping out white in what could almost be a blacka-moor's face. For there was yet another world above the fiery sea, made up of roiling clouds formed from the thousands of smoke columns that spiralled from all the points that burned, shedding soot like rain, covering everything. Yet where the men were not black they were yellow, from strange things that had burnt, as if some great creature had voided the contents of its guts.

He faced front again. 'Has it rings, Master Walker?' he called, and the youth, always the keenest at each beginning, turned from the front wall.

'It do, sir,' replied the youth, squinting up into the eaves from near the front door.

'Good lad.' It made it much easier, to grab rings that house-holders were meant to install for this eventuality and often didn't. Otherwise they'd have to snag the ridge-beam and that was some-times hard to get a grip on. 'Hook 'em,' he ordered the men beside him, ten to a pole, 'then we'll haul away.'

'You will not!' The man who bellowed this had flung open his front door. Now he roughly grabbed young Walker and shoved him down his front steps. 'You will not tear down my house. By what right do you think you may?'

Pitman stepped forward. 'By right of necessity, sir. Slow the fire here and –'

'I'll take my chances with the fire. God may preserve me and mine as it has others, for I am a righteous man.' He took another step down and flapped a hand at them. 'Move on, I say.'

'I am commanded –'

'By whom, ye rogue?'

'By Lord Craven, who is commanded directly by His Majesty –'

The man was on his front path now. He looked up and down the street. 'I don't see 'em,' he said. 'If the king himself comes and asks me I may consider it. Until then,' he drew himself up, 'I am king here!'

Pitman was about to give him one minute to clear his house, and damn his eyes, when Walker, who'd come to stand beside him, tugged his arm. 'Look,' he said, jerking his head up.

Pitman did, and immediately looked down again. 'Well, Your Majesty, you are about to sit a fiery throne.' He pointed. 'Righteous you may be but God has not spared you.'

The man spun about, looked up and cried out. A patch on his roof was aflame. It was the danger, Pitman knew. That despite all his efforts a burning cinder – or a pigeon – could jump twenty houses and set the twenty-first alight.

The householder turned back, his voice and attitude quite changed. 'Help me put it out, fellows. I'll pay you most generously.'

'Oh, we'll help you,' replied Pitman. 'We'll give you two minutes.' Then he turned to his men and shouted, 'Hook 'em!'

As the constables obeyed, the man ran back into his house and came out again shortly after with three women – his wife and servants – and some children. Clutching the little they could carry, all weeping, they ran away down the street.

Even in the short time he'd allowed, the roof had been near engulfed in flaming red. It was hotter near the front wall, and tar was beginning to drip down upon him, but Pitman stayed there shouting directions until both rings were engaged. Then he ran back and took up rope.

'Heave! Two three! Ho! Two three! Heave! Two three! Ho! Two three! And . . . *Heave!*'

They flew backwards – the front wall fell out, the flaming roof collapsed and the side and back walls tumbled in with a roar, offset by the higher-pitched crack of shattering windows. They dragged the poles from the rubble, then slapped at themselves and each other, extinguishing the sparks that had flown out in the abolition. 'Poles, boys,' he said. 'Next one.'

They worked on, even as it grew dark – if a city lit by such a conflagration and bright as a summer's noonday could be said to darken. House after house fell in dust and rubble, while others took spark and burned. Only when they reached the junction where Bread Street ran north did Pitman allow rest – and that because Lord Craven, assigned to command the fire post in this area of the city, arrived with reinforcements and, to the delight of all, bread and ale.

Pitman slumped on the ground, gulping both down, turning his head in a slow circle, trying to reckon the destruction, finding it almost impossible. Eastwards, the great arch of flame had passed far beyond where a dying pigeon may have set fire to St Laurence Pountney, whose steeple stood like a lit beacon amidst a ruined land. Over that side of London, the fire appeared to have pushed much further north than where he sat – for no doubt nearer him it had found too much to feed on among the wharves and warehouses upon the riverbank, with their stocks of combustibles – hay, coal, timber, casks of food and liquor – all savouring the air he breathed. He looked south and west to the riverside and saw that the looming bastion of Baynard's Castle was glowing, like a log about to blaze. Closer still, he could feel the heat building upon his face. The beast – he had begun to think of it as one entire living, ravenous creature – was drawing nearer. Painters' Hall, less than one hundred yards from him, was burning, and more heat coming, from the houses they'd destroyed to starve the animal.

He raised his eyes to the yellowing heavens. 'Merciful Father,' he said, 'draw off your mighty wind, I pray you.'

Then someone spoke. It was a voice he knew, though he had not heard it in a while. 'So, Pitman, were you so taken with Betterton's Othello that you thought to play the Moor?'

'Captain Coke!' Pitman cried, swivelling around to reach out a hand which Coke seized and hauled the bigger man up and into an embrace. 'By God, man, but I am happy to see thee!'

'That I can tell,' coughed Coke, his face too close to Pitman's vast and smutted chest. 'Jesu, man, I warrant you need a bath.'

'Let me look at you.' He held his friend at the length of his long arms, studying him up and down. 'I warrant you, Captain, that if I am dirty you are – hurt.' He peered closer. 'I would say you've been burned already, were these wounds not close to healed.'

'I was in a fire. Not this one. In battle.' His eyes darkened. 'Can you spare a sip of that ale?'

'Aye, man. Drink and tell me all.' As Coke swigged, he continued, 'Start with the end, how did you find me?'

'Josiah. It was the devil's own job getting to your house through London. Even though the west of the city has no flames, the streets are filled with those fleeing them, those marching to fight them.' He handed the mug back. 'Most of the streets are blocked by soldiers, those that are not choked with refuge-seekers. I had to dodge and duck about and it is not a part of the town I know well. I came to your house and your son told me you were with the watch, making a stand near here.'

'Where was Bettina?'

'He said she had gone to help some who were burned. I did not stay to enquire more, but came on straight.'

'You did not see the babe?'

'She is delivered?'

'A healthy boy.'

Coke reached a hand and shook Pitman's. 'I wish you well of him. But that brings me to the point, man,' he swallowed. 'Where is Sarah? Is she delivered too?' Pitman sighed, and Coke started, seizing the other's arms. 'Nay, tell me straight. Does she live?'

'She does.' He hesitated. 'Though she is not well.'

'Has she had the baby? Where is she?' Coke's voice rose. 'I must go to her straight.'

'I will take you to her.' Pitman looked over the captain's head. Lord Craven was on horseback, sending messengers off, directing the men he'd brought. It looked like another bout of house-pulling was imminent. 'My lord,' he called, 'may I take a brief absence?'

His Lordship looked down and smiled. 'Pitman, isn't it? The duke told me of you,' he replied. 'I know that you and your watch have been most diligent. But you look exhausted, and these whom I have brought are fresh.' He waved at a group of men, a mix of soldiers and citizens forming to his left. 'Rest a while, return when you are able. Would one-tenth of London's men showed your appetite for this fight.'

'I am grateful, my lord.' Pitman turned to his constables. 'Back to the parish, lads. Eat, drink, sleep if you can. Rally again when the Bow Bells sound midnight.' As they rose, picked up their equipment and began to head up Bread Street – near empty now, for all those who lived around had already fled – he took Coke's arm. 'Come, sir, and we will seek Mrs Chalker – Coke! Damn me, will I never get that right?' He shook his head. 'We shall find her at the Poultry Compter.'

Coke stopped. 'The debtors' prison? Why?'

'For she is a debtor. You both are. Come.'

They walked, and the dirty story was swiftly told. 'Oh, I am a fool. A fool!' cried Coke, striking his forehead. 'Why did I think to buy us a house?'

'You thought to put a roof over wife and child. It was a worthy aim. You could not know that you were buying it from those who hated you.'

'The Saints, eh?' He ground his teeth. 'I will pay them for this.'

'I hope you will get the chance.' Pitman looked around. 'If the apocalypse they have prayed for has not come.'

'You think they are behind this?'

'Its genesis? No. I saw how it began, at Farriner's bakeshop. But its continuation?' He shrugged. 'How they will love this. It speaks to all their prophecies. And it would surprise me not at all if they are doing the opposite of us – hastening, not trying to halt, the destruction.' They'd reached Bow Lane, and St Mary's steeple was above them. 'My house. Let us see if Bettina's returned.' He raised a hand against the captain's protest. 'I must see that my family are well, Captain. And preparing,' he glanced back the way they'd come, where the smoke spiralled high, 'for I fear we will be on the move this night. Wait here, or come, as you will. I will be but moments.'

Coke stamped up the cobbles to Cheapside and out to the middle of the widest avenue in the city. The sight from there nearly had him running, Pitman or no. For the vast dancing crown of flame burned brightest to the east. It had swallowed the Exchange and beyond. Only his uncertainty as to the whereabouts of the Compter kept him shuffling there.

Pitman was indeed not long – and he did not come alone. 'Dickon, you are well,' Coke cried, as the youth ran into his arms.

'Well, enough, Cap'n. Though hot. D-devilishly hot.' He swung out of Coke's embrace. 'Though she was not at Sheere Lane, Sarah.'

'I know. We go for her now. You wait here.'

'Oh no, Cap'n.' Dickon drew himself up. 'I come.'

The gleam in his eye told Coke that this time there would be no arguing. 'Come then,' he growled, setting off at pace, Dickon running beside.

Pitman kept up, though his walk was more of a lurch, propelled by swung foot and stick. 'Can you not tell me now, man, the reason for your burns?'

'Later,' replied Coke, striding on.

Dickon told a little, though his tale emphasised monkeys and leaping about rigging more than burning decks and broadsides.

Pitman learned enough to whistle and shake his head. 'You are a fortunate man, Captain,' he said.

'That we shall see. Which way?'

'Straight.' He chewed his lip. 'I did not think it would have reached so far so quickly.'

Just past the ruins of the Masons' Hall, Cheapside gave onto Poultry. All the destroyed buildings still smoked, and little fires burned in every one. But the devastation had passed over and most that flame could consume it already had. The monster had moved north, seeking better food.

'Here.' Pitman halted before the tumbled-down spars and charred remnants of a tavern. Part of King Charles's face peered up from the ruin, the eyes and crown alone, the rest of the sign burned away.

'Where?' Coke let his arms rise and fall.

'This is – was – the alley that led to the Compter.' Pitman pointed along a tangle of devastation. 'At the top there lay the prison. Come,' he put a restraining hand on Coke who had placed a foot on a blackened joist, 'there may be an easier way around.'

They walked back to Old Jewry, the wider avenue affording slightly easier passage. All the wooden-framed houses between them and the alley had been levelled – if such a rough sea of burnt wood could be called level. Only one structure, made of stone, stood proud of the carnage. 'That's the Compter's storeroom,' Pitman said. 'I conversed with Sarah in it not a month since.'

They picked their way across, their feet burning on the heated wood. The room was only a shell, its walls standing but its roof fallen in and windows melted.

Coke sank down. There'd been some crazy hope in him that Sarah might be where last she was seen. Now, in the ruins of a prison, he began to weep. 'What did she do here, Sarah? How did she live?'

Dickon stepped close, hovering a hand over his guardian's shoulder, finally letting it drop. Pitman looked where the Knight's side had stood. Where he had come into a room and seen Sarah lying on a table between two men. It was nothing a husband ever need have in his mind's eye. 'She *lived*,' he said fiercely, 'for herself and for the soul she carried. I warrant she lives still. Look, Captain, there are no bodies here. We'd see what's left of 'em, if there were. Trust me, for I've seen plenty. They got out before this place went up.'

'But where to?' Coke wiped his nose. 'Would they have been moved to another prison?'

'Mayhap. But the rats who ran this place would have put their own safety before their wards. She may be both safe and free.'

'And with child? How close was she to her time?'

Pitman sucked in air. 'Bettina says as close as she herself.'

'So she could be fleeing with a babe in arms?' He rose. 'I will seek until I find them.'

'Captain,' Pitman stepped nearer, 'I would help but I fear the flames will overtake even my home soon and I must get my flock to safer ground.'

'Is there any?'

'Aye. The first place you should look: Moorfields. It's open ground, where nothing can burn. Most of the city has fled there.'

'Moorfields? Where we lay in a plague pit, you and I?'

'Yes.' A vision of their escape from Newgate prison the year before disguised as plague victims, of lying among the truly dead and rotting, made him shudder again. 'Yet if we can be resurrected, so can your loves. Good fortune.'

'And you.' Coke took a step away, Dickon following, then

halted. 'I have survived so much to get here. I will find her.' He nodded. 'But if I do, that does not stop the evil that may be abroad in the town. I made a promise to the king to return to fight it. Shall we join again in partnership, Pitman? Thief-taker and thief united to the thwarting of our old foes, the Fifth Monarchy men?'

'We shall. So we will need a rendezvous.' Pitman narrowed his eyes. 'I cannot think that any fire will reach as far as St Paul's and even if it does, God and man will work its utmost to halt it there. Let us meet in its churchyard, if we are able, on the morrow at this same time.'

Coke stretched out a hand. 'A deal made.'

Pitman took his hand and held it. Dickon stepped back and laid one of his on top of those joined. Then, with a nod, they parted.

Blackfriars. Midnight

As he pushed his way back into the city across the Fleet Bridge, through the fleeing hordes, Simeon Critchollow was smiling. 'It is all according to your plan, Lord,' he murmured, feeling the heat as if he was before a bonfire on a Sabbath night. London is the bonfire, he thought, and the Sabbath gives way to Christ's imminent return.

Beside him, Daniel was silent. He'd complained when his master had ordered him to leave their good work in the parishes – rousing the godly, spreading word and flame – for the cause of worldly goods. 'What will puppets matter in the New Jerusalem?' he'd muttered, even as he lifted the bulky wooden boxes and carried them down the stairs.

Simeon had no need to answer: his word was law. But as the fire had drawn ever nearer their lodgings in Carter Lane, the thought of Punchinello and his crew turned to ashes irked him. Though the Saints foresaw a world of the righteous, they could only see some of what that world would contain. King Jesus, returned in the flesh to judge them, would resolve it all. Was it not possible that he would decree a place for every man's skills? For the shepherd, the smith, the tanner? The puppeteer?

His companions were safe now, at a brother's house beyond the Fleet — and he was free to continue the good work. Across the narrow bridge, they entered straight into the narrow wynds of the liberty of Blackfriars, making their way through the ever-present smoke to the Devil's Tavern, rendezvous for more mischief. It was full — from the squalid tenements the populace had come to ransack the inn's cellars. As venial a mob as ever came out of those sinful streets, they were fuel for the Saints' fire.

A renowned liberty slattern was up on a table haranguing the crowd. 'It's the fucking Dutch what done it!' Mad Moll yelled. 'Fifty thousand Hogens landed at Tilbury yester'morn and they fired the Tower.' A great yell rose at this, so she screamed louder. 'They've come to take our freedom. And they're being helped by all those they sent afore, who've taken all our jobs. The weavers, the brewers —'

'The whores!' someone shouted, to huge laughter.

'Aye, the whores too!' rejoined Moll. 'All poxed, they infect our brave boys.'

'Aye,' cried many there, the signs of their own poxing clear in rotted noses and scragged lips.

Many voices rose. Simeon spotted Brothers Tremlett and the huge brewer, Hopkinson, across the room and weaved his way through to join them. 'We needed to do little,' the builder said, inverting his tankard from which only drops ran. 'They've drunk all the beer.'

'This heat will only add to their thirst. And I saw something outside to slake it.' Simeon leaned into Tremlett and whispered. The builder nodded, picked up a lit lantern and went out of the tavern's rear door.

Simeon stood back, listening to the mob's growing fury. After just a few minutes, Tremlett came back and nodded. He was still carrying the lantern – but its flame no longer burned. The puppeteer pulled Hopkinson's arm, and the big man leaned down to listen. Nodding, he stood straight and lifted his musket – many there carried them – above his head.

'Loyal countrymen,' the brewer bellowed, his deep voice quieting the crowd, 'one of them poxy foreigners is outside, e'en now. Worked 'is evil, 'e 'as, and is trying to make 'is escape. Out upon 'im, I say!'

'Out upon 'im!' cried the crowd in one voice. They streamed from the ravaged alehouse and the Saints followed.

The mob easily spotted Simeon's next target. 'Tinder,' he said, as they caught up.

'You think this is tinder?' laughed Samuel Tremlett. 'You should see what he had stacked up in the back of his shop.'

The wine merchant stood on the box of his wagon, trying to steady the two horses in the traces, who fussed and jerked as the crowd swarmed around them.

Moll mounted a crate. 'Where you from, sweetheart?' she called to the man with the reins.

'I am from 'ere. You know me. I work 'ere all my life.'

From the moment he opened his mouth, and foreign sounds came out, people were growling. ''E's fucking Dutch,' someone cried, others immediately echoing. 'Dutch!'

'*Non!* No, I am French. French!' he shouted.

'Also our enemy!' screamed Moll. ''E's going to burn the town down.'

Simeon tapped Tremlett's arm. The builder stepped forward. 'Moll's right,' he shouted. 'Look at his store. Look what he's left us.'

All looked – at the smoke seeping from gaps in the windows. One man ran forward and opened the door – and more smoke gushed out.

''E's fired it! Frenchie's fired 'is house!'

'No, I did not do this. I save my wine –'

He got no further. 'Wine!' yelled most there, swarming the wagon, its body stuffed with casks. The Frenchman was knocked down and pinioned in a rush of bodies.

''Ang 'im!' Moll screeched above the roar and some heeded her, dragging him off the wagon, while others rolled barrels off it and stoved in their lids, dipping tankards borne from the inn.

'Hey! Hey! There's sugar over 'ere,' a woman shouted from an open door opposite. Immediately, others broke those doors down too, rolling out sugar casks and smashing them open. Men and women seized great handfuls, dropping it into their wine. If they never had the coin to drink the sweet sack beloved of the wealthy, today they tasted something near the same.

Someone had found rope. One man used some to bind the Frenchman, another to plait him a noose. Moll, swaying upon her perch, her lips rimed in sugar, yelled, "Ang 'im! 'Ang 'im.'

"Ang 'im! 'Ang 'im! 'Ang 'im,' screamed the mob. The rope was thrown over a crane spar in front of the Frenchman's warehouse. He was hoisted back onto the wagon, the noose placed around his neck.

"Ang 'im! 'Ang 'im! 'Ang 'im!'

The explosion made everyone duck, cry out. Simeon recognised the savour that had filled his nostrils on a dozen battlefields. And he saw, through the smoke, the men who had discharged the volley. They wore the red coats of the King's Life Guards. Mounted on a horse behind the double rank of twenty was the Duke of York.

'What mischief make you here?' James cried into the shocked silence. 'Who is the man you assault? Seize him.'

A sergeant and two of his men pushed roughly through the crowd, mounted the wagon and grabbed the wine merchant. As they pulled the noose from his neck and turned to take him back, the mob found its voice again.

"E's a Frenchie!'

'They've invaded,' others cried. 'They've burned London.' They began to jostle the soldiers, impeding them as they descended and tried to return to their ranks.

"Ang 'im,' Moll screeched again.

"Ang 'im! 'Ang 'im! 'Ang 'im!'

Another shot sounded now – but from a single gun, a pistol which the duke lowered as he shouted, 'The fire is an accident. No Frenchman, nor Dutchman is involved.' Under the cover of the shot, the soldiers forced their way back to their comrades. 'Help defend your homes from the real enemy – the fire. There's a post set up on Ludgate Hill. Report there. Aid your king. Your country. Your city.' He shoved his pistol back into its saddle holster. 'And let us pass.'

The soldiers began to march, the mob giving way before them, many jeering, some spitting on the weeping Frenchman. Behind him in the doorway, Simeon heard a stirring. He turned. 'Open the back door so we can escape,' whispered Hopkinson, pulling back his hammer to full cock, shouldering his musket, taking his stance, 'for I'm going to kill me a duke.'

'No.' Simeon placed a forearm underneath the barrel and lifted it up. 'He is a capon. We want the cockerel.' With a grunt, the man uncocked and lowered his musket. Simeon continued, 'This is our time, comrades. As the fire spreads – as we aid in its spreading – the king cannot help but return to try and save his capital. We will be waiting. We will have both Stuarts at our barrels' end – and end the Fourth Monarchy with two righteous shots.'

He looked out – James was passing, so close he could have prodded him with a stick. 'And for that glorious moment I would we had Captain Blood.' He turned to the Saints beside him. 'Separate and seek again at his haunts – those that have not burned. Tell him if you find him, to meet –' He tipped back his head. A great bell was tolling nearby, and though its peal was rung backwards, like all in the city during the conflagration, its tone was one every Londoner knew well. 'Tell him to meet tomorrow between six and eight bells in the churchyard of St Paul's.'

The Guildhall crypt. 4th September, 10 a.m.

'I cannot.'

'You must.' Jenny bent again, placing a hand under Sarah's elbow. 'One, two –'

She tried, as she had a half dozen times before. As with each previous attempt, her knees locked for a moment and she thought that she could do it. Again, though, when she tried a step, her legs failed and she sank down, only Jenny's strength preventing her from tumbling onto the crypt floor. 'It is no good,' she said, flopping back. 'I used all my strength getting here. I am not leaving this place.'

'Then we're not, neither,' said Jenny. 'Come, Mary.' She reached to her daughter waiting near the stairs that led up to the main hall. 'We'll bide a while yet till Sar's strong again.'

'You will not!' Though she had no strength in her legs, she had some still in her voice. 'We talked of this. How the fire comes ever closer. How we must leave.'

'Yes, *we* must.'

'I cannot,' Sarah said again. 'Look,' she gestured about her. 'Almost everyone has already gone.'

'Not all. Some still think these stones might resist it.'

'Only those who have no choice.' Sarah nodded at those around them. The crypt had been jammed with hundreds not an hour since. Now there were scarce a dozen souls remaining – and all those were old or crippled. 'Yet the Guildhall stones might hold,' she continued, letting her voice brighten. 'So I am better off here than falling down a hundred yards away in the open.' She reached out, took her friend's hand and squeezed it. 'You have to take the chance. And before the chance is gone.'

Jenny looked down to the box beside Sarah. It was lined with the books, the parchment rolls and the sheaves of paper for which the crypt was a repository. They had made a suitable bed for the babe who slept soundly amongst them. 'And you still think to –?' she said, her lower lip trembling.

'Yes.' Sarah kept her voice steady. You are an actress, she thought, bloody well act. 'I cannot let him take his mother's risk. Not when he has a godmother willing to carry him.'

Still Jenny did not move. 'But you promise me – you'll follow on?'

'As soon as the fire passes by, and I am able.'

'It's still madness outside.' Jenny tipped her head to the roar outside. 'Moorfields is closest but there may be no space there. I've a sister in Hampstead. Lives with the landlord of the Spaniards Inn!'

So far! Sarah thought, the village in the country five miles away. But she did not say anything, only nodded.

'Be safer there. Food too. But I'll not stop there long,' continued Jenny. 'Don't like my sister, we always fall to quarrelling. Was a whore, found God, forever nagging me about the trade.' She sniffed. 'I'll come back, soon as it is safe. But who will take the mite if'n –' She flushed, as red as her hair, 'if'n you don't come for, ah, for a few days, like.'

If I don't come at all, is what she's saying, Sarah thought. Who indeed? She had no family by blood, beyond a few cousins in St Giles, and she would not send her son to that cesspit nor into their care. Yet she did have another family, one she'd chosen. 'Take him to the playhouse. Ask for Mary Sanderson – no, Mary Betterton now. If it's burnt out, they will return – and it is where the captain will seek me, I suspect, if . . . *when* he returns.' Sarah reached and lifted the baby from his cot. He felt so heavy, though she knew that he was not. 'Please. Take him now.'

Jenny did not reply. And in her silence the noises came loud from outside – the crazily pealing bells, the distant cries of 'Hi! Hi! Hi!' that showed that someone at least was still trying to fight the inferno. Above them all they heard the beast-like roar that had filled every citizen's ear since dawn two days before. Flames devouring a city. Getting closer. 'I beg you, Jenny, before I –' She broke off.

'Very well,' her friend said, stooping to snatch up the child, so firmly that he woke. Immediately he began to wail.

'Hush now,' said Sarah, taking the little waving hand in hers. 'Hush.'

Jenny pulled him free, her mouth set in a line, and began to gather what they'd taken from the Compter and the shops near it, and what they'd picked up along the way. It took but moments and too soon she was finished. She turned back, and Sarah could see her tears. She knew she must not yield and join her in them. Not yet. 'Here,' she said, reaching up, and Jenny stooped, bringing the baby's face level with hers. 'Fare thee well,' Sarah whispered, running her fingers down the silken skin of his forehead. 'Remember me.' Then she shoved the child away. 'Go. May God keep you. May God keep you all.'

'Amen.' Jenny crossed herself fervently. Then, slipping the baby into the sling that Sarah had fashioned, setting it upon her back, seizing her one bag and her daughter's hand, she strode to the stairs.

A moment more, Sarah thought, watching her child wriggling in his cloth prison. One moment more.

Yet they did not disappear. Jenny stopped halfway up the stair. 'Have you a name for the mite yet?' she called.

She hadn't, for she'd believed the parting she feared must come would be harder if she had to say his name. Now she knew she was wrong – for nothing could be harder than this. 'William,' she replied, her voice still strong. 'His name is William Coke.'

'William,' echoed Jenny. She nodded and left, leaving Sarah at last able to sink down and weep her fill.

Moorfields. 10.30 a.m.

William Coke woke from a dream of fire, to fire. He jerked suddenly – no gentle waking for him – reaching all around, for whatever was lost to the dream. His hands hit Dickon, with whom he'd been entwined, but the boy just grunted, turned his back and slept on, leaving Coke to rub his eyes clear, allowing him to see – at first not the terrible scene spread out before him upon Moorfields, but the one beyond it, over the city wall.

'Holy Christ, does the whole of London burn now?' he gasped.

'Nearly all. But that occasions no need to take the Lord's name in vain.'

Coke took his gaze from the fire that appeared to reach right up and unite with the smoke clouds it formed across the width of London, and looked on the man who'd spoken – a portly, dog-collared rector, his back against a cart, his arms wrapped about a woman and a girl who slept.

Coke came up onto his knees, his head still wrapped in dream and exhaustion. 'What time is it?' he muttered.

The man pulled out a watch. 'Half past ten o'clock.'

'Ten?' How had he slept? He'd not got through the Moorgate until at least three of the morning, so jammed was its narrow entrance with those that had fled, and what they brought. And he'd not got far into Moorfields before he was overwhelmed by the sight – a sight lit like the middle of the day by the thousand fires that had become one. The area beyond the wall was jammed with refugees, and what little they'd saved. Thousands upon thousands beyond the count, cramming each space, trampling the greensward, heaped up on the paths, crouched under hedges. Animals, from pigs to cats, ran everywhere. He could not remember how he'd found a piece of earth to stand upon, let alone lie on. And then, looking down, he did. For the earth he knelt on was mounded, dry, and the little grass that had grown upon it was torn and scattered.

He was kneeling on a plague pit. Probably not much more than an arm's push through the crumbly earth, hordes of his fellow Londoners lay dead. He could see white traces in the soil of the lime used to dissolve the flesh more quickly. And he remembered coming to the only piece of land near the gate that had not already been colonised. The earliest comers had feared to rest on their relatives. Those who followed had not been so particular; every space was swallowed up now. Besides, thought Coke, perhaps it was easier for me. I lay *in* a plague pit before, after all.

He shook his head hard and stood. How had he allowed himself to sleep when he'd come in search of Sarah? How had he given up on that? Then he remembered – for now, as during the night, hundreds of voices called for their missing ones. His voice had added to the chorus of the lost for just a while, until he was overwhelmed. Dickon had dropped down, curled up, too exhausted to move further. They had not slept two hours in their ride from Dover. They had not slept at all since reaching the devastated city the previous dawn. Ah, now he remembered. He'd thought he could lie down for a minute, ten perhaps, no more. And he'd woken five hours later.

'Dickon? Wake! We must go. Dickon!'

He nudged him with his toe. The boy tried to curl up into himself for a moment, grumbling. Then he sat up. His eyes, taking in the scene, widened. 'But — where?'

Where indeed? Coke looked north, over the rough camp Moorfields had become, the vast crowd roughly camped upon it. Again he heard the innumerable cries. 'Water, for the love of God, water!' 'John? John Woodbury? Has any seen him? 'Agnes?' 'Mary? My Mary?' 'Peter?' The thought of Sarah there somewhere made him take a breath, to add his voice again. But he withheld it. It would do no good. And he realised that if Sarah was out here somewhere — or upon Finsbury Fields, or Smithfield, east or west, which rumour had told him were also filled — at least she was safe enough. But if she was not . . .

'Listen, lad,' he said, crouching down. 'You carry on the search here. Keep calling.'

'Me? Why?' The boy sat up. 'Where will you be to?'

Coke nodded towards the great arch of flame. 'There.'

'No, C-cap'n,' Dickon replied, standing too, brushing earth off his clothes. 'I come with you.'

'I forbid it. The danger —'

'We face it together.' Dickon set his shoulders, looked his guardian straight in the eye. 'I'll not be left.' Then a grin transformed his grimness. 'Don't worry, Cap'n,' he laughed. 'No monkey to chase in there!'

'You rascal!' Coke gave the boy's head a gentle slap. 'Come, then.'

It was but a short walk to Moorgate; still it took time to weave through the sprawling crowds. But the gate was mobbed on this side by carters trying to get in – Coke had overheard that the price for a cart and labourer had risen to forty pounds, a work-man's wages for a year – as well as the far bigger mob t'other side trying to get out. A harassed corporal and three men were trying to regulate the flow each way to universal abuse. They watched the masses trudge out for close on a quarter-hour. Old men and women were being carried on mattresses; children were borne on backs or shoulders. Disaster had reduced all classes to only one – the homeless – and mixed them entirely. Here an alderman in a beaver coat, a gold chain of office around his neck, walked next to a scabby, one-eyed beggar. There a lady in what must be her favourite, most expensive gown, her hair held in tortoiseshell combs, followed a large, flame-haired woman in the roughest of smocks. She pulled a crying daughter in one hand, held a sack in another and she also, Coke saw when she passed close, had a black-haired baby in a sling upon her back. The child slept, to Coke's envy.

The sight brought him straight back to Sarah – Sarah, so near her time. Past it, perhaps. 'Come,' he said, turning away from the gate. 'There must be a swifter way in.'

They found it, in the lane to the west that ran parallel to the wall. It was called the Postern and led to the small gate of the same name that gave entrance or exit to no more than two abreast.

Because no cart could get through here it was less crowded. Coke pushed up to the soldier controlling the flow who looked his sailor garb up and down and said, 'Off to seek your fortune, shipmate?'

'A wife in there. In labour.'

'Go on then. Good hunting.' The soldier stepped forward, shoving a man back, so that Coke and Dickon could squeeze through – and halt off the road to the side.

But where to hunt, Coke wondered, as he stared at the wall of flame that stretched from east to west and seemed, even as he looked at it, to be advancing towards them. It could be but a few hundred yards off; less in some parts, perhaps. It must have breached Cheapside, the widest, richest avenue in the city. Its width would have given some hope that the fire would halt there, with nothing but cobbles to burn. But the monster had leapt the gap to burn on, seeking easy prey.

It was Dickon who pointed nearer to them. 'Wassat?'

Coke looked. Perhaps two hundred paces away, one of the tallest structures in London stood like a castle in a blackened wasteland. He knew the Guildhall was the very centre of the city's industry, the place where the guilds would meet, discuss and feast. He also knew that it was made of stone, while all around was wood. If there was a place that men might rally to fight it would be there. And, with a sudden lurch of his heart, he realised too that it lay almost directly north of the Poultry Compter. Between the prison and the sanctuary of Moorfields.

'Swiftly now,' he said, and he and Dickon began to run, their faces getting hotter with every step they took, wind-borne cinders catching in their hair and their clothes slapped away as they ran.

Most of the heat was coming from the place they sought. The

Guildhall stood alone in a sea of burnt timbers, for every shop, tavern and chapel that had abutted it was gone. Now it looked like a fire army was sending its hordes to attack, flame sweeping across the paving stones and devouring the marketplace stalls, slapping in waves against the great stone base, crawling up its walls to melt stained glass and push in to devour the wood within.

But he'd been right. Men *were* making a stand here, a double line of them passing leathern buckets from a well that somehow had not run dry, the end man throwing water on the fire at the corner of the building. Beside them, brass syringes were being dipped in tubs, filled and squirted at the flames' base, a gallon at a time gushing forth. Coke could see that they were having some success – at least in this small part. He could also see above their heads the fire pushing into the building at points where men did not fight.

Screams drew his eye. 'There's people trapped in here,' cried a man, his body entirely black, stepping from the western entrance, pointing back and down. 'The crypt is part caved in. Help! Oh, help!'

Though his scarcely healed skin hurt still, and flame tormented every dream since he'd nearly died on a fireship, Coke barely hesitated. He may not be able to save Sarah, but he could save someone. Then, in another part of the inferno of London, perhaps someone would save her.

He knew better than to order Dickon to remain. 'Axes and rope!' he cried, seizing both from the piles that lay about. With his ward at his heels, he joined a troop of men rushing towards the entrance. All shied at the flames lapping around the wooden doorframe. All took a deep breath and plunged in.

The great hall was ablaze in various parts for it was near all wood inside. Timbers fell from the hammer-beam roof, exploding in sparks upon the richly rugged floor, wool crisping and wafting acrid smoke into their faces. All coughed and choked, then Coke saw the man who'd summoned them in, standing at the top of a stone staircase, driving his axe into a wedge of fallen timber there. Coke and others rushed to join him, chopping in their turn. Beams were halved, ropes attached to the pieces and these dragged off. It looked that in moments the entrance would be cleared, the people screaming below freed.

'They fall! Give back! Run!'

Coke looked up through the smoke. Two great statues tottered on flaming plinths, leaning further and further out over them. Gog and Magog, he knew them to be, guardians of the city – forsaking their watch now, plunging down. Grabbing Dickon by the collar, he ran back and threw himself down against a wall, arms over both of them. He heard the statues smash, heard cries of agony and looked up to see the twin monsters shoot sparks up to the dissolving roof. Other cries were still coming from the crypt and he staggered, near blind, through the smoke. Heedless now of the cinders that burned him, he saw that the statues had only narrowed the stair, not closed it off entirely.

'A line here,' he roared, slipping a length of rope around his chest, executing a swift hitch, grateful for his brief seaboard education. 'Make it fast to a pillar,' he said, throwing the one end to Dickon, who'd also learned about knots. 'I'll get all below to follow the rope,' he said, and then, taking a huge breath, he stepped down into the smoke-filled chamber.

At first it was more sound than sight that guided him –

283

coughing, pleading people whose outstretched hands he brushed, seized, clamped to the rope and sent staggering to the stair with a shove. Then some crash further into the crypt and a sudden rush of air blew much of the smoke away, flushing it out as if through a horizontal chimney. Suddenly he could see.

And he saw her.

For just a moment he wondered if the smoke had taken him, or falling timber crushed him — that he was dying and having a dream ere death, a wonderful dream if so — because there was no doubt that it was Sarah — Chalker that was, Coke as she had become — lying with her back against the crypt wall. Her face was wan, her auburn hair blackened with soot; she was wearing some ill-fitting and filthy smock and he had never before seen anyone, anything more beautiful.

The sight halted him, the pure shock of it. And as he stood there, gaping, the rope attached to him being jerked and tugged by those that fled, she looked up and saw him. Wonder and disbelief moved over her face, a mirror to his. And then he had thrown off his rope, leaving it to others behind him, and he was across, pulling her up into his arms, enfolding her in an embrace that dissolved into a kiss. Her lips tasted of soot and smoke and he didn't think he'd ever tasted sweeter.

They broke apart, as more warning cries came. 'How?' she said — all she could say. 'How?'

'Later,' he coughed, as smoke again enveloped them. 'We must go.'

'I —' She sagged against him. 'I can't walk.'

He bent, caught her up and carried her out of the burning crypt, out of the burning building, into the light.

He thought they were the last to leave. Dickon was at his heels, uttering wondering, wordless cries. They kept going until they reached a patch of paving that did not smoke, a wall that somehow still stood. There he set her down and crouched before her, staring, unable to speak, just as she seemed able to do no more than stare at him.

Dickon, though, was never wordless for long. 'We found you, Sarah,' he cried, as he leapt around them both, 'we d-did, we did.' He let forth a huge yelp of joy, jumped, landed, then looked at her. 'Have you any nuts for me?' he asked, quite solemnly.

Sarah laughed. She could not help it and she could not remember when last she had. 'Marry, but I do,' she said, and reached into the pocket of her smock. With a cry of joy, Dickon ripped open the little cloth bag and began immediately to crunch the hazelnuts within.

With his silence they both found some words.

'How —?'

'Where —?'

Coke reached out, seizing her hand. 'The baby,' he said, looking at her distended belly beneath her smock.

She laid her hand upon it. 'Gone. This is just —'

'Oh.' His face sagged. 'Oh, my love, I am so sorry.'

'No, no!' She clasped his hand to her. 'He lives. I gave birth yesterday, in the Compter.'

'He?'

'Aye, William. You have a son.'

'Truly?' His smile gleamed a brief white in the black of his face, then vanished. 'But where —?'

She squeezed his hand and tried to rise. 'We must seek him. A friend carried him away when I could not follow.' She fell back. 'Ay! Give me but a moment. We will go together.'

'Where to?'

'Moorfields.'

He thought back to the crowds, the endless crying of names. 'It would be a miracle to find him there.'

''Twas a miracle you found me.' She tried to rise again and fell back. 'Jesu, mercy!'

'I do not think we could wish for two such miracles in a day,' he said.

'But we must try. We must!' With a huge breath she rose, and got onto her knees. 'There. Let us go!'

She tried to stand and he helped her. But when she wobbled there, he said, 'Sarah, hearken to me. Moorfields is a mob of lost souls twenty thousand strong. More –'

'But still –'

'Did you arrange any rendezvous there?'

'No. Yes! Not there. At the playhouse. Jenny is to bring the babe there if –' she swallowed, 'if I did not find her before.'

'Then it is to the playhouse that we shall go.' He overrode her protests. 'Sarah, my love, you can barely walk. Besides, Moorfields will not yield our child, you have to believe me. And rendezvous must – must, in these times – be kept.' He put a finger to her lips to halt her argument. 'Do you trust this woman who you gave the babe to?'

'I do. Entirely. We have been through . . . much together.'

There was something in the way she said it, the way she looked away. Her ragged smock. Some lines of grey in her hair. 'Oh Sarah, I am so sorry,' he said.

'For what?'

'For . . . everything.' He sighed. 'I should have —' He broke off.

She took his hand again. 'You were cozened, William. Our enemies sought vengeance upon you. Upon both of us.'

'And I vow I will have mine on them,' he said. 'As I vow I will make it up to you.'

'I will hold you to that.' She smiled. 'Beginning with the wedding night you owe me.' She gripped him tighter. 'Now, come. Help me. I do not think we can stay here.'

Behind them, the Guildhall was aglow, flames shooting from its every aperture and through its roof, the building lit from within, for its walls still stood. And men were still at it, in lines with buckets, and squirting syringes.

He helped her, but the going was slow. Yet they'd not gone more than twenty paces before Dickon gave a cry and skipped away through the smouldering ashes of what had been the yard of a church — and returned rolling a two-wheeled cart. 'Look!' he cried, turning the vehicle on one rim, spinning the other wheel. 'Will it do, Cap'n?'

'Bravo, lad. It will do very well.' He looked at Sarah in his arms. 'Your coach, milady.'

They returned the way they'd come. Arms of fire stretched out either side of them and would, ere long, link up to enfold what remained. But for a short time there was passage through them, back to the postern. The crowd had thinned, and the soldier soon greeted them with a delighted 'Found her then?' With his help, they put the cart on its side and squeezed it through.

London beyond the wall was as yet unburned, though the smoke was still thick and all could see that huge approaching arc of fire and hear the roar of its destroying power. Forewarned, constables of the parishes they passed through were mustered with equipment, and there were many cries of 'Hi! Hi! Hi!' with men dashing past to attend a roof that a blown spark had reached. They walked in near silence, as if both understood that there was too much to say and that now was not the time to say it. Dickon, though, was as unrestrained as ever and from his chirpings that alighted on various things like a butterfly upon a bed of mixed flowers Sarah was able to gain at least some of their tale.

'Oh, Captain!' was all she said, when the talk passed on to fireships, and the role of monkeys upon them.

Though the streets were busy, there was not the same crowd of refugees that had gone straight north. In an hour's push, they arrived at the Duke's Playhouse.

'Mrs Chalker!' cried Thomas Betterton when he saw her, then struck his forehead. 'Ah! I apologise, sir. Mrs *Coke*. I should know that, since I gave away the bride. Delighted to see you both, uh, well.'

He was studying the arrivals, all three of them blackened head to toe with soot, his nose wrinkling. 'You have obviously emerged from the inferno. Praise the heavens for your deliverance. What's the news? I hear the king and our patron the duke are in the forefront of the fray –'

'News can wait, Tom,' said his wife Mary, elbowing him aside to reach Sarah. 'My dear, come,' she continued, taking Sarah's arm. 'We've water to wash with, and ale to drink. Food, too. You must be parched, and starved, all of you.'

'Oh indeed. We've opened the playhouse doors to so many old

actors.' It was not his best delivered line, if Betterton intended to keep his disdain from it, continuing, 'We've quite the mob of 'em in the dressing rooms. Pray, join them.'

It was indeed a scene more like a party than a funeral, with many sat about, some as soot-ridden as the newcomers. Sarah was immediately swept up, cleaned up, her smock exchanged for one of her old costumes. Coke and Dickon were offered new clothes too, though he declined for both of them, taking only a pair of better boots apiece, and contented himself with sponging down what he had. He was not concerned about going back into the city wet. It was a furnace and he would be dry, and dirty again, in minutes.

For go back I must, he thought, snagging a satchel and, between bites and gulps, filling it with some crusts, nuts, cheese and two bottles of ale. The idea of rising from the chair he'd sunk into and venturing again into that hell was daunting. But he knew he had no choice.

'But why?' Sarah said when he came to tell her. The actresses who'd been fussing around withdrew at the anguish in her voice.

'I made two promises. Betterton reminded me of one – to my king, who is indeed out there striving to save the city, to halt the fire within the walls. For if we do not,' he shrugged, 'it could rage past and destroy Whitehall and Westminster – here. All of London, within and without the walls, will be consumed. I would not see that.'

She stared at him, then nodded. 'And the second promise?'

'Was to Pitman. Aye, I found him in the heart of the fight and 'twas he who told me of –' he faltered, 'of you, and your travails. He guided me to the burnt-out Compter, then returned for his own family, his parish. I promised I would go back to help him.' He took both her hands. 'Listen to this, Sarah. He believes our enemies, those who practised so upon us, are about their mischief again out there.'

'The Saints burned down the city?'

'Not that, perhaps. But all their prophecies point to an apocalypse. One that is foretold to happen now, this year, even these days.' He nodded to the world outside, to the roar of devastation, distant yet distinct. 'I do not know if this *is* the apocalypse – but it will certainly do until the real one arrives.'

She laughed, as he hoped she would, and he rose on that, still holding her hands. She hugged them hard. 'You will not – not take too many risks?'

'I?' He smiled.

She did not. Instead she hugged him fiercely. 'I mean it, Captain. I have lost enough. I will not lose you.'

'You will not. Trust me.'

'I do.'

They kissed, he bowed, then made for the door. Dickon leapt up there. 'Are we off, Cap'n?' he asked, his mouth crammed with food.

'I am. You must stay here, safe.'

'Ha!' Dickon obviously thought that was the funniest thing in the world for he sprayed bread and cheese onto his captain's breeches.

'Come then,' Coke sighed, leading the way. A thought came when he passed Thomas Betterton. 'Sir,' he said, 'do you possess a brace of pistols?'

'I do.'

'May I borrow 'em?' He saw the man hesitate. 'You know I am the king's man. His Majesty asked me to return in arms.'

'Oh, indeed.' The player went and returned with a box – and a sword. 'Thought you might need this too.'

'I am grateful, sir,' Coke replied, buckling it on, 'for I have a feeling that I will.'

St Paul's Cathedral. 6 p.m.

How is it still there? marvelled the man so many sought, the man of blood. It looks more like a carrack in a black sea than a cathedral.

The flames had devoured almost every structure around it. A few discoloured stones remained; a wall here, a steeple there, a brick doorway giving entrance only to ruin. The fire had moved on, leapt the Fleet river two hours since, mocking the puny efforts to halt it there. Now it raged in districts beyond the ditch, above and below Fleet Street, ravaging both foul Alsatia and the fine lawyers' chambers of the King's Bench with indiscriminate joy. Yet somehow it had bypassed the cathedral.

Until now. Even as Captain Blood watched, he saw yet another flame under one of the boards that covered the much-holed roof. Though men were up there, precariously perched, drawing up buckets on ropes from below and hurling water as fast as they were able, he could see their efforts would be futile.

'Old St Paul's is burning down,' he sang to a popular tune about a different London landmark, adding in speech, 'and a good riddance to it.'

It was not so much that it was ugly, its great square and spire-less tower and multiple patchings giving it the aspect of a bunched and mottled toad. He had visited cathedrals in Europe, in order to study the houses of his enemy, the Antichrist, the Pope. Most, he would grudgingly admit, had at least some grandeur, some beauty about them. St Paul's had none. But since it was also the centre of the Anglican faith he despised, the sooner it was reduced to ash the better.

The stone tower he occupied had survived the devastation of its church, St Austin's, its blackened stone steps allowing him to mount to its bell tower, even though the bell itself had melted and covered his perch in lead, only now beginning to harden again. It still gave him the view, not only of the cathedral's unfolding destruction, but the churchyard to the north and the one house that still stood there. Where his brother Saints would even now be gathering, according to the youth, Daniel, he'd encountered.

He stared at it, marvelling how some confluence of wind, some diligence of man, some indulgence of God had left the house standing. Before it, men scurried, shouting, and running at the cathedral with buckets, ropes and axes.

Not long now, he thought, picking up the weapon beside him, putting the hog-back stock to his shoulder, lining the front and rear sights up on a man standing just in front of the house, his hands on his head. 'Pff!' Blood breathed out on the sound. It was as if the man felt something, so suddenly did he drop his hands and run.

Carefully he put the gun beside him, and took out and placed his monocle to his eye, the better to study the weapon's breech and the letters engraved on steel upon it. One Christian Reich had made it in Westphalia and it was the best thing Blood had brought back from Holland. It was a Müller-Büchse, a type of wheel-lock — far better than a flintlock, for it so rarely misfired. Best of all, it had a rifled barrel. A hunter's gun, it hardly threw at all, unlike a smooth-bored musket. He would not have attempted what he must do with one of those. With this superb tool, he knew he could make the shot. One hundred and fifty yards perhaps, with the wind following straight and not swerving the ball at all? He'd knocked a seagull off a roof in Harwich at two hundred yards in a crosswind with this weapon, just for the practice. But I am not hunting seagulls today, he thought, and licked his lips.

There was a stirring near the churchyard's entrance. A larger group of men was pushing in, armed with tools to fight the fire, several dragging a sled on which a large brass squirt was fixed. These newcomers looked organised, determined. Not surprising, perhaps, since they were in the presence of their king.

Charles, his brother mounted beside him, rode into St Paul's churchyard. Dropping the monocle into a pocket, Blood picked up the gun, laid it in front of him, resting it on the lead-covered stone before him, and lined up the sights.

'Pff,' he breathed.

St Paul's Cathedral. 6 p.m.

'He told me he would be here,' Daniel said, squirming in Simeon's grip. 'He promised.'

'And you told him the house on the north side? As I instructed you.'

'Yes. Yes!' Daniel wriggled out of the grip, rubbing his arm.

'Hmm. He'd best come soon. For I fear the king will. And Captain Blood would not want to miss that.'

Looking through glass that was bowed but not melted, Simeon peered again from the one house standing on Paternoster Row, out into St Paul's churchyard. As soon as he'd seen it, he'd known that God had preserved it especially for his Saints – for this moment to come. It was the perfect place to view the destruction of the cathedral – as the king and his brother must realise. Rumour had put Charles at every scene of greatest destruction during the previous three days: Baynard's Castle, the conflagration of the Exchange, the gutting of the Guildhall. He would surely come as the very centre of religion in his kingdom burned. He would try in vain to stop it. He would stand before them here.

Yet, despite all the scurrying before it, not one person had tried to enter the house. The roof had been scorched, its beams charred. People had learned that the inferno could pass by, breathe on a house merely, and then move on. But within hours the structure would still tumble into a smoking ruin. He would not have taken shelter here had he not had this purpose. Had he not been sure that King Jesus kept this house for his Saints.

He looked at the others now. Hopkinson was rechecking the muskets. He had been the champion marksman of the regiment. A hunter still, he'd lost none of his skills. Tremlett, if less accurate, had always been steady under fire. He had vouchsafed that, when the two of them aimed for the king, he would shoot the Duke of York. At twenty paces, how could any of them miss?

Daniel, who'd come to peer through the window, suddenly cried out. 'There! There! It burns.'

They all looked out. The cathedral roof was indeed fully alight now, the fire spreading fast. But under the growing roar, Simeon heard something else. 'It is time, brothers,' Simeon said, stepping away. 'As we used to say in the regiment: "Raise your weapon to the enemy and your voices to God."' He went and picked up his musket, as did the brewer and the builder. 'Our Father,' he began, and the others joined in, 'who art in heaven . . .'

The noise he'd heard was growing outside. Not only the panicked shouts of those trying to stop the inevitable – but the cheers for someone approaching, someone special. But he did not stop the chant. There was time enough to finish the prayer and kill a king.

St Paul's Cathedral. 6 p.m.

'Will they save it?' asked Coke, staring up at the roof of St Paul's and the fast-spreading flames.

'No,' replied Pitman, lowering the flask, the last of the beer now drunk. 'I have seen enough these last days to know the way of it.' He reached out a hand, and Coke pulled him up. On his feet, the big man bent and rubbed at his leg. It had begun to plague him mightily, for he had been pushing it too hard. 'And do not think of getting too close to it. When my own parish church of St Mary's caught, the lead near took my scalp in its melting.' He touched the oozing burn on the top of his head, then peered to the corner where the churchyard joined the end of Cheapside and what had been Paternoster Row. Bizarrely, one house still stood there, curtains in its windows, no less.

'Who are these?' Coke said, pointing. Men were marching around the corner, soldiers in the main. Following behind them was King Charles II.

'Come, Captain,' said Pitman, setting out. 'It's time you kept your promise to your king.'

'I'd rather sleep,' said Coke, following him and pulling Dickon up, who was transfixed by the burning cathedral. 'Still, if there's any man who has the power to fight this fire, it is probably he.'

They were halfway to the king when the explosions came: the first above and behind them, the second an instant later. There'd been explosions all day, with men using barrels of gunpowder to hasten the destruction of houses by blowing them up. This was not like that. This was a gunshot and first it had the pair ducking, then running, to the crowd ahead and the men mounted within it.

Simeon gave the commands, as he had when he'd been sergeant to the regiment.

'Cock,' he said, though he did not roar it as he had on battlefields. 'Aim.'

The window frame exploded inwards. They cried out, all except Hopkinson, now unable to, lead ball having taken away his face. He was flung back, his own gun firing as he fell, his bullet going high as if he aimed at the roof of flaming St Paul's. Simeon and Tremlett were too shocked to shoot, and immediately blinded by gunsmoke. Daniel, holding the back door open for a speedy retreat, screamed, 'Hurry!' Both men dropped their muskets and ran out past him.

'Where?' yelled Tremlett.

Simeon did not answer, only ran. He had seen what they'd done to Colonel Rathbone and other martyrs at Tyburn tree. He would outpace that if he could. Yet even as they reached Amen Corner, and felt the heat on their faces from Newgate prison still aflame, he turned and saw that they were pursued. A large man came in a strange, quick lurch, another tall man beside him.

'Pitman and Coke – the devils!' he hissed. 'Faster.'

'They make for the bridge!'

The paths along the Fleet Ditch were always a jumble – of ropes for the tied-up wherries and skiffs; of barrels, broken crates, spars; and of lean-to shelters for those who could not even afford tuppence for a floor in the liberties nearby. Yet it was clearer now than at any time Pitman had passed along it, for, like all the detritus-strewn streets of the city, it had been purged by fire. Soot rose in clouds as they ran, their faces turned away from the Fleet prison as they passed it, still raging in flame.

By the time they cleared its end, Coke was about thirty paces in front, Dickon slightly ahead of him, both able to leap the charred timbers and smoking coils Pitman's leg forced him to step over. They were gaining on the three ahead, who were slowing because of the great press at the bridge – a crowd of humanity, wailing and shoving in their attempts to cross, driven by terror and by the great heat, coming from all around but especially from the cathedral fully aflame now on the hill above them.

As the three fugitives drew near, there came a huge explosion. Pitman, at the end of the prison yard, looked up in time to see fireballs bursting from St Paul's. One came hurtling down to pass just above his head and smash into a wherry tied up in the ditch, turning it instantly to flaming kindling. He saw what had caused it, as the boat sank spluttering into the filthy waters, but could scarcely believe it – it was a chunk of building stone, he could even see a mason's mark on its edge. God's house had been transformed into missiles.

Screams from the crowd now scattering before him showed that it had become something else too – a river of lead. 'Jesus save us,' screamed one woman, lifting her skirts above the flood as it were a puddle she wished to cross, screaming more as the molten metal encased her feet. A man snatched her up, shouting in agony in his turn. People broke every way, fleeing the heated stone falling from the sky, the shifting, scalding ground. Flight opened a passage to the bridge where there had been none before, and those they pursued took it, shoving aside any who paused to look back.

Both Coke and Dickon had been slowed by the mob's scattering. Pitman caught up with them and, forcing themselves to enter the glistening metallic pool, they ran with soles burning, leather dissolving, toes crisping, to the bridge, then across it.

Their enemies were still in sight for many of the houses that would have hidden them were smoking ruins now. Certain buildings nearby still stood because of their stone walls – St Bride's church and the huge Bridewell, once a palace, now a prison. Both contained the flames that consumed them from the inside, hot as a smith's furnace. No man could stand near one for long – unless he had to.

Its intensity made them draw up for a moment, their hands

raised in feeble effort against the glare and the heat. 'Where do they make for?' shouted Coke, above the roar that had filled London for days.

Pitman peered, coughing through the swirling smoke, and saw those they pursued again. 'There!'

Coke and Dickon looked. There was one row of buildings still standing. Somehow the shelter given by the twin fortresses of church and prison, some vagary of wind and flame, had preserved them – though it could not be for much longer. As they looked on roofs were catching fire, one by one. Even so, the three ahead vanished between the smoking houses.

'Shall we leave them to God, Captain?'

Coke looked up at the bigger man, then down at Dickon. He did not see how any could survive the maelstrom closing in; while the heat that held him, from the soles of his scalded feet to the crown of his crisped head, made him want nothing more than to flee. But a memory came, a recent one – his first sight of Sarah, waiting to die in a burning crypt, having given up her baby – their baby! The men ahead had put her there. It was not something he could leave to anyone else. Not even to God.

He drew one pistol. 'Nay, I will see this through. You go back, if you will. One of us should. Bettina . . .'

'. . . would never let me hear the end of it if I abandoned you here.' Pitman looked to the pistol. 'Haven't a spare one of those, have ye?'

Coke passed one across, pulled the second from beneath his cloak and drew his sword. Dickon looked at the pair of them, then reached into his boot cuff and pulled out a dagger. 'C'mon then, Cap'n,' he cried, 'into the f-fire again.'

Side by side the three of them entered the lane.

The roar diminished only a jot, the heat too, but in contrast to what they'd come from it was like stepping from midsummer heat into a monastery's cool cloister. They each took the first unscorched breath for an age, felt the relief . . .

Then, in a moment, it was gone with the flash of a gun pan, an explosion of powder which sent a ball so close between the two men that both lurched sideways. Coke kept moving, taking Dickon with him into the shelter of a doorway, Pitman going the opposite way into another. The lane was narrow, the houses' eaves near joined above into a running arch. 'I think we've found the rat's nest,' Pitman shouted. 'Do we let the fire smoke 'em out?'

'And us too?' The respite afforded by the cobbled lane had been brief indeed. Coke could feel the hot wind rising, as the flames neared. 'I've fought in streets before. One should draw their shot –'

He'd no sooner said it than it was acted upon. 'Hi! Hi! Hi!' Dickon shouted, giving the fire-fighters' cry, launching himself from the doorway, rolling onto the cobbles like a tumbler, leaping to his feet, all within the two heartbeats it took Coke to scream his name.

In the time before the three shots came.

The boy straightened up. He did not move for a moment that seemed endless, staring to where the smoke rose from windows, the two men up already and moving towards him.

'Dickon!' Coke yelled again, his voice cracking.

The boy looked up at him as he closed in. 'Missed me, Cap'n,' he grinned, 'just like them Hogens.'

A moment of relief, then all three were running again. Enemies needed time to reload or pick up another gun, time that Coke and

300

Pitman ate in great strides to the door of the house. No other shot came, as they flung themselves each side of the entrance. A swift glance showed Coke a narrow entrance hall hung with gunsmoke, and a stair leading up to where a door now slammed.

'The officer leads?' offered Pitman, with a wave of his muzzle.

Coke took a deep breath, then ducked into the hall, pistol pointing up the stair. ''Tis clear,' he called, and the others followed in. 'There,' said Coke, pointing his gun at the door. Muffled sounds came from behind it.

Pitman cocked an ear. What remained of his eyebrows rose. 'Are they . . . praying?'

One of them was. And loading his pistol even as he testified.

'"And the fourth angel poured out his vial upon the sun; and the power was given unto him to scorch men with fire."'

'Brother Simeon!'

'"And the fifth angel —" No. No! "The *seventh* angel poured out his vial into the air; and there came a great voice out of the temple of heaven, from the throne, saying: It is done."'

'Brother!' Tremlett grabbed his arm. 'The back window. We must flee.'

'No!' Simeon jerked free. 'We do not leave here. We have no need.' With his boot, he poked Daniel who crouched on the floor. 'Cease your weeping, boy. Join me. Both of you. Raise up your voices in gladness.' His eyes shone, in fervour, in reflected fire. 'This is the time foretold. This is the apocalypse. Fire has scorched the world and King Jesus comes.' He threw his arms wide. 'It is done.'

'It is —' Daniel tried to rise, but fell back. 'I can't! I can't.'

'The roof's afire,' Tremlett called. They looked up, to the smoke streaming in. The builder moved to the back window and tried to open it. When it would not give, he kicked it out. 'Come, brothers. There's a way through here.'

'The way is here!' Simeon screamed. 'Have you no faith?'

'Stay if you want, you mad bastard,' cried the builder, putting one leg across the sill. 'But I want to live.'

'And you shall, brother – forever,' said Simeon and shot him.

Tremlett plunged from the window. 'No! No! No!' wept Daniel, curling up on the floor.

A voice came from beyond the door. 'The house is afire,' the man called. 'We can get you out, if you come now.'

Simeon crouched, putting his arms around the weeping youth. 'Shh! Shh! Daniel, hush. Hush!' He rocked him. Smoke was fast filling the room and both coughed hard. 'The kingdom of heaven is upon us. Enter into the New Jerusalem.'

'No!' screamed Daniel again, surging up. He was big, bigger than the man who held him, and he broke free, staggering to the door. 'I am coming,' he yelled through it. 'Do not shoot me!'

'Oh, ye of little faith,' said Simeon sadly, lifting, aiming and pulling the trigger. But the pan flashed, nothing more. Jerking the door open, Daniel stepped out and tumbled down the stairs.

Simeon was up in a moment. Coughing hard, he stepped forward, kicked the door shut and staggered back to the table. Five boxes were in a row upon it. He slipped the lid off the top one.

His oldest friend was within, the one who'd never abandon him. 'Eh! Eh! Eh!' he croaked, lifting the battens, pulling Punchinello out by his strings. He held him standing, swaying upon the table.

'Where'sa thata —' he began. And then the roof fell in on top of him.

He was knocked down, but clutching his puppet to him, Simeon forced himself up, shaking off the beams that pressed in on him. Everything was burning now. He was burning.

But did not the martyrs burn for you, King Jesus? Will I not be raised up with them?

White agony took him. He did not know where he was. Somehow he was still upright. Somehow he was at the door. Somehow he remembered the words.

He was not sure if he had a tongue left with which to testify. But he spoke nonetheless. '"And fire came down from God out of heaven . . . and devoured them!"'

They had just got Daniel out onto the cobbles, Dickon sitting on him, when the door above crashed open and a fireball burst out. It rolled down the stairs, flames expanding as it came. There was another sound in the roar of it, some shriek from within. Leaping back, they could see shapes dissolving. For the briefest of moments, what was left of two faces showed — one with a great hooked nose, one with a nose smashed in and a scar above it. Then these turned into one, blended by fire.

The house was nearly gone. But the others beside it to the east had still not fully caught. No one had voice to call, nor need. There was only one path from the conflagration now, and they took it.

Part Five

———◦———

AND I (JOHN) SAW THE HOLY CITY, NEW
JERUSALEM, COMING DOWN FROM GOD OUT OF
HEAVEN, PREPARED AS A BRIDE ADORNED
FOR HER HUSBAND.
The Revelation of St John the Divine 21:2

The water in the great tub had turned tepid, yet Sarah lingered. It was the coolest she'd been in – she could not remember how long. Since the fire, of course – and the Compter cell which had been ever hot, airless and rank with the odours of the inmates, herself included.

Mary Betterton had added essence of orange to the water and given her a rich soap to scrub herself. 'It's my husband's own. Uses it to take his paint off after *Othello*. Comes all the way from Castile. Bergamot, or some such in it, he says.' She'd giggled. 'Wait till he catches a whiff of you. He'll be furious.'

She had to get out soon, she knew. Not because of the water – for her baby. At the thought of him, she placed her hands on the tub's sides, levered herself up and stood straight, letting the water run off her. She was a little stronger, but was it enough? It would have to be. In normal times, the walk to the outlying village would take four hours. But the times were not normal and neither was she. Yet she felt if she took it steady, she would make it, perhaps in twice that time. Set out at dawn, which could not be long away, and she'd be there by noon.

Hampstead. That's where little William is, she thought. At that inn where Jenny's sister lives. The more she'd considered it, the more convinced she'd become. All the reports from the open spaces beyond the walls were of terrible places, with little water, no food and scarce a yard of land to lie upon. But she knew Jenny from close acquaintance in the Poultry Compter. She would forever seek to improve the present situation. And she had the strength of a plough horse. She would have pushed on to where there was food, a bed, some comfort and in spite of a scolding sister. Two children to carry would have slowed her not a jot.

There were some linens to dry herself upon, hanging from pegs on the theatre's bathhouse wall. As she rubbed herself dry, she realised that she felt clean for the first time in near three months and that it was truly a glorious thing.

There was a soft knock upon the door. Raising a sheet to cover herself, she called, 'Mary? Is that you?'

'Nay. 'Tis I.'

The voice, though muffled by wood, was his beyond any doubt. With a delighted cry, Sarah crossed to the door, unlatched it and opened it wide – onto a black apparition. 'Well, Master Coke,' she said, staring, 'you are more a Moor than Betterton will ever be.'

His smile and his eyes were all that showed white in the blackness of his face. 'Coke's my name – and my colour, sure,' he laughed, throwing his arms wide. From them soot fell, yet did little to diminish the amount that covered every part of his clothes and skin, blackening him from the crown of his head to his fingertips. 'Yet, madam, I am sure if you try you can still find my lips somewhere in the dark. You always managed it at night.'

He stepped forward. She raised her hand, halting him. 'Why, Captain, there is nothing I'd like more – had I not just rid myself of my own dirt.' She dropped the hand. 'And were other urgent matters not pressing us.'

He halted, his arms lowering. 'The baby?'

'Aye.' She moved back into the room and lowered herself onto the tub's edge. 'We must go get him, William, as soon as there is light.'

'Sarah, I thought we decided, that to search on Moorfields –'

'He is not there,' she interrupted. 'Ever since he was born I have had a – a sense of him. Even when he was not beside me.'

'Then where is he?'

'Hampstead.'

'The village?'

'Aye, or an inn near it, anyway. It is called the Spaniards.' At his chuckle, she frowned and peered at him. 'Do you know it?'

'I should.' Teeth shone again in the dark. 'For I launched half a dozen robberies from its front parlour. Why there?'

'That's where Jenny has taken him. She has a sister there. I thought to set out with the light.'

'Walking?' He came closer. 'Clean again you may be, my love, but are you also strong?'

'No. But I warrant if I take it slow, I will make it now. My fellow players have fed as well as bathed me. I have even slept. And perhaps with your arm to support me?'

She reached out a hand to him and he took it, squeezing her fingers. 'I think I can do better than that. My horse, Thunder, is in a stables not far from here, where the fire has not reached.' He lifted her hand, kissed it, leaving a smoky oval imprint upon her skin. 'Let me undertake this mission for you, Sarah. I can ride there and be back, with fortune, before noon.' He smiled again. 'With our child.'

'Nay, sir. He will need me, need feeding and I –' She shook her head. 'I will not sit and wait. Can you hire an extra horse?'

'Even had I the coin, every horse in London not privately owned has been conscripted to move goods away from the flames.'

'Then I will ride with you. Thunder is huge –'

'But will not be able to take a side saddle in addition to mine. And it's a long way for you to ride before me.'

She thought a moment, then smiled. 'I will not need a side saddle. There are advantages in this current fad in plays for women to be in breeches.'

'Do you mean –?'

'I will dress as a boy and ride behind you.'

Coke returned the smile. 'Very well. Though we will make a sight, you and I. The comely clean youth and the –' he indicated himself, 'monster.'

'Easily remedied, sir. There's water here,' she replied, her hand dipped to its surface. 'And if it is not in its first cleanliness, marry, it is still much cleaner than you.'

'Ha! Well, indeed. I would welcome the chance to bathe.' He looked down. 'But then to put on again these scorched and ragged things?'

'Oh, I am sure that if the players can accommodate a boy, they can also dress a man.'

They set out with the light, tiptoeing past a snoring Dickon, a note left for him with Mary Betterton as to where they were going and when they hoped to return. If he woke, he would run beside the horse all the way to Hampstead. But Coke knew his ward was exhausted and needed his rest. He could have done with more himself, but at least after his bath he'd taken a couple of hours' sleep and been woken at dawn by Sarah to ale, bread and cheese.

What a pair we make, thought Coke, as they walked, slow but steady, up to Holborn. Sarah had thought it best to fully assume the role of a youth, and had tucked her hair up under a hat, complete with green ostrich feather. The rest of her was soberly, if richly clad, in a chestnut jacket and breeches. Coke, however, had been given one of the few costumes that fitted his tall frame — a fop's peach doublet with a superfluity of lemon lace. He had rejected the petticoat breeches that were the natural partner to the peach and had beaten the worst of the soot out of his own, much damaged pair. Mostly, though, these were covered in thigh boots, the only footwear that fitted him, his own shorter boots so encased in the melted lead from the roof of St Paul's that it felt like walking in armour.

The street they passed along had not been caught up in the main conflagration, though many houses had been singed by wind-borne sparks, and a few stood in ruins, with men amidst the charred timbers, stamping out embers. The great fire was still present in distant explosions, where houses were being blown up to deny the fire growth. It was also there in the thick smoke cloud that hung not far above their heads.

'The wind's dropped,' Coke said, pointing up, 'otherwise all would not be so still above us. A blessing — for if God had kept plying his bellows, the flames would not have stopped till every house from Whitechapel to Westminster was burned.'

As they walked, he told her of events since they had parted – the pursuit of their main enemy and his flaming end. 'I suppose he died thinking the Saints had got most of what they desired. An apocalypse indeed, though King Jesus has yet to appear. I think we would have heard of it if he had.'

'And Pitman is certain these were the same foes who practised so against us?' she asked. 'Who got me into prison, and you into the arms of that houri?'

He stopped. 'Sarah, I cannot tell you how foolish I feel. How sorry –'

'Nay, William.' She shushed him. 'You were gallant, as ever. If there is a good flaw to have it must be that. I would not have you were it not for that flaw. I do not blame you. Does the thief-taker think we are clear of these Saints now?'

Coke began walking again. 'We cannot be certain. One of those we pursued was certainly that bastard builder, Samuel Tremlett. The house we chased him into was destroyed and he must be dead. He may have heirs, though.' He shrugged. 'There's also a certain Irish captain I'd hoped to meet again. He may not be about, or he may also be ashes now.'

They reached the stables, tucked behind Furnival's Inn. The harassed owner, with horses to hire out, left Coke to the saddling and he helped himself to a thick blanket, double folded, for Sarah to perch on behind him and atop Thunder's rump. Still, when he lifted her up and she straddled, he saw her wince in pain. 'Are you certain?'

'Certain, sir,' she replied, taking a deep breath. 'Come, let us go find our boy.'

He had ridden the route often, for some of the finest opportunities awaited a road knight somewhere along the Great North Road. Reasoning, however, that the areas directly above the city itself would be jammed with the displaced, he took them wide and by narrower ways to the village of Islington. This was as crammed with folk as if it was fair day; but there was no revelling, just several thousand who'd made it this far, camped in whichever space they could find, surrounded by whatever little they'd been able to save. At least the countryside around provided them with some food, and the inns were busy. Coke shuddered to think what people must be suffering closer to the walls, at Moorfields and Finsbury.

They made good speed along Holloway for Thunder had not been run out for a while – Coke could only bless his stars that one of the few things for which he'd provided before being snatched away was his horse's care for some months ahead. The roads were still dry from the hottest of summers and the gelding took them at a pace.

The hill up to the village of Highgate taxed even him, so Coke reined in at the summit to let him drink. He helped Sarah down and as he led Thunder to the trough, she walked a few paces off to ease her cramped limbs. 'Merciful Jesus,' she said, her voice desolate.

He turned, and saw what she saw, gasping in his turn. Under a brown cloud that roofed the whole metropolis, fed by a thousand coiling columns, lay a devastated land. Fires still burned, though in isolated places now, the biggest around what Coke thought might be the Cripplegate. Mostly, though, the flames had gone out, for they had gorged on all they could and the wind that had so fanned them had died. Yet from the Tower in the east to halfway down Fleet Street in the west, from Moorgate in the city's northern wall all the way to the Thames, lay a blackened wilderness. There were a few, a very few, buildings standing, churches or tradesmen's halls that a trick of wind, a thicker stone, a caprice of flame had saved. But tens of thousands of structures were gone, from hovel to palace, tenement to tower. The very earth smoked, as if some vast marsh exhaled foul and noisome breath, curling up around the thousand steeples and chimneys that yet stood, though the buildings they served were ash.

It was not his city, yet the sight saddened him. It was Sarah's and she wept.

'Come, love,' he said, gently taking her arm.

He helped her up, mounted again in front of her, and clucked to Thunder to walk on. They rode along the hard-packed track from Highgate westwards, grateful that the trees of the encroaching heathland obscured all except that louring cloud.

Emerging from a copse of elm, at the top of the next rise, a whitewashed building stood.

'The Spaniards,' Coke called over his shoulder. He felt her hands, that had grasped him firmly the entire way, tighten to the point of pain.

They rode into the yard. Since it was a coaching inn there were various vehicles about, some so stuffed with goods that they must have come from the disaster. Sarah could hear the roar of people within the building as trade was being conducted. Coke dismounted ahead of her, reached up and helped her down. 'Wait for me,' he said, 'while I see Thunder into the stables.'

'I will go ahead,' she replied.

The place she entered was indeed crammed with people, many

of whom showed their status as refugees in mismatched clothes, smut-daubed faces and singed hair. A mix of peoples merged, lords and commoners united in the euphoria of survival. They gave way good-humouredly to her shoves as she passed through the crowd, her gaze seeking everywhere. She pushed up to the trestle, waving away the tankard that was thrust at her. 'Jenny Johnson?' she shouted. The man looked at her and for a moment she felt her heart thump. What if she was wrong? What if Jenny had not come? Then, to her joy, he raised his eyebrows to the ceiling directly above.

She found a narrow staircase. It led to a corridor of plaster walls, with half a dozen wooden doors along one side. 'Jenny?' she called, though her throat was suddenly weak and she had to clear it. 'Jenny Johnson?' she called louder.

A moment's silence, then an oath from behind the door nearest her. Someone crossed within and the door was flung open. 'Sarah!' Jenny cried, pulling her friend into an embrace, smothering her in her bosom.

'Is he —?' Sarah began, then had her answer in a high yell. Knew it now as the most glorious sound she'd ever heard.

Another woman held the baby, an older, stouter version of Jenny. She had a mug in her hand, and a spoon. 'The mother?' she asked. ''Tis as well. For I can't get this little mite to take any ewe's milk.'

Sarah was across the room in a moment, bending and scooping up her son. The baby yelled louder at the sudden jostling, then calmed down as Sarah sat with him and fumbled to open her young man's doublet. That first yell had not only produced joy; her breasts, swollen with milk, had flooded on the sound. The boy appeared quite content with that.

Jenny and her sister fussed around her, commenting, gossiping, questioning. Sarah didn't answer much, couldn't think of anything to say or do, beyond staring at the wonder in her arms. But she did look up, to the footfalls on the stair, to the door they'd left open. To the man standing there.

With a little difficulty, she plucked the baby from her breast and held him out. 'William Coke,' she said, 'meet William Coke.'

17

AFTERMATH

One week later

It wasn't convenient. But Pitman had insisted.

'A short visit only, Captain,' he'd said. 'I know 'tis the Sabbath. But if we get the business out of the way first, then we can fully focus on God.'

Coke wished to focus on nothing and no one save his wife and his son, having to make their own way to St Paul's in Covent Garden. At least they were not alone – for the entire Pitman family was with them, and Dickon too. But Coke did not understand why he must spend even a part of the day of young William's christening in the company of the Under-Secretary of State. And then to be kept waiting an hour by the rogue, as the bell sounding in Scotland Yard testified. 'Truly, Pitman, I must go. Sarah will not tolerate any tardiness on this occasion. I have been away enough, as you know.'

'A few moments longer, please. The ceremony is yet an hour off. And I need Sir Joseph to understand that you are an equal partner in any enterprise we undertake for him. In case one of us is,' he tapped his leg, 'laid up again.'

'Undertake? Pah!' Coke grumbled. 'I am reconsidering our partnership, sir. I did not agree to join in your work to become a damned spy. The plan was to take footpads and highwaymen, begod.'

'And we will, Captain. Yet we are victims of our own success. We have now thwarted two assassination attempts, on duke and king. Marry,' he laughed, 'maybe we've been summoned here to be knighted.'

'Pitman, do not jest. I have —'

His further remonstrance was interrupted by the door opening. 'He will see you now,' said a bespectacled secretary, passing them and leaving the door ajar.

They rose and entered, blinking against the sunlight blazing through the window behind Sir Joseph Williamson at his desk. Towers of paper covered it; one of which, taller than the rest, began to slip sideways at the vibrations of the large thief-taker's approach. Pitman's hand averted catastrophe.

'I thank you,' said the Under-Secretary, leaning to remove some sheaves from the stack to make an equally precarious stand next to it. 'I am, as you see, drowned in reports. The nation will have an answer to the cause of the late fire. Sit, both of you.'

Pitman sat in the chair indicated. 'The cause is not in doubt, sir. It began with a baker's carelessness in Pudding Lane. Trust me, I was there soon after.'

'I know that, uh, Pitman. As do you and any man of sense in the realm. Alas,' he indicated the mounds of paper, 'others do not. Including the baker himself, who claims the place was fired deliberately by rivals —'

'He would say that, wouldn't he? Hardly going to help his trade being known as the man who burned London down, is it? What will that say for his buns?'

He and Coke laughed. Sir Joseph did not. 'Oh, you would be surprised how many crave that title. I have confessions here,' he jabbed a finger, 'from one Robert Hubert, a Frenchman, clearly a Bedlamite, who claims he started the fire for the glory of our enemy, France. Another here from a ten-year-old apothecary's boy, Edward Taylor, who swears it was he and his uncle who lobbed fireballs through Farriner's window to begin the blaze, for mischief's sake alone.' He sat back. 'Then there are all the accusers. Everyone is suspect, but most especially the nation's enemies. Those without – the Dutch and French – and even more, those within – the Catholics of course. Some even testify here that the papist Duke of York was the arsonist because,' he picked up a paper and read, '"he wore too cheery a smile as he feigned the fighting of the flames". Ye gods!' He dropped the paper and picked up another. 'And then of course there are the fanatics. Yours and – uh, Captain Coke, is it? – particular field of expertise.'

As he said it, he glanced behind him, to a door ajar there. It was the tiniest of looks but Coke, who'd raised his hand to block the glare from the window, thought it odd, and looked at the door too. 'Not mine,' he declared, sitting up. 'I intend to leave them well alone, and desire of them the same for me.'

'Though there is some truth there,' said Pitman. 'They did not start the fire, certainly. But I am sure they helped spread it. It was, after all, the divine sign they'd been waiting for.'

'Ah yes. The day foretold in the year of the Beast.' Williamson licked his lips. 'At least that's past.'

'Forgive me, Sir Joseph. But there's still near three months left of it to run.'

'You are right.' He peered over his spectacles. 'Have you concerns? Did you not kill their leader?'

'Saw him killed, aye. But we have killed their leaders before, and others arise to take over. They are a snake with many heads, the Fifth Monarchy Men. Which brings me to another point. We did not fulfil the second part of our mandate.' Pitman nodded. 'We did not bring you Captain Blood, or vouchsafe *his* death.'

'Ah yes.' Sir Joseph cleared his throat. 'It is for those matters that I have summoned you here. To pay you, for your services to date. And to inform you that the second half of your mission has been terminated. You are no longer required to hunt down the Irishman.'

As he spoke, he opened a drawer, took out a purse and placed it on the desk. He also, Coke noticed, gave another tiny glance to the door behind him. It was the second time he'd done it and the captain felt hairs rise upon his neck.

Pitman lifted the purse, frowned. ''Tis lighter than I'd hoped, Sir Joseph. Why are we not to pursue him still? Did you not, in this very office, tell me that Homo Sanguienus was the most dangerous man in the realm.'

'He has been dealt with, sir. That is all you need to know. Now you have your orders and your reward, you may go.' The Under-Secretary reached for another folder of papers, bound in string, and put it before him on the desk. 'I have much other business with which to deal.'

Muttering, Pitman tucked the purse within his cloak and rose. Coke did too – and squinted. The harsh sunlight was now reflecting off something on the desk, hidden until this moment by the folder Sir Joseph had just picked up. Shifting slightly to the side, Coke saw what it was: a monocle.

He stepped swiftly around the desk. Sir Joseph rose, crying at him to halt. He did not, but marched to the back door and threw it wide.

Sitting on chairs in a small, windowless room were two men.

'Captain Coke,' said the elder of them, rising.

'Captain Blood,' replied Coke, drawing his sword.

'Stop!' shouted Sir Joseph. 'Put up, I command you.'

'So this is the rogue, is it?' Pitman loomed in the door behind the Under-Secretary. 'He was masked when he stabbed me in St Paul's.'

''Tis him. And his whelp,' replied Coke, not lowering his sword.

Blood raised his hands, open-palmed. 'I am unarmed, sir.'

'As was I when you had me tied in a chair in Holland.'

'Put up, I say!' Sir Joseph came closer. 'Would you have me call the guards?'

'You've not seen the captain with a blade, sir. Both Bloods would be dead before your men got here.' Pitman put a large and restraining hand upon the other's shoulder. 'I believe the only way you can prevent him is by an explanation.'

'And swiftly too,' added Coke.

Sir Joseph's eyes showed fury but he took a deep breath. 'We apprehended the Bloods in Harwich as they landed. We kept the son, while the father —' he hesitated, 'did us some service in the protection of His Majesty.'

Pitman whistled. 'So it was you who shot the villain in St Paul's churchyard. You were not shooting at the king?'

'If I'd wanted to kill him, the tyrant would now be dead. Pff!' Blood replied, blowing out his lips. 'But so would my son,' he glanced at the boy who was staring hard at Coke's sword tip, 'and not swiftly, I was warned.'

'So now you are a double traitor, eh?' Coke said. 'To the realm and to your brothers?'

The Irishman's eyes narrowed. 'I am no traitor. I am loyal to my causes. And if I sometimes reach . . . accommodations with my enemy,' his eyes flicked to Sir Joseph, then back to Coke, 'that is the nature of the spying trade, sir. As I am sure you are soon to discover.'

'Trust me, I am not.'

'Now that is all the explanation you will get.' Sir Joseph shrugged off Pitman's hand and stepped forward to place his own on Coke's sword arm. 'You will put up, sirrah, and leave the business of the realm to me.'

Coke stared a moment longer, then sheathed his sword. Both Bloods sighed, lowered their arms, and the elder stepped forward. 'Will you shake hands, captain to captain?' he said, smiling. 'No hard feelings, eh? It was just the trade.' When Coke simply stared back, he offered his hand again. 'Come, sir, if we cannot be friends, can we not be honourable enemies?'

Coke looked at the hand, then up into the Irishman's eyes. 'Perhaps. Once we are even.' And with that he drove his fist straight into Blood's jaw. The man flew back, smashing over the two chairs, crashing to the floor. His son cried out and threw himself down beside his father.

Coke stepped closer, peering down at Blood. 'You asked me once if you'd broken my jaw with your blow. I replied that you had not. Can you so reassure me?'

322

Nothing but moans came from the floor. 'Thought not,' said Coke, as he turned and walked from the room.

William Coke's christening was at St Paul's, Covent Garden. The actors of the King's Company, their playhouse nearby on Drury Lane, had adopted the chapel, and some from the Duke's Company joined them there each Sunday. Many from both sets of players attended the ceremony, delighting that he, who would perhaps be the newest recruit to their ranks, displayed the required playhouse lungs by yelling throughout the ceremony and most especially when the rector poured water on his head.

'I baptise thee William Aethelred Pitman Coke,' pronounced the priest, needing to bellow, player-like, to be heard. Sarah glanced up above their screaming child to her husband, one eyebrow raised again at this second name. He just shrugged. 'My father's,' he'd told her when the matter was first discussed, 'and every Somersetshire Coke going back from before the Conquest. On this matter, madam, I will not yield.'

The godfather, standing near, simply smiled. His own son, in Bettina's arms and as quiet as young William was loud, had been baptised in their Baptist meeting house in a secret ceremony only that morning – for they were still not permitted to meet, even in a ruined city. As was their custom, the name he was given was biblical: Eleazar. Though the father suspected that, like him, the boy would reduce it still further and forever be correcting those who would append 'Mr' with 'That's Pitman to you. Pitman to all.'

The second godmother simply grinned. Jenny Johnson was enjoying the company of the players. Indeed Betterton had even offered her a small role in their next production.

With London still smoking, and people needing sustenance, Sabbath rules had been relaxed and every tavern and inn was open. The congregation retired to one on King Street nearby where the baby's head could be 'washed' again, though liquid was not poured onto him this time – he'd only just ceased shouting from his first dousing – but in great quantity down the players' throats. Many toasts were made to fortune and a long life. The Dutch and French were ritually damned, the king huzzahed. Before very long, instruments appeared – mandolin, fiddles and fifes – and dancing began.

They stayed for a time, and enjoyed it. But when Coke caught Sarah's eye across the room and raised an eyebrow, she nodded, rose and joined him. 'You could stay,' he said. 'Pitman and I can deal with this.'

'Nay. It's my life. Ours,' she corrected herself, hoisting a now sleeping baby.

In the end, everyone came – the entire Pitman brood, all in their Sunday best, surrounding the two mothers who walked behind with babes in arms, the captain and the constable slightly ahead. 'Anything more?' asked Coke.

The taller man shook his head. 'The parishes have received the instructions amongst many others and there is yet so much to be done. But the authorities are concerned that when the prisons burned down, most of the prisoners escaped. They will be tracked down. Murderers, thieves –'

'Debtors,' finished Coke. 'Well, we shall see now if there is still one debt to honour. At least Isaac has disclaimed his, now he is fully recovered.'

The streets they passed through first had not been touched by the fire, the cataclysm being evident only in more people being about, with refugees having found shelter where they could. As they proceeded further east, though, the signs were there – in an occasional burnt-out shell where a house had stood before a wind-borne spark had fired it. And as soon as they stepped from under the eaves of narrow Magpie Yard and onto the wider road at its end, a very different sight appeared.

Fetter Lane, running north–south, was the westernmost boundary of the great fire. Behind them, most houses still stood; before them – hardly any did. They all regarded the devastation, and even the chattering children were struck silent. The sight Coke and Sarah had seen from Highgate was even grimmer close to, with smoke still curling from a thousand scorched cellars, and charred timbers leaning together like a fleet wrecked by fireships. Yet not everything was the uniform black of soot. Everywhere, different things had been consumed, leaving their residue – grey from the riven and calcified stones, red from powdered brick. As far as any could see, multi-hued dirt had settled over the city like a thick and filthy blanket. Everywhere, people moved upon it like fleas, seeking, beginning to clear – and to extinguish further flames. The main fire may have been put out, but even within their sight they could see a dozen smaller fires, with men clustered about them.

It was not a wilderness any would choose to walk through. But both men had tried and failed to dissuade their families.

'Come then,' the big man called and led the way. Their destination wasn't far, though the way to it took time as they had to go around the jumble of the streets, the remains of pulled-down houses, the remnants of lives lived within them. The children fell upon items with delight – here a scorched poppet, there a partially melted glass figurine – and were commanded to put them down. Another game could not be stopped – the constant dancing that was required to walk over ground still glowing with embers.

Yet when they reached their destination, all fell silent, aware of the attention of the two men upon what was before them, and that of the two women who joined them.

'Well,' said Coke, unable to say more.

The house he'd bought for Sarah was, like all the others around it, a gutted shell. Most of the brick had withstood the flames, though the back wall had collapsed and the roof joists had burned and fallen in. Because it had been unoccupied, the dirt and soot within was a uniform black: no possessions, no wall hangings, no tapestries had dissolved, no glass lay melted on the floor. But it was a ruin nonetheless.

'Door arch stands, husband,' said Sarah at his elbow, an eyebrow raised. 'Do you still wish to carry me over the threshold?'

He was prevented from replying by the children's shrieks. He looked to where they pointed – and indeed a monster did appear to be emerging, as covered with soot as Coke had been only days before.

'Bastards,' the apparition muttered. 'Bloody –' The man ceased speaking when he saw them. 'Your pardon, sirs. Ladies,' he said, taking off his hat which let fall yet more dust as he did. 'I did not see you there. In sooth, I have little sight for anything but my,' he looked back, 'disaster.'

'Yours, sir?' said Coke. 'How so?'

The man looked to spit, noted the women again, and thought better of it. 'This house, sir, and the three each side of it – my father and I built them and they were near complete before the fire. Now –' This time he did not withhold the spit. Wiping his mouth, he continued, 'The worst of it is that not only did my father die in the flames, they took all our records too.'

For some reason, Pitman felt that the man looked sadder about the latter loss than the former, a feeling confirmed when he murmured a condolence.

'Aye well, by his belief he is in a far happier place now. His new Jerusalem. For 'e was one of those, whatcha-ma-call-'ems. Saints!' He spat again. 'But the bastard's gone and left me in his old bloody Jerusalem.'

'I take it,' said Coke, 'that you are not of his beliefs?'

'Nay, despite how often 'e tried to impress them on my arse with a switch. Apologies, ladies,' he said, not looking sorry at all, as the children giggled. 'But it 'as been a trying time,' he added with a sigh.

'Sir,' said Coke. 'I am sorry for your troubles. And I hesitate to add to them. But you are standing in my house.'

'Yours? Are you –?' he pulled out a small, black leather note-book, 'Coke? William Coke?'

'I am.'

'Ah.' The man scratched at his chin, letting fall more dirt. 'And I suppose you'll be wanting me to rebuild this for ye?' He swallowed at Coke's silence. 'Did you pay my father the joist money?'

Coke thought of the forty guineas he had not paid because of the conspiracy this man's father and his saintly friends had caught him in. He thought of the results of that: of the fireship; of Sarah giving birth in the Poultry Compter; all that he could have lost.

But he let none of those thoughts show on his face. There was a reason that he usually won at cards. 'I did indeed.'

Somewhere under the blackness, the man paled. He looked down. 'I see. Well, the contracts burned, of course, so –' he muttered, then shook his head and raised it. 'Nevertheless. I will honour what my father promised you. It may take me a little time –' He straightened up. 'But if you will give me that, I will finish the 'ouse for you.'

Coke turned to Sarah. For a moment they just looked at each other. Then she shook her head.

It was what he hoped. Turning back, he said, 'No, sir. We no longer want it.'

'I see.' The man looked dismayed. 'Then you'll be wanting your money back. Twenty for the signing, and forty for the joist? I could fight you in court, say you must have this 'ouse or nothing.' He shrugged. 'But that was my father's way, not mine. I'll pay you back if, again, you will but give me the time.'

Not so long before, and if he'd met the man upon a highway, Coke would have happily taken sixty guineas from him over a gun's muzzle. But the man was not his father. And, like so many that week in London, he had lost enough. 'I'll tell you what, Master Tremlett. When you sell the house again, you may send me twenty guineas back. The other forty – perhaps I will call upon you for that also, someday, when your fortunes are quite re-established.'

'Sir! Oh, sir!' the man's smudged face showed a little white with a smile. 'That is most 'andsome. Most 'andsome. I can see you are a gentleman.'

'On occasion.' He nodded. 'Good fortune from the rubble, Mr Tremlett.'

As they walked away, Sarah took his arm. '"Most 'andsome",' she echoed, in perfect mimicry. 'And most 'onest too, my 'usband.'

'Almost,' laughed Pitman, coming up. 'Though I admit surprise, Captain. For a highwayman you have some scruples.'

'Former highwayman. And a family man now. I must set my son an example.' He reached to run a fingertip down the babe's forehead, then sighed. 'Though as a family man I worry how I will provide.'

'Why, William,' said Pitman, stopping, 'we talked of this before. All those prisoners running free? They must be taken again. And I suspect that all their former rewards will be offered, or close to.' He threw his arms wide. 'Indeed, I believe we are entering the golden age of thief-taking.'

There was general laughter, while Coke pulled at his moustache. 'I suppose something good should come out of all we have been through.'

'Aye.' The thief-taker smiled. 'You know what is said: "Tis an ill wind that blows nobody some good.'

'And what book of the Bible is that from?' asked Sarah.

'Nay, 'tis only a common proverb,' said Bettina, taking her husband's arm. 'Though you'd think it was scripture, Pitman is so given to quoting it.'

'Just as long as it is not from Revelation,' said Captain Coke. He looked beyond them all, to the devastated city. 'For I think we've had quite enough apocalypse. Don't you?'

Author's Note

As with my last novel, *Plague*, about the great pestilence of 1665, so with this one: I only had vague schoolboy knowledge of the Great Fire of London. Research opened my eyes and imagination to the horrors of the cataclysm that swept the city from the early hours of 2nd September 1666 to its conclusion four days later.

London is my city. Son of a Londoner, if I was not myself born there I grew up there. I love it and the longer I am away from it, the more I feel the need to write about it – my last three novels have been set in the city. I know it well – perhaps better than most because after school my 'gap year', 1974–5, was spent there as a motorcycle messenger. Based in a Soho that was still very much 'sin city', I learned all sorts of interesting things. The naive schoolboy grew up fast. And learning meant getting to know my way about London really well. We were paid per ride, so the faster you could finish one . . . this led to a deep knowledge of alleys and cut-throughs, not all of them strictly legal. It also led to a lasting distrust of black-cab drivers who appeared hell-bent on eliminating messengers as a species.

Somehow I survived. And at the end of 1975, I went to the Guildhall School of Music and Drama to train as an actor. First based just off Fleet Street, we then opened what would become the Barbican Arts Centre. So I studied in the very heart of what had been devoured by flames. Alas, I was too up myself as a budding thespian to pay much attention to all the history around me. And though not much remains of Restoration London – destroyed by that fire and by the second 'Great Fire' of 1940 when Hitler tried to burn the city down – I kick myself now that I didn't spend more time absorbing what survived. But it is still there and gives me every excuse to return and research the city I love.

All my novels are very personal to me. My life inevitably creeps in. And I do have one 'fire' event, one of my earliest and clearest childhood memories: waking up in our house in Los Angeles, joining my mother at a back window. 'What's that?' I asked, staring up at a huge column of smoke, coiling from the Hollywood Hill. 'Fire,' she replied. It was the start of the Bel Air Fire of 1961. We were evacuated, excitingly we spent a couple of nights at a motel, and the flames passed within four hundred yards of our house. Hardly Cheapside in 1666 but . . .

I also included two very personal stories – to do with birth. Sarah saves her baby's life when she recognises that the skin over his face is a 'caul' – the amniotic sac that sometimes gets stuck over a newborn's face – and rips it off to let him breathe. Just as my grandmother did to save my mother. And Sarah hearing her husband's laugh in her son's first cry? My mother always claimed she knew me straightway because she heard her father's laugh in my initial wail.

Telling the story from multiple viewpoints – heroes and

villains – allowed me to encompass a fairly wide chunk of the Fire's extraordinary detail. And I was most fortunate to find, in a second-hand bookstore in Hampstead and just when I needed it, 'the' book. There always seems to be one that arrives at the right time, and though I'd read a couple of others, perfectly good in their own way, none came close to the massively detailed handling of the subject I discovered in *The Great Fire of London* by Walter George Bell, first published in 1923. Mr Bell not only gave a superb pre-Fire study of the city, but he also filled the pages with anecdotes and characters, gleaning the best of all the observers at the time, distilling Evelyn and Pepys but above all taking me street by street, church by church, hour by hour through the four days and the aftermath, in prose always clear and witty. And he made me smile often. ('One mistrusts a versifier,' he said of the dramatic poetry of one fellow on the destruction.)

One fact puzzled him as it does me: the death toll. The official death-roll, in the Bills of Mortality, was six. Six, of which the first and most reported was Thomas Farriner's maid! This seems impossible given the speed and totality of destruction and is disputed by many. It seems more an error in addition, or a deliberate under-reporting. Evelyn certainly disagreed, testifying to the stench of so many bodies coming from the ruins.

One myth that people always bring up when I tell them what I'm writing is: 'Oh, but the Fire was a good thing in one way because it got rid of the filth that the plague-carrying rats thrived in.' Uh, no. Though black rats love dirt, it was not its absence that diminished them but the growing strength of their cousin, the brown rat. This relative newcomer breeds in a shorter amount of time. It outbred the black, killed them all, replaced them . . .

and the brown rat doesn't host the plague flea that did the actual infecting. The Stranglers were quite right to celebrate this hitherto unsung hero in their album *Rattus Norvegicus*.

Ah, London! Whatever its tribulations in whatever period, it always rebounds, stronger than it was before. And I shall keep returning to it, in body as often as I may, and certainly in my novels.

C. C. Humphreys, July 2016
Salt Spring Island, BC, Canada

Acknowledgements

As ever, so many people have helped hugely in this endeavour. Since *Fire* is a loose sequel to *Plague*, nearly all those I already owe a debt to are still aboard with the publishers on both sides of the pond. In the UK, there's the wonderful team headed by Selina Walker at Century; Georgina Hawtrey-Woore, who became my main editor for reasons explained below; and Kate Raybould, who saw the manuscript through to the conclusion. In Canada, at Doubleday, I am still well taken care of by my publisher Kristin Cochrane, by perspicacious Amy Black and by super publicist Max Arambulo.

I had one sad parting during the process: Nita Pronovost, the editor I so enjoyed working with on *Plague*, decamped to another publisher just after she gave me my first set of notes. I missed her, but benefited hugely from her final thoughts.

My family – wife Aletha and son Reith – were as always most supportive and forgiving of eccentricities. Yelling 'Fire!' rather than 'Plague!' in the middle of the night made for a nice change. And this while Aletha was busy opening our new venture: Café

Talia on Salt Spring Island. Yes, on top of plying a quill I can now draw a fine latte. (Though I mainly do the dishes.)

Lastly, I'd especially like to thank the man to whom this book is dedicated, my agent, Simon Trewin of WME. Simon not only handles all the business side with aplomb, allowing me to write for a living, he is also a great brainstormer of ideas. *Plague* and *Fire* would not be here without his sudden flashes of inspiration. I have no doubt he will continue to keep me and mine fed for the foreseeable future – no mean trick in the turbulent world of publishing.

To these, and all my readers who give me such strong feedback, many thanks.

Further Reading

The good thing about writing books set a year apart is that the background reading is already done. So most of the texts I read for *Plague* were still useful for *Fire*. The first three below, especially the wonderful one by Bell, made the difference.

ON THE FIRE:
Bell, Walter George, *The Great Fire of London* (London: Folio Society, 2003)
Hanrahan, David. C, *Colonel Blood* (Stroud: Sutton Publishing Ltd, 2003)
Tinniswood, Adrian, *By Permission of Heaven* (London: Pimlico; new edition, 2004)

ON LONDON:
Ackroyd, Peter, *London: The Biography* (London: Chatto & Windus, 2000)
Hyde, Ralph (ed.), *The A to Z of Restoration London* (London: London Topographical Society, 1992)
Picard, Liza, *Restoration London: Everyday Life in London 1660–1670* (London: Weidenfeld & Nicolson, 2003)
Porter, Stephen, *Pepys's London: Everyday Life in London 1650–1703* (Gloucestershire: Amberley Publishing, 2011)

ON THE TIME PERIOD:
Capp, B.S., *The Fifth Monarchy Men: A Study in Seventeenth-Century EnglishMillenarianism* (London: Faber & Faber, 1972)

Friedman, Jerome, *Blasphemy, Immorality and Anarchy: The Ranters and the English Revolution* (Ohio: Ohio University Press, 1987)

Gyford, Phil (ed.), The Diary of Samuel Pepys, www.pepysdiary.com (advertised on the gyford website)

Hill, Christopher, *The World Turned Upside Down: Radical Ideas During the English Revolution* (London: Penguin Books, 1972)

Miller, John, *The English Civil Wars: Roundheads, Cavaliers and the Execution of a King* (London: Constable & Robinson, 2009)

Palmer, Tony, *Charles II: Portrait of an Age* (West Sussex: Littlehampton Book Services, 1979)

Pennington, Donald and Keith Thomas (eds), *Puritans and Revolutionaries: Essays in Seventeenth-century History Presented to Christopher Hill* (Oxford: Oxford University Press, 1978)

Purkiss, Diane, *The English Civil War: A People's History* (London: HarperPress, 2006)

ON THE PLAGUE:

Defoe, Daniel, *A Journal of the Plague Year*, with notes by Louis Landa and introduction by David Roberts (New York: Oxford University Press, 2010)

Porter, Stephen, *The Great Plague* (Gloucestershire: Amberley Publishing, 2009)

ON THE THEATRE:

Etherege, George, *The Man of Mode*, translated by John Barnard (London: Bloomsbury Methuen Drama, 2007)

Fisk, Deborah Payne (ed.), *The Cambridge Companion to English Restoration Theatre* (Cambridge: Cambridge University Press, 2009)

Speaight, George, *Punch and Judy: A History* (West Sussex: Littlehampton Book Services, 1970)

THE BIBLE:

Daniel and *The Revelation of St John the Divine. King James Bible.* (Nashville: Holman Bible, 1973)